320 Down

320 Down

❖

Christopher J. O'Bryant

Copyright © 2010 by Christopher J. O'Bryant.

Library of Congress Control Number: 2010901939
ISBN: Hardcover 978-1-4500-4270-3
Softcover 978-1-4500-4269-7
E-book 978-1-4500-4271-0

All rights reserved. No part of this book may be reproduced or transmitted in any form or by any means, electronic or mechanical, including photocopying, recording, or by any information storage and retrieval system, without permission in writing from the copyright owner.

This is a work of fiction. Names, characters, places and incidents either are the product of the author's imagination or are used fictitiously, and any resemblance to any actual persons, living or dead, events, or locales is entirely coincidental.

This book was printed in the United States of America.

To order additional copies of this book, contact:
Xlibris Corporation
1-888-795-4274
www.Xlibris.com
Orders@Xlibris.com
73893

Dedication

James O'Bryant   Stephanie Murray

The best parents I could have ever wished for. This book is for you and all the things you both sacrificed for me over the years.

ACKNOWLEDGMENTS

Writing a novel doesn't just happen, and I had to bother a lot of people to make the characters inside these pages seem much smarter. I hold a debt of gratitude to many people for their support and encouragement, but a few names do stand out, namely Robert and Elaine White, Nathan and Stacy Macias, Barry and Susan Schwartz, Heidi Holt, George Galdorisi come to mind immediately.

Anything incorrect in these pages, is all me, and has nothing to do with the many people who gave generously of their knowledge, and was most likely the product of my fevered imagination trying to make the story just a little bit better.

*

Photo credits are courtesy of Nathan Macias Photography

Prologue

Breakdown 0.0

March 1, 1999

"So I'll go with you," he said from behind while she looked out at the city. Washington, DC, was cold, just on the brink of rain. She didn't want to be having this conversation and wished he'd just take it like a man and move on. As usual, Jerry missed the point. When she said she was leaving to take the other job, he thought government service was all she meant. He didn't realize she was leaving him too.

She stood by the window, not wanting to turn and face him. She knew the moment he saw the look in her eyes, it would be clear to him. He could read her, at least at moments like this. Years of growing and living together had taught her that. He could be utterly clueless about her most of the time, but the moment the subject turned to their relationship, or the prospect of its ending, he knew immediately what she was thinking. Of the two of them, he was far more emotional, always was, and she knew he always would be. She was soft spoken most of the time, a watcher. In her field of choice, it made her an excellent investigator, but at home, in the heart of life, it sometimes meant she came across as cold. Her expertise was in psychology, a field she mastered with one small exception; her own relationships. Once she was involved, her piercing analytic skill dulled considerably. An old professor once told her it's very hard to turn one's perceptions inward, to separate oneself, and form objective opinions. He told her few ever managed to succeed at it. She hadn't. And that was why, after almost twelve years of being with Jerry he'd always managed to say the right thing at just the right moment, with his eyes full of tears and his head hung low to get her stay, even when she was ready to leave.

"Jerry . . . ," she started to say slowly, still facing the window, still avoiding his stare as she watched him step closer in the reflection from the glass.

"It's OK, Dawn, I understand." He was behind her all of a sudden, his hands gently cupping her shoulders, positioning himself right behind her to fill her every curve. "You've been through a lot, and I'm not going to think any less of you if you don't want to stick it out. We'll find a way to make do. We always have."

The sigh she let loose was real but not a sign of relaxation, not relief from his words. The sigh was only from sadness. This side of him, the kind, innocent soul who captured her heart back when she was a teenage girl in high school, was hard to resist. The problem was she wasn't the same scared, naïve girl she was back then. Little Dawn Marie McCafferty was all grown up and found the big old scary world wasn't so scary after all. Not if you were willing to take the chance to embrace it. With every year of growth she stepped out further and further, and all Jerry did was follow at her heels. She knew he wasn't leeching off her, not purposely. He loved her with all his heart but he just wasn't the man of her grown-up dreams. The older she got, the more she wanted to live out a romantic fairy tale in which a dark stranger, the hero with the dark side and sparkling eyes of myth and legend, would sweep her off her feet. Instead she was with Jerry, the "stand by your woman" man, eager to please and resigned to existing in whatever kind of lifestyle she created for them.

He was educated; she'd made sure of that, practically whipping him every step of the way to getting his degree. But his majors changed wildly with every new academic quarter, so he had his degree but no real skill, or the drive to pursue a real career. He worked as an office temp, making a decent wage, but nothing like what she brought home. His last words still echoed through the vast landscape of her crowded mind; he was wrong and she knew it. He didn't understand; in fact, he didn't even have an inkling of what was going on inside her head. She was sure he'd run screaming out of their apartment if he did. Despite all her skills, despite the voluntary therapy she was undergoing, when she closed her eyes she could still see Simon Walter's face, very clearly as her two dead-on shots ripped through his chest. The image played out inside her eyelids like a never-ending movie scene that only served to remind her she was a murderer.

Officially, she wasn't. Everyone told her that. If she hadn't fired those two critical shots when she did, three men would have died by Simon Walter's Uzi. So while Jerry sat around some air-conditioned office one day, counting paperclips and making small talk at the company water cooler, Dawn hefted up her nine millimeter and blew a man's chest away. She had done the right thing and she knew it beyond any shadow of a doubt. But realizing a man was dead by her hand didn't sit well with her, even four months, three days, and four hours after that fact.

"Jerry," she said, trying to keep her voice steady and light hearted not wanting to clue him in just yet to what was coming. She wanted to break the news to him gently, to finish her words before his tears obstructed what she was trying to say. "I think we need to talk about the future."

"I know, babe, and we will. We'll pull out the bankbooks and we'll see what we have to do. Maybe I'll even have to work a little overtime at the office, but that's OK."

"They want me in Sacramento in two weeks for procedural training."

"Two weeks?" He didn't mean to stammer, but his words fell from his mouth jagged and shaken.

"Yeah," she said, still looking outside as he moved in even closer to her body. "It seems the NCUA has a lot they think they need to teach me before I can become an active field investigator."

"You sure, hon? I mean, I thought you liked being a cop."

"I did, Jerry, I did." And that was true; she very much liked being a field agent but not an agent who needed to shoot people. Her training had never taken her that way; she never intended to be a field officer originally. She had gone to school to learn psychology, where she toyed with the idea of opening up a private practice listening to bored housewives ramble on about their wasted lives. That was her college idea, at least: easy work for a lot of money while she partied on into life. Back then she had also fantasized about raising two perfect children with Jerry, who would be a hardworking bread winner providing his family with a large house and all the amenities money could buy. Like a lot of people's college fantasies, however, hers had proven to be nothing but smoke and mirrors. During one of Jerry's many academic transitions, he had gotten involved in the law enforcement division. Bored out of her mind one day, Dawn went with him to class. Listening to his instructor speak inspired her deeply, passionately even. She liked psychology and, in truth, analyzing people and emotions had always come easily to her. Suddenly there was a way to apply her skills that made sense to her. The next quarter, only a few credits shy of graduating, she started pursuing a minor in law enforcement. It came as no surprise to her when Jerry switched majors again once she started doing better in class than him.

After graduating, Dawn began training with the FBI, and for that interim with the bureau she was away from Jerry for the first time since they began dating years earlier. She was already an active, working agent, checking backgrounds, by the time he managed to graduate. She believed at the time and, somewhere in the depths of her mind still believed, he only actually graduated so he could follow her to her new post in Washington, DC. Jerry, her eternal shadow, following her everywhere she went, with or without the sunshine.

"But I just can't be an agent anymore."

"OK, babe, the NCUA it is."

The National Credit Union Association was a federal organization that watched over credit unions in much the same way that the FDIC monitors banks. The NCUA insured deposited monies to make sure the average credit union member was safe and remained secure. A month and a half ago Dawn heard from an old friend that a new investigative post had opened. She knew the work at the NCUA wouldn't be anywhere near as exciting as the cases she worked for the FBI but it wouldn't be a matter of life or death, either. The people she would be investigating would amount to fraud. No murder, no rapes, no terrorists. She would start going after the white-collar criminals of the world.

"Jerry, how long have we been dating?" She knew the answer but, for some spiteful reason, needed to hear him say it.

"Twelve years."

The thought raced into her head immediately, *nine years too long*, but it was a thought she would never voice. She loved him and always would, but her love had slowly changed over the years and the passion had died. She didn't know how he didn't notice; perhaps it was simply because they had sex on a regular basis. She'd known more than a few men who mistook active sex for desperate love. Most men never understood that women need, want, and desire sex, too. "Twelve years," she repeated into the window, her breath fogging up a small section of glass, blurring her own reflection, "Twelve years."

"Have you ever cheated on me, Jerry?"

"What?"

He moved his hands off her shoulders and reached around, taking her in his arms so he could hug her warmly. "Are you kidding, Dawn? Baby, I've never even thought about cheating on you. You're everything I've ever wanted in a woman."

In terms of the perfect male-pattern fantasy Dawn knew what Jerry meant. She had been blessed in life with an exquisite figure, slow, sensual curves and a healthy amount of cleavage that, even when she aged would never sag too much. She was naturally athletic, participating actively in any sport that her hectic schedule permitted and jogging three to five miles each morning, no matter what. She was 5'6," though her height was adjustable depending on her shoes. She kept her hair long, not wanting to be one of those women who finds a career and suddenly cuts her hair as short as the men in the office. At work, when on duty, she simply kept her hair up in a neat, professional style. It allowed her the best of both worlds. She could look as professional as any agent on call but within minutes; transform herself into the epitome of what a man considered a woman to be. She kept herself well-tanned, even in the cold winter months she wasn't the type to wear clothes to show off her body, but for the few people who did see her in revealing items, she was going to be damn sure she looked good in them.

She could look in the mirror and see every genetic error. Some men said she was beautiful, but she never really believed them, mostly because Jerry never told her. He wasn't the type to toss out compliments easily, and because she had been a shy child, she rarely complimented him either. These issues were a few of the many things she was starting to address with the therapist she was seeing to help her through shooting Simon Walters. In school, she had to go through mandatory therapy as well. That was easier though, she was young and didn't have the issues she did now bottled up inside. She learned to play head games better than most in her class and sailed through the psyche evaluations with ease. These days, she knew the right things to say and could still play the games needed to get back to active duty, but now she wanted to talk, she wanted to be heard. Communication was never Jerry's strong suit, and speaking from the heart was always difficult for him to do without tears welling up. In the confines of the therapist's office, Dawn was allowed, for the first time in her life, to voice her feelings without having to worry about hurting his. She could be herself, the person she was afraid to be most of the time. She caught the doctor looking at her once or twice; he liked her long blond hair, her deep blue eyes, and the athletic body she only hinted at with what she wore to her sessions. She liked to know that men looked at her from time to time, and assumed that most women felt the same.

The therapist was deeply concerned about her relationship with Jerry, and on the day he said it to her, she burst out laughing, telling him she'd been concerned about it since she was twenty years old but always found a reason to stay with him. The doctor confessed he was amazed at how long they stayed true to one another, and, in a fit of honesty she told him about the other men in her life. The dirty secrets of herself she'd never planned to share with a soul, though with where she was emotionally, it seemed as good a time as any to admit to them.

Dawn knew she wasn't a saint and never claimed to be, though she could tell from the look in Jerry's eyes that this was exactly the way he viewed her. They started dating when she was seventeen and probably still saw her the same way she'd been back then. They were high-school sweethearts who intended to be "together forever." It was when she was nineteen, though; a tall, dark stranger awoke something in her that Jerry could never have dreamt of. She hadn't meant to cheat on him; it was just one of the things that happened, one of the times the games she liked to play got out of control. She didn't think of herself as a victim. She knew what she was doing and deep down she knew she wanted to cheat; however, words like "cheating" and "infidelity" weigh heavily on a woman's soul in the dead of night when the silence of darkness surrounds and only your conscience can be heard. In the twelve years Dawn dated Jerry as her supposed one and only, there had been five other men, never for lengthy periods of time but short, quick encounters that burned hot and fiery for a few months and then fizzled into nothing. Unlike the death scene of Simon Walters, Dawn never replayed her sexual memories of past lovers. They were indulgences from her past, not something she longed to do again. She wasn't the type of woman to pine for a man.

Despite her question she already knew the answer: Jerry wasn't the type to cheat. They were both virgins when they began to date; his entire life experience of sexual satisfaction was with her. When they were together, she knew it was an act of love on his part. He was working to satisfy only her, and she to satisfy him. Jerry picked this trait up at an early age; the other men, she noticed, didn't figure this out until they were older. When she turned twenty-five she took a field assignment from the bureau that pulled her away from Jerry for five months. She'd been placed with a forty-year-old agent who had recently divorced his wife. It was in his eyes that she had first seen the possibility of being with an older man. It took two months and a half-bottle of vodka to start their secret affair, but the three months that followed were the most sexually intense of Dawn's life. It was been the first time she actually considered leaving Jerry for another man.

The older agent took on a different assignment, and they stopped seeing each other. He claimed his religion didn't allow him to carry on the way he was with her. Jerry was spared that time by a religious complication that had nothing to do with her or how she felt.

The therapist really got Dawn thinking, pulling her from her comfort zones and mental safety nets. He asked her hard, pressing questions she didn't have answers for. He wanted to know why she was afraid of being alone, afraid to commit, and why she wanted so desperately to hurt the man she was supposed to be in love with.

"Why would you even ask that, Dawn?" Jerry's voice sounded shocked.

The truth would be so easy to tell him, she mused to herself as she straightened up and out of Jerry's embrace. "I was curious, that's all." She also knew the truth would devastate him. She had been true and faithful to him for the last eighteen months and she just couldn't find any reason to tell him what a fool she had played him for time and time again.

"Well, don't be. I'm not a cheater. OK?"

"OK," her voice was quick and sharp, her tone indicating she didn't want to discuss it further.

"What's gotten into you tonight? You seem so stiff . . . tense?"

"I've had a lot on my mind."

"About the new job?"

"No, Jerry I've known I was going to take this job from the moment they offered it." There, she thought, *at least the first part was out*. It wasn't a major thing, although she knew he'd react to it. She hated playing this mental game on him, hated the fact she was already working several sentences ahead of him, trying to stay focused and control the conversation, unlike the times she broached these topics in the past. If she was going to end this, she was going to do it right. The time had come for her to take charge of her life, and the major factor in her decision to start the new job with the NCUA in a new city was the fact that she could very literally start her life over, at least as long as she didn't take Jerry with her. It wasn't easy for her to do it, because she still loved him. The problem was it was no longer a passionate love, or one that thrilled her. She loved Jerry in a platonic way now, not as a soul mate. She didn't want to hurt him but she knew their time together really should have ended back when they were twenty. The last nine years had been filler space for both of them; he was just blissfully unaware of how far they had fallen apart. Tonight she was determined to tell him.

"A month?"

"Yeah, want a drink?"

"What?"

"I'm thirsty, I want a drink. I'm gonna get myself a beer; I'm in the mood for one. If you'd like one, let me know. I'll get you one, too." She kept her voice even, controlled.

He stared at her reflection in the glass, trying to study her but realizing he couldn't from the poor reflection and then finally shrugged his shoulders, "Sure. Whatever."

She drifted down the hardwood floor of the hallway leading to the oddly shaped kitchen at the back of the apartment, facing a vacant alley. The kitchen was circular and mostly inconvenient for cooking but it was entertaining to show to friends and associates when they stopped over for the first time. As it appeared to all, that whoever designed this kitchen had no idea what someone was meant to do within it. As she moved down the hall, slowly and deliberately, she could almost feel him starring nervously at the back of her head, a sign that he was starting to get scared even though he didn't know exactly why. As she reached the doorway where she would cross out of sight she heard him lean back against the old, rickety bookcase to wait for her return.

"So why didn't you tell me a month ago we'd be moving?" His voice wasn't clean; it had a nasal quality rising up at its edges, not a whine exactly, just the misplaced fear of the unknown. He could always sense when something was wrong, when she was maneuvering for something. He just wasn't sure what it was, and that concerned him.

Opening the fridge she pulled out two chilled bottles, light beers with the twist off caps that Jerry liked so much. Looking in the cooler she saw how little food they actually kept. They either ate out or made TV dinners. The extent of cooking for either of them consisted of macaroni and cheese or maybe the occasional tuna fish sandwich. "I didn't know how to tell you."

Still waiting for her in the entryway, he called out to her, "You know, there are still people I need to tell, too."

This was the part she dreaded, where it got angry and ugly. She needed to make him mad for this to work, which was her best line of defense to stop his tears from coming. Then she'd be able to get through it. That was what had stopped her so many times before; she couldn't stand to see him cry, or bring herself to break him down that much. That, more than anything else, was why she would never tell him about the other men in her life. He wouldn't get mad at that, at least not at first. He'd be hurt but it would take him years to step up to anger. That was why tonight was orchestrated and she was playing him for all he was worth.

"Who?" She walked back into the hallway. Her eyes were cool and collected, for the first time in front of him giving away nothing. She had already taken the first hit of beer from her bottle and was offering him up the other. He took it reluctantly, as his nerves continued thinning.

"People, friends, call my mother . . ." As he rattled off the inconsequential list, she took another drink of beer, defying his claims with a dead look in her eyes. "And work," he blurted out rashly. "I need to tell the people at work."

"It's a temp job, Jerry. If you decide not to show up tomorrow, they just replace you, no big deal."

"Is that what this is about? My job?"

"I think if it was about anything it would be about your lack of a job."

"Well, excuse me," Jerry said, starting to raise his voice, not caring, as he usually did, about disturbing their very close neighbors, "that I don't have a fancy, high-paying job with the goddamn FBI or that I'm not being headhunted by the *NC-fucking-UA*. I'm just a regular guy trying to get by!"

Dawn didn't squirm as she always had in the past when cowering to his raised voice. She knew he would never do anything but she had always stepped down from his raised voice as a courtesy to let him feel like a real man when he got angry. Tonight she wasn't worried about that so, instead of yielding, she simply took another hit from her bottle as he looked at her harshly.

Against her eyes, Jerry started to melt. He'd yelled at her, something he knew he hadn't wanted to do. His job was a point of frustration between them and always had been. He couldn't understand why she needed him to be in some job he hated. He liked working by the day, playing it fast, loose, and easy. He instantly regretted his angry words, and a second before he started to apologize, she pulled the half-empty bottle from her mouth sensing his shifting emotion and said, "Would you mind keeping it down? We do have neighbors, and I doubt they want to hear you whine." She needed to keep him angry but the moment she finished her line she realized she'd gone too far.

His left eye was the first to tear, and, instead of saying anything more, she walked into the living room and sat her bottle down on the coffee table as she slumped down onto the couch. He didn't move, just stood there in the hallway, trying to maintain his composure. She leaned her head against the back of the couch and tilted it slightly toward the ceiling. She wasn't looking at him but she could hear the first telltale signs of sniffling.

"I'm sorry, Jerry. I didn't actually mean that."

His voice was very shaky as he hovered on the brink of losing it; the first few tears were already starting to trickle down his face. "What is with you? You're not usually like this."

In her head she whispered, *"But it's not usually over."* It was another line she could never bring herself to say. "I'm being a bitch, Jerry, and I don't mean to be." Her eyes closed, tired of looking up at the foam-crunched ceiling.

Jerry stepped gently into the room, heading toward her; Dawn didn't open her eyes but waited for him to sit next to her. The pattern was starting up again: he was coming to her side like a scared child, and she wasn't stopping him. This was how he kept her; this was when she started realizing how mean she was being to a simple little boy in a man's body who just wanted to love her with an unconditional love he gave willingly and that she tarnished years ago through her discrete encounters. Even now, she asked herself how she could leave him.

He slowly wrapped his arms around her and leaned his head into her chest, like a baby animal nuzzling its mother. His grip was tight but not forceful. Dawn's arms were down by her sides and she dug her nails into her suit pants so as not to instinctively reach up and return his embrace. The decisions and the arrangements were already made, and while this was certainly the hardest step in changing her life for the better it was the most necessary. Dawn understood that, no matter how much growth she made as an adult, she was still seventeen-year-old Dawn Marie McCafferty. Still plagued by the scared, innocent little girl she once was. Looking at herself, which she did most often through Jerry's eyes, she was still the girl he had first gotten together with all those years ago. She was tired of being a child in a dysfunctional relationship, tethered to a past she no longer wanted to live. It was time for her to grow up and move on, and whether Jerry wanted to accept it or not, she knew it was time for him to do the same. They had created a codependent relationship. She counted on him for constant emotional support, because with him around she would never have to be alone. She knew he would come running at her slightest whim. She had taken the role of the dominant figure and allowed him to hide from his fear of confrontation. As long as they stayed together like this they would never change; she would continue cheating on him until it got so risky that she would make him find out, just to provoke him into a reaction.

It had to end somewhere.

"I didn't want to tell you a month ago," she whispered into the night as his trembling arms wrapped even more tightly around her, "because I wasn't ready for you to know."

"It's OK," he said, between short, gasping breaths.

"I'm a different person now, Jerry, and I don't know how to explain it to you. I killed a man. Someone who was out there, walking around alive and healthy, isn't anymore, and it's all because of me."

"It's OK, baby, I still love you. We'll get through this. You didn't do anything wrong."

"You don't understand what I'm saying, and I'm doing a terrible job of communicating it." She opened her eyes and looked at the scared man-child hanging onto her, both physically and emotionally. "I know I did the right thing when I shot him; that's not the question anymore. I've dealt with that. I mean, it still affects me that I killed someone, and I think that will continue to affect me and the actions I take for the rest of my life, but I'm comfortable that I made the right decision that day."

Her hand reached up as she ran the tips of her nails through his tangled hair. "This is about my life, the decisions I've made, and the decisions that still need to be dealt with. I think I was in such a rush to grow up when I was choosing my life that I may have made a few errors. I need to start looking at what I can do to be happy. I can't just exist anymore."

"I . . . I don't understand."

"Why haven't you ever proposed to me?"

"You said you didn't want to get married until you were ready for kids and you've always said you wanted to wait. Every time I've asked about kids you've told me 'next year' or 'not now.'"

"Why do you think I keep putting it off, Jerry? You know I've always wanted to be a mother and I used to want to be a young mother, but here I am at twenty-nine, and the chances of that happening are growing slimmer by the second."

She felt his grip tighten as he whispered reluctantly, "You put your career first."

"No, Jerry, I just put you second."

She didn't need to look at him to tell he was turning pale, or to see his tears were falling in earnest. His breathing became forced. "We can't go on like this," she said as quietly as she could.

"C-c-counseling . . ."

"The reason I didn't tell you a month ago that I was taking the job as Senior West Coast Claims Investigator for the NCUA, Jerry . . . is because when I go . . . I'm not taking you with me."

"Dawn . . ."

"Shhh . . . ," she said quietly.

"I don't want to lose you," he said, his words blurring against the coming hysteria.

She didn't know how to tell him he already had.

* * *

Breakdown 0.1

October 3, 1998

"I'm looking for a man who will take me somewhere in life, Tom, something that you'll never do at this rate!"

Tom stared down at the floor of his condo in a suburb of San Diego. The closest thing they had to a fall season had hit, and it had been raining throughout the day. The chill was still hanging in the air. The patio door was still open, since the evening chill only brought the coastal temperature down to about seventy. He wore a pair of loose shorts and an old T-shirt that hadn't really fit in a decade. He was drinking a Pepsi while sitting at his dining-room table, looking up at a girl fifteen years younger as she broke up with him. He knew he should care and should be reacting, saying all the right things to get her to stay, but at the ripe old age of thirty-eight, he just couldn't bring himself to care.

He could barely even think about what she was saying. His mind had been a million other places in the past few hours. Her name was Jenna, and she was leaving him. He couldn't blame her, really. They didn't love each other, and what brought them together wasn't some wave of romance or passion but loneliness and desperation. They were two lost souls trying to find shelter from life's brutality.

Tom Williams wished she'd just get through with it. He didn't need a lecture from a woman who hadn't even been alive when *The Godfather* came out on film. There were other things on his mind at the moment, and hearing he didn't really have a future wasn't going to help. The notice he'd gotten in the mail that day softened the blow of his recent news a little, but not enough. What Tom wanted from Jenna that night was comfort; that was why he'd invited her over. Like usual, though, they had jumped right to the sex part, hot and steamy but with a careless disregard for passion. They were both old enough to know how to make love, but neither one of them cared enough to make the effort. What happened when they got together was more like something out of *Animal Kingdom* than a romance novel.

He wanted to tell her his grandmother died the day before but he just didn't want to share with her something so very private, at least not with her in her current mood.

"So that's it? You're just going to sit there and drink your Pepsi like nothing matters?"

"What do you want me to say, Jenna?"

"Do you even know what you want out of life, Tom? Do you? You're stuck at a dead-end job you hate, you've just been passed over for the supervisory position you wanted, and you transferred departments at the Credit Union to get away from that bitch who got the job that should have been yours! Christ, Tom, was that the best your lawyer could do?"

"I'm very aware of where my life is at the moment, and Megan did the job she was hired for. OK? She's a very good attorney."

"How can you say that? You're a creative man, Tom! And you're going to Collections, for Christ sake! You're going to start repossessing cars and suing people!"

He was supposed to say it now, he thought; tell her he loved her. They would both know it was a lie, but it would be a reassuring lie they could both steal a moment of comfort from. Then he could tell her about his grandmother, and she'd cry and cradle him in her soft, gentle arms, and after a few hours of talking to one another quietly in the dark they would have sex again. Then he could tell her about what he'd received in the mail that day, and how things would soon change for him and, indirectly, for her.

"It pays well and I don't have to work for the bitch, OK?"

"You're a PR man, not a repo man."

The next set of words mattered most, he thought, he needed to tell her it was just temporary until he shopped his résumé around and found another marketing/PR position. She'd believe him, even though he would know it was a lie. He knew all the right things to say; he'd said them dozens of times before to different women who had occupied the same argument at different times in his life. This time was different, though, he was sure of it. But he wasn't focused right now, and a part of him didn't care what she thought. He didn't want to talk about this right now, but he knew she wouldn't let up. He looked up at her and smiled weakly, hinting not to get into this with him. "Not anymore."

"Why are you doing this? I thought we had something here?"

He finished his drink and looked up into her eyes. He wanted her to go. He'd loved his grandmother deeply, and she was dead, and he wanted time to grieve without having to justify his life at the same time. Jenna was a momentary diversion from a night of a few too many beers that lasted way beyond its prime. Tom's life was starting to fall apart, and he knew it, knew he needed to make changes. Getting rid of Jenna was just the first step. The second would take considerably longer to set up.

So they talked about life, and they broke up, and he never bothered to tell her about the registered letter he got with the check for $98,000 dollars, his portion of his grandmother's estate. If things had gone well he would have taken her to Hawaii for Christmas, but instead he was thinking he'd just go buy the Corvette he'd always wanted. All he had to do was the hard part, saying all the right things to break up with her so he wouldn't have to bear any guilt from their breakup, and then the task of deciding what color the Corvette should be.

There would always be another Jenna; there always had been before.

* * *

Breakdown 0.2

June 22, 1998

Flowers were placed on the grave.

It was nighttime and no one was allowed in the cemetery so late, but he had no place else to go. Nothing left for him to do but stare at what was physically left of the woman he loved, perhaps the only good thing to have ever really happen to him in his entire life. This was all that was left.

Everything he had was her, and without her he was nothing all over again. Even when she was in his arms he never realized how much he loved her. The sensation was almost overpowering. Now he couldn't even figure out what the point in living was.

He swore he was leaving and that he would never again come back to her grave. This wasn't the way he wanted to see her. He would rather look inside his head and recall the collection of memories that showed her living and breathing, laughing and dancing, not a dead husk of flesh, slowly lowered into the ground with a dark-gray marking for people to come and grieve. That wasn't who she was to him, not how he would remember her.

He would remember their wedding, all the small moments of the time they were together. That's what he would keep in his mind and, more important, in his heart. Those precious moments between them that mattered most.

But he would forget the promise he made to her back when they first got engaged, although when he thinks about it, he's not really breaking his word.

She'd made him swear that as long as they were together, he'd never break the law again. It was a promise he willingly made to be with her, but they weren't together anymore.

Now all bets were off.

Coming up Short

Coming up Short 1.0

March 8, 2000

Jim Krieder was a morning person, always had been. There was something about watching the sun come up in the morning that filled him with a sense of accomplishment, the kind that he had trouble expressing to most people. Every morning he got up and was at work by five.

He was a senior comp-op for the Hillsborough Industrial League Federal Credit Union. It was a big title that really meant he made sure that the Credit Union s computer systems stayed on line and that everything in the Informational Services Division ran smoothly. It was always dark in the privately owned building when he arrived. He was the first one in the building every day. Of course, the main reason for that was he was the one to disperse quite a bit of the morning workload to the varying departments and branches. He would go through the morning files, which were really just masses of reports the closing sys-analysts generated at the close of the previous day for the Logiterm System which they operated on. He would collect, collate, and then distribute, based on the principles of importance and who would be coming to work the earliest. For Jim it was pretty much the same day in and day out. He'd been working for HIL Fed, as most workers affectionately called it, for the last fifteen years.

Every morning Jim walked through the office and turned on the lights and the copier and the few other internal office pieces that were shut down when the last shift left. Before he ever went into his own office to start the collating process he would make himself a nice, strong cup of coffee while reading the comics out of the newspaper. Most of his supervisors knew he completely wasted the first ten to fifteen minutes of his shift, but he was a good enough employee that they overlooked it. Besides, he knew a large part of this gracious understanding was that no one else wanted to come to work at five in the morning.

Jim loved it. His office had a window that faced the sunrise, and he long ago adjusted his desk so he could watch it each morning. He'd sit in the makeshift break room for the computer department until he finished reading the two-page comics section in the *San Diego Tribune*. A childish pleasure he'd never quite grown out of. He'd fold the paper back over, leave it sitting on the center of the table, and approach the coffee machine. With his cup in one hand he would switch out the pot with his gigantic cup and then fill it right up to the rim before switching the pot back under the drip. It made for stronger coffee, which many of his coworkers learned the hard way when they took a drink from the wrong cup and tasted his "sludge," as they liked to call it. Relaxed from the comics and ready for the sunrise, he'd walk down the hall to his office. He could never honestly explain why the "motivational" signs on the walls of the long hallway amused him. When he was hired by HIL Fed he had been brought in to work in the Computer Department, but now it was called Informational Services Division. They did the same things, but they were called something new. The signs on the walls reminded him of the upper management's incessant need for meaningless buzz words that seemed to be saying something when what they, in fact, did was complicate what was working just fine originally.

Yawning as he walked into his office, Jim saw three extra stacks of reports on his desk and his computer blinking with an urgent e-mail message. All clear signs that a very long day awaited. He shook his head and sat his cup down as he pulled off his blazer and hung it on the coat rack on the side of the room. "At least it's not Monday," he whispered as he turned to face the stacks of reports that each rose up three feet from the top of his desk.

He didn't know where to start looking at the stacks. The night team was mostly young, punk kids, trained at trade schools over the course of five to six months and led to believe they'd make wages close to Bill Gates and never work an honest day again. The truth was, a few million other people had the same idea at exactly the same time as everyone else, so the computer market was flooded with marginally trained computer techs and network specialists. The price for their services dropped considerably unless they also had practical experience, so these kids went in search of real work and mostly found themselves taking jobs they felt were beneath them, while searching for the careers they felt they deserved. Jim had met a few of the night shift guys, and they seemed all right, mostly competent even. But they looked at him like he was over the hill and should be put out to Pasture. To them, anyone who was out from school for longer than a year and a half was a dinosaur in the computer field. The kids all thought they should have his job and salary, never stopping to consider that people like Jim had laid the very foundation for their own careers.

He spun around in his chair and clicked the mouse to read his e-mail. The name wasn't familiar at first, but realized it was one of the night-crew kids. He took a quick drink of his coffee, knowing he would need the fortitude of pure caffeine coursing through his system to deal with whatever these kids screwed up. In his eyes, they were always leaving behind some mess they didn't know how to fix. They didn't want to work any overtime; God forbid they stay in the office past one am to make sure there wasn't a problem. Mostly, what they couldn't solve was a clear sign of their own ignorance about the Logiterm Program that the Hil Fed financial system ran on. The great problems that perplexed them for hours in the evening or early morning hours usually meant about five minutes of cleanup work online in the active entry screen. He'd then wait for Doug Law to walk in, go into his office, and tell him the story. Both would laugh hysterically at the night-crew punks and wonder what happened to good old-fashioned knowhow that seemed to be completely lost in the Gen-X workforce.

Doug Law was the senior vice president in charge of Informational Services, which made him one of the most powerful people in the Credit Union. He had come on board about a decade ago, and he and Jim struck up a quick friendship. They were about the same age and thought alike, which helped the Credit Union to function. They shared the same disdain for these kids with visions of striking it rich in an already overcrowded industry. Like Jim, Doug knew that once these kids were out looking for a job starting at a hundred grand for about six months they would be willing to settle for forty something with the Credit Union along with a hell of a benefit package. They weren't terribly loyal but at least most of the time they got the job done.

Suddenly Jim was thinking about catching an early golf game after work and maybe see if Doug could get away early to join him. It was about then that he noticed the time stamp on the e-mail that floated across the screen: 3:57 a.m.

"What the . . . ?"

He read every line of the e-mail and then turned to look again at the stack of reports on his desk. A crazy thought ran through his head, and with a shaky hand he picked up his phone and dialed the conference room for the computer operators department. The informational services division was spread out into three locations; two were on the main site, across the hall from one another under heavy security doors, and the third was a few blocks away in an unmarked building that stored the backup files and ran on a skeleton crew. The phone rang twice before someone answered.

"Jim, is that you?"

He looked back over at his e-mail for the name of the sender. "Martin?"

"We are so fucked!"

They hadn't left yet. These guys who wouldn't work twenty minutes past their shift to fix a problem they themselves had created were still in the building more than four hours after they were due to leave. Suddenly the weight of these reports meant something to Jim, and he could feel a chill starting to work its way down his spine.

He paused for a minute, collecting his thoughts, rereading the e-mail, looking down at the top report. "Have you done a full diagnostic yet?"

"We'd have to shut down the active interface, Jim, for a full diagnostic. We had no idea how long that would take. It could bring the system down for the entire day! We don't have that authority."

"No," Jim said evenly, starring at the screen, trying to keep his heart from pounding. "But I do."

He looked again at the stack of paperwork in front of him as he heard Martin ask if he was sure. "Prep for shutdown and hold off for twenty minutes while I go over what you've already done. Got me?"

"Sure, Jim, sure . . ."

He hung up without saying good-bye.

Thirty minutes went by before he picked up the phone again to call Martin back. Martin sounded groggy and ready to pass out but too scared to let himself go. Jim was brief on the phone and he could already hear his voice becoming curt, but with what he was seeing he didn't really care. "It's me. Shut the fucker down."

"Jim . . ."

"My authority! Do it." With that, he set the phone down in its cradle and turned around to look into the rising sun. His hand was shaking, his nerves on end. He wanted to scream, and a part of him wanted to laugh at the absurdity of the situation. He wanted to believe he'd just lost track of the date and he'd turn to see it was really April Fools' Day but he knew better.

He picked up the phone again and dialed a number he knew as well as his own. It took four rings before the sleepy voice of Emma Law picked up. "H-h-hello . . ."

"Hi Emma, its Jim . . . I need . . . I mean, uh, can you put Doug on the line?"

"Jim? Is everything all right? It's so early."

"I need to talk to Doug. It's important."

It took a minute to make Doug alert. He'd managed to sleep through the ringing of the phone, and not being much of a morning person made him even less pleased to have to talk to someone. "What the hell is going on, Jim? Do you have any goddamn idea what time it is?"

"Doug," Jim said quietly, "I think you better get in here. Now."

"What in God's good name are you talking about?"

"We have a problem."

Even through the receiver, Jim could hear Doug's angry sigh, his building frustration. "Then fix it!"

"That's the problem. As far as I can tell from going over things, nothing seems to actually be broken."

"What the hell are you talking about?"

"Nightshift never left; they're still here going over everything, and I've ordered a complete shutdown of the system. When the branches open in a couple of hours they won't be able to log on, and to be honest, I have no idea when they will be again. This is big, Doug, and you need to be here and be briefed before Carlson walks in."

Hearing the CEO's name perked Doug up, which was the reason Jim used it. "Jim, what's going on here? You shut the system down? The live system?"

"Uh huh."

"Why?"

"Night crew noticed something big, Doug, really big."

"For God's sake, what is it?"

"We seem to be missing 320 million dollars, without any accounting for where it went, or even when."

For a full minute there was nothing but silence. This was the first time Jim had stated the problem aloud, and hearing the words only seemed to make it worse.

Doug's final words before hanging up were simply, "I'll be there in half an hour. Have the coffee ready."

* * *

Coming Up Short 1.1

March 8, 2000

They sat in Randolph Carlson's office, drinking coffee, and looking like they'd just been blindsided by a truck.

There were three of them at the moment, but more were coming; soon they'd have to move to the conference room because there wouldn't be enough room for everyone who needed to be included. Randolph Carlson had been the CEO of HIL Fed for three years. He was brought in when the previous CEO retired because he'd impressed the board of directors with his strong skills and progressive growth platforms. He was a number cruncher from way back; his degree in accounting was from the University of Texas and he didn't believe in remaining idle. He saw a new world of opportunity in modern technology, and he was hell-bent on bringing Hil Fed into the new millennium. Despite his good-old-boy looks and rather round gut, he'd proven himself to be dangerously effective in whipping the Credit Union into shape after its many years under a CEO who was timid about the future, much less preparing for it. Under Carlson's leadership and guidance their assets had soared to more than a billion dollars in record time. It impressed everyone. Because it was a local credit union in San Diego's active financial market, no one thought Carlson would be able to make Hil Fed develop as fast as he promised. But he did. They became one of the top forty credit unions in the United States, and everyone knew Carlson wouldn't be satisfied until the only credit unions above Hil Fed were national. "You know, its days like this I really wish I could spike this up with a little something stronger," Carlson said.

It was a joke, and both Jim and Doug knew it, but they didn't have the fortitude to laugh. They nodded and attempted to smile.

"After speaking to you on the phone, Doug, I contacted the other Senior VPs and told them they were included in a mandatory meeting that started twenty minutes ago. Not too many found the humor in it. Sally tried to argue with me, saying she hadn't been notified so she shouldn't get in any trouble. Amazing how some of these very smart people can't see the goddamn forest for the trees."

He took another sip of his coffee and then looked back across the table. "We know anything else yet?"

Jim straightened a little in his chair and recapped the morning's events until he finally got up to the new information. "The system is down for now, and we're going over everything from yesterday from before the closing report ran. I'm having them look through every single share account and general ledger; so far we have nothing."

"Then let me follow up with a CEO-type question, which I need to have an answer for when the shit really starts hitting the fan for us. We're a credit union, people helping people, all that shit. How long will the system remain down? People are gonna want access to their accounts."

"We don't even have a projection right now, Randy," Jim said quickly.

"Do the members still have access to their funds?"

"Downtime limits apply," Jim replied quickly, wanting to get back to the real issues, "so people won't be too adversely affected, but with a complete shutdown like we did this morning the FDR hookup won't work. Anyone who tries to use their Visa or Visa check card will be automatically denied."

Doug leaned forward again, his voice reassuring and calm. "However, we're linking up yesterday's file so people can have approval for our members that way. That should be a go within the next two or three hours."

"OK," Randy said in a big Texan drawl, "here's the other big question I want to ask before we get overcrowded. What happened to the money?" He took another drink of coffee, listening to their silence. "OK, fair enough. No answers yet. Last question, then."

"Yes?"

"I've never had anything like this happen before. We have a lot of money missing and a potential PR nightmare on our hands that could ruin us all, and I'd imagine there're a lot of laws and procedures we're supposed to be following at the moment, so my question is, what do we do next?"

Doug stood up at that point allowing Jim to relax a little. This was where Doug would start using the big buzzwords that Jim hated so much. He'd spent the last half hour downstairs helping Doug prepare what he was calling an "Action Plan." But all Jim could think about was the problem at hand. No matter what they called it or what they said, the money was missing, and Jim couldn't help but feel that the answer was right in front of his face.

* * *

Coming up Short 1.2

March 8, 2000

Dawn was pushing herself extra hard this morning. Turning thirty the month before managed to scare her more than she thought it would. She was now officially at an age she once thought she would never live to reach. She was running the river trail in Sacramento and had just passed the Train Museum. She was getting ready to head away from the freeways and the noise. She had taken the long way to get down to the river and to the Old Town section. She was already an extra mile beyond her usual stopping point and she was sure that she would feel it in her legs well into the evening as they reminded her she wasn't twenty-one anymore.

Tying her hair back into a ponytail was a trick that always made Dawn feel a little younger; that, and she was wearing her skimpiest pair of running shorts, the pair that best showed off her tanned and toned legs. The sports bra she wore held her tightly but still managed to show off her figure. She always attracted attention when she wore this outfit and therefore usually saved it for the days she needed a positive lift to her ego.

She'd been away for the earlier part of the month; a fraud scam in Oregon, she'd been dispatched to look into. She hadn't returned to town and her apartment until last night. It was only when she looked at the calendar that she noticed what the date was. It was one year and seven days ago that she broke Jerry's heart. Something she still hadn't quite forgiven herself for doing.

He'd suffered a breakdown after Dawn left, although a few of their mutual friends told her it was nothing too serious, he still needed help. Jerry's mother had always hated her, felt she programmed her son away from the life he was supposed to have. But as much as she hated Dawn she still took her money every month to help pay for Jerry's medical bills. Psychiatric help doesn't come cheap, and with Jerry not having a real job, there was no medical insurance to absorb the cost. She'd felt guilty and sent money but, she couldn't bring herself to fly back to Washington, DC to see him, and his doctor really hadn't wanted her to, either, saying Jerry needed to learn to be strong on his own. So for four months after she left, she sent a check to his mother, never receiving a single thank you.

After six months Jerry went back to working and started to look like he was going to really try to put his life back together. She received an e-mail from him during the summer that sounded incredibly positive. She gave him a quick reply, wishing him the best. The problem was his e-mails had never stopped.

Jerry wanted desperately to get back together with Dawn and was still offering to move out to California. Anything to be with her again. She was trying to be nice, because she didn't want to do anything that might set him off again but she knew she didn't want to have him nearby. She knew how he was; if he was anywhere close he'd be at her side constantly, smothering her. It wasn't that she wasn't lonely sometimes; it was one of the hazards of being single, and Dawn understood that on a very basic level. It was one of the many reasons she stayed with Jerry for so long. The fear of being alone was a powerful thing, and breaking out from under their dependent relationship was one of the hardest things she ever did. How simple it would be for her to get back together with him; a familiar touch on a lonely night might be an easy trap to fall into. A trap would be exactly what it was though. One night would be all it would take for Jerry to assume that last year was forgotten and that they would be together again forever. There wasn't any part of her that didn't still love him, but if she was sure of anything, it was that getting back together was something she did not want to do.

She was feeling all of the emotional turmoil that went along with turning thirty. Single at thirty to most people meant being over the hill and having no hope of ever finding anyone. She didn't really believe that, but the thought still hung above her like a specter in the night. She leaned her head into the run, sticking to the well-marked trail for joggers and bicyclists, ignoring the bums who made their evening homes in the bushes by the river. She wasn't worried about them; she'd been trained to defend herself by the FBI and could fend off any half-coherent bum the world could throw at her. She did not think about the death of Simon Walters or anything else that happened last year in Washington and knew she would be able to focus on the moves she'd been taught with the bureau if suddenly needing to defend herself.

The beeping started as the city started to disappear from her peripheral vision. The one item of technology she brought with her everywhere, even jogging, was her cell phone. When she ran she didn't want to be bothered with music. This was her time; she didn't need a Walkman to tune out the world around her. She would just close down a good portion of her senses and focus on herself. It was like she placed a barrier around herself, shielding her mind from the world at large. If she had the choice she wouldn't even take the phone, but her job required it. She was on call for emergencies because it allowed her far more flexible hours and it really didn't matter because they only called with the really big stuff. It was a private number that she gave to no one; that way she always knew it was business when it rang.

She stepped off the runner's path and flipped the phone out of the belt loop she had fixed to the small of her back. As she stopped running, the sweat started. Strangely, even during her toughest workouts, the sweat didn't usually start until afterward, at the moment her body finally relaxed and she lost her intense focus. Her breathing became heavy and labored, and streaks of warm sweat dripped from the pores around her hairline. It was only marginally annoying. She grabbed the small phone, flipped it open, and brought up to her ear.

"It's Mac." She always answered the digital line that way, with a short version of her last name that she didn't often go by or even particularly like. Still, it made for a short, grunt-like greeting that most of the male employees who called her seemed to both understand and respect.

Dawson's voice filled her ear. Dawson was about fifty going on a hundred. He was also about as overweight as one man could be and looked like he was ready to die at any given moment. But he was one of the few people back at the main office Dawn honestly liked. He was old school and said what he thought, no matter how politically incorrect it might be. His first name was Josh, but no one ever called him by it. "Hey ya, Toots," he said in his usual gruff snarl that was far more good natured than anyone gave it credit for. "Get your ass into central and pack a suitcase. You're hitting the road."

"How soon?" She was purposely being short, wanting him to know she was busy. She also still felt more than just a little out of breath.

"Let me put it to you this way: Neal mentioned something about sending a car to pick you up from your place because you drive like the little old lady from Pasadena."

"Neal can kiss my ass."

He roared into the phone. He had a large, boisterous laugh that filled any room and seemed to reverberate off walls to form its own echo. Most people found it contagious. "Hon, we both know he'd like nothing better. But he's still your boss."

Dawson was one of the few people around the office who knew that Neal Johnson, Dawn's direct supervisor, started seriously hitting on her about five months ago, to the point of bordering on sexual harassment. Dawn knew it stemmed from his own loneliness; he was recently divorced, and his ex had taken both his young children and moved back home to North Carolina. He was a serious workaholic and really had very little opportunity to meet people in general, much less single women. He was forty-seven but still in rugged shape that showed he utilized the private gym his rank and stature commanded. Something about Neal just turned her off, something she couldn't quite put her finger on. So she turned him down when the advances started. What she hadn't known was that he was already telling people he was after her.

By nature, Dawn flirted, not seriously but a little here and there. People like Dawson knew it was just a game; people like Neal didn't. It passed the time, and anyone who could find intelligent ways to make it fun got flirted with more than others. Despite the fact that Neal was a rather arrogant little piss-ant of a man who viewed himself as some form of second coming, he was well educated. He also had certain street smarts and was quick on his feet. His senses may have dulled from riding a desk too long, but he was still an interesting man to talk with on occasion. When Dawn first met him she didn't have a clue divorce was on his horizon. If she had she never would have flirted with him in the first place. She could see by his very nature that he played for keeps, never just for fun, and even the most casual smile between a woman and a man meant something to him. So he asked her out, and she said no, and he assumed she was playing hard to get. The professional relationship between them had been slowly deteriorating ever since. "Tell him I'm not at home."

"He knows you'll have the phone with you and he'll just have me pick you up wherever you're at."

"Tell him anyway; let him think somebody's getting lucky." Dawn's evil little smile caught the eye of a passing jogger, a man in his late forties who grinned as he went by. Dawn winked at him and watched as he blushed.

"You'd rather I didn't."

"And why's that?"

"Because he's planning on going with you."

She was slowly walking back down the river, approaching old town again at a much more leisurely pace. A scowl crossed her face at the mere idea of traveling with Neal. "I beg your pardon?"

"I guess this one's pretty big."

"Shit, he's really going? He never leaves the office. This could prove to be a large pain in my ass!"

"Sorry."

"Don't say you're sorry, Dawson. It's not your fault." Dawn could feel the coolness of her sweat as she walked along the trail, and the breeze coming off the river was still fresh with a morning chill.

"Still and all."

"It's OK," she said resigning herself to what was coming, "I've traveled with him before, survived it then. I'll survive it now."

"So, do you want me to have you picked up at your house or someplace else?"

"I'm on foot, down by the river. Even if I had the energy to run back to my apartment, the motivation wouldn't be there. Expect twenty minutes for me to even get home, another half hour to pack."

"He's really going to hate that."

"Tell him I'm a woman. I take longer to get ready. A guy like him, that's an excuse he'll understand."

"Didn't say he wouldn't understand. Just that he wouldn't like it."

Dawn was back in the old town section, where people milled about aimlessly, walking casually by the river, eating ice cream, and wasting away the bright, sunny morning. "So give me a clue, Dawson. What's so big as to get him out from behind his desk?"

She was still walking along the river when Dawson told her; she stopped instantly, almost dropping the phone. "Did you just say what I think you did?"

"Uh huh."

"Screw it, I'll run back. Have the car meet me in twenty-five minutes."

"You got it, toots." He laughed as he hung up the phone, not feeling at all bad that he didn't wait for her response. He knew her well enough to know there wasn't going to be one. She had already closed her phone and started running home. He laughed for another reason, too. He'd already dispatched a car to meet her in forty minutes.

She wasn't like most of the people he met around the NCUA; she didn't do what she did to obtain monetary rewards, promotions, or special titles. She did what she did because she was good at it and, more than that, enjoyed it. She loved the chase, the hunt. She was never happier than when the drama was at its highest point. He couldn't think of anything higher than the loss of 320 million dollars. If paid out, it would be the largest fraud claim the NCUA ever dealt with. They'd want full effort on this one, and more important they'd want someone's ass in a sling when the investigation was done. Not that it would matter to Dawn, Dawson knew; all she cared about was solving the case. He knew that for Dawn McCafferty, the game had just officially begun.

* * *

SETTLING IN

Settling in 2.0

March 8, 2000

They were in the air before they said a word. A good portion of the time before that he'd spent with his ear buried in a phone. She wasn't entirely sure if he was talking business or personal and didn't really care enough to eavesdrop. Neal was dressed in a full suit and tie. Unlike Dawn, his job was filled primarily with administrative duties. He ran his own little world and enjoyed his Monday-through-Friday, eight-to-five job. Of course with him, it was more often six-to-six. Even here on a plane, when he could enjoy some downtime, he was dressed like he was ready to meet the governor. He wore a heavy gray suit with the thinnest of stripes weaved in and a tie that Dawn was pretty sure didn't match. His hair slicked back in an effort to conceal the growing bald spot at the back of his head. Since Dawn hadn't really wanted to travel with him anyway, she considered his silence a bonus. There were three of them: Neal, his toady, Marc and her. Marc was a climber in the organization, or at least hoped to be. He possessed no special investigative talent but he had a stunning ability to kiss ass that could amaze anyone. Neal, like most people who entered into management positions, needed someone to validate him. Gone were the days when work and commitment mattered. In today's world, the true corporate world of modern-day America, employers threatened constantly that the door was a single step away and that any employee could easily be replaced. No one's supervisor believed in giving praise, so supervisors took it from underlings who were willing to fawn all over them. People like Marc made Dawn sick to her stomach most of the time. But on this occasion she was glad that the few things Neal had said en route to the airport were to him.

In her head she thought of other things, diversions she taught herself to focus on to pass the time on long flights. She would construct riddles, sometimes ones that could eventually be solved. She wasn't bound to a book when traveling because she had the vastness of her mind and she liked to see what limits she could push it to.

"This will be the largest robbery we've ever had to deal with."

Neal's voice bordered on excitement but refused to go over the edge. His official response couldn't be excitement. She knew he was thinking of the press. If they managed to catch the thief, he'd have a whole new level of political distinction and a promotion practically guaranteed.

"Are we sure it's a robbery? The way Dawson set it up for me, all we know at the moment is that a lot of money is missing."

They had to be careful how they spoke because they were still in public. The NCUA wasn't big enough to charter private flights. They used commercial transportation and even though they were in business class for the relatively short flight down to San Diego they didn't want to say anything too clearly. Some things still needed to be discussed, though, even if they knew the answers.

"That much money isn't a technical error, Dawn. No one misplaces that much, especially not all at once. Somebody took it."

The thing was, she agreed with him, but her investigative skills told her to keep it under wraps. As is always the case, if you want something to happen you can make it happen with enough effort. She was afraid if they both went in gung-ho looking for a thief they'd find one, whether the problem was a computer glitch or not. The foundation of good investigative work was to not jump to any conclusion, no matter how minor, until the facts were present to support it. At the moment, the only fact they had was that 320 million dollars was missing, and no one at the Credit Union knew where it was or how it went missing. It could still be anything. Sure, Dawn knew somebody was behind it, could feel it in her gut already. But she wouldn't allow her investigation to become suspect. She would play by the rules, and the first step was getting to San Diego, reviewing the facts, and then making her official determination. "I thought you always said anything could happen." She wanted to play with Neal a little to make him uncomfortable in front of his toady. She resented him being here on her investigation. She knew Neal too well to not know he'd constantly interfere with the case in an effort to appear like he was essential to the investigation process. That way, when all was said and done, he was covered either way. If they caught the thief, which Dawn was sure she would, he'd take full credit for it and simply name her as his chief investigator. If they were unable to find the thief she'd take all the blame when the NCUA covered the Credit Union's actual loss.

That was why they were all on the way to San Diego. Truth be told, there wasn't one person with the NCUA who really cared that some credit union screwed up and lost a lot of member-owned money. What they cared about was that the financial insurance on those members' funds didn't come from the FDIC like commercial banks; it was the NCUA who covered credit unions. If they couldn't find the money, the Credit Union would be forced to liquidate its assets and purge its reserve accounts, and then the NCUA would be forced to issue a check for approximately 300 million dollars. The effects of this outcome would be long term and devastating to the economy as well as to credit unions everywhere. Once word hit the streets, Hil Federal Credit Union would fall apart. Members would lose faith, and the company would be out of business within two years at best Instantly losing anything they would have once called a market share. Mass layoffs, the closing of branches, and a very poor reputation would be inevitable and the rest of the credit unions nationwide would be tarnished with the same brush. Banks would jump on it. They'd talk about how credit unions couldn't safeguard money like they could. The NCUA was a federal organization, so Washington DC would also feel the blow. Legislation for credit union rights would be trampled under the weight of this happenstance, monies would be questioned and consumer rates would be affected because of the strain on the government. As insignificant as $300 million dollars might be in Washington DC, the amount would still be noticed, and its loss would still breed enough resentment that it would take years to wipe away the stigma surrounding the event.

So they really had no choice; they had to find out who committed the crime. But that wasn't their only objective because the NCUA wasn't, by nature, a criminal investigation unit. They were in place to watch over credit unions and protect the money on deposit for members. Dawn knew what her objectives were, even if Neal hadn't clearly stated them yet, they were three fold: first, find out how it happened, and make sure it could never happen again; second, find out who had done it; third, retrieve the money. This was Dawn's future. Most people would consider this turn of events to be the end of any fun she might hope to have, but in her eyes, it was just the opposite. This was what Dawn lived for. This much money meant she was up against one of two things: a lucky amateur who'd go down in a heartbeat once the heat was on or a serious player who would actually pose a challenge because they was ready for what would happen next. They wouldn't be ready for her, though, she thought. *No one ever was.*

Neal and the toady, and probably everyone else involved, wanted the amateur as their adversary. Dawn wanted the serious player. She'd been gone from the FBI too long and hadn't had a serious challenge since joining the NCUA. For the first time since signing on, she saw a case that presented itself with the life drama she craved. It was all she could do to hold back her excitement. If Neal wasn't on the plane, she knew there was a good chance she'd be bouncing up and down in her seat, waiting anxiously to land, like a child waiting to play. The game would soon begin in earnest.

"Anything can happen," Neal said weakly, looking out the window, "but we both know that a credit union of that size didn't make an error like this."

They sat in silence for a few more moments. Dawn could tell that even Marc was getting antsy under its weight. "So why are we working this together?"

"What do you mean?"

"I mean, why us? Why didn't you send Schoreder in on this if you were coming? The last time we tried working together, it didn't turn out so well."

"We're both adults, Dawn," Neal said, as his usual arrogance crept into his voice. "I assumed we were both ready to try again."

"For the job?" Her tone was flat and even, revealing nothing. It was a staggering weapon in the unending battle of the sexes. She would remain still, and the monotonous quality of her voice would get those around her to start talking wildly to fill the silence.

"Of course, Dawn." His teeth were already starting to grind. "I can take no for an answer."

He shifted uncomfortably in his seat, wanting to drastically change the subject and move on with the conversation. "We'll have a car meet us at the airport. It will take us straight to the Credit Union while Marc goes to get us lodging at one of those executive suite places. I'm told there are a number of them near the Credit Union's main office. We'll meet up with some executives from CUNA as well." She knew that CUNA stood for the Credit Union National Association, which concerned itself with all things relating to credit unions. Image and public relations were high on their list of priorities. They'd be concerned about the long-term, or even short-term, ramifications of the situation. "Undoubtedly, they'll be annoying us at every turn and wanting a speedy resolution."

He couldn't bring himself to stop talking, not when she just sat there staring at him with her wistful blue eyes. "Other law enforcement types will be involved, though we aren't making an official announcement yet. The local authorities aren't being brought in at all, just us and the feds. Because of the negative PR quality to this, we don't intend to announce this until after we've at least conducted the preliminary investigation. Investor confidence is crucial."

"Is our star highest?"

"I beg your pardon?" he asked, delighted she was speaking again.

"Who's at point on this? The feds, CUNA, or us?"

"We are. I talked to a friend over at the federal building en route to the airport. He found out you were on the case and said he'd give us some time to get to the heart of things. They'll only step in if we screw up. Sometimes your reputation with the bureau really comes in handy."

"I suppose it does."

"Look, I know you don't like me throwing around your name or past, but in this case, we can show the NCUA is just as effective as any other government agency." He was starting to talk like he was standing before the press. She hated it when he did that.

"How's it going to work?"

"What?"

"The investigation."

He shook his head, a sign of his growing frustration. "Like it always works. We investigate, we find the bad guy, we press charges, and we turn it over to the courts."

"When I'm sent in, it's usually as lead investigator, like my title states. With you on scene, am I just here to keep the feds at bay?"

"You're still lead investigator, and you'll set up the parameters. I'm just here to maintain integrity."

"You don't think I would do my job with integrity if you weren't here?"

"That's not what I'm saying, Dawn, it's all a political show. I'm here in case things go badly so I can verify that you did everything by the book."

She looked forward, down the aisle of the plane. "And if we succeed?"

"I'll give you a gold star."

"Oh, goody," she said dryly, knowing he hated to be placated, "something to look forward to."

* * *

Settling in 2.1

March 8, 2000

They were all gathered in the executive boardroom on the fourth floor of the Hil Federal Credit Union building. A cold, impersonal aesthetic dominated the room in an attempt to convey an image of grand deals and executive power. This was the world Dawn was slowly getting used to during her time working with the NCUA, a world she disliked. They were all gathered around, the same people who existed in a hundred other credit unions she'd seen. Men and women of all ages and all sizes, all programmed or, at the very least, conditioned to speak identically. They were all looking at the small team of NCUA and CUNA people who'd come to save the day. Dawn wanted nothing more than to take charge and tell them exactly what to do but no matter what Neal said, she knew better. They all had to make their speeches first, exchange glances, and establish the pecking order of authority.

The flight from Sacramento had only taken about fifty minutes and as Neal promised two cars were there to meet them. One took Marc to the hotel, and the other took them to the Credit Union. Dawn knew the drill: they'd meet and greet and shake all the hands, say all the right things. Then they'd promise fast results. They'd do a quick review of the situation with the actual facts at hand and call for a support team of trained auditors, the ones Dawn usually referred to as "the suits." She was young and pretty and could therefore get away with the off-handed remark in the mostly male trenches of CPAs working as auditors. They were necessary in an investigation like this. Dawn had no intention of wading through miles of pages containing nothing but small numbers and odd abbreviations; she was there to look for a suspect. She'd count on "the suits" to find the number angle. She wished only to concern herself with the people angle.

    Neal was still annoyed with her for taking so long at the airport, as his gruff manner during the ride over clearly illustrated. She didn't care, though, nor did she bother informing Neal what the real delay was. Since they flew commercial she couldn't take her firearm on board, and with 320 million dollars at stake, she refused to work without a gun. Dawn knew Neal didn't like guns very much, and truth be told, neither did she, at least not anymore. But her bureau training taught her to always be prepared by having a gun on a case like this, whether she thought she needed it or not. Trying to get a piece through proper channels would have taken forever. The last phone call she made before the car pulled into the driveway at her apartment building was to the local FBI office. Her contact list was still strong, and she let them know an abridged version of what was going on. They knew her permit to carry a concealed weapon in the state of California was still valid and managed to find a gun available that no one else was using. She knew it was a request that wouldn't have been honored for many ex-federal agents but she still enjoyed some of the privileges her former life afforded, being known for saving two fellow agents didn't hurt her reputation. A female agent she knew only in passing was waiting at the exit gate and motioned to the closest bathroom. Inside, she handed over the piece to Dawn without a word. Two clips followed, and by the time Dawn placed all the gifts in her purse and looked back up, the agent was walking away.

    She stepped into a stall and, as quickly as she could, did a safety test on the weapon. The first rule of a firearm was to make sure you understood the weapon you were going to carry. Dawn wasn't able to start firing to get a true feel for it but she loaded it and got used to its weight in her hand. She had always been meticulous about her guns back in the bureau, mostly because she grew up not particularly liking them. FBI training showed her another side to the myth of personal firearms. She certainly knew the mental power a person with a gun held but she learned firsthand the joy of shooting and hitting the target. She would never be the markswoman she would like to be but she knew she was good enough to get the job done. Simon Walters discovered that as well.

    By the time she got out of the bathroom and the three of them walked to the baggage area, her delay had managed to push Neal's buttons and patience. It took forever to get their bags, which did nothing to improve Neal's annoyance. Dawn's ten minutes in the bathroom had thrown his time schedule off by half an hour. On the car ride to the Credit Union, he obviously wanted to ask what the hell took her so long but was afraid of what the answer might be. It amused her to no end how squeamish men got when women talked about what they did in the bathroom.

They were shuttled off to the Credit Union in a hurry. Walking into the boardroom, Dawn couldn't say she was surprised to see so many people. She'd always known that nothing brings out a crowd like tragedy. The people in the boardroom could smell ruin in the air. Their careers, their lives, everything. They all secretly wanted to be the one who saved the day, salvage the situation, but the Hillsborough Industrial League Federal Credit Union was well beyond any internal version of salvation. She knew the moment they had decided to bring in people from the outside the writing was on the wall.

She stayed quiet when she entered the room and let Neal wax political with the others. She didn't care what any of the names were scattered about the room. In the next few days, she would get to know them all better than anyone else ever had. For now she was more than happy to consider them all strangers and suspects. Besides that, she wanted to listen to them first, hear their words and try to pick out, if not sense, their inherent weaknesses. It was a fairly easy task to accomplish. Walking in a full stride behind Neal made them all think she was just his assistant; letting him take the lead like he really knew what he was doing allowed her to drift quickly into the background. The people from CUNA, or the one, lone FBI representative sitting silently in the far corner of the room, might have known who she was, but even that wasn't sure. For now, it was Neal's turn.

"Hello, I'm Neal Johnson; I'm the chief administrator for the West Coast Investigations Unit of the NCUA. Pleased to meet you."

"Hello, Neal, my name's Randy. I'm the CEO 'round here. Hope you don't mind jumping forward to the point where we're all on a first-name basis, but I'm having a hell of a day."

They shook hands firmly, each trying to convince the other that they were the bigger man. Looking on from a slight distance, Dawn knew that neither of them could ever back up the handshake they offered.

"I understand, Randy."

"So tell me something then, Neal. You here to save my ass?"

Neal wasn't used to a man in Randolph Carlson's position speaking so openly. He was used to far more of the useless, ceremonial bullshit, and even from across the room, Dawn smiled at the small trace of discomfort that crossed Neal's face as he talked with a man who held a position of power and still managed to speak his mind.

"Actually," Neal said, trying to take a solid lead in the conversation, "I'm here to stop us from writing a check for three hundred-plus million dollars. If that happens to save your ass as well, then hey, I'm all for it."

"Just as long as I know where you're coming from."

Neal took a quick look around the room and then turned back to Randy. "I think it's best if I speak to them all up front. Save the introductions for later and cut to the chase."

"Let's get to it, then."

"How about introducing me?"

Randy stepped up to the hard oak boardroom table and slammed his two palms down flat on it. The thundering sound rattled the table and silenced the room instantly. Dawn watched him closely, loving his style.

There were easily thirty people in the room, all dressed in their professional best and most looking very worried about what was going to happen next. Dawn reached into her purse and pulled out a small notebook and a pen. She wasn't going to take notes; she was going to start listing her plan of action. The first thing she wrote on her to-do-list was, "Get company roster of employees."

"Attention, everyone," Randy bellowed with a voice that wasn't filled with his usual confidence. "The show is about to begin. And this is one you do not want to miss."

He picked up a glass of water and took a quick sip to clear his throat. "When I first got hired on here, I promised you a grand ol' time. I remember it clearly. Told a few of my big Texas stories and even got a few chuckles from those who didn't normally let loose a laugh. Every once in a while, I'm reminded of my first few weeks and the boastful promises I made. Now, sure, I never did cover the back parking lot in Astroturf so we could start our own football team and I didn't turn the boardroom here into a cow patch like I threatened on more than one occasion. But I promised you I'd take this credit union to places it had never been before. Today is no different."

"Today we're facing a problem like we've never had to face; hell, like no credit union has ever had to face. I promised you once I'd bring you a three-ring circus and now I'm here to tell you I was just the opening act. We're in the spotlight now, so I'm gonna introduce you to the fine folks from the NCUA who intend to make sure we all still have jobs by the end of the week."

"The gentleman from the FBI has told me the NCUA will get to handle the first wave of investigation, mostly because he has full confidence in their abilities in this particular area of investigation, namely credit union theft, but has assured me that the bureau will be working in conjunction with them. With that in mind, I'd like to officially introduce you to the ringleader of this circus, a gentleman by the name of Neal Johnson. Neal?"

No one clapped as Neal stepped up next to Randy, and watching him step up, Dawn knew it annoyed him. He shook Randy's hand again and looked out at the mixed group of people united by fear and panic. "Hello, everyone," he said coolly. "As Randy just said, my name's Neal Johnson, and I'm not quite a ringleader but I am an investigator for the NCUA and I am here to find out what happened to your money."

Dawn refocused completely on her notepad. Number two on the list was obvious: she wanted a credit report on every employee. It was expensive, but completely necessary in this case, she thought. She wanted the names of everyone who had worked on their computer system, whether permanent employees, temps, offsite consultants, whatever. The first wave of interviews would be with the online programmers on staff. She knew she needed to be logical, build a network case, just like they would back at the FBI. She couldn't afford to be sloppy. Too much money was at stake for this not to be watched closely. That was why Dawn was setting things up to happen the way she was.

". . . So as you can see, we bring a lot to this table to offer the Credit Union in its time of need. Already, we have two dozen people flying in to help us with the background work. But what I really want to talk to you about is values, namely the values of what a credit union stands for."

She tuned him out again. He was speaking for the media, even though none were present. It was a habit of his that she utterly detested. She didn't want to waste her time or energy listening to him; she needed to find that quiet place inside her where she would have the strength to solve the problem. Still, she made it a habit to occasionally listen to a few of Neal's words here and there, just to make sure he was still saying nothing she cared about listening to.

"Dawn?"

Her eyes opened, which surprised her since she hadn't been aware they were closed. She was sure Neal thought she'd been napping, but nothing could be further from the truth. She knew how to enter her own head, to basically shut out the entire world around her and focus only on her most basic thoughts.

Opening her eyes, she saw the room looking at her, waiting for her to make her move. She didn't need to be drawn a picture; she knew she'd just been officially introduced. She smiled politely at the room and stood. She glanced at her watch and saw that she'd tuned herself out of reality for almost twenty minutes. If she hadn't been in such a public setting she'd have been very proud of herself for the length of her discipline.

"That's me, Neal. Thank you." She dropped her notepad to the table gently. "I hope you'll all excuse me if I don't walk to the head of the table. Mainly because I think it would be a waste of energy, since what I have to say will be brief. I'm not the public speaker Neal is. I'll be the lead investigator on this case, and for some of your departments, I will be the biggest pain in the ass you've ever encountered, and you will grow to hate me."

Her voice was cool and stiff. She wanted to throw up walls around herself to shut out everyone and she wanted to put them in a position to try and breakdown those walls, right from the beginning. Being a woman was still a challenging thing; even in the year 2000, she had to work twice as hard to get half as far. She needed everyone in this room to know she wasn't going to be a pushover.

"I feel it's important to tell you this because I don't care if you hate me. What I care about, all I care about comes down to three things: find out how it was done, stop it from happening again, and catch who did it. The rest is all crap. The rest is your concern, not mine."

"Some of you I will speak with in teams, others I will talk to individually. In some cases I will ask very difficult questions, some of which you may not want to answer. Again, I don't care." She let her words hang for a moment so they could absorb what she meant. "My goal is to solve this."

She stepped away from the table, stretching her legs and walking around the boardroom. "Our first order of business here is to prove that a crime has actually taken place. I believe it as much as anyone else in this room. However, in any investigation I conduct I will base my conclusions on facts. Therefore, we must prove that a crime has been committed. We need to eliminate any chance of an internal or computer error. The moment that is accomplished, we will actively begin a network criminal investigation. Neal and I will be spending a good portion of the rest of the day making sure it wasn't an internal error. By this evening, I suspect we'll be looking for a criminal."

It pleased her to know that Neal was already sinking down into his chair. He didn't like it when she came on with what he called her FBI persona. It made him uncomfortable seeing her take charge so easily, watching her carelessly disregard the feelings of the people who surrounded her. Neal was a people person; she was not. For her it worked in a way that troubled most people deeply. She was effective.

"I know that if I polled this room it would be ripe with theories and ideas but I can almost guarantee you how it happened. The trick is narrowing down the details, because no matter how careful whoever did this might have been, the details always show them up in the end."

"Again, I thank you for your time and attention today. I'll speak with you all later."

Without making eye contact with a single person, Dawn stepped up to Neal, who was holding onto a pathetic attempt at a political smile as he stared at the speechless group of important people. She leaned down and, without taking the slightest effort to muffle her voice, said, "It's time to get to the computers."

* * *

Settling in 2.2

March 8, 2000

It was after Doug Law finally left them alone that Dawn was able to get into the files. Neal wasn't there, which pleased her. He'd stayed with the executives, saying he wanted to smooth over the rough edges she'd left behind. Doug agreed to escort her down to the bottom floor and walk her into the secured area of the building until they got her a badge of her own.

He leered. He tried to be subtle, the entire ride down in the elevator and then even more as he was fixing her up with a magnetic key badge to get her past the security doors. The upside to the experience was meeting Jim Krieder. Dawn liked him; he was competent and less worried about his job security than any other person she'd met since arriving. He walked her through how to read their reports in a scholarly way, not an elementary one. She appreciated it. Most of the credit unions she worked with had some guy trying to play the role of the big man, showing the little lady how they did things. Krieder cracked a few jokes and even pointed out the things he hated. With his aid and her previous knowledge, she was up to speed within an hour.

He looked tired, and she knew why. He was old school and had no intention of leaving until he had some answers. Dawn also liked the fact that he was leaving her alone, wasn't peering over her shoulder every time she made a notation in her notebook. It was six thirty when she got through the main stack of paperwork and looked up at him empathetically. "So, this is really your job, going over all these numbers?"

"Day in, day out."

"I think I might kill myself."

He chuckled as he put his feet up on the desk that faced her. He'd given up his desk to her, wanted her to have full access to the same resources he did. He spent a lot of time in the outer office using the workstation desk for the small things he still needed to get done. "I guess I'm not much of a people person. I'd rather spend my time with numbers."

"You married?"

"Once."

"Not anymore?"

"She liked people, didn't much care for numbers. Liked one person a lot. What I didn't know was that person was my best friend."

She moved one of the mammoth stacks of paper out of her way to get a better view of him. "You ever hook up with anybody else?"

"Nobody else was her."

"Yeah," she said, smiling at him from across his desk, "I could see how that would get in the way."

"You want a cup of coffee?"

"A man actually offering to get me a cup of coffee? What a concept."

As he got up from his chair, Dawn could see that his back was bothering him from the way he winced as he moved. She also saw the bags under his eyes. "I guess I lack the proper amount of testosterone. You want any crap in your coffee?"

"Black."

"My kind of woman."

Watching him walk out, seeing how tired he really was, she couldn't help but ask him, "You know it's not gonna get solved tonight, don't you?"

"Nope." And with that, he twisted around the corner. Definitely old school, she thought, a man who believed anything could be solved if he just worked a little harder. A dying trait, especially in men her own age. They all wanted everything handed to them on a silver platter like it was owed to them. She was always trying to explain to her mother why this was one of the reasons she hadn't dated anybody since moving to Sacramento. She couldn't find anyone she felt was worth the effort.

When he walked back in, holding two steaming cups of coffee, he asked briskly, "solve it yet?"

"Just about."

"Good. I need to get my beauty sleep."

She took the coffee from him, smiling as she watched him sit back down and prop his feet up again. "Thanks again for letting me use your office."

"Figured you had to work someplace, and hell, a pretty young lady such as yourself working out at the main station wouldn't have gotten a damn thing accomplished. All these wannabe computer studs would have been all over you from the get-go."

"I can handle myself."

"Oh," he said, blowing some of the steam away from his cup, "of that I have no doubt."

"So, who did it?" she asked, smiling, wanting to see what his reaction would be.

"Hell, I thought that's why you were here."

"No theories?"

He was laughing again, not a belly roll but a heartfelt laugh that rolled loosely out. "I'm not paid to give theories. I'm paid to give answers."

"And in the absence of true answers?"

"I've been told repeatedly in the past to just keep my damn mouth shut."

"What if I told you to open it?"

"Why should I guess," he asked boldly, "when I can tell you already know the answer?"

She stopped smiling but not because she wasn't happy. It was just the opposite in fact; her eyes sparkled brightly to let him know that he was right. "The money's missing."

"That I already knew."

"No trace or record, just gone."

"Again," he said, perking up a bit, "that I already knew."

"But it's clearly missing, and not just in arbitrary amounts a computer screen says should be there. We have money missing from accounts all over the membership base. What I think was a nice touch was the fact that none of the affected accounts are missing more than a hundred thousand dollars."

"Just within the legal limit of what the NCUA has to cover per person."

"Exactly. Whoever did it didn't want to hurt the membership; they only wanted to screw the government out of the money. And they were smart enough to make sure of it."

Jim took another drink from his steaming cup. "So we got a smart, compassionate thief. Is that what you're telling me?"

"Can I ask you a question, Jim?"

"You gonna ask me if I did it?"

"Nope, I already know you didn't do it."

"How?"

"A million, small little tells. The things you say, the other things you don't. I imagine you're a pretty crappy poker player, Jim Krieder."

"Well, I do always tend to lose when I play with the guys." He shook his head again, thinking about everything she said, and then looked back up at her. "Sure, Dawn, you can ask me a question, if I can call you Dawn."

"Yes, Jim," she said almost methodically, "you can call me Dawn. My question is this: how many lines of code were entered into your computer system last year?"

"Last year? You mean throughout the calendar year of 1999?"

"Yes."

"I can honestly say I have no idea."

Her smile was starting to form again. "More than, say, the year before?"

"Well, sure, last year we had the great Y2K threat that all the simpletons were so worried about."

"Uh huh . . ."

"You know, hundreds of people last year went to town meetings about what would happen, about how the computers would stop and we'd all turn into mindless savages. People went crazy just thinking about the whole Y2K thing. They called in, they wrote letters. They whined to their congressmen and generated a media storm, and we all know how the media loves to stir things up, especially if they can do it for a profit." He was shaking his head, partially in frustration about what the Y2K alarmists were like and partially laughing at their ignorance. "So the computer geeks of the world united and started to produce about a million quick fixes to calm everyone's growing concerns. The problem came from the fact that a few scam artists picked up on the paranoia and decided to become millionaires. I can't think of any large company around that wasn't upgrading and loading tons of new code into their machines for the better part of the year, especially during the last six months of 1999. I don't think there's anyone in this organization that could even begin to tell you how many lines of code were entered last year."

"Uh huh," she repeated, letting a silky smile slowly cross her face.

For a moment Jim found himself caught up in just the look of her, in the sheer seductive quality of it all, and then he realized what she was getting at. "You think someone loaded in a virus?"

"Nope. I know it."

"How?"

Her smile fell a little. She was starting to get playful. She could feel it inside herself and she couldn't help it. She had missed the thrill of the hunt since leaving the bureau, the thrill of piecing together a mystery. "The way people just know things, Jim. I can't prove it yet, probably be quite a while before we can. If it's what I think it is, we'd be looking for a few harmless lines of code that's probably buried like all hell in the first place."

"If there was a virus, we'd have noticed it; we run daily checks for them."

"How do you check for a virus?"

"The usual ways, I guess: we look for programs whose file size has suddenly grown without a reason and we watch for virus-specific code lines, code that is found in all viruses. It's not like in the old days. Viruses are a lot more difficult to hide than before."

She took a drink from her cup, savoring it. "This is a special blend, isn't it? Something you brought in from home?"

"Uh huh . . ." he said, mimicking her in a good-natured way, "I hate the regular stuff the company supplies."

"It tastes much better."

"I'm glad you approve."

She sat the cup down between two high reaching stacks of computer printouts and looked across at him. "Name of the computer system you use? Logiterm, right?"

"Yup."

"Does it ever increase in size dramatically in the course of a day?"

"The mainstream program?"

"Yes."

"Depends."

She was smiling again, that same delightful smile that so many men had fallen for over the years when she used it properly. "On what?"

"How many new accounts are created, how many transactions our members make in a given day versus the purge dates on the system, how many new loans are made and funded, and how much general ledger activity there is. There are a lot of variables in that question."

"Not really," she said playfully. "You already answered what I needed to know."

"I did?"

"Uh huh. You've officially told me that the Logiterm Program System can dramatically increase in size during the course of a single day."

"Wait, you think someone loaded a program virus and stored it inside the mainstream Logiterm program?"

She continued, still smiling, playing him with her eyes, "You wouldn't have been able to catch it on the live program, no matter how hard you were looking for it. It would have been a Trojan horse, sitting almost out in the open."

"There'd still be a trace record. The opening of a new account would appear on a generated report."

"How about reopening an old account that had recently been closed?"

He stopped and sat there, staring into her eyes, his mouth half open, wondering about the possibilities she was laying out on his office table. "Well, there'd still be a report," he finally came back with, "but not one most people would pay any attention to."

"And then you have a virus in the mainstream system that cannot be found, at least not until it's ready to execute."

"You'd still need to be a hell of a computer jockey. To load a program up into the live system, it would still have to be put through the operating system. You'd still need to have the trigger program on the operating system. Otherwise the virus would remain dormant."

"OK," she said. "Assuming I'm right, and assuming we have an individual smart enough to upload this kind of a sophisticated virus into the Logiterm program, how many lines of code would you need to execute it?"

He started to laugh. She'd led him in a huge circle. "No more than two or three. Maybe even just one."

"A needle in a haystack."

"Especially," he said, shaking his head, thinking about what she began the conversation asking, "after all of the miles of code lines that were entered into the system last year."

"So, what do you think?" She was teasing him; she already knew the answer.

"Sounds like about the best theory I've heard all day, and I tell you, I've heard a number of them since I got in this morning. One thing's nagging at me though, Dawn."

"What's that?"

"If the virus was put in last year, why wait so long to execute it? I mean, hell, it's March. Why not just snag the money as soon as you could and run?"

"Whoever it was had time to kill, Jim." Dawn was leaning back in his chair now, looking casually up at the ceiling as she let her mind roam through the many possibilities open to her. "And they were waiting for something; at least that's my theory."

"So, what's the next step?"

"I bring in about a dozen guys to look over your shoulders until they find those three or four lines of code hidden in your working system, and they keep working until the code is found. Once we have the code we see if we can narrow down who put it in."

"We can track anyone who was on our system inputting code once we locate the code we're looking for."

"That's good to know," she said, as her mind seemed to wander for a moment.

"But you don't believe it?"

"No, too easy."

"I told you, computers are a lot more sophisticated than they used to be. It's hard not to leave a little electronic version of fingerprints when you do things on a network."

She nodded as she continued looking up at the ceiling. "I agree with every word you're saying, but," she started whispering, "the crime is too good, too smart, and too big to get nailed on something like that."

"I read in a crime novel once that every criminal makes at least three dumb mistakes in committing their crime."

"Then all that means is that the novelist in question was too damn lazy to let the hero do some actual police work to find the bad guy. Some criminals are very smart and some never get caught. If you doubt it, go tour a police department's unsolved case files; it'll scare the hell out of you."

"You don't think this one'll get solved?"

"Oh," she said slowly, closing her eyes, "with this much money at stake, it'll be solved. Sooner or later, the money will surface. The only question is if I'll be able to solve it before the NCUA has to pay out the money."

* * *

Settling in 2.3

March 8, 2000

He was staring at the computer screen in disbelief; he couldn't believe what it showed.

He'd never before seen so much money in one place, much less at his disposal. He smiled a dark, rich smile, the kind that worried his wife back in the days when they were still just dating. It was a smile that said he was up to no good. That was why it worried her so deeply. She hadn't liked to think of him going out to do bad things but she had known the dark fire that burned inside him, how prone he was to playing the hand life dealt him. He'd gotten in a little trouble before but always managed to avoid direct contact with the police, even during his closest calls. His skill with a computer had also always amazed her, and she'd been sure there was a way to put his talents to legal use. He never worried about getting caught, though; he always assumed he was too smart to get nailed like the other hackers he'd seen online.

Starring at the screen, he wondered how much trouble this would get him into if he actually got caught. All that money floating across the computer, all the money he needed to manage. If he were caught, if anything could be traced back to him, it would mean life in prison or a life on the run. The game he was starting would be exceedingly dangerous, especially now in its beginning stages when everything could still be traced rather easily.

It would be so easy, he thought, to take it all and disappear, to never be seen or heard from again. It would still be risky, because they would never stop looking for the money, not with that much missing, but in his mind, he assumed he was smart enough to do it. That wasn't the kind of man he wanted to be. Not the kind of man he would be.

He wasn't planning on running. But the thought was there all the same, tempting him. Still, he was going to do just as he promised: he'd keep the money moving, like a child playing with a balloon, making sure it never hit the ground.

With the computer setup he created, it would be simple. He'd been waiting for this moment for almost two years, and perhaps it could be said a lifetime before that. He'd designed the program he starred at on the screen just for this moment, relishing it. It was dangerous, just the way he wanted it. He would live on the edge again, just the way he lived before he was loved.

He knew the easy part of the plan was getting the money.

Now the money was here, sitting right in front of him in all its digital glory, begging to be spent and abused.

He pushed the execute button on the screen with his mouse, beginning the next stage, knowing the hard part of the plan was just beginning.

* * *

DOLLARS AND SENSE

Dollars and Sense 3.0

March 9, 2000

Day Two:

D awn looked up at the overcast sky as she ran. The morning radio announcer said the fog would burn off by early afternoon. The sun was still stretching its way across the sky, and the twilight like darkness was clouding the newborn light. It looked like the setting for any of a dozen horror movies she'd seen growing up. She was running, maintaining her daily exercise ritual, in the back of the hotel complex where she was staying. It was scenically connected to the back of a medium-sized park that was mostly abandoned at this early hour.

In her mind, she was still going over the day before, trying to lose herself in the rhythm of it. Over thinking wouldn't help her solve the crime. Feeling her way through, using the skills they can't really teach you in school was where her answers lay. The trick was getting there. It was no different back at the FBI. Too much thinking could easily lead to missing something vital. She couldn't help but wonder if she hadn't already missed something, due to the combination of jetlag and staying up far too late inside Jim Krieder's office drinking coffee last night. She should have added cream and sugar, she thought.

It took Dawn forever to convince Jim to leave. As much as she liked him and enjoyed talking with him, she knew she did her best work alone. What she didn't know was a way to tell him that so she sat with him, as he went over all the facts they had on hand with her, until he was finally too tired to stay. She watched him walk out the door and saw that it was already a quarter past nine. It was almost ten by the time Neal came walking in.

"You look tired, hotshot."

"I'm not."

He smiled. As much as he really wanted to hate her for the way she talked to him, he couldn't. He liked her spark, her utter lack of fear over his title. No matter how much power he held, he knew from Dawn McCafferty he would get nothing but her honest opinions and thoughts. "Solve the crime yet?"

"You're the second person to ask me that today."

"Whatcha tell the first one?"

"Nope."

"Shit. Does that mean we have to stay here?"

"Hmmm, you don't like sunny Southern California?" she asked, without looking up.

"I'm a Northern California kind of guy. Being this close to the border makes me nervous."

"Prejudice or you just don't like good carne asada?"

"Everyone's prejudiced against something, and I prefer Italian food."

"I'll keep that in mind."

"So, I've left you alone for a while. Just the way you like. Find anything?"

She looked up at him, thinking about how she could actually feel the caffeine in her system from the three cups of coffee she'd downed in the last few hours, the slight jitter coursing through her system. "It's a virus."

"You sure?"

"As sure as I can be without proof."

"So you want me to bring in the code-finders as well as the suits?" The suits were the auditors who tore through the books and ledgers and went over all the numbers stored and logged in the Credit Union's records. The code-finders were the guys who literally pored through the miles of code contained on a database looking for things that shouldn't appear. They were a different kind of weasel in an investigation like this.

"Yup."

"We bring in this kind of man power and the budget for this case is going to skyrocket."

She was reaching instinctively for the coffee cup. It was empty, and she knew it, but her instincts told her to take another drink, a sign that her mind was already starting to work on a different wavelength. "10 percent, right?"

"Beg your pardon?"

"The investigation can cost up to 10 percent of the amount in question before any cost accounting need be performed or has that changed recently?"

"You want me to blindly approve a thirty million dollar cost ratio for your investigation?"

"You'd be within procedure to do so."

"Procedure never accounted for a blind theft of three hundred million."

"How much can I have, then?" Once again her eyes drifted to the ceiling.

"How much do you want?"

"Already told you that."

"I'm not giving you thirty million dollars, Dawn!"

"Then how much will you give me?"

He found himself looking at her. He always liked it best when she wasn't looking directly at him. He could gaze at her smooth, elegant features, the way she moved her body, the way her hair fell against her face. "You can have a million."

"Won't be enough."

"Make do . . . we'll talk again when it runs out."

"The code lines will be buried," she said, closing her eyes, resting them.

"We'll find them." He sat down in the chair that, a few hours earlier held Jim Krieder. "You think maybe you were a little harsh with the Credit Union staff earlier?"

"Not here to be liked, Neal, here to get a job done."

"Look, Dawn, I know you're a damn good investigator, the best we've had around in years. Your experience with the bureau sets you apart. That's why you're on this case. I have the utmost faith in you to solve it. But the NCUA's main job responsibility is to regulate credit unions. That means we're on the same team as these people. Whether you like them or not, it'd make things a hell of a lot easier if you at least tried to play nice with the other children."

"One of those nice little children you speak so affectionately of is currently 320 million dollars richer."

"Innocent until proven, or so I thought."

"I haven't accused anybody yet."

"Yet?"

Suddenly, her eyes were open and looking right into his. "Did you get me the keys to the employee files?"

"I have the keys, yes. Mark Dryerson, their Senior Vice President of Human Resources, gave me a set and asked me to be very discreet with them."

"They all say that, Neal. It's in a training manual somewhere that all HR people have to read."

He smiled at her, shaking his head. "Well, aren't you just all daisies and sunshine this evening."

"You gonna give me the keys or not?"

He pulled the keys out of his pocket and tossed them onto the desk she sat behind. She picked them up and held them in her hand, as if judging their weight. Looking at her he asked, "Who are you going to start with?"

"The computer geeks. They're the weakest links in any financial company's security. I'll branch out from there. And I need you to call up to Sacramento for me. I need something that'll be easier to get up there, certainly faster."

"What?"

"I want a current credit report run on every employee of this goddamn credit union. On both current employees and anyone whose worked here over the last nine months, maybe a year."

"You fishing?"

"Uh-huh," she said, starting to stand up, the keys firmly gripped in her hand, "but don't worry; I plan to lay some good bait."

"I was afraid you were gonna ask for complete profiles on the entire staff."

"Nope," she said, breezing past him, "only on those who meet a certain criteria."

"And what's would that criteria be?"

She was almost out of the office as she called back, "I'll let you know tomorrow."

The jog wasn't going to be as long as she would like. Too much work and too small a park were going to limit her. No matter what Neal tried, the budget on this case wouldn't be a problem; procedure would back her, no matter what. When she left Neal last night, it was so he could go over the reports stacked on Jim's desk. She'd left sticky notes for him just to make sure he'd be able to follow things. She hadn't made it too easy though, because she wanted enough of his time taken up to leave her ample opportunity to go over the employee files up in the Human Resources Department. As promised, she reviewed the computer department first and hadn't found anything serious. She'd need the credit bureau reports to confirm any suspicions she had, but this gave her a nice idea of the department employees' backgrounds.

She left the office with no better an idea of who might have done it than when she arrived but, thanks to the files, she did have a better idea of who some of the key players were.

Marc was waiting outside in a rented car and took Dawn and Neal to an executive hostel, a mini-condo for working professionals on assignment. It was a high-class apartment with decent furnishing that was run similar to a hotel. They had a front desk and maid service, but the inside of each of these living areas was a functional environment. They had a kitchen and a secret closet that held a washer and a dryer. The bed was fairly comfortable, and there was enough room for Dawn to stretch out without feeling claustrophobic. Neal's unit was about six doors down. And considering the amount of space each unit occupied, that was a fair distance. The park separated them from the business district and from the nearby residential area and kept them in a quiet spot Dawn liked at once.

Being able to continue her ritual of morning jogging was just an added bonus. Even now, as the sun came up, Dawn saw traffic on the road ahead, the masses slowly motoring into their day shifts, clogging the open roads and clouding the air with sickening fumes. Every commuter was just waiting for their one big chance to free themselves from a daily life of having to answer to someone. Dawn knew that somewhere out there was a man or woman who found a way to break free of the grind; found a way to beat the system.

Having 320 million dollars meant being your own boss, but stealing meant a life on the run. That was what she needed to focus on. Who would have access to load the virus? Who wouldn't mind spending the rest of their life on the lamb?

She stopped and looked at the bleak faces she could make out behind the morning dew-stained windows. Men and women waiting in a motorized line to go to places they didn't really want to be for the better part of their day. Occasionally a man in one of the cars would glance over at her and stare a bit too long, but she ignored it. Her outfit wasn't particularly sexy, just shorts and a T-shirt. She was wearing a jogging bra beneath the T-shirt to make the run easier. She suspected it was her long blonde hair that caused the men to stare. Men loved blond hair, the longer the better, and no matter how sick she got caring for her own long locks, she knew she'd never convince herself to chop them to a more manageable length. Her long hair had managed to charm more than one man into revealing information he didn't want to reveal, and as long as Dawn maintained her looks she was going to utilize every advantage they gave her. This morning she was more interested in the cars though, or, more appropriately, the people inside them.

"That much money would be useless," she said aloud while looking out at the traffic. "We'd be able to track it as soon as it surfaced."

Turning away from the traffic, Dawn walked on the damp grass into the center of the park to where the kids' jungle gym was. "All the executives are automatically suspects, but it can't be one of them; they'd all be too easy to trace."

She turned her head back around to the line of cars. "But maybe," she said quietly, "it was one of them."

She began jogging back to her new living space, her head full of ideas. She was suddenly very ready to get to work.

* * *

Dollars and Sense 3.1

March 9, 2000

Tom Williams Corvette came racing into the parking lot about three minutes before his shift started. For anyone who paid attention, this was nothing new. It was no secret Tom was no longer doing the work he'd dreamed of, and delayed getting to the office until the very last second. The 1999 Corvette just made it a little easier for him to make it in under the wire.

Even after arriving to work, he didn't rush to collections; instead he strolled leisurely through the front lobby and drifted into the fully staffed deli to get his morning drink. He'd go into the main office branch and say his good mornings, taking the time to notice any new hires or temporary employees who might have started. It was an everyday occurrence to see Tom roaming the halls, seemingly without anything to keep him occupied, and more than one person remarked over the years they wanted his life of leisure. Tom wasn't a lazy man, though; he was intensely focused. At thirty-nine, he was a professional bachelor, and most people didn't think there would ever be wedding bells in his future.

Tom's hair was still coal black, except for the occasional stray hair that grew in ghostly white. He often joked about what he'd look like when he went completely gray. He always boasted how distinguished he would look, though no one ever claimed to believe him. From a distance he was liked, and he knew it. Most people found it hard to actually hate him. He had a fairly decent sense of humor, and could keep most people talking, but he knew it was all surface chatter. Inside, where it mattered, he wasn't trusted at work. Too many rumors, too many suspicions about when his star was on the rise within these walls, and how it all abruptly changed to accusations and his rise became a fall. A different CEO made many loud promises about where he would wind up, but when that CEO retired, all the old promises were forgotten, leaving Tom to fight for a job that he'd have walked right into a few years before. A job he lost.

He knew most people would have left to find a sunnier place where the dark shadows of their past and even darker rumors wouldn't follow. He didn't leave, though, wouldn't. He didn't want to let them know they'd beaten him. So he stayed to prove the rumors wrong and to make life as uncomfortable as possible for the person who screwed him over. He joked that he was a petty man, although he knew the more popular theory was that the only reason he didn't leave was that no one else would hire him.

For a year and a half, he'd been away from the department he'd originally hired into. The department he loved and the work he'd dreamed of doing his whole life, away from the coveted title of PR man for the marketing department and hiding in the collections department doing repossessions. The bad guy, he called himself when anyone asked. "I'm a professional bad guy."

But he could deal with being the bad guy because; at least on the surface, when he dealt with fellow employees they at least acted like they were still his friends. Anymore, that was good enough.

Today wasn't a day he was looking forward to as he slowly started up the stairwell, which was about a thousand times quicker than the single elevator at the center of the building. He'd actually clocked the elevator once when he'd first been hired to see who could make it up to the fourth floor the quickest. He and his friend David both left the main branch on the first floor at the same time and headed for the administrative office on the fourth floor. David took the elevator while Tom took the stairs. Tom won the bet by a full forty seconds and ever since then took the stairs religiously. As he walked up he started to actually think about what the day would bring. With the system shut down all day yesterday it would mean absolute chaos today. Every deposit that was manually taken in the day before would have to be processed now the system was up. While Tom wouldn't have to do any of the posting, he would be forced to endure hundreds of calls from the branches regarding collection members who were sneaking in deposits. He could already feel a long day in store.

His desk was cut into a cubicle in the midst of the chaos of the fourth floor. The collections office was cast out and away from the administrative side. Collections, as is so often the case with an organization like Hil Fed was a department mostly forgotten about. The mere fact that they even needed a collections office was frowned upon. It was a necessary evil though. The very nature of his work strayed from general credit union philosophy, or at least so the big guns seemed to believe. Tom, for his first few months in the department tried to plead its case, to argue that working in collections was about working with members through their difficult financial times, up to the point where they would have to stop and protect the well being of the membership. His words fell on deaf ears, so he finally stopped trying to change anyone's mind. He even learned to enjoy the seclusion and fear that came with his newfound stature. Whereas once, everyone in the organization knew his name from the work he did in marketing, his ad campaigns, and his slick copy, he was now known as the harbinger of certain doom. His phone no longer rang because people wanted to know how he was doing or if he wanted to hit happy hour with the gang; instead he was called to answer legal questions and to help other people cover their asses.

Tom was a different man than before. But then, rumor and innuendo have a way of ruining a man's career and changing him completely.

Cruising down the fourth floor hallway, he saw once again the boardroom was filled with people. As no meetings were scheduled on the company roster, something big was clearly going on, but he was well past the point of caring about what. He didn't even try to peer in the door, despite the fact that it was ajar. He walked silently toward the collections office.

Inside, he found, once again, he was the last to arrive for work. It was an all-too-often event, he thought with amusement as he said his cheerful good mornings to everyone and slumped down into his chair.

"Tom," Judy's voice called out, as soon as he had managed to find his comfort zone in the chair, "can I see you for a moment?" Judy Tanin sat in her office facing away from the door, looking right into her computer screen. She was the manager of the collections department and held the title for the last four years.

More from instinct than anything else, Tom cocked his head to Samantha Johns, who sat to his immediate left. "What'd I do now?"

Sam was coming ever nearer to retirement age. On her next birthday, she would turn sixty-four, and she swore up and down to anyone who would listen that she was going to walk out the front door on her sixty-fifth birthday without ever looking back. Tom knew Sam long before he'd transferred to collections. She'd met him the first week he'd started at HIL Fed, when he was what she called a 'punk kid." He was basically an office intern back then, twenty-one years old and still in college. Sam had been working for the Credit Union since the mid-1970s, which constituted most of her working life. They'd become friends over the lunchroom table; both liked to argue endlessly about subjects that had no meaning and both were about as sarcastic as they came.

Tom also knew that a large part of his working in collections came from a conversation with Sam right before everything started to sour for him in marketing. Sam smiled as she leaned toward his cubicle and said, "God only knows, buddy; you're on your own."

"Gee, thanks." The smile he flashed back was genuine, as he stood and marched into Judy's office. For him it was always an odd sensation to step into her office. It always took him back to the first time in September of 1998, when he was suddenly left without a friend in the world and everyone with any power within the Credit Union deserted him. "Hey, J, how are you?"

He first met Judy Tanin right after she came onboard four years before from a sister credit union just outside of town. Their first meeting took place in his office down in marketing. At the time, he'd been swamped and needed to get some basic info from her to do a write-up in the company newsletter. It was a cheap attempt at company propaganda, and he told her exactly that when she walked in. She'd laughed as she sat down, not really believing that anyone in a position was so straightforward. Their meeting, which was originally scheduled for twenty minutes, lasted damn near four hours. They were the same age and shared a number of similar interests. They became casual friends, to an extent several people suspected them of having an affair at first. Nothing like that ever took place between them. She was happily married with a beautiful little girl. They just happened to speak the same language.

Today wasn't like that day though. Tom now worked for Judy, which meant he had to tow whatever line she laid out. In all fairness, he knew she cut him a lot of slack in completing his work and, furthermore, knew he owed her a lot. At a moment like this, he knew he'd been caught doing something. He just wasn't sure what.

She spun around in her chair as he took a seat in the chair nearest her desk, "Heavy traffic?"

"Not by the time I leave the house, no."

"What am I going to do with you, slick?"

He smiled richly at her, in a way that always made her smile back. "Well, a raise would sure be nice."

"Start showing up on time, then." She was trying to remain stern but she could feel the corners of her mouth starting to curve.

"I'll do better, I promise."

She shook her head, laughing, "So says the man who knows I don't usually get to work until an hour after you're scheduled in. I won't know whether you're lying or not."

"Well, that certainly helps with my sincerity in this issue."

"I don't need your sass, Tom. It's crazy around here right now."

He leaned into the desk, not wanting his voice to carry into the outer office. "What's up?"

"I'm not at liberty to discuss it."

"That big, huh?"

She was looking him directly in the eyes, smiling widely now. "You never did learn to take no for an answer, did you?"

"That's the reason I thought you liked me so much."

"You thought wrong."

"Come on, J, does it have to do with us being down all day yesterday?"

"I could lose my job for spreading a rumor like this."

He had both his elbows down on her desk now, stretching his head across it, "Hell, if it's a rumor, what's the problem? The busybodies who populate this place will have it all around the water coolers by mid-afternoon."

"The system is back up today. I've been told by our rep in Info Sys department that we shouldn't experience problems accessing Logiterm today."

"So why were we down all day yesterday?"

"I told you, Tom, I can't tell you."

He leaned back in his chair and cracked his voice a little as he said, "You're killing me here. Give me something."

"It would be a bad thing if I did."

"So? Be a little bad, see what happens. Maybe you'll even like it?"

"Ask around, Tom. Most people would suggest I've already used up most of my bad points where you're concerned."

"Yeah, but there's another point to be considered, boss."

She was leaning back herself now, almost sinking into the deep, plush leather of her executive chair. "And what's that?"

"You want to tell me."

"No, I don't."

"Sure you do, or you wouldn't even be entertaining this conversation."

She stared at him for twenty-three seconds exactly, by her view of the clock right behind his head. "You're too damn smart for your own good, Thomas Williams."

"Yeah, yeah give me the dirt."

"We're running short."

"What?" He could feel the breath leave his body as he said the word.

"We've come up short on the books, and no one can find it."

"Jesus," he said, feeling his heart starting to speed up. He knew he didn't have anything to worry about, but at the same time, it was like his past was suddenly there, catching back up to him. "Am I a suspect this time, too?"

"They have nothing, from what I've been told, which is why they've brought in an NCUA investigator, a really tough bitch, if the executive team is to be believed."

"Well, for what it's worth, I wouldn't believe them."

"No," she said, "I didn't think you would."

"How much are we down?"

"That's not been said, at least not to the managers yet. Only the executive team knows the exact amount."

"That means it was a lot. I mean, the NCUA and silence, it has to be a whole lot."

"Yeah, I suppose it does," she said.

"Thanks for letting me know," he said as he stood up. "I'll make sure to establish a better alibi than before."

"Yeah, do that, Tom. Oh and one more thing."

"Uh-huh?"

He was at the door to her office when she spun away from him. "Don't be late for work anymore."

* * *

Dollars and Sense 3.2

March 9, 2000

What wasn't she wasn't seeing, Dawn wondered as she stared out from the fourth-floor window into the employee parking lot? There was a scratching at the back of her skull, something telling her it was all right before her eyes and she was missing the obvious clues. She wasn't a computer genius but understood the basic philosophy that if you take money from one place, it has to appear somewhere else. Like water flowing from one cup to another, it must be dispersed. Even if the water was spilled, you would be able to see the traces of water in the dirt, at least until the ground absorbed the water and it disappeared forever. She was in the accounting department, standing at the window to Craig Peterson's office. His office was rather small considering he was the senior vice president of finance, or so she thought. It was cluttered and messy, littered with stacks of paper layered with dust from having sat too long. Craig was retrieving some old logs she wanted to look through, so she was just looking out the window until he returned.

"One cup to the other," she said aloud, as if giving her words weight and meaning, letting the sound of her own voice settle into her ears. "If it was pulled from the accounts, where did it go?"

It was almost three o'clock in the afternoon. Dawn had spent her morning listening to a bunch of people telling her what she either already knew or strongly suspected. The suits and the code finders had been shuffled into the executive boardroom, which was now nothing more than their unofficial office. Dollar amounts were pulled from accounts seemingly at random. There wasn't one account that was missing more than a hundred thousand dollars. The thief hadn't wanted anyone but the government to be hurt by this crime; the skill of the program was evident, and Dawn found herself almost salivating to catch whoever created it.

Once the money was pulled from the member accounts it fed into a GL account. A GL stood for a General Ledger, an account that was alive and active on the Logiterm system just as any membership account was, except no one but department staff had access to them, and even then access was limited. The job of the accounting department, more than anything else, was to make sure the GL's always balanced. There was no set amount of GL accounts the system could hold; new GL's were created as needed. For some reason, a new GL had been opened at some point in the previous week, and on March 7, 2000 it pulled exactly 320 million dollars out and away from various membership accounts and then closed itself out, somehow making the money disappear in the process. It was a grand trick, Dawn thought. It all came down to a flick of the wrist, smoke, and mirrors. The money went to the GL and was suddenly gone. What Dawn wanted to know was when exactly the GL was created and how the money disappeared without a trace. Craig left his office to get the report showing new GL creations. No matter how good the virus was, it couldn't have found a way around all the monitoring programs. Dawn knew she would track the money down somewhere.

"Money's got to go someplace, quickly," she said again. It couldn't just disappear. Even if the GL closed, the money would still basically be in the Credit Union's system. "Are you hiding inside somewhere?" That didn't feel right to her; leaving it in the system would be foolish, because sooner or later the thief would have to know the virus would be cracked. They'd need to get the money as far away as possible. Keeping it here at the Credit Union for too long would only lead the investigators right to the money.

The GL's were all named at Hil Fed and had a corresponding number code. To create a new GL, even a temporary one, within the system the creator would need to give it both a number and a name. The Logiterm System could automate a new GL when needed, but even with the automation it needed a name to approve the file. As Dawn stood there, thinking about the money, she knew it wasn't impossible to create a GL through the virus program; however, this meant the virus was even more complex than she'd originally thought. It had the ability to approve and respond. It created a character descriptive number and a name for the GL The thief wanted to leave a trail, had specifically named and numbered the GL, as if to say something about him or herself. Vanity was this thief's weakness, Dawn thought, *vanity.*

The GL's number was 600000-6.6; from a ledger sheet printout the number would only appear with non-zero characters, and therefore the full abbreviation of the number code would go down to 666, the sign of the devil. When Neal learned that fact, he started tossing around all sorts of wild theories about Satanists and midnight millennium cults. But Dawn wasn't buying it; she took the numbering as a joke, and the name of the GL proved it to her. It was something that Neal hadn't picked up on yet and she didn't feel the need to share. He could read it in her summation report she'd do later that night and give him in the morning. The GL was named Mammon, and just thinking about the elegance of it made her smile. Mammon was something pulled from more biblical times, from an old saying that implied that one could not serve both God and Mammon. You could not worship both material possessions, such as money and God. By choosing the word *Mammon*, the thief had chosen to worship money over God. To Dawn that meant a devil worshipper was improbable. The mere knowledge of what Mammon was implied the thief was not only well-educated, but had a sense of humor. This case wasn't about religion.

As Craig walked back into his office with a binder packed with reports, Dawn remembered what one of her FBI trainers said her greatest weakness was, the fact she had trouble understanding the religious beliefs of others. She knew one day this weakness would surface to hurt her in an investigation, but she suspected it wouldn't be this one.

"I have the creation date," Craig said as he flipped open the book on the desk. Dawn stepped up right next to him and followed his finger as he ran down one of the many columns until he stopped on the GL named Mammon. "There, do you see it?"

She was staring right at it and couldn't help but smile, "Yes."

The creation date was listed as 03/01/2000, 00:07:34. The Mammon GL had been created on March 1, just seven minutes after the end of February. Looking beyond the date-and-time stamp, though, Dawn saw a "G" listed in an italic font, something that the majority of GLs didn't have next to them.

"What's the G stand for?"

"It means it's a ghost account."

"I'm sorry," she said, looking right at him, trying to make it clear to him what he was saying didn't mean a thing to her.

"A ghost. It means it's a wash GL, created for a temporary holding purpose, not meant to be open for more than a day or two, really. Listed as a ghost . . ."

He didn't need to finish the sentence; he'd said enough to clear it up for her, and she stepped away from him, shaking her head and finishing his thought for him. "So it won't be totaled into your daily reports, right?"

"Right. We don't want to throw the Credit Union off balance for money that may not be ours, money we're just moving around because of changing investment portfolios or incorrect federal wire deposits that occasionally happen. There are actually several circumstances in which ghost accounts are created, so you see, they aren't unusual in an operation such as this one."

"When are the ghost accounts audited?"

"Three times a month, just to check up on them, make sure none were accidentally left open. It happens on the tenth, twentieth, and last day of each month. A list generates during the closing reports on those predetermined days."

"How many people know about the ghost accounts?"

"Not many, we don't exactly advertise them. Don't imagine most people would care."

She was thinking about the money again, even as she asked about procedure. The money needed to get away. "Is it common knowledge among the employees?"

"Only if you're in accounting, really. I'm sure a few others know as well, but we don't broadcast it.'

Dawn turned her head to look at him again and could tell he was staring back at her, almost transfixed, although she couldn't tell if he was staring from attraction or because he wanted to know what she was thinking. Her mind was abuzz; the ghost GL was created in the early morning hours on March 1, right after their report on the ghost GL's would have run, and all the money was taken by March 7. It meant something. First, the employee knew about the accounting audit policies and knew they would need to get the money out of the Credit Union before the tenth of the month report was run. Why take seven days? Why risk taking so long? Why not just do it the moment the new GL was created? Unless, she suddenly thought, you wanted to do it slowly. Looking back up at Craig, she said, "You can do wire transfers, right?"

"Sure."

"Are they automated? I mean, done through Logiterm?"

"Just about everything we do here is done through Logiterm, Dawn, and I suspect I know where you're going with this question. We already checked our outgoing wire logs. The missing money wasn't in there. I don't think Randy would have called in the NCUA if finding it was that easy."

She started to head toward the door of the office, starting to beam. "Craig, the entire Logiterm system is suspect right now. Don't believe everything you see in your printouts."

At the doorway she briefly turned back to look at him. "Do I need to dial nine for an outside line?"

"Yeah," he whispered back, trying to think about what she was saying.

Dawn went to the first empty desk she found and grabbed the phone, hitting nine and her Sacramento office number. She was almost oblivious to everything going on around her, even the man who walked right past her with leering eyes. She was someplace else, solving the crime and people like Tom Williams didn't compute to her when she was at this place inside her head. She sensed him though, immediately on some base level, feeling he was unimportant and not really worth her attention. He was struck by her well-toned and tanned legs. The slit of her skirt was clinging to the desk and revealing a bit too much leg, and for a moment he was transfixed by the sight. Composing himself, he ran his eyes up the length of her body until he was looking directly at her face, smooth and gentle but with a feeling of life about it. He knew from just a glance she wasn't some spoiled rich girl who was given everything. She had a few years of real living behind her, he thought. He even liked how she completely ignored him. His eyes stayed on her as he navigated his way through the office to the desk he had business at, and Dawn was none the wiser.

She was saying something into the phone as he reached Cindy's desk, but he was too far to hear what it was. He couldn't tell if it was because of the distance between them or if she was intentionally keeping her voice low. Cindy was another long-term Credit Union employee. She'd been there only a year or two less than he; he could never remember for sure how soon she came in after he'd been hired. They knew each other only in passing, really, but they always got along, and she was easy enough to talk to when he could avoid hearing about the usual tragedies of her domestic life. "Hey, Cindy," he said, stepping up to her desk, "how's it going?"

"Busy, Tom. How about you?"

He almost missed Cindy's question because he was trying to eavesdrop on another conversation. Even from across the room he was eyeing Dawn, checking her finger for that all-important wedding ring, desperately wanting to know if she was single. "I'm fine," he finally replied shifting his attention. "I'm here for the Martin's check . . . is it ready yet?"

"Yeah," Cindy said with a smile, "Its right over here."

Tom's eyes weren't following Cindy, though, as she began to dig through the masses of invoices covering her poor desk. He was keeping his gaze on the blonde in the short skirt, and under the weight of his stare, she finally lifted her eyes and took notice.

"Hey, Cindy," he said, almost a whispering.

"I'm getting it; it's here somewhere."

"No," he said, smiling, "not the check, the girl. The blonde over there on the phone. Who is she?"

"Auditor, I think, from Sacramento. Don't know her name, sorry."

"We're being audited already?"

"I guess," she said, still searching for the check. "I'm not really sure, but I think we must be. We've all been told to comply with whatever she wants."

"Hmm, interesting."

"Listen up, Dawson," Dawn said with her usual lack of charm, "I need someone to get on it." She gave him a few seconds to complain about his already overburdened work schedule before telling him he didn't really have a choice in the matter. "Get someone over to the Federal Reserve immediately; tell them I want to know about every outgoing wire from the Hil Fed Credit Union since February 29."

"Can't you get that from them? I mean, hell, Dawn," Dawson said in his usual nasal whine, "it should be in their computer?"

"Their computer is compromised, so to answer your question, no." The man from across the room was still staring at her, not as obviously as some, but enough so she knew he was doing it, like a guy at a bar when he was trying to figure out if he should approach or walk away. She turned away from him, freeing the slit of her skirt to better cover her leg again. The last thing she needed was a potential suspect trying to come on to her while working the case. After all, the way she saw it, everyone was a potential suspect. But as she finished her conversation with Dawson she instinctively started listening to what he was saying. And when she found that none of Tom's words carried over well enough she turned her head slightly to see what else she could learn. She wasn't sure why she was doing it, he was most likely a nobody, but the intense way in which he looked at her, enough to draw her out from her inner thoughts, and away from the place where she thought she was about to solve the crime, or at least get another step closer. Not many people could do that without direct interaction, but he'd been able to do it just by looking at her.

Tom stopped after watching her after another moment, Dawn's turning her back to him signaled her disinterest, and so he focused his attention on the woman whose desk he was half sitting on. The woman was handing him a check, taking it with a laugh and a smile.

"Told you I had it," she said, feeling proud of herself.

"I never doubted you for a minute, Cindy. Though I wonder, do you have my other check?"

She looked puzzled for a second as she started looking down at her ledger printout. "I only see Martin's."

"No, the other check, the one for seventeen million?"

"Jesus, Tom . . ."

They both chuckled a little, as much as anyone can ever do about a running joke that's gone on for far too many years. He said a few other things and then walked directly out of the office, only casually glancing at Dawn this time, more to admire than leer

The moment Tom was out the door, Dawn told Dawson she needed to go. She was off the phone and across the room at Cindy's desk in a flash. "Hi, I'm sorry." Dawn was going to play this cool; it meant nothing, and she knew it. She was just being overly cautious. "What's your name again?"

"Cindy."

"Hi, Cindy," Dawn said putting on her most sincere fake smile. "That man you were just talking to, what was that I heard him say about a check for seventeen million?"

"Oh, that?" She could barely contain her laughter. "That's just an old joke Tom can't let go of. It started out back when he was in marketing, called up here one day, asking for a check for some committee the Credit Union was making him sit on, and told the girl who was cutting at the time, that while she was at it, she might as well cut him a check, too, for seventeen million."

"Seventeen million?"

"Yeah, Tom always says if he was going to steal money, it would have to be enough for him to disappear. He told me he sat down and calculated it out one day and, God knows how he came to it, but seventeen million was his magic number."

"Really," Dawn said, a little too lost in thought.

"It's just a joke, though," Cindy blurted out, fearing this woman was an auditor and might be getting herself or her department marked down. "Tom's worked for this credit union since he was twenty-one years old, I think. Started as an intern in marketing or something. He'll be turning forty any day now. He just likes to goof around; he does that a lot. You'd have to know him. He's not the type to take much seriously."

"Yeah, sure, I just thought it was odd. Seventeen million."

"Sure, who wouldn't? I mean, if I didn't know Tom, I'd probably think it was a little odd myself." They both started laughing, although Dawn's laughter was a bit more crafted, and completely fake.

"What should I have expected from a guy in marketing, though, right? They're all a bit loony, from what I hear."

"Even loonier in collections."

"Collections?"

"Oh, yeah," Cindy said casually, as she reigned in her laughter, "Tom's been in the collections department for about a year and a half."

"Well, I suppose for either job you'd need to be a little off center."

"Ain't that the truth?"

"I saw him point at me, though. What was that about?"

"Oh come on, a young woman such as yourself, you should know the answer to that one," Cindy winked up at Dawn. "He was asking me what I knew about you."

* * *

Dollars and Sense 3.3

March 9, 2000

As Dawn walked back into the boardroom they were using as their office, she picked up a company roster, one of the many that were scattered around the room, and found the collections department. "Thomas Williams," she whispered to herself and waived to Marc, calling him over.

"What's up, Dawn?"

"I'm getting ready to pack it in for the day and head back to my room. I'll compose my status report from there and forward it to Neal by secure e-mail."

"I'll let him know."

"I need you to do something for me before I leave."

"Sure."

She wrote down five names on a piece of paper and handed them to him. "Go to HR and get me these personnel files."

"I don't think the HR director is gonna like that very much."

"If he gives you any shit, Marc, add his name to the list and scare the hell out of him."

"You're a real hard-ass, Dawn, you know that?"

"Just get me the files, Marc." She was already turning away from him and grabbing the phone. "I need to ask Jim Krieder a few more questions."

As she suspected, Jim was still at his desk and still valiantly searching for his own answers, Dawn watched Marc leave for her files, but the truth was she didn't care about the first two names or even the last two names on the list. All she really cared about was reading the file for Thomas Williams and learning what she could about his request for seventeen million dollars.

* * *

Playing the Odds

Playing the Odds 4.0

March 10, 2000

Day Three:

"Well," Neal said with an edgy quirk to his voice as he poured his morning cup of coffee, "it's a stretch."

"Maybe so," Dawn replied standing just outside his kitchen unit, "but right now he's the best we have."

"You really think he did it?"

"Would I be here talking to you so early in the morning if I didn't?"

Neal looked instinctively at the clock on the wall, showing five minutes before 6:00 a.m. He was better now, more alert and had some coffee coursing through him, much better than when she pounded on his door at 5:15 a.m. telling him she had something. "We're three days into the investigation, and as I recall, you once told me that the first forty-eight hours are the most critical. How do I know you're not just grasping at straws, trying to look good?"

"It's the first twenty-four hours, Neal, that's when everything's freshest. After that the clues and evidence all start slipping away at a phenomenal rate. The moment you hit the twenty-fifth hour on a serious crime, things start to look bleak if you don't already have a suspect."

"So here we are on day three. Why this guy?"

"He fits the profile."

The coffee wasn't going to be enough, Neal suddenly realized. He could see the look in her eye, the thrill of the hunt burning through. "I wasn't aware we had a psychiatric profile complete yet?"

"In case you've forgotten, Neal," Dawn said in a tone dripping with mock sincerity, "my degree is in psychiatry."

"So enlighten me, Dawn." He said as he pulled out the chair at the small table in his makeshift kitchen. "Tell me about our thief?"

"Do you really want to know, or are you just stalling to find the time to clear the sleep out of your eyes and head?"

He took another long drink from his cup, thinking about how perceptive she was. "Both, so give it to me already."

"He doesn't need the money. That's the first thing I'm willing to state about our suspect. He wants it but doesn't need it."

"No one needs 320 million dollars."

Dawn decided there was no point in standing. He was going to need to be convinced, especially considering that he was just sitting there looking at her. She pulled out a chair opposite him and sat down the personnel file in front of her. "This wasn't a dumb-luck crime, Neal; whoever orchestrated this didn't do it by chance or on a fluke. He was smart enough to know we'd be looking for the people who were heavily in debt. This guy doesn't need the cash. Hell, I'm not even entirely sure he wants it."

"Hell of a risk to take if you don't need the cash, Dawn, even more so if he doesn't want it."

"Smart people commit crimes, too."

"OK, so you don't think our John Doe needs the money. What else?"

"We have his name," Dawn said, making direct eye contact with him.

"Fine, you have a suspect; explain to me, though, why he is our suspect."

"This guy doesn't need the money. He's smart enough to pull it off, has a grudge against the Credit Union, but doesn't want to see innocent people—in this case the members—lose any money."

"And this guy fits that criteria?"

"Close. He's close enough, at least from what I've read, but I still want to know more about him."

Neal's coffee was quickly growing cold. He was too busy listening to her. "What's his name again?"

"Tom," she said boldly. "Tom Williams. He works in the collections department."

"Let me ask you this, Dawn, how's a guy in the Collections department upload a King Kong sized virus into the active Logiterm system without anyone taking notice? I mean, hell, don't they have checks and balances for this kind of thing?"

"Glad you asked, Neal. His most recent employee evaluation gives us that. He's worked here for quite some time. But his last review had an interesting comment on it."

"Are you going to make me beg to hear what the comment was?"

She was smiling broadly again. "One of the performance measures he had to complete, before his next review, was to help automate the collections department."

"Meaning?"

"He was one of the people who worked on creating the collections tracking software on the live Logiterm system to help streamline the daily collections activities."

Neal shook his head as he pushed his coffee cup aside and stood up. "OK, I'm still not with you 100 percent on either the profile you've suggested or the motif, but you're right, Mr. Williams had opportunity, so go ahead. Give him the full work up." He walked over to the bedroom to get his shoes as he turned around to watch her get up from the table. "Get into his life; see if he's a real suspect."

"There's more."

At the doorway to his room, Neal really didn't want to hear it. He wanted to put his shoes on and get over to the Credit Union and start examining the information on Tom Williams himself. "What's that?"

"Eighteen months ago, he was almost fired. He got written up and created quite the scandal, at least if the documents in the file are to be believed."

Neal walked back into the room, approaching Dawn slowly. He was thinking about what she was saying, trying to find a way to second-guess her. "And why was he almost fired?"

"He was accused by his former supervisor of embezzlement and taking bribes from outside vendors."

"You've got to be kidding me."

Dawn was leaning against the main door, smiling with a slick satisfaction. "Now why would I do that?"

"Why didn't they fire his ass?"

"Turns out that the marketing VP couldn't sufficiently prove her claim, because even though there was money missing they couldn't establish a direct link to Williams. The vendors, needless to say, denied making bribes, and Mr. Williams wrote several letters in his defense, including several from Mr. Williams' attorney. It seems he and his attorney were willing to take the Credit Union to court to prove his innocence. It further appears the Credit Union cut a deal with his attorney and relocated Mr. Williams from marketing to collections. I don't have the details yet, they don't seem to have all of the documentation in his file. I'll need to go over to Human Resources again and ask for their legal files to find out what really happened."

"So he got away with it before. That's why you think it's him?"

"No."

With that Dawn opened the door and walked without a care in the world and like a child chasing after his mother Neal rushed out the door calling after her. "Then why do you think it's him?"

She was carelessly walking down the hallway as she said, "What I think, Neal, I can't prove, and I know you don't like to hear ideas I can't prove."

"Try me; despite how early it is, I'm in a pretty good mood."

She stopped and turned around. Her smile faded, and it was clear she was deadly serious. "I think he was innocent eighteen months ago, which is why no one could actually prove his guilt. It was the reason he fought so hard to defend himself, and probably the reason he kept working at the Credit Union."

"I don't get it," Neal said weakly, staring down the hallway.

"He was innocent. Everybody thought he stayed on to prove his innocence, I think he stayed for another reason."

"Revenge?"

"I think stealing this much money and pretty much guaranteeing the financial ruin of the organization that turned its back on you after eighteen plus years of service to them would be a pretty decent version of revenge. Don't you?"

"Give me five minutes," he said, retreating back into his apartment. "It's time we took a very strong look at who this son of a bitch is."

Dawn watched Neal go back inside and then walked back to her room. The first problem was solved, she thought. She knew in her mind who committed the crime. Now all she had to do was prove it.

* * *

Playing the Odds 4.1

March 10, 2000

Fred Halstead was the FBI agent stuck sidelining the investigation, and he could care less about solving a crime about money, even an amount this large. He was career army before his tenure with the bureau started and didn't suffer fools lightly. Dawn immediately assumed Fred drew this assignment as a punishment for what was obviously a surly attitude. Her previous involvement with the bureau allowed the NCUA much more freedom with the investigation than they would normally have, and Dawn knew without it being said that Fred was told to defer to her. He was a grown, burly man with a lifetime of military training who wasn't used to answering to a woman half his size. Dawn knew he hated it, and probably hated her as well.

Fred listened to Neal talk about Williams, and remained stone faced throughout Neal's very weak presentation of the highly circumstantial findings they were proposing as evidence. Neal kept his good-boy smile going the entire time he spoke, and when he was finally through, Fred Halstead looked up and said, "Fine. Let's arrest him."

"We don't have evidence yet," Dawn said, as she crossed the table in the small conference room they retreated to for privacy. "If we pop him now, he'll walk from the charge."

"Look, lady," Fred said trying to remain gentlemanly in a certain military kind of way, "you're running the show, but with what you have, we can get the warrant and get his ass off the street. Isn't that what we're here for?"

"No," Dawn replied coolly. She knew what he was thinking and even expected his answer. "We're here to get the money back and make sure this can't happen again."

"Over getting the criminal?"

"If necessary, yes."

Fred snorted at the answer and shrugged violently in his chair. Dawn was still walking around the table when he added, "Trust me, you pop him now, put him under a few bright lights, and he'll crack. You get the whole story firsthand and the money as an appetizer."

"How about that, Dawn," Neal chimed in. "In this carefully crafted psyche evaluation you've created, what do you think about his breaking?"

"Won't happen."

"You don't know what you're talking about."

She took a moment to flash Halstead her best smile; the one she used to charm people, mostly because she knew it would make him feel uncomfortable. "He's got 320 million dollars hidden somewhere, probably with an off sight accomplice, maybe an ex-girlfriend or maybe a new one. If he goes down he'll think he can trust her to keep the cash until he gets out. And on a money charge, even one of this size he will get out while he's still young enough to spend it. If we arrest him, we'll get to meet his lawyer firsthand. He'll refuse to talk without the mouthpiece present, and he'll plead the fifth or outright deny everything."

Dawn's eyes were burning right into Fred's; she wanted him to understand what she was saying to him. "So the DA who gets the case will have to push this through the court system with nothing but circumstantial evidence. That brings it down to whether or not the jury believes he's guilty. If the jury acquits, he walks away scot-free and can start spending his ill-gotten gains openly, and we can do nothing about it, ever. If he does actual time, he'll get a light sentence in an urban country club like jail because it's white collar. Because this case was all based on circumstances, the judge will go light. And when push comes to shove, we won't have the money back, and again, he gets to spend the money upon his release. Worse though, while he's inside his minimum-security prison, maybe he tells a few of the other cons how to do his little magic trick. In the end, we all lose." She turned back to Neal with a look that cornered him into a decision either for or against her right on the spot. "We're not arresting him yet."

"Then," Halstead muttered, "what are we going to do?" His frustration was apparent he wanted to make a bold move, not listen to the subtle details.

"We're going to get into his life, and to do that, I need a little help from the FBI."

"What do you want?"

Dawn smiled again and responded with a word that at least intrigued Fred, not that his interest surprised her terribly. After all, to Dawn, he looked like the kind of guy who enjoyed surveillance.

* * *

Playing the Odds 4.2

March 10, 2000

For Tom Williams, it was like any other day, though after Judy directly mentioned it the day before, he had the good sense to come in a few minutes early this morning. Something he planned to do as long as the NCUA auditors were in the building. Tom knew how the system worked. All the bigwigs were acting like they actually worked and started keeping regular schedules. That meant until the NCUA left, department managers would be in between 8:30 and 9:00 a.m. None would take advantage of the executive/exempt package, the one that stipulated as long as they worked two hours in the course of a day, they could get paid for all eight without using any of their vacation time.

It also meant that most of the department heads would suddenly want to know what their employees did, just in case one of the auditors wanted to know. It was the same every time the auditors showed up; the managers went running around like a bunch of chickens with their heads cut off. They forced their presence into every outstanding project so they could look like they were actively involved in the office. The truth was usually very different; the department heads were like phantoms that occasionally walked through the overcrowded departments. They appeared to dole out new assignments with impossible deadlines and then disappeared behind closed doors, where they wrote speeches crediting themselves for all the work their underlings accomplished. They were good at making it sound like the world revolved around them, but no one in senior management ever bothered to notice that the departments always seemed to work just fine despite the fact that the department heads were always in one pointless meeting after another. Tom learned long ago to shrug it off. It was a system that had been in place at Hil Fed for as long as he could remember, and he knew it wasn't any better anywhere else.

To excel in the business world didn't require talent; good self-presentation was all that was necessary. Smoke and mirrors were an easier way to achieve career advancement. Tom was the kind of man who still wanted the fruits of his labor to speak for him, and it cost him almost everything he held dear. All he retained was his pride, and he knew they were after that as well.

He stepped into the branch at 8:10 a.m., and walked up to the front counter. The sleepy-eyed teller smiled at him and typed his account number into the Logiterm system before he could even open his mouth. He smiled back at her; she had worked in the branch about six months and had memorized his account number after only a few weeks. It scared him to think that he'd given her so many opportunities to call it up that she was able to do it. Tom was one of the employees people joked about at financial institutions: an "account junkie." He did transfers almost daily, depending on how many checks he wrote. He ran a tight account and knew everything happening in it. He hadn't balanced a statement in seventeen years, and had no intention of starting anytime soon. He checked his account daily at work from his computer. Overrides enforced automatically within the system prevented any employee from performing a transaction on their own account; however, there was a way you could view your account without being able to affect it. He entered that screen to check out his account at least twice a day, and on most days considerably more.

The teller's name was Tesla. She was a lovely young woman with a thrill for life and adventure who enjoyed a good joke of any variety. Tom liked her and often brought in his newest humor material to try out on her first. He liked to make her laugh. Her fiery hair and boisterous laughter pleased him to no end. If she hadn't been married, or just twenty-one he knew he'd be after her for a date in a fierce and determined way. She was married, though, and quite happily at that. But Tom still flirted, and knew he always would, at least as long as they both worked in the same location.

"So, what's the deal?" she asked. "Geek night isn't until tonight."

He was resting on the teller counter, forcing his eyes to stay open as he smiled back at her. "Geek night" was an inter-office joke a friend of his started many years earlier when it came out that Tom, despite his advanced years, still actively collected and read comic books. His friend started referring to the night the comic books were released as "geek night," and the phrase stuck to the point where Tom now just proudly declared what his hobby was to anyone who was listening. Most of the people who knew him weren't too surprised by it and found his mirth about the subject hilarious. Tesla was one of these people. "It's not, but I had to pay a couple of bills."

"Gee, paying bills on the day before pay day, and having the money in your account to do it? What a novel concept."

"What can I say, Tes? I don't like living paycheck to paycheck anymore. That's a young man's game, and I ain't as young as I used to be."

"You're not that old, Tom."

"I'm closer to forty than I am to thirty. Hell," he said, starting to laugh, "I'm closer to forty than I am to thirty-five these days."

"You're too hard on yourself, Tom."

"Well, thank God somebody is."

Telsa started to laugh, and Tom found himself smiling because of it. She was one of the few women left he could be himself around. In this age of rampant political correctness, people had lost their sense of humor to the extent that a joke was no longer considered a joke. A single sexual reference could stop an entire office from getting a damn thing accomplished. It was a hard thing for Tom to wrap his head around. He didn't think anyone should be put in a position of listening to a subject they didn't want to hear about, but at the same time, it just didn't seem fair to hold an entire office hostage because one person was hung up about sex. Telsa wasn't an uptight person; her dark sense of humor clearly enjoyed a good dirty joke, even those directed at her. The only danger of playing with her was that she was more than likely to turn the joke around on you if you weren't careful. Tom wasn't scared of that, though; he had a quick wit and didn't mind losing, as long as the game itself was fun. But the truth was he didn't lose very often.

"So what's the transfer, stud?"

"$87.50 from savings to checking."

"Done! You're all set."

"Thanks, Telsa, don't know what I'd do without ya."

"You know, one of these days they're going to start charging you per transaction. Then what will you do?"

"Go broke." He smiled good-naturedly and stepped away from the counter.

"Hey, Tom," Telsa said.

"Yeah?"

"You heard what's going on around here?"

"What do you mean?"

"All the auditors, everything that's happening on the fourth floor?"

Tom leaned his head in across the teller counter and spoke softly, "From what I heard, doll, somebody fucked up, and now we might all pay the price."

"What do you mean?"

"That's all the details I have. Sorry."

She frowned a little. "You'll tell me when you know something?"

"You bet," and with that he walked away. He walked out the main door without looking back, remembering Judy's words from the day before. Whoever these auditors were, they weren't doing a very good job at staying low profile. Everyone knew that once the branch staff started asking questions, everybody was in on the secret. As far as Tom could tell, the only thing the auditors were doing right was keeping it enough of a secret so no one knew which questions to be asking.

He hit the button for the elevator. After all, why not ride up in luxury today, he was still early and had time to kill.

The fourth floor was abuzz with activity, and he couldn't help feeling just a little of the tension that was spreading so rapidly through the building. The word was starting to leak. His boss wasn't the only one communicating that money was missing. The boardroom was suddenly off limits, and meetings scheduled to take place there were being cancelled or rerouted. There was a general recklessness in the air, and it was slowly affecting everyone. Even stepping out of the elevator, Tom felt like he was walking onto a B-movie horror set, right at the end just before the slasher leaped out to kill the brainless coed. He'd already heard a few rumors circling by the end of the day yesterday; the one he liked best was the one about how the computer was shut down to stop a live feed of money from being automatically deleted and destroyed.

He didn't even bother to look at the boardroom as he walked past. He just quietly entered his own department and began his day.

* * *

Playing the Odds 4.3

March 10, 2000

Dawn was sitting in the office of Mark Dryerson, the senior vice president of Human Resources going through their in-house legal files, which concerned itself exclusively with employee issues. She waded back through it until she came to the rather bulky section on Thomas Williams and his run-in with accusations that could never be fully substantiated. Mark Dryerson was nowhere to be found. As soon as Dawn stepped into the office, he made an excuse to leave, telling his assistant to provide her with whatever she needed. In other offices, the code-finders were going line by line and page after page of code, working over every last number of the Credit Union's financial statements. Their computer techs were combing the active system, looking for any kind of virus that might be lurking online. Dawn wasn't concerning herself with that end of the investigation. She knew the truth of it was here; crimes came down to people, and Dawn was sure she'd found her criminal.

Right after being promoted to the position of vice president of Marketing, Laura Netzly filed a report with the senior management team stating money was missing for no discernable reason from the special Marketing promotional accounts. By the time she finished typing the four-page memo, she drew an elegant, if unprovable, claim that the man responsible for the embezzlement was Thomas Williams. In a follow-up memo dated the next day, she further accused him of taking bribes from outside vendors for preferential treatment. The memos were well-drafted and demonstrated a polished writing style. But to Dawn they read a lot like a witch hunt, which made her curious. It all seemed like smoke without a fire.

The section of the legal file regarding Williams made very clear that, when he worked in Marketing, he was given a lot of professional leeway. Under the previous VP of Marketing, Tom was rarely, if ever, questioned, Netzly's memos strongly suggested the previous VP was incompetent and let Williams get away with anything he wanted, including possibly setting up a funnel for fraudulent activity. Wild accusations were made, and Williams was sent home with pay to wait for the board of directors to come to a decision about his future. To his credit, Williams refused to go down quietly, hiring an attorney who began writing several letters in his defense, copying everyone, including the board of directors to their home addresses. At one point while going through the file, Dawn discovered several years of Thomas Williams's tax returns, all presented along with bank statements and excel spreadsheet records that Mr. Williams had maintained over the years; he'd submitted them to show exactly how he lived and afford the things he owned.

A detailed savings plan for many years filled his bank accounts and enabled him to buy a condo in a good part of San Diego. A letter dated after the credit union's investigation closed indicated a deceased relative left him a fairly lucrative part of her estate, which was also the reason he was driving a Corvette free and clear. Dawn thought it was a very nice touch including that letter to the credit union after the fact. Almost like he wanted to rub their nose in it.

His alibis and excuses were all very neat and tidy. The accusations were muddled and seemed to rely heavily on innuendo and suspicion. Sitting in the HR office, Dawn became sure that eighteen months ago Thomas Williams was indeed set up. The question was how did she prove the missing money was his means of revenge?

She closed the file and returned it to the HR assistant and leisurely strolled back down the hall toward the executive boardroom. She passed right by the collections department. She stopped outside the door for a moment, thinking about the situation, and then shook her head clear and returned to the boardroom. As soon as she stepped through the door, Marc held up the phone and said, "Dawson's on the phone for you."

She muttered a quick, 'thank you,' as she grabbed the phone. "What's up, old man?"

"Sixty-four million dollars a day for five days totals 320 million, right?"

Dawn felt her knees starting to give a little, so she gracefully pulled out a chair and sat down. "Talk to me, Dawson. What have you got?" She knew, though; she'd known the day before when she'd had him start looking into it but, before she could say anything in front of either Neal or the FBI, she needed proof to back her up.

"On Wednesday, March 1, at exactly noon, sixty-four million dollars was transferred to the Cayman Islands via federal wire transfer, using all of the proper automation codes for Hil Federal Credit Union."

"Go on." Dawn was looking across the room, watching as Neal chatted with the Credit Union CEO. To her it looked like they were sharing locker room jokes while struggling to remain reserved in this professional atmosphere. It was the modern version of a good ol' boy chat.

"On Thursday, March 2, sixty-four million was transferred at twelve twenty-two in the afternoon in the same way. On Friday, March 3, another sixty-four million was transferred at twelve forty-four in the afternoon, also in the same way."

Dawn was scribbling everything down onto a yellow pad that had been left on the boardroom table. "I'm listening, keep going."

"On Monday, March 6, at 1:06 p.m. a fourth wire transfer of sixty-four million was completed, and then finally on March 7, at 1:28 p.m. the fifth and final wire for sixty-four million was sent. Each of the transfers went to a different account number at a different bank down there, but all of it went to the Cayman Islands. Total up five days worth of transfers at 64 mil a pop, and like I said, you hit 320. Good hunch, Dawn."

"Yeah," she said, looking down at the yellow pad, "I knew the money had to get out of here somehow." She was clearing her head, prioritizing her facts and follow-up. "Dawson, I want you to take copies of whatever documentation the Federal Reserve gave you. Fax down one set to me at once, then overnight another copy so I can be holding a hard copy in my hands by tomorrow."

"You got it, hon" he said joyously, knowing that despite her current gruff voice she was very happy with herself and the sudden change of flow of the investigation.

She hung up the phone and flagged over both Neal and Halstead. "Dawn," Neal said uncomfortably as he stepped up, "we're kind of busy right now. Can it wait?"

"I know where the money went."

Halstead, who, for the most part, didn't want to talk to Dawn for any reason, suddenly found himself sitting down next to her and hanging on her every word, ignoring Neal and whatever plan he might have been trying to hatch. "Where is it?"

"I doubt it's still there, but I know how it left the Credit Union and where it went to. My question to you is this: do you have any really good connections down in the Caymans?"

"Well," Halstead said, smiling, "I'll see what I can put together. Tell me what you have."

"You bet, but before we do I think it's time we called together a few people, namely the CEO, the CFO, and the guy who runs the computer department, because, I tell you, none of them are going to like what I have to say."

* * *

Playing the Odds 4.4

March 10, 2000

They all sat listening to her. Dawn presented how it was done slowly; making sure they could all follow along. Listening to herself, she thought she sounded like an elementary schoolteacher, trying to explain why "i" comes before "e." But they were listening, hanging on her every word. Craig Peterson was the most unnerved in the room. The other Credit Union officials were just getting mad, but Craig knew that as the senior vice president over finance, when the axe fell, it would be right on his neck.

Dawn felt sorry for him. He seemed like a nice guy and did the best he could the day before to help her get the information she needed. Unlike most people he hadn't just assigned a flunky to explain the system to her; he took the time to do it himself. Given what she was saying, she was fairly confident that, once the money was found and recollected, Craig Peterson would lose his job, but they were past the point of saving people's jobs now. It didn't matter that a very elegant crime was committed, that it sideswiped the entire foundation of the Credit Union. When the public relations people took over at the end of the investigation, heads would roll. For any financial institution to survive in the fast-paced market of the late '90s or the new era of the 2000s consumer confidence was a must. Credit unions had been building strength and support within their memberships for ages now; losing a large sum of money would tear apart that trust. The board of directors would start handing out final notices, the modern age equivalent to the pink slip. No one would be able to walk away quietly, as the PR people would be announcing to the media and anyone else who cared to listen that the people who allowed the tragedy to happen were gone. Names would be named, and even though it all came down to the fact that the Hil Federal Credit Union was the victim of a very high-tech and sophisticated crime, some careers would never be salvaged. Craig Peterson would be only one of the people whom this fate would befall. In fact, as Dawn looked around the room of senior vice presidents, the chief internal auditor, and the CEO, she wasn't sure any of them would survive.

"It appears that the Mammon GL was active earlier than we previously believed." Her voice remained low. She knew they were all ready to burst from frustration, and there just wasn't any profit in antagonizing them.

"How is that possible, Ms. McCafferty? I thought the money didn't disappear from anyone's accounts until the seventh of March?"

"Up until this morning, that's what we believed as well."

Randy Carlson was letting his gut stick out as he sat with one leg up on the chair in front of him. He looked damn comfortable, despite the fact his career was on the line. "And why is that, exactly?"

"I had someone check with the Federal Reserve for outgoing wire transfers from your institution, several were found."

"We do a lot of business with wires through the Federal Reserve." The voice came from the senior vice president of the branch network, Megan Hertigin. She was the one who oversaw the branch operations of the thirty locations Hil Federal Credit Union offered.

"Not usually for this amount of money, though."

"How much are we talking, Dawn?" Carlson asked, with just the hint of his Texan drawl thrown in for good measure. Dawn instinctively smiled back at him as she answered.

"Sixty-four million dollars a day for five consecutive business days." The room went deathly silent as they all did the quick mental calculations. All of them came up with the figure in an instant. This was their missing 320 million dollars.

Robert Fetzer, the senior vice president of Lending, looked fiercely across the room to Craig Peterson. "Why the hell weren't we notified of this, Craig?"

The sad truth was he already knew the answer; everyone in the room did. Dawn could see it in their eyes, no matter what emotions or actions they played out for the theatrics of their peers. Her general theory of a super virus clearly explained this interaction wasn't about them trying to understand what happened anymore; this was where the play for survival began. Robert Fetzer was just the first man to go for the jugular. It didn't take a nuclear physicist to figure out the virus caused much more damage than they ever imagined. Robert's cold, verbal snap from across the table was about blame and how he planned to take none of it. It was only a matter of time before the rest of the people in this room would make similar accusations about Craig as well. That was the way things worked in the real world of corporate America. Craig cleared his throat, knowing that yelling at this point wasn't going to help anything. He looked across the table at Robert, very aware that every eye in the room was staring right at him, and as clearly and steadily as he could, spoke. "We reviewed our generated reports, Robert. We don't show any wires such as the ones Dawn described. A wire of that amount would have been cause for suspicion in and of itself, even for a credit union of our size."

"I'm stupid," Randy said aloud as he stood up from his seat, laughing "I really am, Ms. McCafferty, or can I just go on ahead and start calling you Dawn again?"

"I was surprised you started calling me by my last name as it was, Randy."

"Well, since this all seemed so formal. Well, I thought it was best." He walked up to the front of the room, right toward her. "To hell with that, though." At the front of the room he turned to face his coworkers, the only faces he really knew in the Credit Union. Sure, he knew the managers and vice presidents, but when push came to shove, the only people he really dealt with in his official capacity were in this room, all staring up at him, wondering what he was going to do next. "I've said it before and hell, I'll say it again. I'm dumb as a box of rocks in a lot of ways. Chasing down a criminal in cyberspace, I think you'd have to look pretty darn hard to find somebody dumber at that than I am. So maybe somebody in this room can explain to me what the hell happened here. I mean, I thought all of these damn reams and reams of paper we print on a daily basis was to make sure we knew what our computer system was doing. So can somebody please clear this up for me?"

Doug Law remained seated as he started to talk, and Dawn let him cover the technical side of the questions. He was certainly better versed in computers than she was. As the Senior VP of the computer department, he was fairly certain to lose his job as well. "Well, from the kind of virus Dawn is describing, it laid in wait until something prompted it to open, Randy. Once it opened it created a system wide glitch, and, as far as I can tell, pretty much took over our system without anyone knowing about it. And then, when it was done, it wiped itself out without a trace."

"But the reports . . ."

"If we lost control of the system, Randy, the reports would only print out as they were directed to."

"Randy," Dawn said quietly from his side, "there were a number of problems here, and our thief seemed willing to take advantage of them all. First you gave them opportunity, namely the whole Y2K scare that panicked America for no reason last year. You had miles upon miles of new code being entered into the system, so there was no way to suspect that a large sum of code being entered in on any given day as being abnormal. Second, with the way your accounting department balances GL's, it gave the thief a full ten days to do what he wanted before anyone would have noticed it was happening. Third, your fully automated system, which was used to cut down on employees and save on costs, allowed for the system to wire your money away and erase the fact that it was done."

"But if the money was being wired out on a daily basis, Dawn, why the hell didn't we notice it?"

"You have an automated system, Randy; the computer created ghost numbers to inflate accounts so no one would know anything was missing. The system did this for the first seven days of the month, until it reached the dollar amount it wanted, and then erased itself. At that point, the ghost numbers didn't exist anymore, and everyone could see you were short. This is why when your system ran its reports for the day ending on the seventh; you were missing 320 million dollars. Whoever did this planned it very carefully and, as far as I can see, left nothing to chance."

Randy was still smiling, but there was an edge to it that showed exactly how uncomfortable he was feeling. "Neal says you have a suspect, wouldn't tell me anymore than that. Is it true, do you know who did it, Dawn?"

"I have a suspect profile and I've found someone whom I believe falls comfortably within its parameters, but nothing concrete yet. Nothing we're willing to base an arrest on yet."

"Who is it?"

Dawn was smiling back at him now, ignoring everyone else in the room as she focused her attention on him. "It would be grossly premature for me to announce a name at this juncture of the investigation."

"Dawn, is it one of my employees?"

"Yes."

"Then premature or not, I don't give a huge rat's ass! I want to know which one of these assholes has their goddamn hand in the company till!"

"I can't prove anything yet, Randy, therefore if I drop a name to you, what are you going to do?"

"Do? I'll fire his ass!"

Neal stood up at the back of the room, making no effort to approach. Instead, he wanted to hear the sound of his own voice as it spanned the distance between them. "That's exactly what she doesn't want, Randy."

"To see the guy fired?"

"I want to see him arrested, Randy. Fired is secondary to that. If you fire him, he'll deviate from whatever his plan already is; he'll change to make sure he doesn't get caught. If we don't fire him, just toy with him instead, he'll think he's getting away with it; he'll stick to the plan he's constructed, and then we'll nail him when he goes to collect the money. Besides, I'd rather monitor him, track his computer time, his phone calls, basically know every keystroke he makes." Dawn heard the sound of her voice; to her it felt like she was suddenly competing with Neal, something she didn't particularly like.

"Fine, I won't fire him," Randy said abruptly, "but I sure as hell want to know who it is!"

Dawn flashed a quick look to Neal, who shrugged his shoulders. "I think it'll be OK." Dawn nodded her head and stepped back toward the door.

"I'll need to speak to a few managers directly," Dawn said quietly. "See if the employee has any consumer loans with you; ask a few questions of the people who know him."

"Who is it?"

"Remember," she said quietly, "the name can't leave this room, and nothing can be done about it just yet."

"I understand."

Dawn knew Randy was lying about understanding but she told him anyway and marveled at how much the man's face dropped as she spoke.

* * *

Playing the Odds 4.5
March 10, 2000

Dawn walked into the collections department at 1:15 p.m. and with sheer presence distracted everyone from what they were doing. She carried a steno notepad with a pen safely tucked into the spiral binder. She hadn't really given much thought to what she was wearing. When she got up in the morning, her only goal was to corner Neal before his morning coffee, and present her suspect to him. She wasn't the type of woman who spent a lot of time thinking about her clothes. To her, it was a great day if she could wear jeans and a T-shirt, something comfortable and easy to move around in. But throughout most of her professional life she hadn't been able to dress like she wanted. In the FBI they hadn't wanted her wearing T-shirts, though at least they'd let her wear jeans from time to time. The NCUA was even less accommodating. They didn't want their agents, even field agents, dressed like they were headed out for a day at the park. They expected professional dress at all times. For Dawn that meant dresses and skirts, tailored suits, and worse yet, fitted slacks. None of these choices thrilled her. Wearing the slacks always made her feel old, and she thought the tailored suits just looked foolish on her. That left dresses and skirts. The problem with most dresses was they restricted her movement and reaction time. In blue jeans she could do whatever she wanted; she could be rough and tumble. She could run or even get into a fight if the situation called for it. She resolved to abide by her company policy, whether she liked it or not, but to do so within her own sensibility.

Dawn knew she had nice legs; it was one of the many reasons she ran every morning, and worked out in the early evenings. Her body was tight and lean and she secretly liked the way she could use it to capture people's attention. While she certainly believed she looked her best in tight jeans, she learned walking around in a short skirt usually did the same trick. The shorter the skirt, the more range of movement she had. At the bureau she was careful to keep her skirts around company guidelines; she remembered reading something about how a skirt couldn't be higher than three inches over the knee. Now her skirts and dresses averaged around five inches. Some went higher others a little lower. All showed off how elegant her legs looked and to a certain extent how much time and care she spent to make sure they continued looking the way they did. At the home office many of the other female employees had secretly complained to Neal or other supervisors about Dawn's short skirts, but not surprisingly, nothing was ever said directly to her about it. Neal was usually too busy staring at her legs himself to say anything. She was hardnosed, and most people didn't want to directly deal with 'that woman' from the FBI. Those that did were blown off; therefore, all complaints about Dawn's appearance were directed to Neal. And with Neal they were promptly forgotten.

Over time Dawn got fairly lazy with monitoring the length of her skirts' on a daily basis. Some she brought were really far too short for the office, but knowing her boss wouldn't say anything about it didn't really motivate her to make changes in the way she did things. Today's skirt was one of those. It ran to the higher side of Dawn's legs, showing off exactly how long and sensual they were. She'd been too busy today to notice but every man she'd passed was distracted by its length. The skirt was part of a matching set, along with a blouse and blazer style jacket that wrapped around her. It was powder blue and brought out the natural blue of her eyes. The moment Thomas Williams looked up, his eyes locked in on Dawn, until he forced himself to blink; breaking the hypnotic effect a woman's legs can have on a man. A dark grin crossed his face, and, with his eyes still closed he tilted his head upward so he could look up to her face, and only then did he open them.

Everyone else in the room was waiting for Tom to say something. Working in an office with five women came with certain perks. Any attractive woman who walked through the door would be greeted by Tom. It was an unspoken rule of the department. His coworkers had started to worry about Tom in the past year and a half; the man who once carried a reputation of a womanizer hadn't so much as dated a single woman since coming to collections. They worried that after everything that happened in marketing, a part of him died. He was still a fun guy, who always had a joke and an easygoing manner, but his coworkers were concerned that he was no longer living for the future and instead concerned himself only with momentary survival. It was a bleak existence at best, and those who knew Tom best said they could see despair in his eyes. Thus, when a pretty woman walked through the door, it became almost an obligation for Tom to do the talking. Everybody talked about fixing him up, but very few actually did. He still liked talking with women, but there seemed to be very few he was actually interested in anymore.

Tom's smile was still present as he rose up from his chair and extended his hand. He wanted to believe his smile was what garnered her attention and made her sway over to his desk, but he could tell she was looking at him from the moment she came through the door. In that dark part of his psyche he wanted desperately to believe it was because this blonde haired beauty from parts unknown was secretly attracted to him, but he knew better. Her arrival awakening a survival sense, because she was staring at him not with a hunger born of desire, but the look of a cat that's just spotted a mouse. His smile remained steady as he extended his hand to her. She was slowly walking toward him, extending her own. "Hi," he said, in his most charming of voices, "my name's Tom. Can I help you with anything?"

Tom was very aware that everyone in the office was staring at them. He also knew they were looking for the wrong thing. His coworkers were studying for signs that they should start match making, Tom was trying to figure out if he should start worrying. He understood one's past was a very hard thing to escape and knowing what Judy told him, he suspected that his name was starting to come up once again. She lightly took his hand and demurely looked him right back in the eyes. "I know exactly who you are, Mr. Williams, and what I'm looking for now is to speak to Ms. Tanin."

Surprised by her bold statement, his eyes widened and her grip tightened. She half expected him to shrink back and away from her. Instead, his smile only grew as he tried to cover for the shock in his eyes. "Well, hang on then," he said, slipping his hand free of hers. "I'll see if she's available."

"I'm more than capable of introducing myself, Mr. Williams."

"I'm sure you are, but we have rules around here."

A smile crossed her face for just a moment. "And do you follow them?"

"When it suits me," Tom chuckled gracefully, stepping around his desk and behind her. Dawn remained still, unconcerned by his movements. Everyone in the office continued to watch, waiting to see exactly what kind of dance would play out. No one was surprised to see that Tom lowered his gaze to check out the woman's well-shaped rear, the moment he stepped behind her. The glance only lasted a second or two, but his cheeks reddened just slightly as he breezed by and into Judy Tanin's office. She was leaning back in her plush leather chair, looking up at him and shaking her head in amusement.

"You could have just sent her in?" She was trying to hold back her laughter and keep her voice low because she suspected this was Tom's way of flirting. He smiled back attempting to stop blushing before he turned back around. He stepped right up to her desk.

"I know how you hate surprises."

"Who is she?"

"The auditor."

"Does she have a name?"

"Well," Tom said with his ever-growing smile, "don't they all? Not that I ever bother to learn them."

"Jesus," she said, exasperated by his piggish joke. "Just send her in."

"Will do, chief." With that, he spun around and, in to the doorway of Judy's office, met Dawn's look eye-to-eye. She raised an eyebrow at him when he didn't speak right away; she was curious if he was trying to study her as much as she was studying him. She was about to open her mouth when he motioned for her to step forward. "Ms. Tanin will see you now."

Dawn stepped forward methodically; keeping Tom's eyes locked in her gaze, and was astonished when he didn't yield. Most men, she had learned, were cowards in brute's bodies. They could crush beer cans in their hands but couldn't think their way out of difficult situations. Put them under the weight of a heavy stare and most men would break or at the least show signs of strain. As far as Dawn could tell, Tom Williams was enjoying it. "Thank you, Mr. Williams."

"My pleasure, Ms. Auditor."

She slid past him, running the edge of her shoulder just barely against his chest, as he moved forward from the doorway out of her way. He was slightly turning his head to take a look into the office, hoping for one last glance at the sultry auditor before she settled into the chair at Judy's desk when he realized she wasn't moving away from the door but closing it. Suddenly, instead of having a clear view into Judy's office he was looking at the polished oak door, left to wonder what might be going on inside. Knowing for certain he wouldn't like the answer. *After all*, he thought, *why else would she know his name?*

Inside the office, Dawn could feel the weight of Judy's stare at her back. It annoyed most people when she took command of their office, especially when the office she barged into belonged to another woman. There was an order to things in life that couldn't be changed. Women were forced to fight very hard for their accomplishments and trained by experience to know that once achieved they needed to work twice as hard to keep it. Women, by nature, didn't really trust one another, with friends and family as about the only exception. Dawn knew the smart play to this scenario would be to come in humbly, sit before the broad desk of the collections manager, and act like it all really meant something, and after a few idle minutes of chit-chat, ask if she could shut the door and get down to business. The problem was, she just didn't have the patience for it at the moment; the investigation was stimulating, and she wanted to slowly peel back its layers. She wasn't in the mood to playact. She mused in her head that it was probably her own reaction to being stuck in a small room with a woman she didn't know. Dawn also knew that what she was doing was far more important than anything the collections office might be working on at the moment. She knew that Judy Tanin wouldn't agree with that for a second, but Dawn was there to set her straight nonetheless. To do that, Dawn decided the best way to get the information she needed was to set the pecking order right from the beginning. She turned with what her father referred to as her 'anti-smile,' not quite a smile but not necessarily a frown. It had an odd effect on most people over the years; many suggested she looked like a mannequin when she used it. Judy was staring right at her, the chip on her shoulder already forming watching as Dawn came charging into her office. She opened her mouth and, in a tone that was more brisk than professional, asked, "What is it I can do for you?"

"My name is Dawn McCafferty. I'm a special investigator for the NCUA. Undoubtedly you've already heard that a crime was committed recently within the Credit Union."

"Yes," Judy said, as she motioned her hand to the empty chair. "I've heard it was a large loss that your people are investigating. Please, have a seat."

"Thank you." Dawn took the chair for the sake of Judy's ego, even though she didn't really feel like sitting. After settling herself in and adjusting her skirt to make sure she was sitting as a proper lady should, Dawn returned Judy's gaze. She could tell that Judy wasn't used to having such an intense look being directed right at her. "I'm the lead investigator," Dawn said in her easiest tone, trying to give the woman before her a chance to get comfortable, "and I need to ask you a few questions."

"Certainly."

Dawn clicked her pen on and flipped the steno pad open. She was aware of the tension in the room where she so easily sat; about to ask unknown questions that would be hard to answer. Undoubtedly all of the managers were already talking about the idea of missing money, wondering if they would be contacted, maintaining a tight network so they would know if interviews were starting to happen. It was quite clear that Ms. Tanin hadn't expected to be first in the interview lineup. "I understand you had a rather large computer upgrade near the end of last year. Is that correct?"

"Well," Judy was stalling trying to phrase her words correctly, not wanting to show any weakness that this investigator might misinterpret, "it was implemented at the end of last year but it had been in the planning stages for well over a year before that time. In fact an almost useless beta version was running on Logiterm for about five years prior. We used it for mass mailing of preprinted letters."

"Sort of like an old data feeder?"

"Pretty much, yes. The bigwigs . . ." she threw in lightheartedly, hoping to see Dawn crack a smile. Instead Dawn sat stone faced, waiting to get the information she wanted, ". . . wanted something more formal for our system, so this upgrade was specifically designed. Needless to say it was approved by several different people many times over before actually being uploaded into production."

"The original system used off Logiterm was mostly for data feeding, but the 'bigwigs', as you call them, wanted more. By more, what is it you mean?"

Judy wanted to scream an obscenity at the top of her lungs but knew better then to let it show. Dawn McCafferty wasn't going to yield anything, and that meant Judy would have to play this even more carefully than she thought. "Well, it means they wanted us to go paperless, to not use our old flying system of cash pay cards. Cash pay cards were basically lined eight-by-five-inch cards that we used to keep all of our notes on, a system this credit union used for collection purposes for almost thirty years. But in this age of automation, we felt we needed to raise the standard of efficiency."

"Were you satisfied by the system you got?"

"It was sufficient but despite the time it took to get inputted, it was still rather rushed because it all had to be done while we were working on our regular collections activities."

"Did you do the programming yourself?"

Judy sat back a little deeper in her chair as she looked at Dawn, wondering where she was going with this line of questioning. "I helped design it, certainly, but

I'm not a computer programmer. Most of that was done either by the Logiterm programming techs or by our own information services department."

"When did the system, the current system, first come online?"

"Monday, December 6."

"For everyone or just for you?"

"Everyone had access to it at once, but Tom was the first one to utilize it as a regular collector. We wanted Tom to go in and beta-test it, see if there were any kinks in it before we all started using it."

"Tom?"

"Yes," Judy said confidently, "Tom Williams. He's one of my collectors and very proficient with computers. He helps most of us out periodically in the department. It saves us a lot of time from having to call up Info Sys for every little thing that might creep up. He was the best choice to play test it as he was most likely to find any hidden errors or problems."

Dawn hadn't written a word on her pad; she just looked at Judy, holding the pen stiffly. "You said before that your informational services department or Logiterm did the bulk of programming on your new collection system. Is that correct?"

"Yes."

"Who did the rest of it? An outside vendor?"

"No, Tom worked on it as well."

"With the actual programming?"

"Not too much. I believe he wrote a little of the code, but it was a hassle for him to do so because anything he did still had to be approved through Info Sys, whereas anything someone from Info Sys wrote could just be loaded right in."

"But since Tom did write a little of the code, and I assume, was very hands on with the project, he was a perfect choice for beta-tester, right?"

"Exactly."

"OK, let me just make sure I have this straight: no one could have accessed the new collections system until December 6 of last year?"

"Not really. I mean, most of the early testing was done on a simulation of the actual live Logiterm system, but I believe it was operational a few times during the course of the latter part of the year."

"There were times when this untested system was uploaded and usable before the actual release date?"

"Yes."

"Do you remember the dates it was active?"

"I have most of the dates written down."

"Most?"

Judy smiled, trying to insinuate how busy she was on a daily basis. "I made it a point to record every time the system came up, but there were times that Info Sys would activate it for only a few minutes when they'd call Tom to test something out. I really can't be certain I was notified of every single instance it went online."

"Or by whom?"

"I'm sure Logiterm would record that information. You might want to check with Info Systems."

"I'll do that. Now let me get back to something. Was there ever a point when any transaction in your collection system wouldn't have been recorded by the Logiterm live system?"

"Not that I can think of."

"Is Tom a qualified computer programmer?"

"No, he's just very good with computers."

"Good enough that you let him help shape the way you would be working for years to come."

"I trust Tom. He's a good employee."

Dawn looked down at the blank sheet of paper before her. "A good employee? Didn't he come to your department after something of a scandal?" Dawn looked up slightly, just barely enough to see Judy's entire body stiffened at the mention of Tom's relocation.

"He had some trouble in his previous department," Judy said, very judiciously, and left it at that.

"But no problems since then?"

"No, none."

"One last question, Ms. Tanin," Dawn said as she folded her steno pad shut, "You personally review all of the Logiterm activity reports, so that way you know what your employees are doing or what they've done?"

Judy stared silently across the desk, letting the question hang uncomfortably in the air before inhaling deeply and slowly answering, "Yes."

"Great," Dawn said as she stood, putting her pen back into the small metal spiral of the steno pad. "I think you've answered all of my questions for now."

Judy got up, shook Dawn's hand, and watched as Dawn walked to the office door and opened it. On the other side, everyone turned to look as she walked confidently through the office toward the department doorway.

Tom sat his own pen down on his desk as she walked by him. "Bye now." His voice was calm, and he started to smile as he watched her heading toward the door. "I hope you won't be a stranger now that you know where we are." For Tom it was a smart-ass answer, something he would have said to almost anyone, but saying it to the beautiful woman in front of him attached a whole different set of meanings to it.

Dawn turned at the door, slowly turning the knob in her hand, and looked right at him. "Don't worry, I'll be seeing you." And with that she left.

A veil of silence enveloped the usual noisy chaos of the collections department. As soon as the door shut, everyone in the department except Judy turned to look at Tom, waiting to hear what he might say. Instead Tom just looked back down at his desk and started scribbling notes on his pad about a conversation with a debtor from earlier in the morning. Samantha finally broke the silence, asking loudly, so that everyone in the room would be sure to hear, "So, you gonna ask her out or what?"

Tom just smiled, fighting to hold back the laughter. "Gee, do you think I should?"

"Let me think," Samantha said with heavy sarcasm. "She was staring right at you from the moment she walked through the door, and then as she was leaving, what was that all about, if not flirting?"

"She had nice legs. I was trying to stall her so I could look at them a little longer."

"Think, Tom, think," she said, throwing a wadded-up piece of paper at him that he didn't even bother trying to avoid, "if you ask her out you might just get those legs wrapped around you."

Everyone in the office was laughing, and Tom's cheeks were turning crimson. Samantha always had a way of shooting from the hip and saying whatever was on her mind; it was one of the many things Tom loved about working with her. With Samantha there wasn't any bullshit; if she wanted something, she told you so. If she wanted you to leave her alone she was the first to tell you to piss off. It made working with her very easy.

"I'll have to think about that, then."

"Think, my ass, get up and walk down the hall after her."

Tom looked up at Samantha, not knowing what to say back to her. He had a sinking feeling in his gut, like he was about to puke. The question was still weighing on him; how did she know his name? He wasn't sure how he was going to get out of this conversation; he knew that Samantha thought she was helping. She'd stay on her point until she was damn sure it was made clear. His escape route appeared unexpectedly. "Tom, can you come in here please?"

The tone of Judy's voice echoing through the office conveyed her stress. Tom worked for her long enough to know her sounds and moods as they surfaced, and he knew today's tone meant trouble. Tom glanced over at Samantha, with his cheeks still warm and red. "Saved by the bell."

He stepped quickly toward the office, and, as soon as he hit the doorway, Judy asked him to close the door. Shutting it, he entered the room and sat at her request.

"Unless you're firing me, I'd rather stand."

"Tom, I'm not going to fire you."

He paced past her desk, walked to the window overlooking the parking lot, and stared down at his Corvette as if it might secretly comfort him. "Then what's happening?"

"She's not an auditor, and I wouldn't recommend you ask her out."

He now regretted not sitting down. His knees were suddenly weak and he fought the urge to throw up. It was like reliving his past, and even without Judy finishing her sentence, he knew what was coming. "Damn shame," he said, choking back his gag reflex while trying to play his best tough-guy act, "I kind of liked the image of her legs wrapped around me."

"She's an investigator for the NCUA and she came in here, as far as I could tell, to ask questions about you."

"You know, when I went to school I was a history major." He didn't turn around to look at his boss but he could feel her eyes on the back of his head. "I remember the line, 'Those who do not know their history are doomed to repeat it,' I guess it was a crock of shit. I know the past but here I am again repeating it. Churchill, by the way."

"I wasn't supposed to tell you about this, Tom. I think I could get into a lot of trouble for mentioning it."

"Don't worry, I won't rat you out."

"Tom, I think it would be wise if you got back in touch with your attorney friend again. I mean, it couldn't hurt."

"Yeah, don't worry; I never fell out of touch with her." He was embarrassed to turn around suddenly; he could feel the tears in his eyes, even as he fought them back. "It just doesn't seem fair, you know? I've already covered this ground. I've already been the accused, but I guess my attorney was right: Hil Fed will never really let me walk away from that black mark, bullshit or not. Once an accused thief, always an accused thief. She warned me that if any till I could get my hands into ever came up short; I'd be their first suspect. I didn't believe her, though. I was just arrogant enough to think I really could start over here. Damn me for being the fool I am."

"Want to go home, Tom? It's late enough in the day. Don't bother to put it down on the time sheet. Just leave. I'll cover you."

He half turned to look back at her. "What, and steal an hour or two of the company's time? They'll probably have me arrested."

"Tom," Judy said, starting to stand, "I'll stand behind you. I want you to know that."

He turned and started walking toward the door, "You might not want to, Judy. Christ Almighty, they might decide to burn you, too."

* * *

Playing the Odds 4.6

March 10, 2000

"I'm sorry, your name again?"

Gail Landsing stretched out her hand awkwardly to shake with Dawn and gave her name. One thing Dawn had to thank the upper management staff at

Hil Federal Credit Union for they had spread around Dawn's authority very well. Everyone she'd met with knew that she wasn't to be put off, and she hadn't yet needed to show anyone her ID.

Gail Landsing was the branch manager of the Credit Union's main branch, which held all of the employee accounts, and the time had come to take a very good look at what kind of financial records they kept on Tom Williams. Dawn was sure, by this time, Hil Fed had already developed a lot of information on Mr. Williams on their own, she was curious of what kind of accounts he kept. So far Dawn had only met Gail once, on her second day when she really hadn't been paying any attention to the many names she was being inundated with. That was why she chose to start fresh by asking Gail's name. To Dawn's surprise Gail stood from behind the desk, extended her hand in a highly professional manner, and began to treat Dawn as if she was soliciting a new membership account.

"And you're the investigator from up north. NCUA, right?"

"Yes," she said pleasantly, "Dawn McCafferty."

"Of course." Gail sat back down gracefully while, with a slight motion of her hand, presented the visitor chair in front of her desk to Dawn. "I see your rounds have finally brought you down to my branch. What can I do for you?"

"I need to look in a few employee files."

Gail immediately looked concerned as she leaned closer to Dawn. "I'm going to have to ask you to hold for just a moment, and please don't take offense to this, but I need to call up to Randy on this one. For anyone else, even someone with a badge, I'd refer first to our attorney for that request. Randy said he wanted you to have access to everything, but there are laws against releasing private information on members, even when they happen to be employees."

"I understand," Dawn said, settling a little deeper into her chair, "I'll wait while you call him."

Gail quickly got on the phone and was patched right through to Randy once Dawn's name was mentioned. Dawn tried not to pay much attention to what was being said, but it was difficult. Despite the fact that Randy was three floors above, she could hear him screaming on the other end of the telephone like he was sitting right next to her. At the end of the conversation, Gail hung up and stood. "For the record, Ms. McCafferty, I object to this."

Dawn looked up, smiling. It wasn't a smart ass smile, the kind she used on so many others who displayed the same reservations about her crass investigative style, but a genuine smile of understanding. She knew Gail was worried about backlash from any employee whose personal information was ransacked in the investigation; because Gail was afraid she would be liable for divulging secrets. Dawn heard similar fears over the years but didn't really let it bother her. She stood and looked right into Gail's eyes, trying to express her understanding.

"Randy has instructed me to allow you access to any file you deem necessary, no matter what my reservations might be. I'm a good, loyal employee, Ms. McCafferty, so I will do as I'm told, but I think it's wrong."

"Noted, Gail, I'll place it in my report. You'll be fine."

With that, Gail seemed a little happier and escorted Dawn to the backroom, where the file room was kept. The only other person besides them in there was an office temp, slowly posting drop deposit from the afternoon mailbag. Gail pointed to the section with the employee files. "There they are. Will you need any help in going through them?"

"No," Dawn said quickly. The last thing she wanted was anyone knowing who her true target was, at least at this stage of the game. The only file she really wanted to see was Williams', but she'd pull out a handful of other files in case rumor of what she was doing got out. "I think I'll be fine as is."

"Well then, feel free to use the backroom. Teresa's the only other person back here today. We've been short staffed lately, and HR doesn't seem to be in the mood to allow us to tap into our budgets right now any more than is absolutely necessary. I really need to stay up front and help out there."

"I understand," Dawn said, and she did. The Credit Union was worried about suffering a tremendous loss, and the last thing it was going to let branches or departments do right now was spend anything other than essential dollars. It was a sound fiscal plan but it sucked down on the front line of member contact. "I'll be fine with what I have. Thank you."

Gail swiftly departed to the front room, and Dawn reached into the employee files, randomly grabbing five that she could care less about. She also handpicked Williams' file and grabbed three more to stack on top of it. Walking into the back room, she sat down at the empty desk opposite the temp, Teresa. They exchanged a few seconds of mindless chit-chat and then Dawn picked up Tom Williams' file and began leafing through it. The file was remarkably thin for an employee with his tenure. Dawn knew already he'd started working for Hil Fed when he was twenty years old; that meant he'd been there for eighteen years and in that time, had only two loan applications on file, and only one of them completely filled out. The other, for a share secured loan, which meant Tom fronted cash in his account against a loan. A handwritten note by a branch employee stated Tom was taking out the loan for a friend, not himself, a woman named Megan. The thought baffled her. How could any guy not need to take out a loan in eighteen years? She'd done more than that in the past twelve months herself. The one official loan app on file was completed when he was twenty years old and working there only three months. Dawn thought it helped her develop her profile of a man who didn't need to steal.

"Gee," a voice said from somewhere in the room, "three guesses say I can tell you whose file it is you're looking through."

Dawn looked up to see Tom Williams entering the room. The odd thing was he didn't appear angry; if forced to describe his expression in a single word, she'd use "amused." He was holding a file in his hand as he rested against the doorway, but his gaze was impossible to miss. He was looking right at her.

Dawn's chair was hard and wooden, the very essence of discomfort, but she leaned against the back frame anyway and stared back at him. "Sure, but the first two don't count."

He released a small chuckle and dropped the file he was carrying into a small tray off to the side of the door. The office temp was looking up from her stacks of posting, unsure of what was suddenly going on, but even she realized the dynamic in the room had changed. "So, want to clue me in?"

"What do you mean, Mr. Williams?"

"You're going to make me work for this?"

"You're making me work."

"Nope," he joked, "you just think I am."

She thought about it for a second and then closed his file. It was clear there was nothing of any value in it anyway, just as it was evident that she could report back to any and all concerned that Judy Tanin had indeed revealed Dawn's intentions to the suspect. "What would you like to know, Mr. Williams?"

"What's the charge?"

The temp looked up as if somebody slapped her in the back of the head, but looked immediately down again, trying to pretend she wasn't paying any attention to the conversation. "There've been no charges filed against anyone last I checked."

"OK, no charges. How about suspicion?"

"There's always plenty of that. Wouldn't you say?"

"Suspicion against me?"

"Now, what makes you say that?"

"Up in the office," Tom said, taking a couple of steps closer to Dawn, "you knew my name."

"I'm good with names."

"How about history? You any good at that?"

"Not really," she said, "I was usually better at math."

"But you know my history, don't you?"

"Some."

"So I'm a suspect?"

"Let's consider, shall we? If it were your job, you were investigating a crime and someone with your history existed, would you consider that person a suspect?"

"Well, no, but then, I know I'm innocent."

She kept her voice dry, trying to contain her sarcasm. "Then, gee, Mr. Williams, you don't have anything to worry about, do you?"

Tom laughed a little under his breath, still looking right her. "You really think I did it?"

"No," she whispered, prolonging her words, "I know it."

"Will you at least tell me what I'm suspected of?"
"You already know."
"Assume I don't."
"If you don't know, why should I clue you in?"
"All I know is that it's a crime, which most rumors suggest that a lot of money was involved."
"See?" She said, starting to play with him. "You knew after all."
"How much?"
"Classified."
"Even to the accused?"
"Uh-huh."
"A lot, though?"
"Uh-huh."
"More than a million?"
"Mr. Williams, I have no intention playing this game with you."
"More than fifty million?"
"Was my first answer in any way unclear?"
"A hundred? A hundred million dollars?"

Dawn shook her head and broke eye contact with him. "It was in excess of that amount. That's all you'll get."

"In "excess" of a hundred million dollars. I wouldn't mind getting that."
"Who would?"
"There's only one problem with your theory."
"You mean, other than the fact you're innocent?"
"Yeah, as a matter of fact."
"I wait with baited breath to hear it then, Mr. Williams."

"My name is Tom, not Mr. Williams. People who want to yell at me call me "mister," but to everyone else I'm Tom, or Thomas, if you prefer. Just, please, not Mr. Williams."

"Mr. Williams, to conduct the business I need to conduct, it's important I keep my communications as professional as possible. Do you understand?"

"If you're right, and I'm guilty, you'd call me a scumbag then, right?"
"I'd call you guilty."

Tom walked all the way over to the desk, and Dawn was alarmed to notice, he didn't bother to sneak a look at the files laid out before her, not even his own. "But you probably wouldn't call me Mr. Williams anymore, would you?"

"You'd be surprised."
"OK, then, do me a personal favor, call me Tom."
"Mister . . ."

"I know, I get it; you want to remain totally professional while you're hunting me down like a dog, tearing through the darkest corners of my personal life. Really,

I understand, but the thing is, I'm giving you permission, call me Tom. It'll make both our lives easier, really."

Dawn smiled warmly at him, in spite of herself. His persistence was entertaining. "Fine, Tom. Happy?"

"Yes."

"You were telling me the problem with my theory."

"Yeah, the one problem with it."

"Other than you're innocent."

"Right. The other problem is I don't have in excess of a hundred million dollars. Honest, my mattress isn't that thick."

"Oh, don't worry, the money will turn up. With this much, it can't hide forever."

"I'd guess not." He sat on the edge of the desk, still looking down at her, staring into her eyes as she looked up into his. "Can I ask you a couple of questions?"

She gently nodded her head. "Depends what the questions are."

"You know my name, right?"

"Yes, Tom, I think we've clearly established that."

"Well then, isn't it every man's right to know the name of his accuser?"

"I beg your pardon?"

"Your name? I'd like to know who you are."

She studied him for a moment, unsure of what to make of him, and then shrugged, "Agent Dawn McCafferty, NCUA. Pleased to meet you." Tom's eyes seemed to take her in, at least the parts of her that rose above the desk line, like he was studying her right back. She asked "What's your other question?"

"Two more actually."

"OK, what's your next question?"

"What kind of guy would be dumb enough to steal in excess of one hundred million dollars and stick around the office building?"

"That's simple, Tom."

"Really?" He marveled. "Please, enlighten me, because I don't have a clue."

"The guy who thinks he can get away with it."

"That much money, though, a man would never be able to hold onto it. I mean, what good is a hundred million bucks if you can't spend it?"

Dawn blinked. The question spoke a lot of truth. That much money was rather useless. She assumed that anyone stealing it would be dumb enough to think they could hide it forever or would break it up quickly enough to stash it. Tom was speaking differently, though, like a man who knew it was inevitable that the money would be traced. That no matter what was done, it would be found. When Dawn looked back up at him, he was still smiling at her. "You said you had two questions. Was that the second?"

"No.'

"Well, you'd better get to it. I've got to get back upstairs. I still have work to do."

"Don't suppose you'd tell me how many other suspects there are."

"Is that your second question, Tom?"

"Nope, I was hoping for a freebie."

She stood up, revealing her legs, and his eyes darted downward immediately before he forced them back to her face. She laughed at the absurdity of it all. "No one else, Tom. I'm convinced you're my man."

"Suspect number one?"

"Yep, must be time to go grab a lawyer."

"Am I under surveillance?"

"For a hundred million bucks, what do you think?"

"So you really are going to start rooting though my life, then?"

"I think we've come to the end of this discussion, don't you?"

"I still have another question."

Laughing, she stacked up the employee files and placed them at the edge of the desk. "You just don't give up, do you?"

"I'm told it's one of my endearing traits."

"You've been misinformed."

"But you'll let me ask the question?"

"You can always ask."

"I need to set up some foundation for it."

"What are you, a lawyer? I thought you were just an average joe."

"I'm being followed, and watched, my private life is suddenly under public scrutiny? That's what you're telling me?"

"I'm telling you that we're investigating you and will be using all proper means to do so."

"So you'll be watching me tonight, then? Since it's Friday, and I'll be away from Hil Fed for the next couple of days."

"I'm getting bored, Tom. I'd suggest you get to your question quickly."

"OK, ready?"

"Yes, Tom," Dawn replied, laughing again at the sheer intensity of his presentation and its good-natured way. "Fire away."

"Will you have dinner with me tonight?"

"What?"

"I asked if you'd have dinner with me tonight."

"Tom, I'm investigating you."

"Yes, and that means you'll be watching me all night anyway. This way you can just do it at close range. You won't be able to miss a thing."

"Well, I'll give you one thing, Tom—I never saw that question coming. Not that it will change my answer."

"Now wait a second, Agent McCafferty, don't answer too quickly here. I know this great Italian place down the street. You're going to be following me anyway. If you're having dinner with me you'll be a part of everything I do, and who knows? Maybe if I have one beer too many, I'll suddenly confess and you can wrap everything up early."

Dawn hadn't met anyone like him in quite some time. With what she just set up for him, she knew he should be scared to death and demanding to speak to his lawyer. Instead, he was suggesting dinner. It was outlandish in the way of a British comedy sketch, especially considering from the look on his face he was deadly serious. "This is ridiculous."

"A lot of things in life are ridiculous, Agent McCafferty. Take my life, for example."

Dawn managed to reign in her laughter and stare back at him as she came around the desk, trying to use her legs to weaken his resolve. To her surprise, he didn't move his eyes from hers. "Tom, let's face it, I've seen your salary sheet. You couldn't afford me."

"You think I stole in excess of a hundred million dollars. Let's be frank, if that's true, what can't I afford?"

Dawn froze, looking at his face as he smiled caringly, taunting her to answer From a voice that was almost not her own, she was amazed to hear herself answer, "OK, you're on. What time?"

His smile brightened. "I get off at five."

* * *

OUTSIDE THE LINES

Outside the Lines 5.0

March 10, 2000

"You must really like operating outside of the lines," Dawn said as she stepped out to meet Tom in the parking lot. The lot was still fairly full, lined row after row with cars of all different sizes and shapes, but Tom's stood out, not just because of its style, but also because it took up two entire spots without a trace of remorse.

"Funny," Tom said, leaning against his Corvette with a shit-eating grin that spanned the width of his face, "I'm fairly sure that whomever you answer to probably feels exactly the same way about you."

Dawn walked right toward him until she was only a foot away. "I can handle them." The problem was, she didn't know if she was lying or not. To say Neal hadn't taken her dinner plans well was an understatement. The moment she left the branch she went to the elevator and straight back to the boardroom, seeking him out and motioning him back to one of the private meeting rooms and closed the door.

He thought it a little odd, but dismissed it as her not wanting everyone to hear what she'd accomplished so far. "So how'd the meeting go with the collections manager?"

"It went well," she said trying to get past that part of the conversation. "I think if push came to shove, she'd protect him, but as long as she sticks to the truth, we can nail him on circumstance on her testimony."

"Good," Neal said smugly. He wasn't the kind of man to worry about details. That's why he hired people like Dawn.

"There's something I think you should know."

"What's that?"

"I—I—I—," she stammered, once again fighting back laughter in disbelief about the entire absurd situation in which she now found herself. She couldn't believe what her answer to Tom's request was now that she was out of the heat of the moment and back in the safety of the boardroom. "It seems, uhm, well, that I have dinner plans this evening."

"Before or after our daily wrap-up?"

"I'm meeting the individual at five. Well, just after actually."

"Before, the wrap-up then? So what you're really telling me is you want to bow out of the meeting tonight?"

"Yes," she said, trying to find her next set of words, choosing them carefully.

"So what's up, Dawn? One of these FBI guys who've been lusting after you got the balls to finally ask you out?"

"No, it wasn't an FBI guy."

"No?" Neal found himself very interested now and set down the printout he'd been looking through. "And I take it that it's not one of the people we brought in, either? I seem to recall they never tickled your fancy?"

"No."

"So you gonna tell me who?"

"That's why I called you back here, yes."

Neal smiled brightly here, curiosity burning inside of him. "Somebody from the Credit Union then?"

"Uh-huh."

"Not the old guy down from the computer department?"

"You mean Jim? No, not Jim."

"Like I said then, you gonna tell me or what?"

Dawn leaned against the door, making sure it was closed and that no one on the outside would be able to hear what she was about to say. "You're really not going to like it."

"A mystery, then. Is this a test, Dawn? I know you've never considered me an A-list investigator, but let's see here. I know he works for the Credit Union, so for me to really mind it has to be someone we're dealing with. I mean, hell, technically you shouldn't be trawling the Credit Union for dates in non-crime-related circumstances, but for you I'd excuse that."

"You're a hell of a guy, Neal."

"It's got to be someone on either the executive team or the board."

She released a quick sigh, shaking her head as he stared right into her eyes, "No."

"Then who else would I care about, Dawn?" He was staring right back at her when it suddenly hit him. His lower jaw dropped. He looked like a deer caught in the floodlights of a truck that was about to run him down. "Unless, oh Christ, you've got to be fucking kidding me, Dawn?"

"He asked."

"What? Are you so hard up for dates that you're willing to look at criminals now?"

"It's not a date."

"He knows that?"

"It's a component of the investigation."

"Like I said, Dawn," his voice rising, "does he know that?"

"Since when does it matter what he thinks?"

"Since the pot sitting in the middle of the table went up to 320 million!"

"He asked me out, Neal. I didn't ask him."

"Yeah, and did you ever hear the word, 'No?' I seem to recall hearing it."

She crossed the small conference room to get some distance from him. "I needed to talk to him anyway."

"In a controlled circumstance, not over cocktails and dim lights."

"Really? Don't you think his tongue might be a little looser after a few cocktails?"

"It's where he'll be trying to place his tongue that concerns me!"

"You're that worried about my personal standards all of a sudden?"

"Dawn, you've got to realize how this looks."

"I don't care how it looks, Neal. I'm having dinner with him and dinner only. I plan to get him to start talking, if not directly about the crime, then indirectly on the subject. For once, we have a suspect who is willing to talk to the investigator. Whether he realizes it or not, I'm a professional and I will get him to talk, even if I have to play him a little to do so. And, as for where he wants to place his tongue, that doesn't concern me a bit. I was trained by the FBI, Neal, trained to defend myself and I happen to be very particular about who gets to come close to me with their tongue, or any other body part for that matter. And like I said, if he has too much to drink, all the better for us."

"It wouldn't be admissible, Dawn. Any lawyer in the world would get this evidence thrown out."

"As you so often like to say, Neal, we're not in a court of law right now. Furthermore, if anything he lets slip helps me find out what really happened to the money in question, we'll use that piece of evidence to convict, not his actual words. The lawyers, no matter how good they think they are, won't be able to touch it."

"I don't like it!"

"Besides, if he confesses or says anything, it's not illegal. He's not under arrest. Miranda doesn't apply if we don't have him under custody. Anything he says can clearly be used against him."

"Does he know he's a suspect?"

"Yes."

He threw the print out across the room and both watched as it bounced off the wall and fell messily to the floor. "Why the hell did you tell him?"

"I didn't." Dawn's voice remained controlled as she looked at Neal with her face tight, ready for any fight he might want to start. "The collections manager told him that I was asking about him, and he came hunting me down."

"To ask you out?"

"So it would appear!"

"This has an extremely bad feel to it. One I really don't like."

"You don't have to."

Neal pulled out a chair and dropped into it. Only a few of the overhead lights were on, and the room was filled with shadows. He was flabbergasted, and it showed. After only a few minutes of conversation, he was worn out. "You're the head shrink here, Dawn. Why would a guy knowingly ask out a woman who's trying to nail his ass to the wall?"

"Some people are masochists, Neal, or just fucked up in the head to the point where nothing ever really makes sense."

"But according to your profile, this guy would have to be smarter than that, or are you changing your profile?"

"Not by as much as a single word." Her voice was confident and strong as she moved closer to the table.

"OK, then, why did he ask you out?"

"Only two reasons I can think of."

"Guilt and innocence?"

"No," she said slowly, pulling out the chair opposite him. "One is that he's guilty as sin and hoping to stay as close to the investigation as possible, trying to form a relationship with me in the hope I'll leak critical information to him. That way he'll know when it's time to really run or if we're nowhere close and he's safe."

"And the other reason?"

"He's guilty as sin and thinks we can't catch him. He wants to stay just close enough to taunt us, like a serial killer sending in clues to the police, the kind of manipulative bastard who likes to play games."

Neal was completely leaning back in his chair. "And which do you think he is?"

"I think he wants to try and mess with us. He's too cocky and not scared enough. Innocent people have an inbred reaction to being accused of a crime; they panic. They can't help it. They know they're innocent, but their gut reaction tells them they're in terrible trouble and need to do something. They haven't a clue as to what, though, so they get really scared really quickly. Point blank, Tom asked me if he was a suspect, and I told him yes. He looked disappointed but not frightened. I pushed further by telling him that he was not only a suspect but the lead suspect, and more directly, the person I think did it. At that he just seemed amused. He acts like it's all a big joke. He's quick on his feet, at least in the verbal sense, and he doesn't think we can trip him up. I think he's guilty as hell, Neal, and I intend to prove it."

"Is that the only reason you're going to dinner with him?"

"Sooner or later, if I can play him just right, he'll slip up. And when he does we can nail him. Dinner tonight is just the first opportunity."

"Is that the only reason you're going out with him, Dawn?"

"What other reason would there be?"

"Well, gee," Neal said, throwing up his hands into the air, "how about this: do you find him attractive?"

"Not particularly, no."

"What? What the hell does that mean? Not particularly?"

"It means I don't think he's ugly. His reflection probably wouldn't crack a mirror, but he's not exactly Brad Pitt either. I wouldn't expect him to wind up as *People* magazine's Sexist Man of the Year."

"So you're entertaining no sexual thoughts about him?"

"That's none of your damn business, Neal, but if it'll really make you feel better, no, I'm not."

"You know something, Dawn? If you're right, you just made a date with the guy who stole 320 million dollars. Have you considered the possibility he might be dangerous? Or that if we do arrest him, his lawyers will suggest he was set up because of a relationship formed between you two?"

"There is no relationship, Neal, no issue for the lawyers to bring up. We're having dinner, and he's well aware of the fact that my intent here is to bust his ass. Secondly, the FBI already has surveillance set up on him. I'll never be placed in harm's way because I'll have the FBI watching over me at all times. There's no chance of anything dangerous happening."

"Dawn, there's always a chance."

"Don't worry so much, Neal. After all I'm carrying."

"You're what?"

She opened the locked cabinet where she'd been keeping her purse, and slid out her 9mm, and hung it in the air.

"I don't recall authorizing you to carry on this assignment."

"I've got a license to carry a concealed weapon anywhere in the state of California, Neal, and like you said, with 320 million at stake, I figured it couldn't hurt to carry my own insurance."

He stood and picked his printout from the floor. His mood had sobered and he didn't want to look at her. Dawn put the gun back in her purse and threw the strap around her shoulder. "I'll be fine, Neal."

"9:00 a.m. tomorrow," he said coldly, "we're gonna have a little information session from everything we've learned about him so far."

"Fantastic," she replied jokingly. "I hope I'll have a lot to add by then."

Standing now in the parking lot Dawn admitted he did have a damn nice car, maybe a bit too dirty for a 'vette to get, but it gave him the appearance he wasn't a slave to his car. "Nice car, Tom."

"I like it."

"Let me guess," she said, stepping up to him, "you got it for a steal?"

"Nope, paid out the nose for it, actually. The salesman really saw me coming."

"Really?"

"Sure," he said, smiling even more broadly, "I've had to steal millions of dollars recently just to keep up with the payments. I mean, hell, this is a really expensive car."

"Millions, huh?"

"Well, in excess of."

"You know, Tom, that sounds dangerously like a confession."

"You really gonna arrest me *before* dinner?"

Dawn found herself laughing almost uncontrollably. Stopping herself from smiling, usually a simple task now seemed damn near impossible when he looked right at her. "I guess that would be pretty stupid."

"Great," he said with mock enthusiasm, "that means I have until I've paid the check to talk you out of throwing me in the slammer."

"That's a pretty tough trick. I've thrown a lot of men in jail in my time."

"I guess I'll just have to do better than them." With that, Tom bounced up off the car and flipped the remote entry system to unlock the passenger door. Cutting slowly in front of her, he grabbed the door's handle and opened it for her. "Please, allow me."

"My, my, a gentleman thief."

"My momma didn't raise any other kind." She took his hand with a nod and smile. To Dawn, the moment was something out of the 1950s, but there he was, helping her sit down, her hand gently clasped into his. Once she was in, he closed the door, and she watched as he walked around to the driver's side, where he slid in as well. He was a pro at the quick entrance to a Corvette, not an easy trick for the novice considering how low it sat to the ground. As he sat she looked up. She couldn't be sure, but it looked like there was a figure on the fourth floor, looking down from the window. Neal, she thought, watching over her, although she wondered how much of his sudden protective nature had to do with the relatively bad decision of going out for the evening with the prime suspect and how much of it had to do with his own resentment that she wouldn't consider going out with him.

"So, seriously," Tom said, looking over at her. She pulled her eyes away from the fourth-floor windows and looked back at him. Her face tightened a little as she began to wonder what this question would be; he'd already proven to her he thought outside the conventional box. Was this where he would start to plead his innocence or toy with the process further? His face was very serious; as if the world depended on the answer to the question he was about to ask. "Is Italian food OK?"

"Yeah," she said, blushing slightly, "Italian's great." If he noticed the brightness on her cheeks he was too much a gentleman to say anything; instead, he faced forward and brought the engine to life. He backed the 'vette out of the parking space and gunned through the lot in such a way that most people would have thought he was looking for an accident, but Dawn could tell he was perfectly in control. This was a parking lot he'd been driving through for almost twenty years; he knew it like the back of his hand. And from Dawn's own experiences she knew a 'vette handled like a dream. If he was trying to scare her, he'd have to do better. The car came to a stop as the parking lot gave way to the street, and he turned again to look at her.

"So are they ready to follow, or do I need to wait for my tail to get into place?"

"I think you've watched too many spy movies."

"Probably, but I'm not very experienced at this kind of stuff. I don't want to seem like I'm trying to lose the people following me. I just speed occasionally. Or wait, should I not admit to that?"

"Don't worry," she said, "they'll be in position. They're pro's."

"OK, but to be on the safe side, should I announce the address of the restaurant clearly? I assume you're wired for sound?"

"You assume wrong."

"Gee, what an ass I must look like?"

"That's a pretty old joke, Tom."

"I'm getting to be a pretty old guy."

Her smile faded, and she looked at him as seriously as she could, "I don't think you're old."

"Hmm, must just be me, then." With that, he hit the gas and pulled out onto the street. "Sit tight and, as Mom always said, 'don't look and you won't be scared.'"

From the fourth floor of the Hil Federal Credit Union building, Neal watched from the board room with a dark, almost savage look on his face. Watching Tom Williams squeal away with Dawn in tow, Neal moved his portable radio to his mouth. "They're on the go. Don't lose them."

The voice box sounded. An FBI field agent assured him they wouldn't, but it didn't ease Neal's nerves one bit. Even after the Corvette was out of sight, he stood at the window watching as if it might return. He couldn't get past the feeling that one of his agents had just been placed in harm's way.

* * *

Outside the Lines 5.1

March 10, 2000

The restaurant wasn't too busy when they arrived, and they were seated as soon as they stepped through the door. Once at their table, a covered basket of bread with a dish of whipped butter was delivered, and the waitress, who looked too young to be serving them anything at all, asked if they'd wanted a drink. Tom lifted his hand toward Dawn and said, "Ladies first."

"No, please, I insist."

Tom looked back up at the waitress, who thought this scenario was no more than a boyfriend and girlfriend having a little fun with one another. "Sam Adams, please." She scribbled the order down on her tiny pad of faded paper and looked to Dawn. "Make it two," Dawn said. The waitress nodded and told them she'd be right back with the drinks.

"Come here often?"

"Not in a long time, actually, but once upon a time I used to come here a lot." Tom reached into the basket, pulling out a chunk of bread, and, without adding any butter, took a quick bite. "Mmm, I missed this bread. Have some, it's truly excellent."

"Why haven't you been here in a while?"

"Would the proper answer be I couldn't afford it?"

"No," Dawn said, grabbing her own slice of bread, "I'd prefer the truth. I've already seen your credit report and bank account records; eating out wouldn't be a problem for you."

"It'll probably seem odd to you. I can go to a movie by myself, no problem. But I have a lot of trouble eating out alone at a sit-down restaurant. So, since I'd have to come alone, I didn't come at all."

"You haven't been dating recently?" She was spreading some butter on the bread, watching as he ate his.

"Not in a while, no."

"How come?"

He seemed to be weighing his answer, or maybe just deciding whether or not to tell her the truth. The bread sat in his hand as he stared lifelessly across the table. Dawn's eyes remained fixed on him, curious about what he might say. "I guess," he finally said, pulling his eyes out of their fog, "I make bad choices."

"What do you mean?"

"A lot of the women I dated, well, they looked really good, at least to me, but . . . but they probably weren't the best for me."

"I don't understand."

"Attraction doesn't always lead to compatibility, Dawn. That's one of the few things I've ever really learned about dating. It got to a point where I started realizing that every choice I was making regarding women was wrong. So I decided to make a different kind of choice: I quit asking."

"A life of celibacy."

"For now."

"Tough life."

"You have no idea."

"How long?"

The waitress dropped off their drinks and two menus. She apologized for not leaving them previously, and Dawn and Tom shrugged her off, telling her not to worry about it. She faded away into the background to give them time to look through the menu, which neither made a move to do. Instead he looked up at Dawn and asked, "How long have I been celibate?"

"Yes, I'm curious."

"October 1998, just shy of eighteen months. A damn long time, all things considered."

"Wow, that is quite a while."

"Told you."

"It's been just over a year for me."

"What?"

"I said it's been over a year." She took a swig of beer as she stared at his shocked face.

"You make bad choices, too?"

"Uh-huh, really bad."

"So you've chosen celibacy as well?"

"No," she said, setting her glass back down to the table, "it chose me."

"Pardon my abruptness, Dawn, but that's bullshit."

"That's a pretty bold statement, considering you don't even know me."

"You're a beautiful woman. I'm sure you've had offers."

"Not as many as you might think."

"But you've had some?"

"Yeah," she said, settling in a little, "some." Gently, she moved her purse further under the table, out of view. The gun was near the bottom; still easily accessible but deep enough that no one would accidentally notice it.

"So you chose not to act on those offers?"

"I guess you could say that, yes."

"So then celibacy was your choice."

"Hard to imagine."

"Why's that?" Tom looked down to see half his beer was already gone. He set it back down to the table and forced himself to let go of the glass.

"I like sex."

"Who doesn't?"

"I'll introduce you to a couple of people."

"No, really, those kinds of people I don't need to meet. I have no trouble not having sex."

"How long does your exile last?" She asked toying with her glass, moving it slightly left and then back to the right, catching prisms of light from the candle in the center of the table.

"Until I can break the mold I seem to have cast my life into, until I get to the point where the choices I once would have made aren't going to be the choices I make in the here and now."

"I have a problem with that."

"Which part?"

"You say you stopped asking women out because you were making bad choices, yet you chose to stop asking women out. How do you know that wasn't a bad choice as well?"

"My best friend, he's married to a wonderful woman, got a couple of fantastic kids, and when I talk to him, he's happy. Honestly and truly happy. Even before the kids, they had something special. You could see it in the way they talked about each other, the way they acted around each other, the way they looked at each other. It was something to see. I mean, I've had a lot of friends get married, and some of them you looked at and you think, "Wow, they're just getting married so they won't be alone." But my friend Bob and his wife, it was like they were meant for each other. Watching them together, I decided that's what I wanted. I was tired of spending far too much money and time making my conquests in dimly lit bars just before closing time, finding girls who were too young to make decisions on their own but, because the law says they're twenty-one can do so anyway. They've never actually lived a day in their life, never had anything really bad happen to them, so when you start talking you realize they don't have a single interesting thing to say. But like most guys I tune out their bullshit stories, usually revolving around what they did their previous semester in school, so they'd wind up in my bed by the end of the night, and I suppose that counts as the first really bad thing they do, because when the next schmuck comes along trying to get into their pants they can tell them all about the jerk they just got over."

"Really," she said, unable to resist the joke, "You're that bad in bed?"

He chuckled and shrugged slightly, "I guess that would depend on who you talked to."

"So some would say you were good?"

"I imagine some people would say anything if given the chance."

"You're an odd man, Tom Williams. Most men would be trying to convince me how good they were in the sack, but you don't seem to care what I think."

"That," he said, grabbing back up his glass, "or I just think you've already assumed the worst about me and I shouldn't bother trying to convince you otherwise."

"Interesting theory. Can I ask you a question then?" Tom hoisted his glass and told her to fire away. Dawn let him take in his drink and started smiling slowly and seductively in a way that was sure to attract his attention, and hopefully lull him just a little. "Why'd you ask me to dinner tonight?"

"I was hungry."

"That's the only reason?"

"No," he whispered, finishing the remainder of his beer and setting the glass back down on the tabletop. "Maybe I think you're a good choice."

"I thought you said you made bad decisions?"

"I have, in my past, but I'm hoping I'm getting better at them."

"You're not," she said, as she picked up her menu and started to flip through the pages. "I agreed to dinner, Tom, but this isn't a date."

"Really? Then what is it?"

She lowered the menu to look back at him; he was smiling gleefully. "It's dinner."

"Between a man and a woman, at night."

"Yes, I am a woman, and you do appear to be a man, but just because a woman and a man go out to dinner does not make it a date."

"Do you often go out to dinner with men who are not your friends, by that I mean, people you don't even know?"

"No, I don't."

"So, when you do wind up at dinner with a man you don't know, or hardly know at all, what would you call it?"

"This isn't a date."

"OK, then, for my memoirs, what is it?"

Dawn's smile was trying desperately to show. Tom was persistent, she gave him that, and not in an annoying way either. She was almost overwhelmed by the sheer humor of his intensity, the way he carried himself and engaged her. She could tell immediately this was the kind of guy who was hard to get mad at, who defused situations with dumb jokes and off-color humor. He carried himself easily, like a good ol' boy out to make a deal at a power lunch. "It's dinner," she said calmly, holding back her smile as best as she could. "I'm the investigator who is trying to prove your guilt, Tom. I'd suggest you remember that."

"I told you already, Dawn, I didn't do it. So at this point, I figure I don't have anything to lose."

"You're wrong. As a private citizen, you always have something to lose."

"Tell me something?"

"What's that?"

Tom had the menu in his hand but was darting his eyes randomly around the room. "Which table has the undercover guys at it?"

"Why, do you want to buy them a drink? It's been done."

"No," he said, beaming, "I just like to know where my chaperones are. Any money I have to spend, well, I'd rather spend on you."

* * *

Outside the Lines 5.2

March 10, 2000

"Repeat," Neal was still pacing around the Hil Fed boardroom. The lights were dimmed so he could see the neighboring buildings better as the night slowly washed over the city. He was frustrated beyond belief, and his nerves frayed. His radio was on and communicating frequently, probably too frequently, with the FBI relay team following her. But Neal didn't care. One of his people was in what he considered a hostile situation, and if the FBI didn't like the fact that he was acting as team leader, they could take a stick and shove it.

He wasn't sure what was bothering him more: the fact that Williams had the audacity to ask Dawn on a date, or that Dawn agreed to go. It was stupid and irresponsible; she was playing a game she didn't need to play with this much attention on them. Neal was warned when he hired her that she was the type to both think and act outside the lines, though he was assured it was always for the benefit of the investigation she was working. She had a definite problem with authority and from his own dealings with her; he imagined she was a nightmare for her parents when she grew up. He admitted, though she was also about the best investigator he'd ever worked with. She had an innate instinct for the job and could second-guess what criminals were thinking. From what he'd been told, Dawn's record with the FBI was not only spotless but something most agents strive to model their careers after. She didn't want a desk job, though; she wanted to be out in the field working and making the day-to-day decisions. Neal knew enough about her to be aware that some of her methods were highly unorthodox; never illegal, but perhaps a little morally questionable on occasion. That was another thing the FBI indicated about her. She liked to play very dangerous games with a lot of very dangerous people, and Neal was told in confidence that she cheated on her previous long-term boyfriend so many times the guys back at the FBI lost count. Neal assumed most of it was bullshit FBI talk, the kind of crap most women endured when they excelled above and beyond their male counterparts. But he'd often wondered if there was any truth to the rumor. He knew she wasn't easy, but something told him she wasn't chaste either. For the last twelve months he'd wondered if her reckless investigation style would surface, and he couldn't help but think that he was watching it in action now.

The radio came to life saying, "'repeat' is a military term for doing the same thing over, Neal. Just thought I'd let you know."

"Funny, smart-ass, real funny. How is she?"

"She's having a great time, according to the guys we have inside; they've had a couple of drinks and were just served dinner. The guys say the appetizers were delicious."

"Yeah," Neal said harshly, "thanks for the update." With that, he cut the signal, and dropped the radio down to the boardroom table, and asked himself for the hundredth time, "what the hell are you doing, Dawn?" But on some level, deep down inside, he suspected he didn't really want to know.

* * *

Outside the Lines 5.3

March 10, 2000

"... The game's almost over; only a couple of people are still active, and the rest of us are walking around in a pack. I mean, hell, technically we're dead already so it doesn't matter what we do. We're walking down this concrete slope, heading toward the front of the campus, when this blinding light comes out of nowhere and we hear this very loud and nasty voice yell, 'Police! Drop your weapons.'"

Dawn was hysterical as she watched Tom tell his story in the most animated fashion she could imagine. Tom's hands were up, and he looked like a conductor before a band, stretching out the music as his story delicately unfolded. "The thing that amazes me most is that none of us did something stupid like run or start talking back. Instead, we did exactly what we were told, and I tell you, you've never seen six little plastic disc guns fly up into the air so quick."

"You're kidding me?"

"No, I wish. We had a closed campus, whether school was in session or out. So technically speaking, no students were allowed on campus once the official school day was over. But we were young and stupid and bravely marched forward. I mean, we couldn't play Disk Gun War at any of our houses, not with the ten of us playing, we didn't have anywhere near enough room to hide in, but the high school campus was perfect. I mean, I went to a large high school, and at night the campus was completely blacked out; they had security lights only on the perimeter of the campus but nothing on the inside. It was the perfect choice: there were places to hide, plan attacks and plenty of space to make the game truly adventurous."

"And to hell with the fact that you weren't supposed to be there?"

"Aw, come on, Dawn; weren't you ever young? Didn't you ever do something when you were a kid you knew you shouldn't have?"

"Most of the stupid stuff I did happened when I was technically supposed to have been an adult."

"Well, I burned it out of my system a little earlier than you did, then. There were ten of us, one sixteen year-old, eight seventeen year-olds, and one eighteen year-old, all running around dressed in black and carrying little plastic guns loaded with those cute little plastic discs, the kind you had when you were about six and thought were great."

"What'd the cops do?"

Tom's laughter was fluid, very real and a little on the loud side. "Well, needless to say, they weren't exactly thrilled about running into us. They'd been told there were a bunch of kids running around with guns on campus and they were looking for gangs or something, not a bunch of white-bread sissies with the latest in Toys-R-Us hardware. They walked us up to the high end of the slope, tossed us up against the wall, and had us assume the position. How we knew what the 'position' was is still something of a mystery, I suppose too much time watching TV as a kid. Now the thing I should point out here is that there were only eight of us at this time; two of our friends were still out running around campus, as far as we knew, still thinking the game was on. They had no idea that the police had shown up to bust us." He waived his hand in the air, as if erasing an imaginary slate so he could proceed with his story. "Anyway, they have us against the wall and they quickly pad us down, realizing, while they're doing this that we aren't the threat the call officer made us out to be. That just pisses them off more; here they are two trained officers being called off their donut watch to come and roust a bunch of punk kids from good homes. So they pick up our guns and unload the ammunition on us, while giving us this bullshit lecture about responsibility."

"Responsibility is bullshit?"

"It is when you're essentially doing the same thing by emptying the discs on us, while we're lined up against the wall."

"Fair enough," she said, lifting her mostly empty glass to him and telling him to go on.

"So then they go down the line, asking us how old we are, and the spacing, the way we were lined up, was perfect. My friend Billy started us off, seventeen, and from there we just went down the row, seventeen, seventeen, seventeen, seventeen, so on and so forth, until we hit my friend at the end of the line, the only eighteen year-old in the group. I swear to you, they came up to him and asked him his age and it was like his voice was possessed by a nine-year-old girl, and he screeched out 'eighteen'." Tom took a quick drink from his glass, looking at Dawn to make sure she was still interested in the story. "The cops loved that. They were cracking up and just laying into him, saying how he must be the mature adult of the group. They hit him with this heavy lecture about how he could be tried as an adult; I mean they were brutal on him. They were going off about how the county's curfew had already elapsed for that night, and all of us minors were in violation. But the thing that didn't occur to me nor to any of us, until later, was that while they were damn curious to know how old we were, they never bothered to ask us our names. They just wanted to blow off a little steam. But you see, we weren't thinking about that, because we were too damn scared. So they yell out from behind us, and keep in mind we were all still lined up, looking straight ahead at the row of lockers in front of us, they ask us if there was anyone else with us. Now, as a group we hadn't ever planned for a contingency such as this, we were all panicked. Not so much by the cops as by the fact, that at our ages they'd tell our parents what we'd been doing, and of course, our parents didn't have a clue as to what we were really out doing. The thing is, though, at the same time, as if on cue, we all did the same thing. We dropped the dime on our two dear friends and, in unison, rattled off their names right down to the middle initial. I swear to you, if there had been a DA there with those cops, we would have been making a unified deal to turn state's evidence."

Dawn knew the story wasn't altogether that funny, but something about the way Tom told it had her laughing out loud in a way she hadn't in a long time. For a reason she couldn't quite explain she had an image in her mind of what Tom must have looked like at the age of seventeen, his thin, scrawny arms raised upward against the cold metal of the lockers at night, all the blood having rushed from his face in panic. The fact she didn't have a clue about who the rest of his friends were didn't matter at all; she couldn't wait to hear how the story ended, as long as he kept her laughing like she was now. A tear glistened in her eye, both from the laughter and from her own effort to remember when she last felt so free to not have to be perfect and to allow herself to act like a child. She knew he was still the suspect, and she knew he was guilty; deep down, she could tell. At the moment it didn't matter, though. Right then, he was a companion who was making her feel human instead of like a hired goon with the faint trace of blood on her hands.

"So, in a choral like performance, our two friends have been named, and I'm sure it was all the cops could do not to bust a gut laughing at us. True criminals we certainly weren't. They called back into their radios to tell their bosses that they have two more floating around campus somewhere. Then they march us up to the front of the campus. Our campus was raised up from this huge parking lot by these mammoth staircases that stretched down in three different spots. We had all parked around the same stairwell leading up, so, in retrospect, I'm sure they knew most of our names from the registrations, but nonetheless, as we're walking down, they're talking about how they might have already towed our cars away. Again, we're scared to death, not of them so much as having to explain this ordeal to our parents. We get to the edge of the campus, right before the stairwell starts to lead us down to the parking lot, and we see how big a nightmare this thing really is. I knew we were dead; I mean I could taste it. There were two main entrances to campus and both were completely blocked off by police cars. Let me repeat that; I don't want you to miss that. Cars. Plural, as in more than one. In fact more authority then I'd ever seen in one place before or since. That was just at the entrance, The bus turn lane, was filled with every manner of law enforcement agency you could ever want: we had the Highway Patrol, the San Diego Sheriff's Department, the Police Department, the fucking Border Patrol, and not to be left out, a SWAT van."

"They called in the SWAT team on you?"

"They brought in everyone who was even remotely in the area. I think they might have even requested back up from the Harbor Patrol, and my high school was inland. It was like the final chase scene in the *Blues Brothers* movie where they're being chased by every cop in the free world. It was frightening."

"How . . ." It was hard to speak; Dawn was laughing so hard. The animated way Tom told the story; it was like she was there, living the experience with him. "How many cops were there?"

"I honestly have no idea, but it was more than I'd ever seen in one place before and more than I'd ever want to see again. I could see why these two cops were so pissy with us; we'd caused quite a stir with our stupid little game."

"So what happened? What did your parents say?"

"Nothing, they said nothing because they never found out. The cops let us go."

"You've got to be kidding me?"

"Nope, I think we'd been such an embarrassment, showing their overreaction, that they were afraid to make an issue out of it. I mean, if something like that happened today, in this day and age, I'm sure we'd have been expelled, but back then—they just let us off the hook. One of the cops got off his radio and told us to get our asses down to our cars and go home, direct quote, by the way. We ran down the two flights of stairs and jumped in our cars right as our two friends came running out of the darkness and joined us. Stunned, scared looks on their faces, 'cause they didn't know what was going on, or how we'd dropped the dime on them. They'd managed to successfully evade the cops where we hadn't and now all they wanted was to get the hell gone, now that they saw us fleeing."

"I can't believe they just let you walk. I mean, why were the cops ever there in the first place?"

"I'm glad you asked," he said gleefully, as he finished off the last of his latest beer mug. "It turns out that night we hadn't been alone on campus. Unbeknownst to us the Junior Varsity Basketball team was in the gym earlier that night, doing Lord knows what, because we certainly didn't hear any dribbling going on. As I recall, we didn't even see a light on, so what they may or may not have been doing remains a mystery. A mystery that I, for one, am more than happy having lost to the ages. But the JV coach was there with a few of the team members; he heard us and called the cops. Now, as far as our recollection goes, Billy and Harry were the only ones who were running in front of that gym, and the exchange they yelled back and forth at one another went something like, "I shot you, you're dead!" "No, no, you missed, I'm still alive." What you have to realize is, both of these guys were about as stubborn as mule's, so neither one was willing to consider the fact that one of them might be mistaken. The coach heard their verbal dispute over death and being shot and called 911 telling the operator there were boys on campus, with guns. And the next thing you know, we were public enemy's number's one through ten."

"That's a pretty wild story, Tom."

"Oh, it gets worse."

"I can't imagine how."

"We were young, stupid, and scared. We all drove back up to Billy's house and sat around watching each other shake when we realized that we never did finish the game we started . . ."

"Tell me you're joking?"

"Well, by that time it was only 11:00 p.m., and our curfews, the ones given us by our parents, the only ones we actually cared about, didn't run out for a couple more hours. We had a game to resolve, and there was this elementary school that was just down the street."

"You deserved to get shot."

"Probably," he said, as he bowed slightly with his upper body, "but that's my story."

"Remind me not to ask you about your problems with authority ever again."

"Yeah, that was only one story. I could go on for hours."

"Why doesn't that surprise me?"

"Well," he said, "you're not leaving me much choice. After all, you've hardly said word one about yourself and seem to be rather protective of telling me anything. In lieu of your lovely voice, I feel it is my obligation to fill the void from your silence."

Dawn couldn't help but wonder how she got herself into this, sitting across from the man responsible for the largest criminal theft in credit union history, listening as he told stories of his previous run-ins with the law. If this were in a movie, Dawn was sure this would be the scene where Tom's nefarious criminal partners came charging in with the guns to take her hostage. This was reality, though. Looking at Tom, Dawn began to see what a contrast he was; just over the course of the meal she'd seen his character change. At some moments his confidence was almost overpowering, and at other times nonexistent. In either case, his humor remained and kept her entertained. She wasn't sure how much of this evening was her studying him or vice versa.

"If you want to know something, Tom, just ask."

"Do you have to get up early tomorrow?"

"What?"

"Do you have to get up early?" I asked.

"Why do you want to know that?"

He chuckled, grinning from ear to ear. "Two reasons, actually. First, I wanted to know how quickly you'd answer an off-the-wall question, and the second, I wanted to know if I should order another round?"

"What time is it?"

His eyes never lowered to see the face of his watch. Instead, he continued to look right at her. His gaze was crystal clear, and he seemed completely unaffected by the beer. "Quarter to eight."

"OK," she said, throwing caution to the wind, a theme she admitted was predominant for the day. "Another round can't hurt." Tom raised his hand and motioned for their waitress, holding up his empty mug and pointing to Dawn's. The waitress smiled and said she'd be right back with refills. "So, do you drink a lot?"

"Depends. What do you consider to be a lot, Dawn?"

"More beer than water."

"Well, then, hell, I've had a drinking problem since I was about fourteen years old. I hate the taste of water."

"OK, more beer than anything else."

"No, then, I don't drink a lot." He winked at her as he settled deeper into the chair and slid a finger across the table pointing her way. "So, tell me about yourself, Dawn."

"What do you want to know?"

"Let's start with everything and work our way up from there."

"Everything, huh? OK, I was born, I grew up, went to college, wound up working for the FBI, and now I work for the NCUA. The end."

"Wow, twenty-five words or less."

"I was taught to be concise. If you want specific information, you have to ask for it, Tom."

"OK, you said you were single. Why?"

The waitress drifted back to the table and set down two fresh beer mugs. Both Tom and Dawn smiled at her as she went about her job and remained quiet until she walked away. "The last guy I dated, it was a long-term relationship, and he didn't take the breakup too well. It happened right as I was starting with the NCUA, moving away from DC and coming out here to California. Everything in the last year of my life has changed drastically, and I guess I haven't been ready to open myself up to any kind of new dating adventures."

"How long had you dated this guy?"

"Since I was seventeen. He was my high-school sweetheart."

"Jesus! Are you serious?"

Dawn could tell Tom was honestly shocked and she found it playfully amusing. "Afraid so. Jerry and I were together for a long time."

"Since high school?"

"Yeah, is that so amazing?"

"Well, considering my longest all-time relationship clocked in at just under a year, I'd say yes."

"Well, Jerry was what I needed in my life for a very long time, and then one day, one day, he wasn't."

"So one day you decided he wasn't right for you, in a forever kind of way, and you just walked out?"

"No," she said with a pained expression on her face as she conjured up old memories, "one day I woke up and realized he wasn't my forever man, and it took me about four years to admit it, and then another couple of years to do something about it."

"Was there another man?"

"What makes you say that?"

"When a woman isn't happy in her current relationship but isn't willing to leave the man she thinks she loves, it usually means there is someone else in the equation, at least for a little while. Sorry, I didn't mean to offend."

"I'm not offended," Dawn said, as a thin smile escaped her lips. "The proper question, though, would be, *were* there other *men?*"

"Really?" Tom leaned forward on the table, very interested. "Dare I ask how many?"

"Over the years? A few."

"A few?"

"In twelve years, five."

"Did he ever find out?"

"Not that I'm aware of, no."

"How did you hold up against that?"

"What do you mean?" But she knew; he was questioning her psyche, which she considered odd under the circumstances.

"How did you hold it all together when you were cheating on him?"

"I did what anyone, man or woman, would do in that situation: I just didn't focus on the hurtful part. I concentrated on getting what I wanted at the time and didn't think about it much when I was with Jerry." In her mind she could see Jerry's face, fragile and weak. She could see him crying when she said she was leaving. She liked to believe, for the most part, that she was past feeling the sins of her relationship with Jerry, about her mistakes and the poor way she ended it, but every once in a while, a memory surfaced, and she couldn't help but feel a slight tinge of guilt.

"Could that have anything to do with why you're single now?"

"No, I'm single now by choice."

Tom's smile brightened a little, "Really? Or do all of the offers you get these days lack the certain sense of drama you've become accustomed to in a relationship, even a temporary one?"

"I say again, Tom, that's a pretty bold statement considering you don't even know me."

"You don't know me either, Dawn and you seem to think I just stole over one hundred million dollars. Rash assessments come with living in our society. And, to address a minor point, I didn't make a statement about you. I asked a question. One you didn't answer."

"You're a cocky son of a bitch, Tom Williams. I'll give you that."

"Right now, I'll take it."

Dawn ran her finger around the top of the mug, thinking about Jerry, thinking about the past and everything that happened, what she did wrong and how she hurt him, whether he'd known about her affairs or not. It was easy to just play him for the fool; he loved her and therefore trusted her completely. Jerry was a very smart man. His problems didn't stem from a lack of intelligence; if anything, it was an emotional problem that made him a bit too whiney and needy at times. She could hear her former therapist telling her about emotional dependency and letting go. She also remembered, when they discussed her sexual roaming, the therapist hadn't chastised her but much like Tom, suggested she needed something she couldn't find in a standard relationship. The therapist used different words, tried to invoke different emotions, but the heart of it was still the same. Whether it was called adventure or drama, it was always the question at the forefront of Dawn's mind. She'd never enjoyed playing by the rules and always thrived on adventure; that was one of the reasons she excelled in the FBI. What she didn't do well was calm down and relax. With her, everything needed to be pushed to the edge. She liked flirting with disaster as long as she was in control and could stay one step ahead. That summed up her relationship with Jerry, and starring across the table at Tom, she found that she couldn't deny the truth. "Doesn't everyone like a little bit of drama in their life?"

"Sure," he said quietly, "but what happens once the curtain falls on your little drama?"

"Well, that depends," she said, lifting her drink. "Do you mean before or after I nail your ass to the wall for theft?"

* * *

Outside the Lines 5.4

March 10, 2000

"What do you want to do then, Randy?"

"You know what I want." Randy Carlson said as he looked out over the high cliffs of his La Jolla home toward the Pacific Ocean and the brilliant display of starlight dancing off the rushing waves. "I want his ass out."

"You told Agent McCafferty you wouldn't fire him."

"I did, yes, but I didn't say anything about his goddamn privileges. I want this son of a bitch to need an override for everything."

Randy turned back around to face the senior management team. They were all sitting uncomfortably in the dark room, illuminated only by the starlight and by the few lights from the neighboring seaside houses. They all had drinks, and none of them were happy.

It had become very clear, very quickly that any hope of privacy with the NCUA hovering about their building was in vain. They'd taken up meeting at Randy's house every night after work to take stock of the situation themselves. They were quickly realizing that there was very little positive information.

Mark Dyerson stood, a bold move in such a tense room, and walked slowly over to his old friend Randy, trying to lock eyes with him. "Randy, how will that look? The moment he realizes he can't do anything on the system he'll call to get it fixed. What then? We either tell him he's lost all privileges or we, well, hell, I don't know."

"Fuck him," Randy said in his deepest southern drawl. "He calls to complain, you tell him we had ourselves a goddamn computer glitch and we'll get it sorted out just as quickly as we can. I don't think there's anyone in the blasted Credit Union who doesn't already have an idea our computer system's been violated."

The seven other members of the executive team all stared at one another blankly and then turned to Doug Law, who sat quietly holding his glass of whiskey in both hands, staring down at the exposed pieces of ice floating there. "Sure, Randy," he said passively, "it'll work for the short term, but what about long term?"

"Long term is that pretty little NCUA agent plants his stealing ass in jail!"

"And what about after that, Randy? We've all been so worried about finding the money that I haven't heard anyone talking about what happens when it hits the five o'clock news. Because once it does, we're all fucked, and whether Tom Williams is behind all of this or not, whether he winds up spending the rest of his life in jail or not, he'll be the only one who comes away from this nightmare looking like he had any competence!"

"Calm down, Doug."

"Randy, I'm beyond calming down. We're already starting to draw lines in the sand, even between each other. Whether you want it or not the board will demand sweeping changes within the executive team and probably in the management team as well. Even if we get the money back we all know it got lost somewhere first, and when money gets lost, heads roll. I run the computer department so I goddamn know for sure mine'll be the first head to hit the chopping block. It seems to me the best thing I could do now is to throw my resume out to the streets and try to jump off this sinking ship before this scenario takes me down with it!"

"Hell, Doug," Randy said, starting to chuckle for the first time that night, "you always did say whatever came to your damn mind, didn't you?"

"At least around you."

"How long do you think they'll let me stay on as CEO? The buck stops here, as the saying goes, and the buck in question will be the jerk I feel when they're kicking my ass out the door. I know it, so do all of you. And anybody with any brains in this room better at least suspect it about their own job as well. We're down to doing the nasty here, Doug. I don't know who'll survive this with their jobs; I'm willing to bet I won't. However, I do know the best thing we can all do is show excellence under pressure, because when it all hits the fan, I at least want to be able to say I did everything I could once the problem was discovered and helped get the situation resolved."

"What's our PR angle?" Lili Jones was a reserved woman despite her tremendous size. She'd gone through just about every fad diet that ever got the media's attention, and none ever worked for her, at least not beyond a few meaningless pounds here and there. Long ago, she accepted she was going to forever remain a large woman or, as the folks where she bought the majority of her clothes would say, a "woman of size." She knew it all boiled down to the fact she was overweight. She wasn't the type to sit around and whine about her misfortune; she liked to eat and she intended on keeping herself happy. She sat on a tight, hard chair that Randy brought in from his dining room and was looking directly at Roland Pressman, the senior vice president of Strategic Planning. It was his direct function to oversee both Credit Union growth and the Marketing Department, which handled the Credit Union's public relations.

Roland cleared his throat before speaking; wishing like hell there was a better answer. "Well, as most of you know, Laura's on vacation this week and won't be back until Monday. She's out of town, and I haven't been able to reach her. I've left messages for her, so as soon as she gets home I'm sure she'll call." Laura Netzly was the Vice President of Marketing, which Roland assumed everyone knew already. "I didn't want to inform her staff about this without her present. From what I hear, the leaks have already started around the building. I didn't want to give any employee actual information."

"So what you're saying is," Robert Fetzer proclaimed loudly, "so far nothing's been done at all to cover ourselves publicly?"

"No," Roland shot back defensively, "we've spoken with both the NCUA and the FBI about keeping a lid on this until we have a better understanding of what exactly happened, and they've both agreed. They don't want to create a public scare that will cause members to go racing for their funds."

Megan Hertigin shook her head and looked at the group around her. She was the senior vice president of the Branch Network and oversaw the day-to-day branch operations. She was another longtime employee who had risen through the ranks, one position at a time. She was respected and well-liked and spent quite a few years working in both the branch atmosphere and the administrative building. In that time, she found herself many times sitting across a barroom table from Tom Williams. "Do you really think," she asked quietly, "that Tom did it?"

"Everybody always did tell me that the son of a bitch was too smart for what he was doing." Randy shook his head and looked over at Robert Fetzer. "What about you, Robby? Williams falls under the lending division. He smart enough to cause us all this much grief?"

Robert, on the spot, suddenly realized that despite the fact that this was all a computer problem, he was involved. The accused was his employee, and the board of directors might just want to blame him as well. Should he tell them that Tom Williams was indeed smart enough to have committed this crime? If he did, he knew they would follow up with the obvious question, why hadn't he ever said anything? If he said he didn't think Tom was capable of committing the crime, what would they think of him then? He took a quick drink from his glass of bourbon and then chuckled. "Hell, he's Judy's employee. I doubt if I've ever said more than two or three words to him since he's worked under Lending."

"OK, then," Randy said, looking back out the window, "to hell with everyone who says otherwise. Cut the bastard's privileges."

* * *

Outside the Lines 5.5

March 10, 2000

"Gee," Tom said sarcastically, "nice place."

"Actually, it sucks; it's a little more than a cheap motel but not quite a fleabag apartment." Dawn's smile indicated she had no intention of letting him have the last word on the matter.

They were pulling into the curved driveway of the Executive Suites, close to the main office of Hil Fed's administrative building. They were still slightly buzzing from the beer and incredibly full from the meal. They'd left the restaurant quickly and he remained a perfect gentleman to her throughout. She found herself amazed at how much she learned about him that had absolutely nothing to do with the case. When the bill came, she asked how much it was, and he said simply that he considered it money well spent, putting his credit card down onto the leather cache for the waitress to take away. Leaving the restaurant, he opened her car door and very carefully drove her through the city streets back toward Hil Fed and more importantly the executive suites. "So," he said restlessly, "how long are you here for?"

Dawn was having fun, despite the fact that she didn't want to. She was a little annoyed at the FBI guys tailing them. She was pleased that Tom hadn't noticed them, but they'd been sloppy all evening. They tailed too closely and sat too near at the restaurant, and at some points during the meal they seemed to stare blatantly at them as they ate. They hadn't figured out their mistake, either, because Dawn saw their car following way too close again on the ride home. Tom's car was in good condition, and she admitted it was a fun ride although she wished he would either show her how fast it could really go or let her take the wheel for a little while. She made good money, but a car like this was what she considered a luxury, something you should only get if you could pay cash for it, the stereotypical weekend car that Dawn wouldn't be able to afford for quite some time. "Is that your way of asking how far along I am in the investigation?"

"Nope," he said, with what he considered to be his most charming smile, "I just want to know how long I'll have you around the building for."

"That's a very presumptuous remark, Mr. Williams. I don't recall saying that I'm sticking around the HIL Fed building for your amusement."

"No, I believe the term was 'nail my ass'."

"Until I've done so."

"That's how long you're planning to stay?"

"And not a moment longer."

He looked out through the windshield with a slight trace of remorse in his eyes. "Which one is yours?"

"Number eight."

"Number eight it is." He slid his Corvette into the spot that said number eight and opened his door. She held up her hand to stop him from getting out. He turned in the car to look at her; half of his face was concealed by darkness and, to her eye, he looked like some medieval hero. At that moment, a sudden and terrifying thought crossed Dawn's mind: she didn't want him to be guilty even though she was sure he was.

"It was sweet at the restaurant when you got out and opened my door, but I'm more than capable of doing it myself." She shouldn't have been surprised, she thought. After all, wasn't he the kind of man who so many times before got her into trouble? The one her parents warned her to stay away from? The kind of man who made her cheat on her ex-boyfriend so many times in the past? She smiled to herself, and resisted the urge to laugh at herself. No one made her cheat, she knew. Just like no man had ever forced her to do anything in her life. She knew that all her mistakes in her life were her own, just like she knew the men she cheated on Jerry with were poor decisions. She was raised to be the perfect little girl, excel in her classes, get good grades, and live a good life, find a career and climb her way to the top. She'd lived that way her entire life, and maintained control. She assumed that was why she set out to find so many troubled men. She had been a good little girl who obeyed all the rules, but when she found one of those men who didn't she found herself intrigued and distracted, curious and wondering. Wanting to be bad for just a little while and break the façade she lived by. The best part about it was no one would ever know she cheated. That was the true joy in cheating on your lover; being bad and getting away with it, the ability to sin with impunity. Tom Williams was just that kind of man, she thought, but he wasn't just a rebel. He was a different kind of troubled man, the kind who walked inside the system, pretending to be one of them, when, in truth, he was the real danger in society. Men who steal with guns and violence are easy to see, but the ones who steal with computers and wit, from the shadows, smart enough not to dirty their hands and walk away clean at the end. They were the dangerous ones. That was who this man next to her was, and she knew it.

"I don't doubt that you are, Dawn, but I was raised as a gentleman."

She thought about that for a moment and lifted her hand from his shoulder. "Whatever," and rolled her eyes with a bit of a chuckle. She couldn't help returning his smile though as he lifted himself out of the car, she couldn't remember the last time someone got the door for her. When her door did open, a rush of cold air curled around her from the outside and sent a small shiver down her spine. "When'd it get so cold?"

He was holding out his hand to help her out of the car, "It's the area we're in; even though we're miles away from the ocean we catch the sea breezes coming up from the seaside swells and valleys. It can get pretty cold at night along this stretch. Not quite as cold as out on the water, but pretty cold all the same."

She took his hand and let him help her out of the car, "The things I learn when I'm with you." She said it wistfully but wondered what his response would be.

"On the contrary," he said. "When I'm with you I learn far more."

"Such as?" On her feet now, she continued to cling to his hand, and only partially because it felt very warm and inviting in the cool wind that surrounded them.

"Take today for an example," he smiled, "I learned I was a felon, probably well on my way to the FBI's most-wanted list."

"I'll have you in jail long before you make that list. Don't worry."

"What a relief; I should warn you, though, I take an awful photograph. My mug shot will look like hell."

"So, you said it can get cold out on the water; do you mean swimming or sailing?"

"Sailing, it's what I'd guess you call a hobby of mine." Their hands were still touching, lightly but enough to feel the warmth between their interlocked fingers. Finally Dawn realized what was happening and gently pulled her fingers free. Feeling her fingers go free, he sidestepped her and let her move slightly away from the car, giving her space.

He closed the door as she moved and positioned himself so he could continue facing her as she walked. "Tell me something, Tom, honestly."

"Sure." He let his rear fall against the car, making himself comfortable. "What do you want to know?"

"What'd you do with the money?"

"My last steady girlfriend," he started to say, while stifling back his laughter, "said I had a damn lumpy mattress, so I've been stealing money to restuff it. It's very smooth and comfortable now."

"Is that so?"

"What do you think?"

"I think," she said blushing slightly, not even sure why, "you're telling me you took the money to tell the Credit Union to stuff it."

"That'd be a hell of a risk to tell somebody off. Wouldn't it? I mean, that much money, that'd be life in prison, wouldn't it?"

"Depends on the judge and the jury, not to mention how good your lawyer is."

"My lawyer's pretty good, or at least I trust her. She's always done right by me before."

"So then," she said again, "if not to tell them off, why would you steal the money, Tom?"

"I didn't steal it."

She shook her head. "You're back to telling me lies again, Tom."

"Probably because you're back to accusing me of things I didn't do."

"Why didn't they fire you, a year and a half ago, when you were accused of stealing before?"

"I was never accused of stealing, Dawn, I was accused, and falsely, I might add, of embezzling funds meant for outside vendors as well as taking bribes from those vendors. Not stealing."

"Semantics. Stealing is stealing, no matter what you call it." Dawn saw Tom shrug and, briefly there was a look about him, standing in the night while a light in the distance shone around his head like a halo, it made him look like a lost, innocent child. The image was so strong she found herself looking away. "Why didn't they fire you?" she asked again to deflect the image from her mind.

"Because, Dawn, I was innocent; like I said, falsely accused. It seems to be a repetitive thing in my life as of late."

The look on his face was such that she really wanted to believe him. She was already sure he hadn't done a thing the first time around. What a great stunt, she thought: the man you once falsely accused of stealing from you suddenly takes you for more than you could ever imagine. "So you never took anything from a vendor?"

"I didn't say that." He lifted himself up off the car door, opened it once more, and slowly reached inside. "Of course, I took things from vendors. Bottles of wine, candy, some bought me lunch, others bought me drinks. It's about networking, and I was as active on that circuit as any other PR guy in the business." He pulled out an old leather bomber jacket from the rear of the car and held it out to her. "Here, you look cold."

"It'll wrinkle my suit coat," she said, but she started turning to let him rest the jacket around her shoulders.

"But you'll still look great, like a million bucks." He couldn't help but take in the outstanding visual of her body. This same tiny suit that had so captivated him earlier in the day when she first walked through the door now left him near speechless. With the night added to the outfit, there was an aura of intoxication, especially with the light buzz he could still feel tingling at the back of his head and that he was sure she was feeling too. It was the way she was leaning into him as he came up behind her, smelling her hair and perfume she wore while working lingering on the light breeze that whipped around them. All he wanted to do was wrap his arms around her. He'd wanted to be closer to her all night, to let out his dastardly side that he shelved for so long. He was the man who always knew the right thing to say, but with her he felt everything he said lacked merit and she'd see right through him. He wasn't sure if it was because he hadn't been this close to a woman for over a year but he knew he had never wanted anyone more. As he set the jacket down over her shoulders he smoothed out the leather creases while gently rubbing her arms. He felt her tense up at first and then relax into the movement of his hands until finally he stopped and pulled them away, not wanting to push too far.

"And you," she whispered gently against the cool of the night, "you're the expert on millions of dollars." His touch had warmed her more than the jacket, but she wasn't about to let him know that, nor her guard down. She told herself this was all just a game to him; he was trying to win her over to impede the investigation. She wasn't about to let that happen. As if sensing her rising level of control, she felt him step back, slowly enough to keep the bond of warmth between them, but far enough away that it was just a whisper of what could be.

"Can you imagine it? I mean, really, having that much money? A million dollars? Or, in this case, one hundred million dollars? What would you do with that much money?"

"Short of winning the lottery, I don't think I'll ever get a chance to find out." She wanted to speak louder but found she was having trouble speaking above a whisper.

"But if you suddenly had it, what would you do with it? A hundred million clear and free."

"That much money never comes free and clear."

"Does that mean you won't answer?"

"Hell," she joked as she pulled the edges of his jacket closer around her, "how would I know?" The jacket was amazingly warm but it only covered her from her hips up; her legs were still exposed to the cold; and she could feel them tensing up. "Tom, do you want me to say I'd roll around naked on it?" She turned to look at him and, for a moment, caught him staring down at her exposed legs.

"Nice mental picture," he said casually, "but I don't see you doing that."

"Maybe I'd surprise you."

"Gee, for the first time tonight I really wish I had stolen the money. I'd offer to lay it across your bed for you."

"No, you wouldn't," she replied, her tone suddenly bold and brash. "You'd wait for me to make the invitation."

"Maybe," he said quietly, "maybe you're right."

"If you were innocent, Tom, why'd you leave marketing?"

"Is that why you think I'm guilty, Dawn? Because I suddenly decided to switch careers? People do it every day."

"No, there are plenty of reasons why I think you're guilty, that's just one of them. It helps to fill in the puzzle."

"I left marketing because the manager and I had a difference of opinion."

"Really?" She asked, as she leaned up against the post of the hallway's overhang. "What was that?"

"I thought she was a lying whore bitch. She disagreed. It made working together very difficult."

"I would imagine." She watched as he sat on the front of the hood so he could maintain eye contact with her without getting too close. "Lying whore bitch?"

"Uh-huh." His bangs dropped a little, sending a few locks of hair down across his face, and drawing immediate attention to his brilliant, green eyes.

"Care to elaborate?"

"I can't."

"What do you mean, you can't?"

"I signed a gag order; unless the Credit Union releases me from my contractual obligation of silence, I can say no more about the situation than what I already have."

"That your boss was a lying whore bitch?"

"From what my attorney says, it falls under private opinion, and as long as I don't try to publish my opinions as fact I'm absent malice."

"You must keep your attorney very busy."

"No, not since she got married, anyway."

"You dated your attorney?"

"Doesn't everyone?" She started laughing and he joined in a few second later, reacting to her laughter, and then said, "We dated several times. Originally in high school, then again when she was in law school, and for a very short time frame while she was rising up the corporate ladder at her firm. Not for a long time, though."

"What aren't you telling me, Tom Williams?"

"That's not the question you should be asking, Dawn McCafferty."

"What is the question, then?"

"What aren't they telling you?"

She wanted to laugh out loud. Did he really think it was the Credit Union that placed him in her view? Instead she retracted her delicate smile and drew her eyes tightly into focus with his. "I'm the one who pegged you as the suspect, hotshot, not the Credit Union."

"You sure about that?"

"Absolutely."

He shrugged his shoulders and smiled until her tightly controlled lips finally broke into a small smile in return. "You don't know me, Dawn, not yet, anyway."

"I will, though."

"Maybe."

"You were up for the same position as the woman who got the marketing job, weren't you?"

"Uh-huh."

"So why shouldn't I just think the whole lying whore bitch line is sour grapes?"

"There are plenty of sour grapes, Dawn, I'm not denying that. But every word I've said is true."

"Can you prove it?"

"Let's not do this, OK?"

She was losing him but wasn't sure why. Was it because she was getting too close to the truth and he was afraid he'd let something important slip? Or was it really a question of a confidentiality agreement between himself and the Credit Union that was ready to throw him to the street? "Do what?"

"Is what happened back then really relevant to what's happened now?"

"As far as I'm concerned, yes."

"Then ask the people who are keeping me silent for the details, although I bet you don't get much in the way of straight answers."

"Like the kind you're giving me now?"

He smiled differently than he had through most of the night, sadly and in a way that seemed to melt her heart. "I wish I could just come right out and tell you, Dawn, I do, but I can't. I'd lose my job."

"They want to fire you anyway right now."

"Only because of what you think, and can't prove to be true. If I talk about things I agreed not to, then they have their just cause. So on the subject of my leaving the marketing department, I have nothing to say."

"How about just a simple question about marketing, then?"

"What's the question?"

"Did you like doing it more than collections?"

His sadness seemed to grow as his eyes faded away from her and into an old memory where he got lost for a moment before answering. "They are very few things in life I enjoyed more than that. It was something I felt I was honestly good at."

"Then why stay and work collections? Why not find marketing work somewhere else?"

"In the marketing game, reputation is everything. Hil Fed took mine away from me."

"Tell me something, Tom," she said, her voice was coming out so smooth it could have been easily misinterpreted as a cat's purr, "did it make you angry?"

His voice came out just as low and soft. "What do you think?"

"So why stay with them at all? Why not start over someplace else?"

"The longer I stay working for them the more I prove I was right, that I didn't do anything wrong. I figure once things have stayed buried for about three years, I can return to marketing someplace else, with my reputation tarnished, sure, but not destroyed. You see, working at Hil Fed dilutes their credibility in suggesting I did anything wrong. I'm just marking off my days, Dawn, or at least I was until now."

She stood up, shrugged off his jacket, and held it out to him. He reluctantly got up from the Corvette and took it from her. "It's cold and it's late. I need to get my rest." He was playing her; she could feel it or least she thought she could. Suddenly concentrating on him and his motives was difficult. His voice sounded sincere, but his eyes showed a man of intense thought and planning. Everything he said could just be a game he was playing, a story he was using to string her along and take her away from the important facts of the case, and that meant she needed to get away from him as quickly as possible.

"Busy day tomorrow?" He asked, returning to his more gentlemanly smile. "Of following me around, I mean?"

"Maybe. Try to do something interesting for me to watch."

"I'll see what I can do."

She moved to step back toward her door and noticed he was moving with her. She stopped immediately and turned to face him. "Going somewhere?"

"Just walking you to your door."

"Let me guess; it's what a gentleman does?"

"So I've been told."

"Then you're off the hook on this one, hot shot. I can get to my place without your help."

"What, afraid I'm gonna try for a kiss goodnight?"

"Maybe," she said, a little too quickly, "a little."

"Well," he said, smiling as if he might break into laughter at any minute, "I'd be lying if I said I hadn't thought about it."

"A thought's as close as you're gonna get."

"Because you're not attracted to me?"

"That's only one of the reasons, Tom." She took a small step back to show that she really was calling it an evening, that this wasn't just some play to see how far he'd push things. She watched and waited for him to make another step forward, but he stood his ground. Suddenly she wasn't sure if she was happy about it or not.

"Because I'm a suspect?"

"You're getting pretty good with your guesses."

"What if I wasn't a suspect anymore?"

"You'd still be facing a long ride home, very much alone."

"Even if I was innocent?" he asked with a look that showed nothing but confidence.

"If I thought you were innocent, Tom, we wouldn't have gone out in the first place."

"So about that . . ."

"About what?" She was pulling out her room key from her purse.

"Tonight, I mean. What was this?"

"It was dinner, Tom, nothing more. I believe we already covered this."

"And if I ask again?"

"I'll say no." She slid the key into the lock and turned it slowly, feeling the weight of his eyes on her. The lock clicked and the door sprung open into her waiting grasp. She hovered for a moment, feeling the warmth inside her room.

"You're sure about that?"

"You're a suspect, Tom. I shouldn't have even come out with you this evening."

"But you did, and let me ask you a question. Did you have a good time?"

"I think that's irrelevant." She was getting confused again and, for the life of her, she couldn't remember the last time that happened, especially on a case. She was trying very hard not to look at him when she heard him say, "But I'm asking you anyway, Dawn."

She shook her head, trying to erase the natural smile from her face. She couldn't do it, though. What was it about this man, she asked herself? "Yes, Tom, I had a very good time this evening."

"Me, too. Like I said, it's the first date I've been out on in a very long time."

"It wasn't a date."

"So you've said; I tend to think otherwise."

"Think what you like; it won't change the facts. Tonight was all business." She felt she'd just given him too many openings for a one liner that she was sure he'd exploit. All he'd have to do was ask why, if it was all business she was suddenly blushing or why she seemed nervous and timid. Any number of other questions could leave her stuttering for a response. Instead he asked her something completely different freeing her from her sudden fear.

"Is that why you're not inviting me in for a night cap?"

"No," she said starting to laugh, "I told you already, I'm not attracted to you."

He'd seen his chance to put her on the ropes and passed it up. Funny to think that this thief might be more of a gentleman than any man she'd ever met in all her years of law enforcement. That he might have honestly be the kind of man she would have liked to meet under different circumstances.

He was smiling like a schoolboy about to get a present. "You know what, Dawn? I think you're the one who's lying now."

"You should at least consider the fact that I'm telling you what I perceive to be the truth."

"Why should I? You aren't extending me the same courtesy about my innocence."

"OK, fine. For the next hour or so I'll assume you're innocent, you still don't get to come inside, though." But her smile indicated that she had indeed considered it, even if only briefly. He could see it in her eyes; in the very way she was suddenly holding herself. That was enough for him, so to let her relax he took another step backward.

"And let me guess; if I press you too hard, or too long on the subject of coming in, you'll pull the gun out of your purse and shoot me?"

"What?" She looked down at her purse, feeling her carefully controlled look falling away to a sudden panic, not once bothering to think about the suggestive words he'd used to toy with her. "How did you know I had a gun in my purse?"

"Simple," he said, while starting back toward his car. "In an outfit like that, where else could you have been keeping it?"

Both laughed and he opened his door and slowly climbed into his prized 'vette. She stood, watching him from her door, until his lights turned on and he backed out of the parking spot and quickly drove away into the night. Closing the door, she entered her executive suite and slumped down into the highly uncomfortable chair at the small vanity desk with the telephone on it, letting her purse slip down to the floor. She smiled to herself about her night and the sheer foolishness of it all and waited, somewhat impatiently for the ringing to start. After all, she knew her boss well enough to know that, much like her father used to do, Neal was waiting up for her.

* * *

Outside the Lines 5.6

March 10, 2000

Neal grabbed up the handset for the radio the moment the speaker told them Tom Williams' car pulled into the Dawn's parking lot and sat anxiously waiting. Occasionally he barked out orders, demanding to know what was happening, to which the FBI lookout man responded that they were standing out in front talking, he was forced to repeat this same message three times.

The FBI man could tell Neal was on edge and, to a certain extent, felt sorry for him, although he certainly wished he'd shut up about Dawn and the suspect. For awhile, as he watched them he thought something might be going on between them, though he was smart enough not to relay that particular message to Neal. Of course, the FBI man couldn't understand how a non-agent wound up with authority over them in the first place. Still, he followed his orders, watched everything happening, and was very glad to give his final message to Neal Johnston for the evening. "Sir," he said loudly over the static backlash running through the speaker, "target is driving away."

He heard an audible sigh of relief across the radio but ignored it to follow through on giving his final order. "Secondary, take the target home. Primary, go write your report up for the morrow. This is primary control signing off."

With that, the radio went dead, and Neal cut the power to the radio and picked up the phone. Dawn made him wait until the third ring before she picked it up.

* * *

The Sum of Existence

The Sum of Existence 6.0

March 11, 2000

Spring was still waiting in the future but the sun was bright and very, very hot in the open air George Town café, where he sat eating his breakfast. The Cayman Islands were a great place to lose oneself he mused generously as he washed down his breakfast with ice-cold bottled water instead of the mango juice they'd try to give him when he ordered.

He was a warm weather kind of guy and wanted to spend the rest of his life living somewhere in the tropics. A new career, he thought, of chasing the sun. It was a silly dream he knew, a dream he would never have thought possible. But suddenly all the rules had changed. Several months ago his biggest concern in the world was making it to work on time, now he was officially unemployed. He'd already stood in line for half a day last week to sign up for the unemployment insurance he never planned to use. His first check was set to arrive sometime next week, but if all went as planned there would be no one around to cash it.

The day was already on the blistering side of hot and small trickles of sweat were starting to bead up on the back of his neck as well as his hairline. It didn't bother him though, after spending a few too many winters back in Wisconsin a morning like this was nothing short of paradise.

The food was expensive, but he couldn't help indulge himself in a few extravagances now. Sitting there his mind raced back over the past two days where he was moving the money around like a child at play. It all seemed comical to him, how easy it all seemed. He'd miss this place, but he knew it was too dangerous to stay. The plan was great, but not foolproof, and he assumed the people looking for the money would be smart enough to look at the obvious escape routes for the cash to have taken. Once they realized the 'how' they'd send people down there in a heartbeat and he didn't want to get his hand caught in the cookie jar. If he played it right no one would ever be able to draw anything back to him. But a chance encounter on the street wouldn't exactly help, so the better part of valor told him to get while the getting was good. His boat sailed at noon, headed to another island where he would catch another boat that led him to an even bigger island with an airport. From there he'd return to Florida and check in to make sure his current computer program for controlling the money was still working properly before his next destination.

On the first day of the crime there was a small system error that took him three hours to de-bug. He figured the three-hour delay cost them thousands of dollars, if not more. But everything had been running smoothly since.

He still worried a little though, he couldn't help it. It had been a long time since he'd committed a crime of any kind, and certainly never one of this magnitude. He'd slept no more than three to four hours at a time since coming down to this tropical paradise, just so he could constantly check his new creation, the "Fund Management Program." Sailing out today was his biggest concern; this would be the longest time period he'd be away from seeing the digital read outs in real time. At sea he wouldn't be able to connect to his server back on the mainland. Sailing meant he would honestly have to trust his programming was sound and there wouldn't be any problems. He didn't like it, but it's the way it needed to be. His partner was right; having an airline ticket to the Cayman's wouldn't be a bright thing to do. As his partner put it, "why tempt fate."

So he didn't. There were a lot of people coming and going from the Cayman's who didn't want to leave a trail. Cash spoke better here than any other language man created, and he felt right at home spending the last of the insurance money his wife's death provided him. The last big bulk of it was sitting in an envelope in his pocket, but it'd be gone in the next ten minutes or so, once the blonde got there. Glancing over at the seat next to him he saw his laptop computer and his carry case that held everything he'd brought to the island. Just the essentials, he'd been told, travel light just in case anything went wrong. It was easier to run if you traveled light, he knew, but he still wanted to live a little large. It was hard for him to believe he was suddenly rock star wealthy.

The blonde took another twenty minutes to show up and walked right up to his table in a sultry manner that was sure to attract attention. He thought it was silly, he already knew the blonde for who she was, the real her. But this was how she wanted to play it, and to be truthful he didn't much care. After today he was never going to see her again anyway. She was just a small piece of the puzzle. The dress he'd given her to wear today looked good on her, the hat preposterous. He'd told her she needed to wear it along with doing her hair just the way it was in the picture he gave her, so his inside man would know it was cool. She didn't know there wasn't an inside man, she was being set up as the big finish, and she would never even know it.

"Howdy stranger."

"Sit your ass down." His tone was harsh, not because he didn't like her, but he didn't want her dragging this along, with her here he was starting to feel exposed.

After their first meeting several weeks back he'd gotten the impression she was flirting with him, and that was something that just couldn't happen. At any other point in his single life he'd have probably taken the next step, but he couldn't risk her suspecting what he was really up to. She'd already made a few comments about drugs; enough that he'd figured out she thought he was a smuggler. As far as alibis go down in the Cayman's, it was good enough. He'd even started playing into it, anything but the truth, he thought.

Without hesitation or pause, she sat down next to him and did her best to look sexy. She was a cheap tart with long blonde hair that was done up in a way she never would have managed on her own, and she was just ditzy enough to agree to doing it without asking why. She wore large, dark sunglasses and a half hat that allowed the top of her blonde head to poke out through the top. She seemed, to his eye, very proud of herself, "it's all taken care of, here's the last of the receipt's and password conformations."

He picked up the stack of folded receipts and transaction slips and quickly looked through it, not caring it looked like he didn't trust her, the fact was he didn't. Right now he trusted almost no one. She looked good, but as far as he could tell the blonde stereotype of the hair color was an accurate assessment of her mental ability. The day they first met, responding to position he'd solicited for online, she'd shown up thinking it was a dancers job for private parties. Before he'd realized what was happening she'd stripped down to a G-string and was beginning to dance to the Jimmy Buffett song the radio was playing. He'd been half tempted to wait for another prospect seeing her that way, but he couldn't help but notice she'd met all the specific requirements they needed for her role in the plan. Her best quality though, she wasn't the sharpest stick in the shed, as his father always liked to say. Smart enough to do as she was told, but not smart enough to question what they were doing. In short, exactly what they needed.

He slid an envelope filled with money across the table, not even bothering to hide doing it. He'd managed to smuggle the money into the country, it was her job to smuggle it out.

"So," she said in a hushed whisper, "do you think there's a chance you might need me again?"

He told her yes, so she needed to keep a low profile. The lines he used were cheesy, and reminded him of something straight out of an old episode of Miami Vice. But to his untrained ear it sounded like he was playing the part of a big time drug smuggler, and she certainly didn't know any better.

He told her to sit there and eat her lunch until he was safely gone, she nodded intently and watched him boldly grab his things and step away. The walk to the dock and the local charter ship he'd booked passage on was waiting. It was funny for him to think back to when he'd given her the first advance of 2,000 dollars he'd worried the plan wouldn't work that he was throwing his money away. Now he didn't care at all about the bundled money he handed off today. It was nothing more than a drop in the bucket. To her it was the Earth, the Stars, and the Moon, but to him it honestly meant nothing. The final payment sitting in the envelope was fourteen thousand dollars. Walking away he knew he'd never see the woman again, most likely because once this was all said and done he'd never again return to the United Sates.

He wasn't a drug dealer or a drug smuggler, but he was a criminal. Again, he thought. Hacking taken to the next level. After all, he had more than the $320 Million dollars now thanks to fluid currency exchanges and the wonderful world of high stakes interest and the way the international investment markets worked.

* * *

The Sum of Existence 6.1

March 11, 2000

The boardroom was stiff and cool as Dawn walked in bright and early Saturday morning. She felt it immediately as she walked through the door. Every eye was on her, watching her, and more importantly, judging her. It was no surprise, by the time she got Neal off the phone last night she was positive as to what she could expect this morning from the other representatives present. She learned to use sex appeal to her advantage in many situations throughout her life, though she never really could see what all the fuss was about when she looked in the mirror. To her the features she saw reflected were plain, worse even than ordinary. She found herself lacking. It was one of the main reasons she'd always worked so hard to take care of her body. If asked she would say her legs were her best feature. If pushed on the subject she would tell anyone asking that her body was the reason men reacted to her the way they did, it had nothing to do with her looks, and quite exaggeratedly would tell them it had absolutely nothing to do with her personality. She confessed quite frankly she usually worked very hard to push people away, not bring them closer. But undoubtedly those that arrived before her this morning had been engaged in conversation specifically about her looks, and how they were being used in the investigation.

By now everyone knew she'd had dinner with the prime suspect. It didn't matter to any of them that it was simply dinner. To the room, filled with men, it was automatically a date. And as she well knew the mere suggestion of a date to a man meant the woman was looking for sex. She knew, in their minds they were picturing her in lurid, titillating posses and situations. It was the way of men, she thought angrily. It bothered her only because she knew she was a better investigator than any of them. She bore no illusions of being the best in the world, not even the best in the state, but of those gathered around the table, sitting in judgment; none held a candle to her ability and they were all looking down their nose at her. She gave a submissive smile, trying to not show how she really felt and took her seat.

"Morning Dawn," Marc said passing her. She smiled, but didn't say a word. She'd requested her own rental car yesterday so she wouldn't have be shuttled back and forth by Marc. Neal, of course, balked at the expense, but reluctantly agreed in the end. Today after the meeting a rental car agency would come by and bring her a car.

The room contained only the necessary people, which was decided politically if not practically. The NCUA, Cuna Group officials, the FBI, and a token representative from the Secret Service, who looked like he'd rather be anywhere but there. In total there were twelve people, and when everyone was seated Neal cleared his throat loudly to announce the meeting was ready to begin. "OK," he said with a grand gesture of his hands, "let's get started and finished. I know we all have better things to be doing on an early Saturday Morning, but until this is all over this is exactly what we'll be doing." He was trying to sound commanding, she knew, but to her ear he just sounded tired. She suddenly wondered what Neal was doing with his free time once she retired to her room. "The purpose for today is to get to know Thomas Williams, who he really is. For the moment at least, he's our main suspect. We know he has a questionable past with this credit union and at one point was under heavy suspicion of corporate embezzlement. For some reason they didn't fire him at the time, and yes, we'll be looking into that as well. But let's just start off easy today, can somebody tell me who Tom Williams is?"

Fred Halstead opened a very thin manila folder and picked up the top sheet. "We have our initial report." Everyone in the room knew that Fred was the current agent assigned from the FBI, and for some reason that gave him a certain respect. "Our suspects name is Thomas Joseph Williams: he is currently thirty-nine years of age having been born in 1961. He drives a 1993 Corvette he owns free and clear He holds deed and title on a three-bedroom condo in Mission Valley; no loans appear on this property. Reviewing his tax returns shows that he came into a large sum of money back in 1998 when a relative died and he received a portion of the estate. He bought the car at that time and paid off his existing mortgage. He still has about thirty thousand dollar in liquid cash between his accounts. Beyond that he has stocks which show him as having another eighty-seven thousand. From pulling his previous tax records even before his inheritance from his grandmother, which was just under hundred thousand dollars, by the way, he'd been investing part of his paycheck in the stock market and caught a big break by investing in stock for Yahoo.com and Amazon.com in their early years. Shouldn't we all have been so damn lucky? He turned the fifty odd thousand that he invested over the years into a whole lot more. From what we can tell he sold off most of it to buy a sail boat that he keeps down at the Harbor. Instead of gambling on what any of these stocks would do in the future, he sold out after he made his killing to make his life better. He's a part of several investment packages managed by brokerage houses and appears to have a partial interest in a downtown commercial property which lists him as having a 12 percent stake. It's all well documented on his taxes. In short," Fred Halstead said taking in a deep breath, "Mr. Williams is worth approximately a million dollars with no debt whatsoever."

Looking around the room Dawn saw Halstead's words were weighing heavily, but in fact it was telling Dawn exactly what she'd expected. What no one else seemed to understand is this was about revenge. The money was only involved because he wanted to hit the credit union where it would hurt them. What she still couldn't get around was what Tom Williams was up to. He certainly seemed smart enough to know there would be no way he could keep the money, not this much. That much money would always follow him like an unforgiving specter, the moment he tried to access it they'd nail him. There was just no way to hide it from people who were looking for it. And with 320 million dollars on the line people would look for it forever.

"He makes about thirty-eight thousand dollars a year from the Credit Union which more than adequately pays his utilities and insurance bills. We did a quick scan of his insurance's, he's covered on everything. Health, car, boat, house, you name it, he's got it. This guy's the poster boy for how someone should manage their money. He's got assets and equity, along with cash in the bank. He owns property and isn't in debt. I'm sorry Ms. McCafferty, but I'm starting to doubt his guilt. This guy just has no reason to steal anything."

"I told you before Agent Halstead," she said quietly, "this isn't about the money. It's about the effect of it."

"Right." The doubt was clear in Halstead's voice, but he followed his orders, his instructions were to follow the instruction of Dawn McCafferty from the NCUA in investigation of the stolen money. He'd been told she was a former agent of very high standing, and agent the FBI hadn't wanted to lose. Having watched her so far he wasn't quite sure he agreed. She seemed focused, but he wasn't sure on exactly what. She was either completely fixated on the investigation to the point where she wasn't thinking about anything else, or she was fixating on the man. If it was the man she was fixating on, the suspect Tom Williams, nothing good would follow. He wondered where it would all lead. He looked down the table at Mike Hutchingson the man in charge of the surveillance team, "I'd like to turn this over to Mike Hutchingson to speak about surveillance before we get into the breakdown of Mr. Williams life."

Mike continued to sit completely still and speak clearly never once referring to notes; He was six foot, seven inches tall, broad, and clean shaven. He wore a crew cut that didn't for a moment conceal the fact he was slowly going bald on the top of his head. He appeared outwardly to be a very strong man who took very good care of his body. His eyes were tight and stared straight ahead with a fierce intensity. Mike Hutchingson wasn't the type of man who questioned the orders he was given. He was a career military man who left twenty years in the Marine Corps to join the FBI. If he was told to do something, it got done, without question or fail. "We began yesterday at noon. We found a similar condo to his, not too far away that was for sale. We contacted the real estate agent and found that the unit was vacant as the owners were already out of state. A deal was cut and we have full access to this unit as long as we need it. The Unit itself is not on the market so we will not have to worry about prospective shoppers either. The unit we occupy faces the back of Mr. Williams's condo; specifically we can see his bedroom window and back deck. When his curtains are open on the patio we can see right through into his living room. His front door can be seen from a distance from a secondary parking lot where we have a van set up to record his comings and goings. The same location that sees his front door can also see his garage door. Therefore we can track his comings and goings without any problems. Per orders we've set up a twenty-four watch. While secondary team was setting up at Mr. Williams' home we set up the first team at the credit union to wait and watch for him to leave work. The longest time Mr. Williams will be out of zone control is when he is in this building; the windows here are mirrored so we can't see in. But we can control his car; which we placed a tracking device on while he was in the restaurant last night."

"After he left Agent McCafferty last night," a man Dawn didn't know asked from the far end of the table, "did he go straight home?"

"Yes, and furthermore he drove the proper speed limit all the way, used his turn signals and obeyed all traffic laws."

Dawn stayed quiet, but in her head she mused about what might have happened if they pulled him over last night. With the amount they drank she was sure he'd have to be above the legal limit, she was fairly sure she would have failed a sobriety test. Not that either of them were out of control, but the current legal limit didn't give a lot of leeway on matters of alcoholic consumption. For most people one drink was enough to knock them over the limit. They could have arrested him last night, she thought, and pulled him completely out of play.

"What about his phones, are they tapped?" Neal was questioning in his most official voice. The agent looked at him and smiled, "Of course sir, no calls received, or made since we established the tap yesterday at 3:00 p.m. Also of note, sir, we have a piggy-back on him through his Internet provider as well?"

"For the non-technically proficient, Mike," Fred Halstead chuckled, "could you give me the layman's version?"

"Certainly, it means we served a Federal Subpoena on his Internet provider that allows us to place a direct link trace on his computer connection. Or to really clear it up, we're exactly three seconds behind him Online. Any place he goes on the Internet, any webpage, we'll see it three seconds after he does. Whether web-based bank or a porn site, we'll see him go there, and we'll know how long he spends. If he opens an e-mail, we see it three seconds after he does. If he has any digital secrets, we'll know them. The best thing about a piggyback is, even if he closes something out immediately, it will still appear on our screen for the exact amount of time it appeared on his."

"Is that legal?"

"We have a court order, allowing it."

"Did he log in yet? Does it work?"

"Yes, He's logged on to the Internet twice since we established this link. Once last night when he got home, and once this morning. He checked e-mail and went to a general posting board on the Internet about, uh, about comic books. A forum for a comic book creator, I guess he's got his own message board, he read a number of the messages, and even responded to a few. Copies are available in the report we'll be circulating later today with all e-mail-and-message-board activity, if you care to read his opinion of the latest issue of *whateverman*."

"And this morning?"

"Just checked e-mail, got some from what appears to be an ex-girlfriend who now lives across the country. She's married now, and was sending him a picture of her children."

The man from across the table looked squarely at Dawn, "Agent McCafferty, are you sure about this guy? So far he hardly sounds like Public Enemy #1?"

"Yes," she said plainly, "I'm positive." She closed her eyes, wishing to wash away the visual overload she was getting from this male dominant room. She wished to just listen to the evidence presented and focus out the clutter the men would insist upon throwing in.

Fred loudly slurped down more of his coffee, from a plastic mug that looked like it held a lifetime supply, "Keep going Mike."

"He was up and out of the house by 10:00 a.m.; he drove down to Harbor and began to clean his boat. At my last report, he was still there."

"We should search the damn boat!" A voice said gruffly.

"Why," another voice snappishly asked, "do you think he's got $320 million stashed in the floatation cushions?"

"Dawn, are you OK?" She heard Marc asking the question in his own snotty way, but chose to ignore him. There was no love lost between them, and she knew his question was presented in the hopes of embarrassing her instead of any real concern. She kept her eyes closed and leaned back her head hearing one of them ask, "How well educated is he?"

"Four years at San Diego State University, no degree though. In fact, he was one class short when he stopped going back."

"Which class," she heard herself ask.

"Computer Science."

She kept her eyes shut, though it was hard with the sudden eruption of noise going on within the room after his missing academic class was revealed. Everybody expected Thomas Williams to be a computer genius who'd just chosen to follow a different path, she understood that. How clever, she thought, the one class he's missing to get his degree would be his best line of defense at trial. It made her wonder how long he'd really been planning to become a thief, or if this was just some far reaching back up plan in life if his career hadn't taken off. She dismissed it, the plan had to have been formed within the last year or two, she was sure of it. The man just used the inconsistencies of his life to facilitate his plan.

Listening to them talk about Thomas Williams was strange now that she knew him as well as she did. To her he was no longer an academic equation, a man she saw on paper. Everything about his life told the men assembled here he was a long shot, dark horse of a suspect; his only link to this crime was the accusation in his past and an excellent motive for revenge. To her though it wasn't so cut and dry, she'd told them all at one time or another, and written it clearly in her case report that this crime wasn't about money, but that was all they could see. 320 Million dollars was blurring the investigation. She was sure from day one that the person, or persons, responsible didn't actually need the money. There just wasn't the usual sense of desperation involved. The theft was a highly sophisticated computer scam, something that would have required precession planning, advanced problem solving skills, and a lot of detailed research mixed with a requisite insider knowledge of how the organization worked. After spending the evening with him she knew he was smart enough to qualify against her checklist, and his position with the company gave him access to the Logiterm system the credit union ran on. He'd been allowed access to the active system and certainly had motive to want to hurt the credit union. The virus had been well hidden on the system too, it would be a lot easier to catch the thief if they knew where to look for the code, but now it was a question of time. Sooner or later the techs going over every line of code would find it, the trigger code buried somewhere in the system, but considering how many thousands of miles of code they were pouring over there was no idea of when it would be found. So with her eyes firmly closed she just sat and listened, ignoring their occasional stares as they all second guessed her motives for having dinner with the suspect.

In listening she learned quite a bit about Tom Williams, though nothing she found as a breakthrough. He had no criminal record and seemed to have never had any trouble with the law, other than the teenage infractions he'd confessed over dinner the night before which she was sure were not recorded anywhere. He was an only child whose parents were still together after almost fifty years of marriage. He'd worked for Hil Fed for the better part of his life, but before that he'd kept a number of odd jobs, one of which was at a Comic Book store. She didn't know why, but felt it might be important. She'd never read many comics, she always assumed that was something for the boys to spend their time and money on. From what she could recall though, comics were of special people doing larger than life things. Men learning how to fly or casting power beams from their eyes in the name of god and country, at least if she remembered her brother's comics correctly She wondered if stealing 320 million dollars would be considered a larger-than-life thing in the eyes of Tom Williams? Was this his vicarious way of living out some childhood fantasy when he found that he would never be able to fly? Instead of being the hero, he'd chosen instead to become the villain? A modern-day Robin Hood, perhaps? Did he intend to give the money away? It was a thought she hadn't considered; perhaps he wasn't smart as she thought and didn't realize that illegal money would never be accepted by a charity. The money would be returned after evidence of the money's origin was presented.

Records showed he took sailing lessons in his early twenties, and frequently rented boats using his credit card. It was always amazing how much sheer data the FBI could gather so quickly when tasked to produce information. The ability to flash a badge and generate subpoenas opened the doors of many of American biggest businesses. On the table in front of her was literally the life in paper of their suspect. They had a copy of his driving records, speeding tickets and a parking violation he'd received when he was in his late teens. They knew when he'd been late on a credit card payment, and had every tax return he'd ever filed. They had a copy of his passport and a listing of every American Customs Counter he'd ever walked through. They had copies of the last year's worth of checks he'd written looking for patterns, and other than the basic bills they learned that he didn't write a lot of checks there were only two places with any frequency other than utilities he wrote every month. The first was a large chain store who kept low price points on CD and DVD's, and the second was to a local comic book store. He only kept two credit cards open, but appeared to only ever use the one from Citibank which he paid in full at the end of each month. His employee file showed that he was, up until Laura Netzly accused him of embezzlement, a model employee, and the few people who were interviewed about him said he was not only pleasant, but cordial to the point of being too helpful. To her mind, when push came to shove, he was just too clean to be anything but guilty.

His parents were still together and lived in Northern California; it looked from their records that he drove up for Thanksgiving and Christmas ever year, via gas receipts. Having worked for the credit union as long as he had, he got three and a half weeks off a year and therefore took two big vacations a year. He would take a week to Maui in October and two weeks to London in late June. Their records showed he maintained the same vacation schedule for the past decade, renting a condo in Maui and a flat in London through the same Internet service companies. The condos in Maui varied on availability of where the service would locate him, but in London he'd stayed only at a residential high-rise called Scala House, at least for the past six trips.

In school, he carried a "B" average in core classes, but excelled in the creative arts. He never participated in any organized extracurricular activities. After high school, there was a dead zone of activity for about three and a half years. He didn't register to college, and for at least two of those three years didn't hold a legal job; at least no taxes were ever paid in his name during that time frame. When he did appear on a tax record again it was from a small comic book stores with an inconsequential income, until finally he enrolled in a local junior college. Eventually he got his job at Hil Fed, and since then has reported no other earnings under any other employer since.

In interviews held with senior management yesterday afternoon it was discovered that few of them knew Tom beyond his days in marketing, or the accusation held against him, they all seemed to know that. Of the entire senior management team only Robert Fetzer, the senior vice president of Lending, seemed to know much about him at all. Even that was limited. Robert told them Tom once had the reputation as a player, but it faded quickly as he got older. He said Tom was known for always showing up with a different woman draped on his arm at each company event, though he speculated the problem with that is, Tom was young and grew up at the credit union, most of the people in a certain sense watched him literally grow up. He made a joke that he wouldn't have wanted people scrutinizing him in his twenties a decade later. Robert followed up saying, Tom went through a random series of women over the years and a lot of fun was had at his expense, but after what happened in final days in Marketing he seemed to withdraw completely, and no one really knew anything about the man anymore. On the work front, everyone thought he was a competent employee, though it was obvious he did his best work back in marketing. Most people thought he was really too nice of a guy to be in collections.

The room fell into questions for a while, but Dawn remained silent. She didn't want to play into it. They questioned his missing computer class, and why any man would stop short of a degree for one class. Especially since Hil Fed offered a reimbursement program for degree programs, the class would have been free to him. They questioned why it was only this particular class. Computers? Dawn just smiled, how could she not? In her head she was thinking, *"What an alibi!"*

As the day slowly drug on she learned the square footage of his house, the names of his parents, friends, and neighbors, as well as what sort of lifestyle he led based on statement activity. The problem was nothing in and of itself made him guilty. He seemed to have none of the dirty little secrets people collect over a lifetime.

When Dawn finally did speak it startled the room, her voice interrupting others, "he used to date his attorney."

"Beg your pardon, Dawn?"

"I said he used to date his attorney, what do we know about her? And for that matter, what do we know about the deal he made with the credit union eighteen months ago?"

Neal cocked his head a little and looked down the table at her, annoyed she was again steeling his thunder "You're the one who brought it to our attention, Dawn, you know exactly what we know."

"Then that's something we're all missing, we need to get a subpoena and check with the credit union's attorney, and while we're at it check with the clerk's office downtown to see if anything was filed."

"Anything specific you want us to look for Dawn?"

"Yeah," she said coolly, "last night it was the one thing he wouldn't talk about . . . the accusation the credit union made. He said he couldn't talk about it . . . that tells me there's a gag order in place. I want someone to find it!"

"OK," Neal said standing, "we'll get someone on that, though they won't be able to do anything until Monday. Right now, why don't we get to the main event?"

"Which is?" she asked, though she already knew the answer.

"Why don't you tell us firsthand what Mr. Williams is really like?"

She looked around the room, realizing she was suddenly on.

* * *

The Sum of Existence 6.2

March 11, 2000

"This is Megan Carter, how may I help you?" Her voice was solid and confident. It showed no weakness and offered no compromise, even in her greeting. Sitting in her elegant downtown office with a view of nothing but other high rise buildings she fought her way into the demanding world of law, a world that was still jaded by male influences, but she was a partner now, the youngest ever at her firm. She liked to let people know from the first moment who they were dealing with.

She didn't like to go to work on Saturday's and avoided doing so like the plague, but she was scheduled to spend her entire work week in trial and she didn't want any errors. Her firm was counting on the verdict, and the client brought in a lot of business annually. This needed to be a slam-dunk, and by the time court began Tuesday morning at eleven she would know all the facts of this case inside and out.

The phone when it rang always annoyed her and usually proved to be no more than an unnecessary distraction, but she answered it anyway in case it was her husband, Alex. Instead the voice belonged to her errant best friend.

"I thought you didn't work weekends?"

"Tom Williams," she said mocking surprise, "you in trouble again?"

"Can't a guy call his ex-girl friend to say hello?"

"Can? Sure. Does, or even will? Rarely. Besides, if you just wanted to chat you'd have left a message for me with Alex."

"He said you were at the office."

"Big case this week, doing my home work."

"So I suppose an affair is out of the question?"

She laughed the moment he said it, no matter how stressed she might get Tom was always able to say something to get her laughing. Tom was a romantic reoccurrence in her life for a very long time, they were together and then they weren't. Their cycle lasted several years, back and forth, sharing each other's bed while they each searched for the lover of their dreams. She was lucky and found Alex, but there would always be a special place in her heart for him. She also knew that Tom was perhaps her best friend in the world, whether or not they were intimate. After all, he was the man who gave her a loan from his own account so she could afford her partnership, something, at the time, even Alex wasn't able to help her with. "Maybe later," she joked, "this week is bad for me."

"Just my luck, day late and a dollar short."

"So seriously Tom, I haven't heard from you in months, what's going on?"

"Well," he started to say as a wave of static overcame the phone and for a moment drowned out both of their voices with a metallic hiss.

"What the hell was that?"

"Static, I think."

"Time to buy a new Portable phone, Tom, I think your digital delight has officially been overused." It was an old joke between them; years ago he'd gone out and spent way too much money on a digital phone for his house, right when they first came out. He'd gone on and on about how much better they were than normal portable phones. That you wouldn't pick up neighbors calls, and the transmission would always be clear and crisp. She'd thought it was a waste of money at the time. She waited patiently for the prices to drop to something a little more reasonable before buying her own.

"I'm not at home Meg; I'm at a pay phone down at Sea Port Village."

"You're calling me from a pay phone?"

"Uh-huh . . ."

"Tom?"

"Yes?"

"Talk to me, Hon, what are you up to? You in trouble?"

"Truth?"

"Yes."

"A lot of trouble I think . . . I'm on a pay phone because I'm pretty sure my line at home is tapped."

"Tapped? Are you in trouble with the law?"

"Trouble's a relative term, but I think in this instance it's pretty safe to use it."

"What did you do?"

"Whatever happened to innocent until proven guilty?"

"Tom," she hissed out suddenly, "you know I'm on your side, but if I'm going to help you I need to know what's going on."

"I'm under suspicion."

"Of?"

She heard him chuckle, his witty sort of chuckle, like it was all a big joke. "I'm not quite sure what the exact charge is, but it turns out the credit union is missing some money . . . they think I did it."

"They think you're guilty of stealing?"

"Sure."

"How much?"

"That's not officially been said, though it's quite a bit. Enough to involve the NCUA as well as the FBI?"

"You're kidding?"

"From what I have been told Meg, well, it's in excess of a hundred million dollars."

"Jesus Christ!" Her voice echoed in the office around her, reminding her how very alone she was in this high-rise building on a weekend.

"Yeah, it's almost like I'm famous now."

"Are they following you?"

"I expect so, but hell Meg, I'm not an expert at this kind of stuff, I don't have a clue."

"You said you were down at Sea Port Village?"

"Yeah," he was speaking quickly, she knew him well enough to know that he was a little rattled and undoubtedly his head was darting around, looking for anyone him who might be trying to listen in. "I came down to clean the boat, I figured all of my phone lines were tapped, so I walked up here to a pay phone . . . I wanted to talk to you about it. Find out how screwed I really am."

"They haven't arrested you then?"

"No. That I would have called you sooner on."

"OK then, Tom, I need to ask a very important question . . . How do you know you're a suspect?"

"The lead investigator told me."

"Shit."

For a minute there was a dead silence on the line, until she heard him place another coin into the slot to keep the call going. She was trying to think clearly, it wasn't every day a client, much less a friend called up saying they'd been accused of a major felony. "When did he tell you this?"

"She told me right before I asked her out for dinner."

"What?"

"Come on, Megan, you heard me."

"It sounded like you said you asked the woman investigating you out to dinner?"

"Uh-huh."

"That's a new one; I'll give you that . . . want to tell me why?"

"She's really cute, nice legs, smart too."

"You are a piece of work. When is this date?"

"What makes you think she agreed to it?"

"If she thinks you're the suspect, Tom, she'd leap at the chance to talk with you without your lawyer present."

"Yeah, good point. I guess I didn't think about that."

"You already went out with her, didn't you?"

"I think I need help though, representation."

She couldn't help the incredulous tone that slipped out, but she knew she didn't have to worry, it was Tom, and she was always able to say whatever she wanted around him no matter what. She knew without a doubt their friendship was unconditional, too much water under the bridge for them to be any other way. "You think? Being investigated for something like this? I guarantee you need it!"

"Will you?"

"Be your lawyer, of course, I will Tom, after all defending your livelihood is rapidly becoming my favorite past time."

"Gee, thanks."

She looked over at the clock on the wall, "we'll need to talk soon."

"Not today, OK."

"Why, do you have another date?"

"No, I told you I need to clean the boat, it's dirty as hell."

"You're being investigated for stealing a hundred million dollars, and you're worried about your damn boat?"

"I like my boat, a lot."

"Did you sleep with her?"

"Who?"

"The investigator?"

"No," he said quietly, "just dinner. She was pretty clear on that."

"Good, do me a favor Tom, don't do it again."

"Don't not sleep with her?"

"You know what I meant!"

"There's a small problem with that Meg,"

"What's that, Tom?"

"I like her."

"No, you don't, Tom, you just like the extra bit of drama it adds to your life, I know you well enough to know that. I still remember what it was like dating you, you're a thrill junkie . . . probably the reason we never lasted."

"And here all this time I thought it was because I wasn't responsible enough for you."

"That I could deal with, you're longing to live on the edge was maddening though."

He looked up from the payphone and around him at the people busily hurrying by. Tourists and local workers out on breaks and lunches, and undoubtedly, he thought, *FBI agents as well.* Hidden amongst the young lovers walking arm in arm and children out in the park flying kites he could just barely see from his position. "Funny," he said, 'I thought you liked it."

"I did, for a time, but the thing was Tom, it wasn't what you needed. You wanted someone to ground you, someone to help keep you in check. I wasn't ever able to do that, with you I was always swept up in the moment and willing to do or try any foolish thing you came up with. I always figured you wouldn't find yourself married and settled down until you ran into a woman who could tell you no."

"Maybe this one can."

"No Tom, this one can lock you up, there's a difference between that and settling down."

He sat silently on the phone to the point where she began to wonder if he was still there and then realized he'd entered into one of his silent, brooding moods where he was totally lost in thought, a thought so deep she'd oft times joke he'd forget to breathe. "We need to talk soon, Tom, I need to hear exactly what's going on . . . and not over the phone or Internet."

"Sure . . ."

"Why don't you come over to the house for dinner tonight?"

"You sure Alex won't mind?"

"Alex thinks you're a kick, and I'm sure he'll love hearing this one . . . what do you say, Hon?"

"I'll bring a couple of bottles of wine."

"Oh, in that case I'll make up the couch."

"Deal."

"Six?"

"I'll be there." He hung up the phone and walked back down toward the docks, spirited out in front of the giant tourist hotels on the harbor. He knew he was being watched, could feel it. He tried to push the thought out of his mind, he knew he still had a lot to do on the boat, especially since he'd have to call it an early day to give himself enough time to get cleaned up and go to Megan's.

He smiled to himself and said aloud, "move along people, nothing to see." Then put more change into the phone, after all, he still needed to make one more call.

* * *

The Sum of Existence 6.3

March 11, 2000

She returned to her rented suite just as the sun was starting to set, exhausted from going over useless facts for the better part of the day. This was the downside to her job, the endless hours of talking, of soothing the minds of all the people who wanted to play at being an investigator. The people were already lining up to take credit for her success. The trouble had been in convincing them that Tom Williams had something to hide. She now had a rented car which allowed her to come and go as she pleased, not having to count on the stupid twit, Marc, to chauffeur her around. That pleased her greatly, mostly because she found herself very uncomfortable at how Marc looked at her. She was never sure if his soft gazes were looks of some school boy crush, or if he was just creepy.

Dawn reviewed the previous evening with them slowly, making sure to never refer to their dinner as a date. She wanted to show herself as a total professional, and never indicate that any attraction or flirtation took place between them. That hadn't changed, she told herself; she still wasn't very attracted to him, at least not in a conventional way. It was the image he portrayed that attracted her, not his looks, but his attitude. He was the bad boy in a three-piece suit, the thief who stole from the safety of the shadows. On paper Tom Williams was proving to be the exact kind of man his parents always wanted her to wind up with. Intelligent, smart with his money, and generally a good person. In reality though he was a criminal, and he was forcing her to do something most men never made her do, she was opening up to him. *To tame him*, she thought, *she'd have to deconstruct him.*

She stopped herself with the key frozen in the lock and thought about what she just considered. Tame hadn't been the word she meant, *catch* was the word. She wanted to catch him, capture him, imprison him. She reminded herself again that no matter how smart he was he was a thief and he'd never be able to spend it. That made him foolish.

Though something told her everything was going according to his plan. He feigned innocence easily, and in his own way admitted guilt. In her eyes it was almost as if he wanted her to know, wanted her to see how smart he was, how clever. The success of actually stealing the money wasn't quite enough, not unless someone else knew about it. That was the hardest part to try and convey to the room of staunch ex-military men who made up the group she was working with. Not that some criminals needed to gloat, they all knew that, but what she was trying to show them was that Tom Williams wanted to get away with his crime, but wanted to taunt everyone with the fact he did it first. He wanted his cake and to eat it too.

She decided this was how she would catch him as she stepped inside. Sooner or later his vanity would creep up; sooner or later he'd give a sign, maybe for the simple reason of trying to impress her. She'd seen the way he looked at her, the way he would fight his own eyes not to stare down at her legs. Most of all though, she'd seen the way he looked into her eyes, she could tell, he liked her.

And of course, she did like him, even if it was for all the wrong reasons. The silly part was, if it wasn't for this crime she'd have never given him a second glance, but because she'd been thrust into his world, she was now very intrigued by the man he was, as well as the man he obviously kept hidden inside. Normally he'd never been able to catch her eye, never be given the opportunity to be the man he was at dinner. The man willing to walk the mental hire-wire and play her Cat and Mouse game of one-upmanship. Now, because of the crime she found herself very interested in getting to know him. He didn't strike her as the type, and maybe it was because of that she was fighting away the sensual thoughts she was suddenly experiencing about him. It was a moot point though; she was single and planned to stay that way. They lived 520 miles apart, and was very soon was going to jail. These factors didn't exactly make for a perfect union. She felt silly suddenly, even entertaining the thought in her head . . . kissing him . . . touching him. "It's not going to happen," she said quietly as she closed the door to the outside world, feeling a tinge of red flush over her face. She reminded herself that he was just trying to play her. The upsetting thing was it seemed to be working. Somehow, she thought, this goofball of a man became entertainingly charming over dinner, and managed to say and do all the right things. The fact that he wasn't playing it safe only made him more exciting in her eyes.

She dropped down her briefcase trying not to think about the reams of questions she'd answered, trying not to think about the questions that hadn't really been about him at all. The ones they'd asked about her, asked in sly ways trying to probe to see if anything had secretly gone on between them last night. It annoyed her, mostly because the questions they'd hinted at were the same ones she'd been thinking of last night as they stood in front of her doorway.

They wanted to know if he'd tried anything at any time where they were out of visual sight of the FBI surveillance team, she assured them he'd been nothing but a gentleman. *Not even when given opportunity,* though she chose to leave that part out. She'd expected a bold gesture, an uninvited kiss at the end, the way his playful flirting was going, instead he smiled and left. Part of her though, she hated to admit, wished he had kissed her. Something told her if she'd kissed him last night, or, more to the point, if he'd been bold enough to kiss her, standing beneath the porch light lingering, their lips touching, separating, she would have gotten him to tell her exactly how he did it. How he got the money and where it currently was. She would've arrested him, of course, but the game would have been ever so much sweeter if he'd kissed her.

Now she was left with the small soft center inside that wanted something she knew she couldn't have. It was driving her crazy.

The answering machine light was flashing and she set down her small leather briefcase and pressed the button.

"Hello, Dawn? It's Tom."

She froze as his voice echoed in the silence of the room. It was a bit too dark for so early in the evening but she ignored that, choosing to focus on the machine and the sound of his voice.

"I know calling you is probably against the rules—someone's rules anyway, not mine, and, you know, I wanted to tell you I had fun last night, even if it was just an investigation for you." She heard the sound of voices in the background, children running with glee. He was at a public phone, she'd been told he was down cleaning his boat; it amazed her that he'd stopped to call. Amazed he'd called to the front desk and asked to be transferred to her room. "I had fun though, in fact I can't remember the last time I'd talked with someone like that. I hope you got what you needed . . . then again, maybe I don't . . . because if you didn't, then I might get to see you again—." His voice paused and she found herself inching forward toward the phone, wanting it to be a live call so she could pick it up.

"—So, here's hoping I at least managed to leave a smile on your face. Good-bye Dawn, I hope everyone enjoyed hearing about our evening."

The beep sounded through the room and she closed her eyes. It was foolish, she knew it, even as she stood there fighting back the smile that waited to part her lips. She couldn't remember the last time someone made her feel this way, unsure, unsteady. She told herself again it was stupid; he was the bad guy in this scenario. She was going to arrest him, but the message was a nice touch, because deep down inside she knew what she really wanted to do was call him back. What she wanted was to hear the sound of his voice. She knew the message should be saved as evidence, but she didn't want anyone else hearing it. It was for her, and before she could change her mind she deleted it, but in her mind she played it over and over, thinking of him as she did so.

* * *

Upping the Ante

Upping the Ante 7.0

March 13, 2000

He got to work extremely early on Monday. Dinner with Megan and her husband the night before left him tired and the multitude of legal possibilities were still swirling in his head. They were watching him, they had to be. That most likely meant his phones were tapped and his life under a microscope. It didn't sit well with him, by nature he was a private man. The idea of being in the public eye was driving him nuts, and even starting to interfere with his sleep. And anyone who knew Tom Williams knew he needed his sleep.

No one ever confused him as being a morning person, he could work late hours without blinking an eye, but getting up before nine left him cranky for several hours. Falling asleep on Sunday evening was damn near impossible, he's tossed and turned all night He lost count of how many times he awoke during the night; just to uncomfortably shift beneath the covers he was entangled in. He finally got up at about 5:30 a.m., an hour before his alarm usually went off to begin the snooze button game he played each morning to drag himself from bed. He went through his morning ritual, and even checked his e-mail and the message boards before leaving. None of his delaying tactics mattered though, he was still at work forty-five minutes early to start a shift he really didn't have the motivation for.

As he walked in from the parking lot, he looked up at the fourth-floor windows, wondering if any of his accusers might already be on duty, watching him from above, like mythological gods passing down judgment in-between reading their morning memos. He wanted to rush up there and give them a piece of his mind, but he knew it wouldn't matter . . . that it would all fall on deaf ears. He was the accused, and anything he had to say would be dismissed as an outright lie. Unless of course, he walked up willing to give them a confession, then they'd listen, he thought.

He was the first person to get to the collections department, and as he fished the office key out from his key chain. He couldn't remember the last time that happened. He'd become the running office joke, how close he could get to his shift without actually being on-time. Opening the door and deactivating the alarm code he wondered suddenly how his coworkers really viewed him. Did they see him as just some has-been slacker? The guy who was there to do the bare minimum and draw his check? Staring over at his desk he remembered how much he hated his job . . . how much he hated this place.

Tom was sure that having dinner with Megan hadn't helped his mood. She was a lawyer, and therefore tended to draw out any and all negatives that might possibly arise from any given situation. Dinner last night consisted of her telling him everything that might happen to him based on the accusation Dawn McCafferty made against him. Of all the options presented to him, he couldn't even find himself afraid of prison. Looking around at the four walls that made up the office he worked in, seeing where his dreams, his hopes, even his career existed, he'd already come to think of this place as something close to hell. There was a very real part of his mind that honestly thought prison might be an improvement to his living condition. It was funny in its own way, by all accounts he was living a good life, had all the possessions a man of his age should, financial security, but at the same time, he couldn't remember the last time he was truly happy. In fact the closest brush with happiness anytime recently was Friday night, at the same time he was finding out his world was getting a whole lot smaller.

Sitting at his desk he began to open drawers, looking for any sign of a search. Looking for any kind of recording device, not that he would have known what to do with it if he found one, it was a work phone and he knew he didn't have a right to privacy at work. His phone didn't unscrew, so he left that alone, wondering if they had a tap on it. The HIL Fed credit union phone system was completely computerized so Tom assumed they'd be able to tap into his line easily, maybe even go back over the past several weeks to see what calls he'd been making from his work line. Not that it mattered he thought, he wasn't trying to hide any phone calls. His brief search turned up nothing, though he could still hear Megan's words echoing through his mind. She wanted to make a statement to the press, but he'd refused. She spent an hour arguing with him, but he wouldn't budge. His thinking was that if they hadn't made a statement yet, why should he? She tried to explain to him the urgency of the situation, but she saw the look on his face, a look she'd come to know all too well back when they dated. It was the look that said his mind was made up, and nothing would convince him otherwise. It was a moot issue and Megan reluctantly let it go, but both knew she'd bring it up again soon.

He flipped the switch to boot his work computer, staring at his own darkened reflection on the monitor, wanting to ask himself who he was. It seemed like he really didn't know anymore. He seemed to be more of a reflection of the man he once was, and he couldn't honestly say he liked who he'd become over the past year. As his image faded into the Windows start up functions he tried to get a handle on where everything went wrong, when he decided to give up and stop living life, and simply exist in it. He now spent all his time waiting for something to come through, like the hapless man who played the lotto twice a week waiting for his ship to come in, spending money he was better off saving. Tom honestly believed that the people who most deserved to win the lotto never did. The people who won would be selfish greedy bastards, for the most part, the kind who couldn't care for the money they had, and would wind up pissing away their millions in a matter of months and left in much the same boat they'd been in before winning.

The really funny thing is, none of it really bothered him until he met Dawn. Until last Friday he'd been more than content to just idly exist, being no more than a character actor in the drama of life. Meeting her seemed to awaken something inside of him he'd long since shut down. All weekend long he'd felt something he hadn't allowed in ages, he felt alone. He felt empty. He knew she was rooting around the corners of his life, undoubtedly listening in on his phone lines and maybe even reading his mail, she was coming after him. It didn't bother him though, he honestly believed he had nothing left to lose. He reached his hand up to the mouse and double clicked on the Logiterm start icon so he could get a fresh start on the day, and with any luck clear his mind. The Windows applications opened without problem or error as it did every morning, but Logiterm through him for a loop all the same. It booted up the just as it always did, and Tom entered in his user name and password like he did every single morning. The next screen after his password was accepted would allow him to dedicate his terminal for his use, this feature allowed him to bypass putting in his password with each and every transaction performed throughout the day. It was a specialized function that not all employees were automatically entitled to. It was a function that needed to be approved by the employee's manager and monitored by the controllers. Despite the importance of the override, and how closely monitored it really was, for the people who used it, the function meant very little. It was something that happened almost automatically, yet today Tom's computer refused to dedicate. The first issue of many that would immediately follow.

It happened before in his time with the collections department. A glitch would happen, or an employee in the Technical Support department would decide his time for the function was up, and suddenly he wasn't allowed to dedicate. It took about half a day to fix usually, and it always annoyed him. He'd have to get Judy to sign off on a form when she came in. He quickly discovered though that dedication was the least of his problems . . . suddenly ever transaction, no matter how minor, needed to get a supervisors override. He was locked out of every account, accounts that on Friday, he was able to gain access to without a thought. Accounts he'd been actively collecting on were suddenly blocked from his view, he couldn't even get in to transfer a payment. It didn't sink in right away, at first he thought his user name had been lost from the records, but then he realized if that were the case he wouldn't have been able to log on in the first place. He hadn't been forgotten, he'd been shut out. This was a message from his corporate masters, they thought he was guilty and cut his teller privileges so he didn't have access to their computer system anymore. He wanted to go off screaming at first, to yell and carry on about how he was being wronged. He heard his grandfather's voice echoing through his head, yelling and caterwauling, talking about how he'd raise the roof off the place if he wasn't heard. Tom's grandfather was a character and a half, and he was pleased that his grandfather was no longer alive to see the state to which his life had fallen. As he sat there, staring into a computer system he couldn't access all he wanted to do was sit back and cry. It was maddening and he didn't know how to stop what was happening. He couldn't help but ask himself why he fought so hard back when they were after him before. It was all happening again, different reasons, different causes, but the feelings were starting to rise up inside. It was like reliving the worst moment of his life. He'd been sure when it ended last time he would never let himself feel this hollow or scared again, but yet here he was staring at a computer prompt telling him he needed an override to enter a collections account. He wondered if they'd be coming soon to tell him he was out of a job. Certainly they planned on at least suspending him until a true determination of his guilt could be made? Isn't that what happened in criminal cases? Isn't that what Megan had warned him about just last night?

    He picked up the phone as he took in a deep breath, quickly dialing up the Technical Support Department before he lost his temper. He very calmly explained to them that his teller privileges were no longer working and that something needed to be done if he was going to participate in any meaningful way at work. They were very polite with him on the phone, even laughed at his joke, and told him they'd look into the problem and get back to him. He knew what that meant in HIL Fed Lingo he was the lowest priority they had at the moment and they'd get to him when they could. "So much for friendly member service," he said aloud for absolutely no one to hear.

    After an hour he got the impression that they weren't going to be calling him back anytime soon. As his coworkers filtered in he explained he'd been locked out and they all gave him their worried faces but acted like it was no big deal. He knew the rumors were already starting to fly, he wasn't sure if they knew he was the one yet, but even if they didn't it wouldn't take long. Knowing he was useless on the computer or actual collection work until his teller privileges were restored, he went around and collected up everyone else filing and began to do the only real work he was currently capable of.

    When Judy came in she could tell something was different in the room, the way they all looked up at her as she came through the door. Tom sat down the filing and walked up to her and said simply, "well, you see, there's been a development."

    She stopped in the center office and looked at him apprehensively, "and that would be?"

    "I've been shut out."

She marched into her office and told him she'd take care of it, but he knew better. The sinking feeling in his gut told him that this was far from over, and whatever authority she thought she had was about to be taken away. He smiled softly so everyone could see, his way of showing he was OK and there was nothing big going on, just another, everyday little inconvenience.

He continued filing, far enough away from Judy's office that he couldn't hear her phone conversation, but he could see her, and he knew she'd been on the phone with more than a single person. Her level of frustration was growing with each new person she spoke with. This was the run around, and sooner or later she was going to run out of track. A part of him wanted to go in and tell her to stop, not to waste her time, but he knew this was something she felt she needed to do. Judy was a woman who enjoyed the privilege of her authority. She'd worked hard to get it at such a young age, and she didn't much like it when anyone challenged it. Tom knew she was setting herself up for a huge let down, but he didn't let it concern him too much, she needed to figure out what kind of place she was working for and exactly how much any individual person mattered to them in the long run. It was a hard lesson to learn, Tom knew it firsthand, he still remembered the sting of finding out himself.

It took about an hour altogether before Judy asked Tom to come to her office, asking him to close the door as he stepped in. Tom fought to keep the sly little smirk off his face. Closing the door meant bad news, now the question was how bad?

"You better sit down," she'd said quietly, partly closing her eyes to avoid looking at him.

"Another of those special little talks, eh?"

"This isn't a joke Tom."

"Funny, it all seems pretty comical to me."

"They've told me that you shouldn't be allowed to do anything on the computer right now, we should limit your duties as much as possible, while still allowing you to be a useful member of the team. If you need something done on the computer one of your fellow employees will have to provide you the necessary override after they've reviewed your work and what you plan to do."

"Yeah, useful to the team . . . Interesting concept to be brandied about this place."

Looking at her he could tell she had nothing to say back to him on this, the look in her eyes told him she was mad as hell. Tom just sank down in the chair, part of him wanting to curl up and cry at the injustice heaped upon him, and the other half wanting to laugh hysterically at how utterly absurd his situation was. He wanted to yell out that this was his life, this silly little existence that seemed to trouble so many people. This was his life, and by all appearances he seemed to be failing miserably at it. "Did you mention to them," he asked with a forced calm "that my entire job was based off a computer network?"

"Yes."

"And they said?"

"They said it didn't matter."

A soft chuckle pushed from his lips and he fought to hold back a much darker smile, the one that so often haunted him, giving away his feelings to any who might be watching. "Am I going to be fired any time soon, Judy?"

"They can't fire you Tom," she said with an obvious sense of having asked the question herself of someone just moments before, "if you aren't proven guilty it would leave them in a terrible position."

"So I'm here out of convenience . . . theirs."

"Tom . . . I . . ."

Tom was looking up at her and smiling, not the smart ass one she was used to seeing from him in tense situations, instead this was his sweet smile, the tender one that didn't usually come out during the light of day. "Sssshhhhh, it's OK. What concerns me is why they haven't let me go; suspended with pay until the investigation completes itself . . . it doesn't make sense to keep me on."

"I don't know, Tom, all I know is what they're telling me, which is damn little. At the very least they should have informed me this was happening to one of my staff, that way I could at least account and plan for it."

He was ignoring her; she was slipping into her management mode. She got this way sometimes, and he'd learned it was best not to listen to the details of what she was saying as it tended to make anyone who worked for her feel like a farmhand. Instead he focused on his own situation, started playing it around in his head. If they considered him enough of a risk to cut his teller privileges, why not just keep him at home. The one place he was sure to stay out of trouble. Perhaps they just wanted to punish him, he thought, force him to continue getting up early every morning and coming in here to feel utterly useless. Though, that didn't make much sense to him either.

Then it hit him. They wanted to watch him, the NCUA, the FBI. They were hoping he did it again, went after more money, that was why he was still there, he thought, that's what they're thinking. The Credit Union got cold feet though and shut him out of the network; he was willing to bet that Dawn didn't know yet. That they still thought he had access to everything. The reason they hadn't gone public yet, they were hoping to bait him into taking more money. "Son of a bitch," he whispered, interrupting whatever tangent Judy was on. It suddenly occurred to him exactly what kind of mousetrap he was in, and how he was meant day by day to get even deeper in it. *No,* he thought, *not a mouse trap, a spider's web that was slowly being wrapped around him.*

"Tom?"

"Yeah?" He responded, but he still wasn't quite listening, his mind turning away, working on his own strategy for what he needed to do. The kind of plan Megan would never approve of.

"Are you OK? You look like you're starting to phase out."

He looked up at her and smiled, a peaceful genuine smile. The plan was starting to come together, the lost details filling themselves in. Part of his marketing training, thinking creatively on your feet. "Did I ever thank you . . . For helping me out before, the last time I was accused . . . when you brought me into your department to cover my retreat from Marketing? The day you saved what was left of my ass?"

"Yeah, you did."

"Good, because I do thank you, for everything you've done and undoubtedly will do. The thing is, don't drive yourself nuts on this one. Here I think both our hands are tied. At least as far as this situation"

She looked tired all of a sudden and let out a small sigh. "Why Tom, why do they think it was you?"

"I guess I fit the profile . . . And I have what they consider to be a history of unscrupulous behavior. It's funny when you think about it, up until now I always assumed I was the traditional square peg trying to be rammed into a round hole. Now I find I was just aiming myself at the wrong hole, I should have gone for the criminally jagged one instead. Show's me for being a registered republican, huh?" She didn't smile at his joke and he could see something was weighing heavy on her.

She stared at him silently, forcing him to read her eyes and it suddenly dawned on him the depths of his situation also revolved around the actions of the credit union. The government agencies were looking to nail his ass, but that didn't mean the senior management team was going to sit around and wait. But mostly what triggered it was the guilt he saw in her eyes. "They've told you to monitor me, haven't they? Turn me into a liability. That way when they fire me I can't say it was about what they've accused me of."

"I . . ." her words froze as she composed herself, speaking extremely slow, enunciating every syllable, "I've been told to keep a close eye on you and your activities, and . . . ," again she paused not really knowing what to say, ". . . I should call you on any and all mistakes, documenting them as I go."

"Gee," he said almost comically, trying to find a way to make her laugh, "who knew my life was so exciting?"

"This is very serious, Tom, you need to quit joking."

"Yeah," he said in a way that lacked commitment, "I suppose you're right."

"Have you talked to your lawyer yet?"

"Do you think I should?"

Judy stood up and walked around her desk, "I think you better do something . . . just to protect yourself."

"I'll think about it . . ."

"Promise?"

He looked at her with his shy and innocent smile, "Promise." He got up and started walking toward the door. "You know, I think I'm going to take my break now, OK?"

"Take some extra time, Tom; it won't be on my report."

As he opened the door he simply said thanks, and then disappeared out of the Collections office.

* * *

Upping the Ante 7.1

March 17, 2000

She watched as he pulled into the parking lot from the fourth-floor window. The glass was tinted sufficiently that she was sure he had no clue she was watching. Behind her, Dawn heard the sound of shuffling paper, Marc going over the reams of legal documentation she'd requested on Saturday, paperwork they were just now receiving from the Credit Union's labor relations attorney. Technically she knew she should be helping him go through it, instead she stood at the window and watched as Tom got out of the car and slowly walked toward the office. The smallest sign of some macho strut in his step, like a man who didn't have a care in the world. At that moment she almost hated him, how dare he be this calm, this cool while under investigation.

She was getting a whole new feeling to this case, something she never liked. She knew that if you scratched the surface long enough, any case would reveal facts the investigator would rather not know. But in this instance, she got the distinctive feeling that the credit union was trying to keep something from her. Not just her, that was too possessive a statement, she thought, they were trying to conceal something from the investigation, something specifically about Tom. She knew, or at least strongly suspected Tom was trying to leak information to her about it in the only way he legally could. But she didn't think she'd be able to find it going through the boxes behind her. She'd dispatched a couple FBI agents to go down to the courthouse and run a few discrete checks on any cases with Hil Fed or specifically Tom Williams. She knew sooner or later she'd get the truth, she just wondered if she'd get to it in time, before whatever game Tom was playing blew up in his face.

"Dawn, I think I got something."

"What is it?" She turned and walked back toward the crowded table littered with legal size files. He didn't look up at her, which was the first sign he might actually be onto something. Marc, despite all of his nasally qualities, which she mostly detested, always took a few seconds to leer at her. It was one of the many things that disgusted her about him. Whenever he was so lost in something it meant there was a morsel, something he was starting to latch onto. "Are you going to tell me, or what?"

"Uh," he said wrestling back through the thick legal document he had open in front of him, trying to find that place where he'd started reading from, "yeah, back here." His eyes scanned over the documents until finally he looked up, focusing directly into her eyes, a beaming sense of pride of having beaten her to what he perceived as a clue. "It's a gag order, this one hasn't been stamped by the court, but it was being prepared for filing."

"About Tom?"

"Uh-huh, it's about what you were talking about, about when he was accused of stealing."

"What's it say?"

Marc tossed the document over in front of her, "neither party can talk about the events leading up to the event, or the aftermath. There's a lot of details spelled out, especially in the way of limiting what your little friend can say to anyone regarding the situation. A lot in here seems to be in regard to talking about the VP of Marketing as well. One Ms. Laura Netzly."

"Mrs. Laura Netzly," Dawn heard herself saying in a rather chiding way, "you really should read the files closer."

"Ms. can be used whether or not the woman is married or not, look it up."

Dawn took the seat next to him, taking up the file, "Ms. is to be used when you don't know if a woman is married or not, in this case we knew the answer . . . or at least *you* should have." She could tell that Marc's face was starting to tighten; he didn't like to teased, and absolutely hated to be proved wrong. Unfortunately for Marc, proving him wrong was something Dawn was able to do on a very regular basis. She started to read and immediately realized that Marc was wrong again, this was a gag order, but one that hadn't been filed, at least not yet. There were no dates listed, and everything seemed to refer back to a confidentiality agreement that was dated back when Tom's job had been on the line. She found herself reading every line, the legalese that it was written in slowed her down slightly, and she would never understand why lawyers felt the need to have their own language.

"We're missing a piece here Marc."

"What are you talking about?"

"When two parties enter into an agreement that one or both would rather not have openly discussed, they include what's known as a confidentiality clause in the contract. Now, in essence the confidentiality clause is mostly worthless, as it's not a document of the court, there's really no way to honestly enforce it without suing, but if you sue on it, you're usually jeopardizing yourself by getting even more publicity. You're only real choice is to file a gag order with the court, but before you can the confidentiality clause needs to be broken."

"Do you think maybe you could give that to me again, maybe in English?"

"There are no dates on this gag order, no specific cause that Tom has broken, yet the credit union had their corporate attorney draft up a gag order, as if they thought he would."

"Is that strange?"

"Very. I mean, think about it, Marc, would you really have your attorney sit down and draft up an order if you didn't need it? How much does their corporate attorney charge for that kind of thing, you have to figure at least three to five hundred dollars to draft this document, maybe more."

"OK," he said as the creases formed in his brow, "when you put it that way, it does seem sorta queer."

Dawn leaned her head back, staring up at the ceiling until she heard Marc ask, "So, what does it mean?"

"I'm not sure, but it smells fishy . . . I really want to read a copy of whatever agreement he and the credit union signed."

"I haven't seen anything yet."

"Keep looking," she said, "It's got to be here somewhere."

She heard the doors to the room open and Neal came walking in with Fred Halstead, both seemed to be lost in a deep conversation, one she had no problem interrupting. She got right in front of their path, "so?"

"So, what Dawn? Could you be a little more specific?" Neal seemed easy going this morning, a clear sign he'd finally managed to get a good night's sleep.

"Is it true that the FBI lost him last night for a few hours?" As soon as she said it she realized Neal didn't know about Tom's unaccounted for time.

Neal's whole body language changed as he spun on his heels looking at Fred. Fred was sucking in air through clenched lips, and tucking his head in for what looked to be a fight. Dawn wanted to laugh, it seemed like a battle of the super egos, and she'd somehow managed to get a front row seat. "What the hell is she talking about?" Neal snapped, not wanting to give Fred so much as a moment to prepare an excuse.

"From approximately 6:30 p.m. through 11:20 p.m. we have no idea where Mr. Williams was."

"Why the hell not? I thought we were paying you're boys to keep tabs on Mr. Williams."

Fred dropped his briefcase down just inches from where Marc was still digging through stacks of paperwork. "He's got a goddamn Corvette, Neal, my agents were tailing at a safe distance in a sedan, a suped-up sedan, but just a sedan."

"What happened?"

"He caught a light on a yellow when my agents were two cars behind, everyone else hit the brakes, but your boy hit the gas. He sailed through the intersection and barely managed to avoid running a red. My agents pulled out his extend-specs, and saw that Mr. Williams continued to move at his advanced course of speed and turned a corner, out of my agents view. That was at approximately 6:30 p.m."

"And how'd we find him at eleven thirty?"

"Well," Halstead said, stalling as he spoke with a stuttering problem he'd never displayed before, "he went home."

"Well," Neal said as loud as he could, "Isn't that just fucking beautiful!"

"We regained visual Neal; it's hard to keep someone in the fishbowl twenty-four/seven."

"For all we know he could have been out burying the goddamn money somewhere."

"We have pictures of him coming in, he was dressed the same as he left, very casual."

"Where the hell did he go then?"

Fred was getting angry now, Dawn got the feeling that despite his initial reluctance he would have been willing to take a small portion of blame just to end the conversation, but the more Neal pressed, the less willing he was to go down alone, so it came as no surprise when he pointed his stubby little finger at her. "Why not ask her, she's your psyche major!?!"

"I've got no idea Fred, that's why we wanted to have him followed."

"What about the transponder?"

Fred lowered his head, "it seems to have malfunctioned."

"Are you kidding me?"

"Sometimes it happens. You put a highly technical electronic transmitting device on the bottom of someone's car and a rock flies up and hits it. Shit happens, Neal. What do you want me to say?"

"Shit happens? Jesus, are you serious, that's the bureau's response to this?"

"Neal," Dawn said softly, "let it go. We count on surveillance for a reason."

"Because, shit happens?"

She smiled at him, trying to stop herself from laughing, "mostly, yes."

"So," Neal was still shaking his head and turned to look at Halstead, "and what exactly were you doing while Tom Williams was running about town without a chaperone?"

"I was going through his message board postings."

"Why," she asked, suddenly very curious as to why the FBI was spending so much energy on something that seemed very insignificant to them the other day.

"Because," he snapped back bitterly, "as far as I can tell, it's the only social life this guy actually has. Besides, if he's here and the money was wired to the Cayman's, I figure his computer is the only way he can move it."

"I thought you said he wasn't doing anything suspicious on the Internet?" Neal asked as he rested one shoulder against the wall and fixed his scowl outward.

"He's not, but he's our suspect according to your lead investigator. For my own money he appears too clean and legitimate, but if Dawn's right about him, that means he's damn smart and we need to be smarter. If he's not doing anything on the net he shouldn't be, not transferring the money or even checking on it, we have to come to one of three conclusions. 1) he's innocent and we're chasing the wrong guy, 2) he thinks he's dumped the money into someplace so safe he doesn't have to worry about it, or 3) . . ."

Dawn was shaking her head as the last piece of the puzzle sank in, ". . . he has somebody else keeping tabs on it."

"Exactly," Fred said with his grim smile looking past the callous eyes of Neal Johnson, "so we're suddenly a lot more interested in who he's communicating with on the net. Though I do have a question for you, Dawn."

She evened her face, looking directly back at him, and answered in a very non-committal way, "yeah?"

"Is he smart enough to speak in code?"

She was in one of her all-time favorite outfits today, and ever so glad she was. Blue jeans and an old, worn out Van Halen T-shirt that used to belonged to her father. She was more relaxed in this garb, more herself. She wasn't playing the pretty little princess that all the boys wanted her to be growing up, not the sweet young thing the dirty old men wanted to gawk at. She dug her hands into her pockets and mulled it over; normally a question like this about a suspect's innate intelligence would be an easy question, something for her to just rattle off. Things were different where Tom Williams was concerned; she was starting to reach the point where she didn't trust her judgment. Whatever it was inside her that was developing feelings for Tom was starting to cloud her judgment on certain, specific aspects of his character. Was he smart enough to set up the scam they were now discussing? Her natural instinct was to say yes, but the idea of stealing money you couldn't use still cast a shadow of doubt over the situation. "Yes," she finally said, "I'd have to believe he'd be smart enough to know he couldn't just spell it out. I don't know how good a code it would be though."

"Well, we now have some people going over every word he types online, whether in e-mail or a posting to a newsgroup or message board."

"Can we see inside his computer," Neal asked bluntly.

"Guy's got a pretty good firewall," Halstead said shrugging, "we can piggy back him on where ever he goes and see whatever he sends, but we can't get onto his system without letting him know we're doing it. And if the firewall's good enough, he might be able to keep us out long enough to destroy whatever it is we might be looking for."

"Shit! How about down in the Cayman's? Are we asking any questions down there yet?"

"I sent out a request to have a couple of the guys ask a few questions, but down there . . . well, we just don't know if we can get anywhere. Their banking industry's a little different from ours."

"OK," Dawn said, "at least we're moving." She knew all too well that the banking laws in the Caymans were very lax and not in their favor.

"But we still don't know where he was last night?" Neal said with the just enough emphases to jab at Frank Halstead.

"No," he said tucking down his chin against his chest, "no we don't."

* * *

Upping the Ante 7.2

March 17, 2000

Tom walked briskly, around the series of parking lots that surrounded the Hil Fed main office as well as the other office parks that existed on either side of the Hil Fed Building. It was good exercise that Tom tried to do at least two or three times a day depending on whether or not he actually took his breaks and lunches. He'd always told people he'd rather do anything other than sit on his ass all day, plus he found it to be very relaxing when he was beginning to feel stressed and needed a little bit of a release. Today he walked hard and fast, trying to clear the anger from his mind, but walking wasn't quite doing the trick today. *There was just too much going on,* he thought, *too much that's taking him right to the edge.* It was like he was starting to feel like a stranger in his very own life, that if he wasn't very careful he would cease to exist at any given moment. It wasn't a sensation he felt comfortable with and as foolish as it was, even to him, he wanted to lash out. He wanted to act childish and cruel, he wanted to hit something, and watch it break.

Up ahead of him was the Hil Fed Building, and at the moment he couldn't think of anything that he would like to see broken more. He swore under his breath and started charging back to the building, walking as fast as he could without allowing himself to break into a run.

Inside he went straight for the elevator without really thinking about it. The walk had been just brisk enough that he was feeling the sting of the air conditioner. He wasn't hot enough to start sweating, but warm all over to the point he decided if he was really going to do what he was thinking, he didn't want to chance the stairs making him perspire. He pressed the button and waited as the meticulous hum began indicating the car was starting to sail down from a higher floor. When the door opened he stepped in without looking back and pressed the button for the fourth floor. The doors started to close and he felt his darkest smile starting to creep to his face, at least until the well tanned hand reached through the narrowing crack of the shutting doors and pressed on the inner release bar to pop them back open. Tom was a bit annoyed as he sunk into the back corner of the elevator car and let his smile fade, he wanted to be alone on his ride upstairs but this happened many times. For the staff of Hil Fed who knew exactly how slow the decrepit old elevator was it was a matter of urgency to do anything you could to get on the elevator before the doors slid shut. You could wind up waiting as long as five to ten minutes until the car would make a return visit to the first floor.

Tom looked up in passing, not really caring who it might be, until he actually saw her face. The moment he did he could feel his leg muscles starting to tense and his jaw grow stiff. He'd never really been the kind of man to believe in hate, but the woman entering the car with a tanned and smug look was enough to bring it out in him. Laura Netzly, the VP of Marketing, the woman who set the chain of events into motion that led him to where he stood now. Her feeble accusations that placed him in the spotlight of the Hil Fed Board of Directors and Senior Management Team, who forced him out of Marketing and ruined his career. He'd successfully managed to avoid her most days since it all happened eighteen months ago. They no longer moved in the same circles and the few mutual friends they shared had long since chosen sides. She always rode the elevator, which had been another reason why he avoided it. Even now, after all this time, he still he hated her for it.

He could still hear her words, accusing him of the very worst things that could be imagined about a man in his previous profession. Accusing him of theft and a callous disregard for the credit union he had sweated blood into for almost two decades. He used to think of them as friends, which is why her words, her actions stung him so deeply. He'd read her completely wrong back in the beginning, and it the long run it cost him everything.

"Well, well," she said letting a certain nasal quality fill her nostrils, "I certainly didn't expect to see you today."

He looked her up and down; she was still a strong, beautiful woman with a long, strikingly lean body. She'd been a high-school cheerleader and still proudly proclaimed, or at least did back when they were closer, she could fit into her old uniform. Her long blonde hair was tied off behind her. Not a reserved blonde either, hers almost qualified as platinum. She maintained herself in what Tom liked to call a false sense of eternal beauty. He knew she was the type who believed in image over substance, and her career track certainly proved it. He couldn't help but wonder how many people she'd stepped on to get to where she was today? After all, he could still feel the tread marks on his back from her harsh climb to the top . . . to the position he'd always been promised. His heart began to beat faster, it had been a long time since they were this close, and he could still sense her bitterness to him, a bitterness he felt he didn't deserve. He was the one who'd been hurt, all around, not her. She looked slightly different than he'd remembered. Her hair a touch shorter and it looked like she'd had something done to it, something professional, something incredibly expensive to show off her new found financial gain, he thought, but there was more. Her tan was darker than usual, she looked almost like what he might call sun drenched, this made her cool green eyes stand out even more. She was dressed in a power suit of the modern-day businesswoman, the kind that showed none of her sensual curves. It gave her the look of being a young, up and comer, and if he were just about any other man she might have been able to convince him of it. He knew her though, all the dark little secrets and truths she'd fight bitterly to keep quiet. "Fall asleep on the tanning bed again?" He knew she hadn't, it was an office in-joke several years back when she went to go tanning at a local establishment and fell asleep on the tanning bed, she'd burned herself something fierce and he'd joked her steadily about it for the better part of a year. Today she didn't seem to remember the humor in it, not that his tone indicated he was going for humor.

"Not that it's any of your business Tom, but I just got back from a cruise."

"What a shame," Tom said with his hurtful smile as the outer elevator doors started to close them both into the small box, "that it wasn't the Titanic."

The moment the doors closed and it was just the two of them her face changed, gone was the professional image, suddenly he was looking at an angry woman wanting to lash out. "Got an interesting phone call last night from Roland, want to guess who it was about?"

He didn't need to guess, he just leaned further back against the corner of the elevator car as he felt the upward motion begin. "What can I say, I'm popular again.'

"I was impressed at first, really," she said nodding her head and making eye contact, "but then I realized you're nowhere near smart enough to pull off a crime like this. Oh, sure, you might have been able to think it up; you've always had a devious mind, but to execute it, not a chance. Want to know why?"

"Not particularly, no."

"First, you're too much of a coward to actually break the law, second, you're too timid to stand up to the credit union who you still secretly feel will come cradle you in their arms, and third, you don't have the technical knowhow or access to the online systems required to pull this off."

"Gee Laura; can I get that in writing? I might need it for my defense."

She turned away from him as the ever slow elevator car began to settle into the groove of the second floor, "not a chance Tom, I want to see them burn your ass."

The door began to shake open and Tom closed his eyes and asked the one question he knew he shouldn't, "how's Karen?" It was stupid and he immediately regretted asking it, but inside, he desperately wanted to know. She stepped out of the elevator looking back at him, a brisk look coming over her face as she stiffened her whole body angrily.

"None of your damn business convict!" And with that, she was gone.

Tom rested his body tightly into the back corner of the elevator, looking out and mentally restraining himself from doing anything. Taking what seemed to be an eternity, the doors to the elevator finally closed, leaving him in silence and his own regret. His anger only grew. It was amazing, he thought, that after all this time, she still had that effect on him.

*   *   *

Upping the Ante 7.3

March 17, 2000

"Do we know anything about these stories he's referring to in the messages?"

"We have a couple guys who are running around to a few local comic book shops picking up some of these comics he talks about." Halstead dropped off another stack of messages that Tom posted online over the past few months. Dawn knew that Halstead had already put a couple of bureau agents on it, having them search for any kind of possible code. She wanted to see them any way, in her head she was already starting to convince herself that there had to be something there the agents would miss, something she'd be able to see.

The messages, so far, all seemed rather boring. They were discussing comic books, their creators, and the suggested meanings of the failing comic book industry. She found one message Tom posted about a month back that suggested the true deterrent for younger audiences reading comics in today society were three fold. 1) A lack of material for younger readers to find as well as distribution problems as the bigger publishers have steered away from the youth market. 2) The advent of the Internet and the Point and click mentality being forced into the youth of America, which was leading to a wealth of children being little more than functionally illiterate. 3) The fact that comic books were perceived one of two ways within the country, generally speaking, first as something only for young children (see problem number one) or second, that they are all smut filled books that should not be given to children.

Dawn could almost hear him saying the words; though in truth during their brief evening together the subject of comics hadn't come up, at least as anything more than an off handed comment. She could tell from reading his postings that this was a subject he was very passionate about, and feeling the weight of his passion made her want to talk to him again, and in that she feared she was missing whatever it was she was really supposed to be reading within the messages. Her mind was starting to move at a whirl.

"How about the people he's speaking with? Do we know anything about them?"

"As far as we can tell there are over three thousand posters on this board and about twice as many lurkers that can clearly read every word printed on screen. The message board service asks for names and e-mail address at sign up, but that's hardly the most reliable information source."

"You'll have to forgive me, Fred, but I don't have a clue as to what you just said."

Fred looked up at Neal with a highly professional smile, the kind that just screamed it was fake, "An online message board has to be hosted by someone who has free space on the net. That's how it works. Now, the people who own the message boards usually make their money selling ad space instead of charging potential visitors or host forums."

"Host forums?"

"Yeah, that's when a private individual or company create a message board and opens it up to a public 'forum.' This means anyone with a modem and Internet access can get to the message board in question. Now, like most company's who run message boards online, they want to know a little about the person before they can start posting responses. The form you fill out to get a user ID, and by that I mean a name that allows you to add to the message boards, is usually fairly simple. They want to know your real name and an e-mail address to contact you with."

"So," Neal said hopefully," we have their names?"

"Not really, there's no way to make sure the names or e-mail they put into the form are accurate. On top of that, if you're just a lurker, you don't have to fill out the form, all you have to do is click on the 'read only' entrance."

"No," Dawn said quietly, "we can see everywhere he goes online, you told me that, we have him piggy-backed, we'd know if he was going anywhere else for information. Whoever it is he's communicating with has to be on this comic book forum."

"Assuming," Neal said sharply, "he has a partner."

"He does, he has to."

"Why do you say that Dawn?" Halstead asked as he took a step closer to her.

"Because otherwise he'd be where the money is."

"So," a voice suddenly boomed into the room with heavy Texas drawl, "you catch me my thief yet?" The group of agents turned to look at the figure of Randy Carlson swaggering in. Watching him lumber forward Dawn saw that pretty much all he was missing was an over sized cowboy hat.

"We're working on doing just that Randy, what can we do for you?" Neal was the politician, and Dawn sometimes forgot how easily he glided into the proper tone of voice needed to walk the thin line of public relations. She watched as he went right up to Randy and slid his hand into a nice firm shake.

Dawn turned and walked away from their close knit group. Her mind still awhirl thinking about who Tom Williams was using as a partner. *For a crime like this*, she thought, *it would have to be someone he trusted implicitly*. Three hundred, twenty million dollars? Who would you trust to hold onto that much money? To Dawn's way of thinking, all Tom did was give his partner 320 million reasons to betray him. She wanted to know about his friends. Family was a dead end; she knew that already, but suddenly the idea of a partner put friendships he might have into a whole new light. She knew he was in the building, the question she now had was how to find a good reason to go talk to him. One that Neal wouldn't have a conniption over.

In the background she heard Neal and Randy exchanging small talk and good ol' boy stories with Fred uncomfortably wedged between them. Her mind, mostly though, was on Tom and the idea of a mysterious partner. She was determined to find a way to see him when she heard the main conference room door slam open.

* * *

Upping the Ante 7.4

March 17, 2000

Tom didn't even bother trying to be subtle as he charged through the double doors leading into the main conference room. The agents on duty at the far table immediately jerked up, ready for any kind of trouble the intruder might bring. Instead of causing any trouble though Tom just stopped and stared in with a cool gaze of contempt for everyone and everything. To Dawn's eyes it was as if he was putting the room on notice. Dawn began to slowly move herself forward, matching a line with Randy, Neal, and Fred. It looked as if they were getting ready for a standoff. They were all shocked Tom Williams would come charging in, and Dawn knew it couldn't mean anything good.

"Can we help you, Mr. Williams?" Neal asked in a reserved tone.

"I'm here," was all Tom said as he started to walk toward them. Dawn knew why Tom remained still and silent after entering and found herself impressed by him all over again. He knew if he came charging further into the room the agents in the back would have instinctively moved to restrain him, so he waited for someone to acknowledge him. Now that someone had he could safely walk toward them, knowing the agents wouldn't do a thing.

"I wasn't under the impression that anyone sent for you, Mr. Williams."

That's when it struck her, Tom may have been talking to Neal, but his eyes were focused in on Randy Carlson, and it wasn't a pleasant look.

"I'm here to face my accusers, isn't that one of my rights?"

Fred took a step forward, sensing the hostility and wanting to form a barricade between Tom and Neal. "Last I checked, son, you haven't been officially accused of anything, so why not simmer down before you give us something, eh?"

Tom continued to look right past Fred Halstead, continued to look directly at Randy Carlson even though he did respond to Halstead. "You're not my father, so lay off on the familiarity."

Halstead nodded at the suspect, "whatever you say, *Mr. Williams*. My point remains valid though."

"Why'd you do it, Randy?"

Neal placed his hand on Randy's shoulder, trying to get him to ignore Tom's baiting, but Dawn could see the fire building up in Randy's eye and the hot headed Texan inside him coming to bear. "Funny, Tom, I d think I might be asking the same goddamn thing of you!"

"So the word did come down from you then?"

Everyone in the room was starting to look puzzled, except for the two men at center stage, arguing more with their eyes and appearance then with any words they might be thrusting back and forth. "You're damn right I did, we should have forced you out instead of allowing you to stay, our mistake, we thought you learned your lesson."

"So now it's off to jail I go?"

"If there's any justice in the world, hell yes! And I just don't think your ex-girlfriend will be able to save your ass this time."

"Well, Hell, Randy" Tom said mimicking his southern drawl, "it all depends who preps the case against me, if it's the halfwits you've surrounded yourself with here at Hil Fed, then I should be completely safe."

"You think you're so goddamn smart, don't you? Well, one day you're gonna learn the better of it, that you can't just go around pissing in the wind without getting a face full of your own urine. You've always been clever Tom, but you've never been clever enough, now have you?"

"Gee," he said with obvious mocking in his voice, "was that my problem? I always thought it was the fact I wouldn't put out for you ? Oh wait, I forgot, I wasn't your type—I never stood a chance!"

"You son of a bitch!"

"OK, enough!" Fred was quick to force himself between them, he could see with the way Randy was starting to tense up that it wouldn't be much longer until Randy through a punch at Tom, and everyone present knew that would cause the case far more damage than good. "Neutral corner's you two, neutral corners! We're all gentlemen here from what I've been told."

Dawn took her chance to step forward and get right in front of Tom's face as he slowly started to turn away from Halstead. "What the hell are you doing?" She asked with a much stronger sense of urgency than intended.

For the first time since he walked in he focused on her, she could see it in his eyes. It was like he was suddenly waking up, looking right at her, seeing her, the rage cleared from his eyes and the briefest trail of a smile crossed his face. "Dawn?" He said it as little more than a whisper barely even a conscious thought. She then saw his face stiffen back up and the swells of rage starting to run back across his eyes. "Did they even bother to tell you what merriment they had in store for me this morning?"

With the mood he was obviously in, she decided to take the tactical approach. "What are you talking about?" Her eyes looked concerned; from times past she was sure Neal would think it was just the calm face she used while interrogating people, but this time around, she was honestly curious to see what got under Tom's skin so badly.

"They shut me out. Completely!"

"Shut you out? What? What are you talking about?"

"The computer system, I can't do a goddamn thing on it without someone else approving it . . . They've made me effectively useless in my own department!"

Neal's eyes rose up and looked over at Randy, who did nothing but stare motionlessly at Tom, which to Dawn indicated a deeper history between these two men. "Is this true, Randy, has Mr. Williams been shut out of the Logiterm system?"

"You're goddamn right he has!" His words were quick, and his tone was tense. Randy Carlson's eyes seemed to almost curl as he stared angrily at Tom Williams.

"I don't believe that was what we discussed, Randy," Neal as ever was trying to be the diplomat, and in this instance it frustrated Dawn completely. Tom knew what was going on, she could tell. His voice sounded hostile, his face even looked it, but the more the conversation went on, the more she noticed the subtler side of Tom's character, the fact he seemed to be in perfect control of his actions. The way he seemed to be intentionally pimping Randy.

"I'm not letting this son of a bitch do it to me again, Neal, not a chance!"

"Gee Randy," Tom said with a rather dry, guttural tone, "is that so?"

"You can keep up with that sass talk all you want Tommy, but it's come to an end this time! Look around ya! That's the goddamn FBI looking into you now, you may have been able to run roughshod over the board of directors, but you ain't gonna be able to do it to them! The jig, as you say, is up! So are you!"

"That's good to know Randy, but can I ask you one last question, you know, for prosperity?"

Dawn, like the rest of the room, was suddenly watching the heated exchange as if they were waiting for a bomb to go off. No one was moving, just watching. Dawn wondered if Tom could intentionally be pulling the CEO's strings so well, or if perhaps her senses were too far off line when it came to analyzing Tom Williams?

"What's that?" Randy looked ready to swing at any second but Tom held his ground, almost taunting him to do it. Fred remained in position, trying to stay between them.

"Does she still taste like me?"

With those six words it all fell apart, just hearing what Tom said and the tone he used made her take a defensive step back, sure of what would happen next. Randy was pure Texan, and everyone knew it. Mentioning a woman seemed to be more than his Texas pride could handle and before Fred Halstead could react Randy thrust a short, quick jab that connected directly into Tom's lower jaw. For Dawn it was like watching it all happen in slow motion, though she could see the actual speed of what happened. Randy's tightened fist plowed directly into the bottom half of Tom's jaw and sent Tom falling back to the floor and the cushion of his own ass. Fred jumped over Randy and pushed him back, a firm, flat palm against his chest coupled with a menacing look on his face telling the CEO to go no further. Neal just scattered as far away from the fight as he could.

Tom hit the ground and Dawn's eyes stayed on him. She knew without looking that Halstead could keep and control Randy; her concern was on what Tom would do next. In her mind's eye, she assumed he'd come charging up some like testosterone-driven male, ready to pound Randy to the ground for the indignity of the punch. She was preparing to run interference for the situation. She was closer to Tom than any of the other agents. Despite the fact that just about every agent she'd ever encountered at the FBI always looked at her as the weak little girl in their ranks, she was more than confident she'd be able to take Tom down before he even realized it happened. Instead she saw Tom simply sit up and look at his attacker with nothing more than contempt. A thin trail of blood was starting to leak from the corner of his mouth and he was raising a hand up to touch gently at his jaw, making sure that no serious harm had befallen him. "Funny, Randy, I'd always been told violence was the last resort of a thinking man's argument, or is it just that there wasn't another option in this case?"

Fred's hand stiffened on Randy's chest, letting him know that he wasn't going to let the man react again as he stayed directly in front of the CEO. It was clear that Randy wanted to come charging into a fight, giving the illusion of a man who had once been a very heavy handed hell raiser in his youth. The short pants coming from his mouth gave away the fact it was several years since fist to cuffs was a part of the ritual of his life. "Get the fuck out of my board room you little cock-sucker!"

Tom struggled to his feet and shook his head in a way to indicate he might still be a little light headed from the blow, "whatever you say, Randy, after all, I'm sure I have some filing left to do downstairs in the office . . . Lord knows that's all you've left me useful for."

"I shoulda fired your ass when I had the chance!"

"That's the thing, Randy," Tom said as he slowly started walking for the door, "You never had the opportunity, and you damn well know it." With that Tom walked out saying, "no matter what you've told this room to the contrary!"

The doors slammed shut and he was gone and the entire room now stared at Randy, Fred most intently of all. He leaned right into Randy's face with the stern look of a career law enforcement officer, "tell me something Randy, when you get all those fancy degree's on your wall, is that to notch off the common sense you fucking lose along the way!?!"

Randy's face which already looked ready to blow from the stress and anger he was feeling inched closer to Halstead's, his voice sounded like heavy foot falls on broken glass, "I beg your goddamn pardon!?!"

"You think he couldn't have had us arrest you for assault if he wanted? You just fucking hit our suspect; don't think for a second his attorney at trial won't try to question our entire investigation now that you've taken a cheap shot at the little punk for some off handed comment! No one will give a shit he taunted you; they'll say the good guys were beating up the suspect. That was about the fucking stupidest thing I've ever goddamn seen! The worst part is, I now have to fill out an incident report, all because you wanted to pull out your dick and show it to the room!"

"What?" He was still panting from the fight that had never really started, but Fred's words were dawning on him. "You're kidding?"

"No," Neal said gravely, "he's not." He took a quick step up to Randy shaking his head in the way a father might do to a small child, "you have no idea how much your little tantrum just hurt our case. Much less put yourself at personal risk if he decides to sue you civilly."

"Fuck!"

"Look," Dawn said rashly as she started to dart forward toward the door, "you can stand around and chastise the Texan all you want! While you're at it rip him a new asshole for taking him off the system and blowing our chance of watching how he works on it, right now I'm going to try for a little damage control!"

"Dawn! What the hell do you think you're doing?" Neal knew she wouldn't answer, which frustrated him even more. Dawn was a calculating woman, and he knew there was always more to her plans than she let on. He also knew she moved so abruptly because he was being left with someone to take it out on. He watched her storm out of the door before turning his attention back to the CEO.

In the hallway she saw Tom leaning up against the small piece of wall next to the closed elevator doors, waiting for the car to open up. The down button already pressed. She came up right behind him and stood silently, waiting for him to feel her presence.

"Come to arrest me?" His voice was a cool monotone that ran smoothly off his tongue.

"I'm not a police officer, Tom."

He turned to look back at her as the elevator doors slowly opened. The blood was smeared under his jaw. He was no longer bleeding, but what bled was enough to make its presence known. "Lucky me." Without another word he stepped inside the elevator.

She moved in right behind him as he pressed the button for the third floor; she could feel her clenched jaw and didn't quite understand why she was so thoroughly frustrated by Tom's actions. She waited quietly until the car doors shut and they started moving down to the third floor. Without warning, she reached over and hit her fist on the "All-Stop" button and the car jerked to a halt between floors; automatically the light in the small car changed from the bright fluorescent's to something darker and more mysterious. Tom tripped on his feet and fell back against the back of the car as it jerked suddenly to a stop, managing only to keep himself on his feet because of his proximity to the elevator wall. He looked up at her like she might be crazy.

"So," she said confidently, "wanna tell me what the hell that was all about?"

It took him a moment to answer, as if he was considering his answer and how much he wanted to reveal. Finally, he simply said, "I can't."

"Fuck your goddamn agreement not to talk!"

"Shit," he said as his hand still lightly rubbed over the obvious sore spot on his jaw, "anyone ever tell you that you talk like a drunken sailor?"

"Don't change the subject, Tom."

"What subject?" His arms were out and his eyes were shut, she could tell he didn't like taking a beating from Randy, he may not have been a body builder or professional fighter, but he wasn't the type of guy to just lie down and take a blow without swinging back. To Dawn this said volumes, it was somehow a part of his plan.

"Who was she, the woman who pissed him off so damn much?"

"Aw, Christ, Dawn . . ." He was shaking his head, not really looking at her, but then his eyes slowly drew open and back to her face, "why should I, am I under arrest!?"

She took a deep step in, getting right into his face, pointing an angry finger right at him that immediately caught his eyes, her voice had slowly been rising with each word she said, but now she wasn't bothering to hold back, "do you want to be!!!? I can arrange for that if you like!"

"Really, what's the charge, getting hit in the face? What's the fine for that? According to you I have the money stashed to pay it, no problem."

"You don't want to play this game with me Tom!"

"It's not a game, Dawn, in case you hadn't noticed, it's my life, a life you and yours think they can just trash the hell up. I'm not playing anything, I'm just reacting to the card's I've been dealt."

"Who's the woman?"

"Who the hell do you think?"

She brought both her hands to her temples and shut her eyes as if trying to fight back a headache, "Tom I just met you, I don't know the in's and out's of your life here at Hil Fed, I have no clue who the woman is."

"What, I thought you said you'd read my file?"

"Someone here?"

"Some investigator."

"Don't push me!" She was looking intently into his eyes when she said it, but then it all became clear, the small little notes in the file, and the off handed comment to Randy. His entire file mentally opened in her head. "You were sleeping with her, weren't you?"

"Who, the woman?" His sarcasm dripped bitterly from his lips, and the drying blood on his chin seemed to illustrate it.

"Laura Netzly, the Vice President of Marketing."

"She wasn't always the VP of Marketing," was all he said as he looked away from her.

"No, according to her file, she used to answer to you, didn't she?" he remained silent as he looked back at her. "Maybe in more ways than one?" He still chose not to answer her, but the look on his face said everything she needed to know. "Tell me Tom, have you made it a habit, dating married women?"

"Am I under arrest, Dawn?"

"No Tom, you're not."

"Then I choose not to answer that question."

"Even if you damn yourself by doing so?"

They were now staring directly into each other's eyes, almost longingly. They were no more than half a foot apart right now, but the distance between their eyes could have easily been mistaken as miles, "why didn't you ever tell Jerry about the other guys you were seeing? I mean, at the end, what the hell does it matter? Just tell him everything, bare your soul, clean it all out. Why carry the guilt around?"

"That's none of your goddamn business!"

"Neither was what happened in the Marketing Department."

"I just witnessed a brawl in an office boardroom over what happened, it's rapidly becoming my business."

"She's married you know, two kids. A boy," he paused for a second, "and a little girl. Her husband's a nice guy, name's Geoff. The little girl's two years old. What happens when it gets out—she sleeps around, huh?"

"You did it, stayed quiet, I mean, to protect her?"

"I did it to protect me."

"From what, a jealous husband?"

"Jesus, Dawn, think, why do you think the credit union dropped the charges they were preparing to file against me? Why do you think they have a signed agreement with me, why do they still have me working here?"

"She recanted, didn't she? Said she might have confused things? The board was satisfied, but your career was ruined, and she got the job you wanted?"

"Close," he said quietly, "she already had the job."

"Because she slept with the CEO?"

"Well, I tell ya, take a look at her sometime, it certainly wasn't her long standing history of work in the Marketing field."

"Do you want to press charges against Randy, for hitting you?"

"No," he said quietly, "what I want to do is fall apart right now."

"What's stopping you?"

"I'm trapped in an elevator with a woman I'm dying to kiss."

She froze, not knowing exactly what to say, feeling a rising heat inside her. She wanted to say something, but the words didn't come. This time it was her who broke their eye contact, tilting her head down and looking away from him. Her left hand delicately touched his chest, while she rested her forehead up against the side of the elevator. He did nothing but stare directly at her, waiting and watching to see what she'd do next.

"That's . . . That's not going to happen, Tom."

"I know." His voice was quiet and still and he closed his eyes and leaned his head back against the elevator wall behind him, feeling her long, extended fingers, slowly starting to close over his chest. In the eerie glow of the elevator light he felt like they were trapped. They stood together, feeling the warmth of each other's bodies for five minutes before she finally propped herself up and away from him.

She looked like she was fighting back a tear, but he couldn't be sure and he knew better than to ask. He watched as she hit the button that restarted the elevator and returned them to the normal lighting. He knew it though, that what he was feeling, he wasn't alone. She was just better at not showing her hand, at least when it came to emotions.

"You're wrong."

She looked back at him, "about what?"

"A lot."

The doors slowly slid open and he walked out, unsure of his destination, moving his hand back to his jaw.

* * *

From the Inside

From the Inside 8.0

March 17, 2000

The week seemed to go by painfully slow, a constant side effect of an ongoing investigation where the real burdens one was faced with was physical evidence that amounted to printouts of digital displays that seemed to go on for miles. Knowing she wasn't the one to go page by page and line by line through the reams of paper, Dawn stayed away from it. She was frustrated not being actively involved, but to her, computer code looked like gibberish. She was better off leaving this part of the process to the computer people they'd brought in. Still, she hated the waiting. She also knew that it was beginning to show, even if just a little.

Since Monday's incident everything remained quiet, though their relationship with Randy Carlson was now somewhat strained. Considering the way both Neal and Halstead lit into him over how he endangered their investigation, she was fairly sure that cooperation from him would be limited at best for the remainder of the investigation. Not that it really mattered to her anymore; the main thing she wanted to use the credit union for was to watch Tom. She wanted to record and track every keystroke he made while at work, her hope was to find him checking his own system making sure that he'd properly concealed everything. At best she hoped he would need to pull information off the Logiterm system. As of right now though, Tom was no more than a glorified file clerk with a business card that happened to say collector. They might as well have fired him, she mused, as she sat at her small kitchenette leafing slowly through the latest report from the computer people. The report itself was six pages long of single-spaced type, all leading to the obvious conclusion that said as of yet no virus code had been found. Obvious, she thought, because if they'd found anything they wouldn't wait to write a report, they'd just call her. She tossed the report across the table and watched as it tumbled slowly to the floor. "How'd you hide the code, Tom . . . How?"

Neal flew back to Sacramento on Wednesday evening and was scheduled to return in the afternoon, he was signing off on their expenses, as well as making the necessary arrangements to set up what would be the largest transfer of funds ever by the NCUA to one of their insured's. There was 320 million of lost money and the NCUA's job was to make sure the general public never felt the burden of that loss. The clock was ticking, and soon they'd have to issue out the money, no matter where they were with the investigation. The only thing at this point that could stop the transfer was if they found the missing money, and they had until the end of June. Until then the credit union would simply ignore the missing money, members wouldn't feel the effects because anymore money was little more than a digital construct of belief. With little more than a quick backtrack of their computer network every account that was missing money was fixed, and the 320 million was transferred over to a General Ledger that was kept negative. Since all the money was insured by the NCUA, what Hil Fed did wasn't illegal, but the fact was over a third of the credit union's membership was using and spending money that at the moment didn't really exist. The credit union had close to two hundred million dollars in liquid reserves and investments, so the likely hood of the sham being exposed to the general public was slim. Still, the government would feel the loss, and certainly the credit union as well, once the story finally broke. Looking down at the fallen report, she thought that June really didn't mean much, but it still lingered all around them. The NCUA would officially seize the credit union and all its assets, liquidate it, and offset the difference. They'd sell off everything, the investments and loans, and then find a new depositor for Hil Fed's members to move their accounts to. Then the great sale would come. They'd auction off computers, servers, desks, and even paperclips if they could find a buyer. Then they'd liquidate any real estate holdings the credit union owned, anything to minimize their loss.

 The end of June, to Dawn, seemed almost an eternity away; the part of her brain that still thought like an FBI agent told her if she didn't have a significant lead within twenty-four hours the case was essentially dead. Tracing money, and the fraud that led to it was a different story. Unlike bloody knives and missing persons there was more of a trail to missing money. More people seemed to be interested in what happened to the money, even above that of human life. It was odd how people reacted to money. Dawn grew up middle class; money was never what she would call abundant, but she never lacked for anything either. She wondered for a moment what it would be like to have 320 million dollars at her disposal, but the number seemed too large. At least the price it would come with would be. To her that much money wouldn't buy freedom, it would only buy a life of worry. Thinking of the money got her back to thinking about the case, and then the headache returned. She was known to get headaches when she had a problem she couldn't work through.

 This case was quickly developing into a very large headache. Right now her head had a slow, dry ache, but she knew that unless something happened, the pain would quickly upgrade to a dry throbbing. For the millionth time she asked herself what she was missing, and for the millionth time no immediate answer came.

"Netzly," she said aloud as she closed her eyes and remembered back to all the notes and memos from her in Tom's employee file. The woman who once answered to him, the woman who later became his boss. A woman he'd once had an affair with The woman who'd tried her damnedest to get him fired, a woman who allegedly slept with the CEO, at least, if she was to believe Tom. She reached across the table and picked up the phone dialing Hil Fed's main line and waited somewhat impatiently until someone from their phone center picked up. The young lady on the line was cheerful and offered a warm greeting that bordered on actual sincerity; Dawn was completely uninterested. "Marketing department please."

A couple of phone clicks later she was speaking to a woman named Corina, who ran the front desk in marketing; rather bluntly Dawn asked to speak to Laura Netzly. Corina did exactly what Dawn expected. In the fast-paced insanity that seemed to have run amok over corporate America, no one wanted to take phone calls, especially if they're the only ones who might be able to solve a particular problem. The person answering the phones on the front line, in this case Corina, was to field and filter as many of the incoming calls as possible. Dawn knew it was coming, and before Corina could get even half way through her litany, Dawn spoke up, "Listen, my name is Dawn McCafferty. I'm a field investigator for the NCUA and I believe that Ms. Netzly might have some information I need. So instead of telling me all the reasons why you can't put this call directly through to your VP, you are going to place my call on hold, get up from behind your desk, barge into Netzly's office, and tell her who I am. Then you're going to tell her that I'll be in her office within twenty minutes to interview her, and if she either needs or wants to verify my identity, she can contact Randy Carlson." Then, before letting Corina get so much as a word in she said, "Thanks, Corina, you've been a big help," and hung up the phone.

As she got up from the table she wondered why she'd been so harsh. Not necessarily with Corina, that would have happened either way, but she wasn't giving Netzly any choice in the matter. Why hadn't she simply called in, played hot and heavy with Corina, and made a reasonable appointment with Netzly? It's what she would usually have done. Was she already siding with Tom? Was that where the hostility was coming from when she thought of Netzly? What was it about this woman that made Carlson take a swing at Tom, and what stopped Tom from swinging back . . . and then refuse to press charges when given the opportunity? Another bit of pain pulsed in her head, another question that didn't seem to make sense.

Too much here was being left unsaid, and she knew Tom wasn't going to say anything, at least not yet. Randy would be especially silent now, but maybe Netzly would be the one to let them in on a few secrets. That was her hope at any rate.

She quickly put on shoes and headed out to her rented car.

As she walked into the Marketing Department, she tried not to think about Tom, tried to clear her head of his words, thoughts, and opinions. If she was going to do this interview she needed to do it as a professional. She needed to enter this room looking for facts that would help her accomplish her ultimate goal, a goal that remained unchanged, to find sufficient evidence to arrest and convict Tom Williams of the largest single heist ever encountered by the NCUA. Corina knew who she was as she entered, her name already circulating, even if the exact reason why she was here wasn't common knowledge yet. People knew, or at least suspected, there was a theft, a large one at that based on how many officials were flooding into the credit union. There were guesses swirling about over coffee stations and water coolers, but no one knew what the magic number was. No one knew they were 320 down. Dawn preferred it stayed that way, at least until the day of the official press conference when they'd have to announce. Until then she liked the cloak of mystery the questions circulating provided her. It tended to make people chatty; they were all hoping Dawn would let slip some torrid little detail. What none of them realized was she used their chattiness to get information out of the people she spoke with; giving away nothing to them she didn't want them to know. Corina looked up at Dawn as she entered and gave a fake but unassuming smile, politely asking how she could help. Dawn smiled back, a power smile, one that said far more than any words would. "I'm here for your boss." She quickly took a deep breath feeling her body tense, making her wonder how much she really believed of what Tom was saying.

Three minutes later, Dawn sat across the desk from Laura Netzly. Appraising her, she noticed a few things; she was a tall, lean blonde with full, pouty lips and deep, dark green eyes that seemed to brighten her entire face. Her dark tan made her lush, long hair seem even blonder. Her face was fairly angular, to the point of being what Dawn would call striking. She was what most of her male friends in life would have called a man-killer. Dawn, in growing up, went through a few man-killer phases herself, but she'd never considered it a defining feature for her. Looking across the thick desk at Netzly told her this was her defining trait. She couldn't help thinking of this woman as a user.

Netzly had a confidence about herself, something that could easily set people off. She was the kind to take charge and not care what the consequences were. In a way that disturbed Dawn a bit, mostly because she could tell that most people could probably easily compare the two of them. The ambitious drive and unforgiving way in which they both set out to accomplish their goals and assignments. The difference Dawn thought was, she hadn't used sex to climb her ladder, she'd used her mind. Netzly was openly a sexual creature; she seemed to almost exude it, even sitting here in front of another woman. She wore her clothes as to show off her slender frame and a skirt that allowed a little too much leg to slip out. Dawn got the sense of this one being a hunter, and to Dawn's eyes that meant she was dangerous.

"So you wanted to see me?" Netzly said politely, looking up at Dawn.

"Yes," Dawn once again held herself back. She was fighting herself from making snap judgments in this scenario they wouldn't do her any good. "I need to ask you a few questions about a former employee of yours."

"How many guesses do I get as to which one?"

Already she was toying with Dawn, which not only helped keep her senses sharp, but also gave Dawn reasons to read things into what she said. She could tell why Tom had both run together and afoul of her. She was what any man would consider beautiful, and she was what any man might consider challenging. Perhaps Tom thought he might contain her, control her even? Or was Tom's goal more base? Without letting Laura sit on her words for more than a second Dawn fired back, "How many do you need?"

"We're talking about Tom, right?"

"Tom?"

"Tom Williams, one of the only two employees of mine who have left since I took over. Tom, the only one to leave my department in shame . . ."

"And innuendo?"

"No," her voice didn't budge, it was something you could tell she wanted to stress, "no innuendo at all."

"So then, Ms. Netzly," Dawn said coolly, "tell me, why did Tom Williams leave the Marketing Department?"

"Because he was a thief, a thief I caught."

"If he was a thief, why wasn't he fired?"

Laura smiled, letting her face show that she actually thought a little something of the woman sitting in front of her. Most of the people coming in front of her hadn't done their homework, this one had. "Tom's a longtime employee, he has a lot of friends here at many different levels of the company, and from what I understand a fairly competent lawyer."

"Good enough to keep a guilty man out of jail?"

"You're the investigator, Ms. McCafferty. Are you telling me that all guilty men go to jail?"

"Not at all, but if you caught him red-handed, forced him out of your department with proof, that would imply to me that he would have been raw meat to the local DA."

"I didn't have a lot to do with Tom's situation, you'd have to ask those questions of the board of directors and Randy who acted as there direct agent."

"You didn't have a lot to do with it? I thought you said you were the one who caught him?"

"Yes . . . ," her voice got a bit scratchy as the first creases wrinkled on her forehead, "what I meant was I didn't have a lot to do with the disciplinary side of it."

"Did you make any recommendations as to what you thought should happen to him?"

"Well, of course."

"And what was that," Dawn asked trying to keep her voice as low key as possible.

"I suggested he should be terminated at once."

"Did you also suggest his actions be forwarded to the DA for possible prosecution?"

"No . . . no I didn't."

"Really, why not?"

The crease on her forehead was growing, Laura didn't much care for the question Dawn was asking, and couldn't quite get a bead on where she might be going. "I—I didn't really know what the proper protocol for something like this was, my main concern was removing him before he caused Hil Fed any irreparable damage."

"Now, as I understand it," Dawn said tamely, "before your promotion Tom used to be your direct supervisor? Did that cause any friction within the department, you rising above him like that?"

"I think it was clear to everyone long before my promotion that I was the most competent and qualified for this position. In fact many people, if asked, would tell you that the only reason Tom Williams looked as qualified as he did in Marketing was because I was there to back him up."

Dawn was trying to study Netzly, read her from the inside out. She was a hunter in her own right, Dawn could tell. A different kind of hunter than Dawn, but the same instincts, they'd just developed in different ways. Dawn knew she was considered hard assed and occasionally bitter, but for her it was from a sense of detachment from the people around her. With the woman in front of her it was about playing people. It was about getting ahead simply to say that she did, she was the kind of woman who had something to prove, and that made her dangerous, at least in Dawn's eyes.

"So," Dawn asked, "you worked closely with him, Mr. Williams?"

"Yes," she said without a moment's hesitation, "very."

"Then why is it you never noticed his thieving before you were placed in charge?"

The look on Laura Netzly's face sunk as the question was asked; she never saw it coming. She'd put herself in a position where suddenly direct questions of her own character could be addressed. Dawn assumed no one on the Board of Directors or Senior Management Team would ever ask such a question; it was something an investigator would look for. And no one seemed interested in tossing Tom Williams to the police back when questions to his integrity were asked. Dawn didn't smile as she watched Netzly's eyes tighten, nor did she give any indication that it was an intentional trap. She just sat there patiently, waiting for Netzly's response.

"I—I," was Netzly's first tentative response as she furiously tried to deliver a reason, "I mean . . . Tom was very good at keeping it concealed, until I actual, I mean, until I was actually overseeing him directly, there would have been no way for me to know what was going on?"

"So, you never went along on any of the business lunches with Tom where he accepted free items?"

"Does this have something to do with the lost money at Hil Fed Agent McCafferty because all of this took place a long time back and frankly I'd be much happier not discussing anything to do with that rather dire part of my early management experience unless absolutely necessary?"

"Actually it does have something to do with what's going on now. My question at least the main one at the moment, why would Hil Fed continue to employ someone they believed to be a thief?"

"I told you already, he had a very good lawyer."

"And Hil Fed doesn't?"

"We have an excellent attorney!"

"Just not as good as Mr. Williams'?"

Laura put her hand out directly in front of her, as if miming she was slamming on a hand brake. "I didn't say that!"

Dawn leaned into the desk just a little, making sure to catch Netzly's gaze intently, "Then why is Tom Williams still working here?"

"There were questions, all right."

"Questions," Dawn asked quietly?

"Questions as to how I gathered my evidence."

"What kind of questions?"

Netzly's eyes tightened down into slits and she stared venomously across the desk, "Am I suddenly a suspect Agent McCafferty?"

"No," she said politely with an almost engaging smile on her face, "but Mr. Williams is."

"Then shouldn't you be asking questions about him instead of me?"

"If Hil Fed had a known thief on their payroll, would you pay out a claim on their behalf?"

"You're saying that unless I confess to blowing the original situation with Tom by being too eager the NCUA may not pay out on our current claim?"

"I'm not saying anything yet Ms. Netzly, right now I'm asking questions."

"The people who were paying Tom off were mostly vendors, good people who's services and products the credit union needed, if we went after Tom in the way we wanted to it would have ruined several of them, it would have made other companies leery of doing business with us. More to the point though, Agent McCafferty, no one working for them would have admitted to any wrong doing as they knew it would only hurt them in both the short and long term. I caught Tom stealing, but had no way to actually prove it. I called him on it, and you know what, he called me a bitch for doing so. I reported the incident and he gets booted out, shipped off to collections where he can play black sheep and whine about how he was so wronged and I got the job he really deserved. A job he would never have been able to handle. I look like the wicked witch and he the tarnished hero, because everybody likes him. The fact is, he was stealing, but there was just no way to prove it. His attorney was willing to drag Hil Fed through the mud for years to come; depositions would have been needed from everyone, current employees, ex-employees, vendors, even family members of employees. It was going to turn horrendously ugly, cost a lot of money and the bottom line came down to the simply realization, if we weren't going to press charges against Tom Williams, his attorney would have filed a case. It was simply more cost effective for the credit union to put Tom someplace where he couldn't cause any real trouble. He was dumped into the unwanted job of a collector, and no one ever guessed he'd last there so much as a month. Collections required real work, something Tom was just not commonly known for. He was a three martini lunch good old boy, the kind you hear about from the past, the way things used to be done when women like us stayed home and raised children instead of going out and being the bread winners. More importantly, the whole situation would have been a Public Relations nightmare."

"So you didn't learn anything from Mr. Williams then? While you were under him, that is?"

"Of course, I did," she said shortly, "Tom did marketing for years, he knew the job, he just didn't seem to have much interest anymore in actually doing it."

Dawn drifted to other topics for awhile, steering away from anything direct, light, fluffy questions she didn't much care to know the answer to, but they soothed Netzly back down. After about a half hour Dawn slumped her shoulders a bit to indicate they were bringing things to a close. "Do you know Randy very well?"

"Randy?"

"Randy Carlson?"

"Fairly well I'd say, I attend most every social function that credit union has, as is my job, which puts us in a lot of situations together."

"Would you classify him as a violent man?"

"Randy? Certainly not."

Dawn nodded her head in agreement, "Would you have any idea then, why he would throw a punch into Tom Williams face right in front of the FBI?"

Netzly didn't breathe as the question was asked, and before answering seemed to spend quite a bit of time thinking about the question. "You'd probably have to ask Randy that, but my guess is he simply wanted to hit him. Randy takes this credit union very seriously, and anyone who messes with it, is messing with him."

"I thought about that," Dawn said as if deeply considering it all over again," but you can't really taste a credit union, can you?"

"I beg your pardon?"

"Right before the incident occurred Tom said something to Randy, he wanted to know if 'she still tasted like him?' Odd, wouldn't you say?"

Dawn was once again starring right across the desk, but this time it was clear that Netzly had no intention of answering that query. "I don't suppose you know of any women that both Randy and Tom dated, do you? Shared?"

"Randy Carlson's a married man, he doesn't date."

"To the best of your knowledge then, Randy doesn't fool around?"

"No," she said in a forced whisper, "he doesn't."

"Well then," Dawn said as she started to get up, "I guess we're all through here."

"I'd walk you out but . . ."

"No need." Dawn was already up and half way out the door, even with her head turned she could feel Netzly's dagger filled eyes stabbing at her from behind as she heard her hand clutching for the phone to call and inform everyone of how terribly Dawn treated her.

Walking out of the office she was sure that the woman she'd just interviewed slept with both Tom Williams and Randy Carlson. That she was also bound and determined to keep both those tidbits a secret, and mostly she could see that Laura Netzly hated Tom Williams.

The question now became, did any of that actually help with the case? Was any of this getting her closer to the truth?

* * *

From the Inside 8.1

March 17, 2000

Neal was off the plane and feeling tight, so tight in fact that when he got off he didn't go directly to the car he'd stashed in airport parking. Instead he went to the small sports bar just inside the airport where his flight landed and ordered himself a tall, cold beer from a local brewery. Neal Johnson wasn't the sort of man who enjoyed being reamed, yet that was what he'd spent the better part of the week having happen. No one wanted to pay out 320 million dollars, and the few superiors he still answered to came down on him in a huff, they wanted to know why he didn't have answers. Why he didn't have the money? When he was going to get it?

He tried to explain the process to them, but they didn't care, all they knew was that they were getting close to having to pay out an astronomical sum of money to a credit union that would have tragic ripples to the mainstream economy, as well as weakening the public trust in credit unions political pressure was mounting. They didn't want that, what they wanted was, 'Neal to do his job."

"Do my fucking job," his voice was bitter as he brought the cool mug to his mouth. He'd lost any hope of getting things under control after he explained Dawn's thought process. They wanted him to press the FBI to make an immediate arrest and let them worry about getting the money. They could hold off paying a little longer if an arrest was made. He told them they didn't yet have enough to arrest; they simply looked at him and told him to get it.

"By whatever means necessary." The bartender looked up at him as he said it, but Neal waived him off. He didn't much like what they said to him, but he understood it. 320 million dollars was a tremendous amount of money, the vast majority of credit unions operating within the nation were starting to hear the news, and the panic was starting. A loss of such a devastating amount would cripple the NCUA, it would publicly smear the good name of credit union's nationwide, and it would force the government to step up and pay out the necessary funds to secure the loss. The kind of devastation paying out 320 million dollars would cause, could cripple the upward financial growth of the entire country for years to come. This kind of blatant computer theft would weaken the public trust of any financial institution, and would probably spell the end of the credit union movement. Everyone back at the main office of the NCUA was worried about that issue more than any other; they spelled it out for Neal very clearly. Once word of this leaked out the banking giants of this world who have for years been laboring to tightly restrict credit union growth by limiting membership ability and placing road blocks against financial opportunities would shift gears. The big banks would abandon their pursuit of legal actions and restrictions; they would instead shift their focus to attack on the credit union industry. They would run huge marketing campaigns saying credit unions would be unable to protect people's money. That in their blatant effort to become "banks," they weren't able to provide a fraction of the necessary security required. In the end, Neal's superiors told him, whether it was true or not, public trust of credit unions would fade quickly against such an onslaught. 'It's been proven time and time again,' they said, 'in research that the average citizen is more concerned about their financial status than their health.' Many large credit unions all but abandoned their initial fields of membership and became just as greedy and self-serving as most banks. Neal could see why his superiors were so concerned about the outcome of this case; he just didn't know what to do about it.

It occurred to him everyone at Hil Fed was frantic to get things accomplished because their jobs were on the line, he hadn't realized until this morning that so was his. If he failed, it was very likely that he could be out on his ass, Dawn too. Not that it would matter to her, with her resume she could get an A-list job investigating somewhere. He was an administrator and had no intention of returning to active fieldwork. That wasn't in his lifestyle anymore, and truth be told, he'd never been very good at it. He suddenly felt like he was under pressure, the kind that breaks men, leaving them shattered and ruined. He wasn't going to be one of those people though, so he sat there with his beer in hands thinking about what he needed to do, and what the obstacles surrounding him were. He tried to think of the best way to push things forward, speed up their timetables, and nail Tom Williams to the wall. One thought kept getting in his way though, *Dawn McCafferty.*

She didn't want to speed things up; she was like a cat with a mouse. She wanted to play Williams and then nail him for everything. Neal's first thought was to force Williams to play the game, he realized somewhere around his third beer that it was up to him. He knew Dawn was a competent investigator, but he was sensing that something was changing in her. The idea that she enjoyed her "date" with the suspect a little more than she should have still rang through his mind as a possibility. He knew nothing out of place happened as they'd closely monitored every step of their evening out, but he couldn't help but wonder if something sparked between them.

At first he'd thought it might just be jealousy on his part, but after Carlson knocked Williams to the ground and she went chasing off after him, he started to wonder. As the third glass of beer ran empty he pulled out his phone and waited for a single carrier beep to allow him to make calls. When it finally beeped he motioned to the bartender for another round and dialed up Marc, his voice was short and terse as he instructed his aide to pick him up. The next number he dialed belonged to the private back office line that was installed in the back of the Hil Fed board room that Fred Halstead was using as his private line. Neal heard the line ring twice before Halstead picked up. The reception bordered on terrible, but Neal wasn't too surprised, he was on a cell phone in the middle of an airport and Halstead obviously had him on speaker.

"It's me," he said into the small mouthpiece, "I'm back from up north."

"Where are you?"

"I'm at the airport, Marc's on his way to pick me up, anything new to report?"

Halstead sighed heavily over the phone, "not really, no. We're monitoring every step Williams takes, we're going over every goddamn e-mail or message board posting he makes, but nothing is leading me to believe we have a case."

"Starting to have second thoughts about him as our boy?"

"Not at all," he said without a moment's hesitation.

"You trust Dawn's instincts that much all of a sudden?"

"No, I trust my own. The guy's guilty as sin on this one, I agree with Dawn, whatever bullshit this place put Williams through in the past soured him to the point where he designed a massive surgical strike against the thing this place cherishes most, their financial assets. She's made me a believer."

Neal shook his head as he watched the bartender placed another beer in front of him, "why is it I sense a 'but' coming in that sentence?"

"But," Halstead with a sense of amusement, "he's smarter than your average thief, he's not looking for thrills, he's looking for revenge, and that makes him a harder nut to crack. We could be forced to chase him for awhile to get what we need. For all we know he threw the money away, after all, he doesn't need it."

"Do you think he has records somewhere?"

"Sure, a scam this complicated? He has to. The program itself would have to leave evidence somewhere. No matter how much you try to delete something off a hard drive, someone who knows what they're doing can get it off. At least in most cases."

He was just holding the glass of dark, amber brew in his hand, looking past it and into the large mirror centered behind the bar, looking at the weary administrator he'd somehow become. "Think there's any chance of us getting a warrant to search and take his hard drive?"

"With what we have right now? Not likely."

He took a long hit at his beer, listening to the silence on the other end, wanting Halstead to wait for his response. "Tell me something, Fred . . ." he paused again, taking another deep drink.

"Yeah?"

Neal closed his eyes, not wanting to look at his own reflection as he continued his conversation, "have you ever illegally entered someone's home before?"

"Neal, can I ask you a question?"

"Go right ahead Fred."

"Have you been drinking?"

"You said it yourself; we need to take a look at Williams' hard drive."

Neal could hear Fred Halstead nervously shifting around in his chair back on the fourth floor of the credit union, "I think we would be better off continuing this conversation face-to-face Neal . . . not over an obviously unsecured line."

"I should be back at the credit union in less than an hour."

"We'll meet then."

"Oh, and Fred," he said before letting Halstead disconnect, "let's not mention this to Dawn, OK?"

* * *

From the Inside 8.2

March 17, 2000

Anna Marks stepped away quietly; wanting to make sure she wasn't heard. It wasn't difficult; the man she was standing behind didn't seem to be paying much attention to anything other than whatever was going on inside his own head. Anna had been sent up from the depths of the research department on what she was told was an extremely urgent and private matter. She knew what she held in her hands; it was account statements for a Hil Fed corporate card. She knew because it was one of her job duties over the past couple of days pulling these statement copies. Two copies of each statement were being pulled off microfiche, one copy was directed to go to the investigative team up on the fourth floor, the other was sent directly to Randy Carlson's office marked private.

The corporate card in question had for over a decade belonged to Thomas Williams, and was a necessary part of his job function down in the marketing department. Not many people outside of management were given corporate cards, but some job functions at the credit union proved to be notable exceptions. Tom's job in marketing was one of those, and now the FBI wanted to know where every dime he ever spent went.

For the Research Department that meant going back over the last twelve years and getting copies of each and every one. The two manila envelopes she held in her hands at the moment were each about four inches thick and stuffed about as tightly as they could get. Her boss told her to walk them right up and hand-deliver the package to either Dawn McCafferty or Fred Halstead. She'd told her boss no problem and walked right up the stairwell to the fourth floor.

Walking into the boardroom was a little surprising for her, no one had been allowed in since the NCUA and FBI took over. They'd somehow managed to clutter up the entire place with people working furiously, going over what looked to be reams and reams of computer print outs. From what Anna heard the Information Systems Department didn't look any better. Walking into the room she put on her small, fragile country fed farm girl look, the one she threw up anytime she started to feel overwhelmed and asked one of the men with a gun slung on the back of his belt where she could find either McCafferty or Halstead. The agent grunted that Halstead was in the back office and that he didn't think McCafferty was in yet. She thanked the man with a bright, toothy smile and gingerly walked to the back of the boardroom. It was as she was started to enter the office that she froze in her tracks.

"Have you ever illegally entered someone's home before?"

She didn't know who the man on the speakerphone was, but she realized quite quickly that this wasn't a conversation she was supposed to hear. Instinctively she backed herself out of the doorway, but kept her body close to the door that wasn't quite closed, listening in to what was said. She could hardly believe it when she heard Tom's last name mentioned.

When the line disconnected she slowly stepped backward and headed to the front double doors. She stepped back up to the man with the gun and handed him the two files. "He's on the phone," she said meekly, "I didn't want to disturb him, could you give him these for me."

The agent looked up and nodded, smiling at her in a way that indicated how cute he was thinking she was. She smiled back, blushing brightly and back-stepped her way out of the boardroom, and kept backing up until she hit the wall opposite the entrance. She stood there for far longer than she should have, and for a moment she honestly couldn't move. Tom's name and the word "illegally" kept dancing though her head in a way that was quickly making her sick to her stomach.

Years ago, if someone asked her she would have declared loudly that she hated Tom Williams for what he did to her, anymore though she didn't blame him for their break up.

She and Tom shared what many would call a whirlwind romance. Something Tom was famous for back then. That was nine years ago though when they'd first met at one of the numerous company functions. They'd kept their affair a secret from everyone as Tom disclosed to her that the previous employee's he'd dated had all been the focus of the entire credit union's attention. She knew he wasn't exaggerating, in the five months she'd already worked for Hil Fed at that time she'd seen firsthand how their intricate rumor mill worked. No one was spared and any tidbit of gossip, no matter how small or unimportant, was quickly shuttled from office to office, branch to branch. Anna was still new to the city and didn't know a lot of people; she at that time was incredibly shy and didn't get out much. She'd heard rumors about Tom, rumors that told her he'd been a bit of a player around the credit union's younger, blonder employees for years and years, but he was the one who finally started talking to her. The only one who seemed to go out of his way to be nice, even if it was just a casual hello as they passed in the hall.

When she'd first started at Hil Fed she found that most of the branches had clicks within it, and these clicks weren't really altogether that friendly. Her first job was as a regional floater, which meant she didn't know from one day to the next which branch she'd be working at. She went wherever they told her to go. That meant she rarely got to meet people or talk with anymore for very long. She was an outsider, even as a regular employee. Tom walked up to her one day while she was sitting at the lunch table and said hello. He hadn't come on like a dime store Casanova; instead he simply spoke to her about meaningless things. It made her feel at ease and she began to talk with him more and more. In talking with her he realized that she hadn't seen much of San Diego and he started to invite her places, all very casual. Not as a date, not at first at any rate. Just places he thought she might enjoy seeing. Over the course of a few meals she decided she didn't care about Tom's reputation, and entered into a sexual relationship with him. In her heart she thought she might be able to change him, even though her mind told her otherwise. She'd been hurt when after just two months they began to drift apart, she'd tried to cling but that only seemed to make Tom uneasy, pushing him further and further away. Eventually he just stopped calling, and they began to only speak at work. For years she resented it, but anymore she was seeing a good man who honestly loved her and she just couldn't hold onto the hate she once kept for Tom. She'd known his reputation and she'd proceeded forward anyway.

She took the stairs instead of the elevator, moving downward, in her mind headed back to the research department on the second floor, but at the same time knowing that wasn't really where she was going. She swung back and out of the stairwell and down the hall past the boardroom and opened the doorway and slowly moved into the room. She walked in with purpose and headed right to his desk. He looked up and she could tell there was a twinge to his face upon seeing her, old memories she suspected. She continued to move forward without stopping and then sat down at the chair by his desk without another word. She felt tense and didn't really know what to say, or if she should even be saying anything at all. Looking over at him she saw him force a quick smile and say, "Hi."

She leaned in close to his ear, and he willingly leaned into her, for a moment it was just like old times, then she whispered, "can I talk to you . . . privately . . . It's important."

Tom Williams looked at her and nodded, he could tell something was the matter, but he suspected she had just found out he was a suspect and wanted to wish him well. He smiled as gently as he could and told her, "you bet." He looked over at the others in the office and shrugged, once he would have told them he was going to take a break, but anymore he wasn't doing any real work anyway, and he knew they didn't really care about his comings and goings, so he just stood up.

With that, they both headed for the door.

*   *   *

From the Inside 8.3

March 17, 2000

Tom came back into the office with a nervous twitch about him, feeling pale and scared. He couldn't believe what he'd just been told, and he wasn't quite sure what to do about it.

He stood in the office as his coworkers looked on, they spoke to him but his mind was far too gone to listen. If they were making any noise, speaking with any volume, he couldn't tell.

He looked up at Samantha and asked to borrow her cell phone, seeing the strange look on his face she quickly held it up for him and nodded. Popping the small phone out of its case and began punching in the number. He had to assume all of his lines were tapped, especially his work phone. On the other end his friend Bob picked up the phone.

"Hey buddy," he said quickly and very forced, "do you still have that key I lent you to my condo?" After listening on the line for a second Tom began to smile, "great, here's what I need you to do, go pick up Eric and . . ."

They spoke for about ten minutes and then Tom hung up and dialed the second of the three calls he needed to make.

* * *

From the Inside 8.4

March 17, 2000

What Dawn really wanted was a drink, Southern Comfort on ice immediately came to mind, but she was still in the credit union boardroom on the fourth floor. Night fell and a quick look at her watch told her it was rapidly approaching seven. The report she held said it all. The two agents down in the Cayman's ran into the usual hassles. Banks down there didn't like to divulge anything, strong-arming tactics and threats eventually led the bank manager to step out to an early dinner and speak to the agents, off the record, at a slight cost to the FBI slush fund.

The bank manager claimed the tapes for the day in question, when the woman came in to withdrawal the money were already erased, so there was no photographic evidence of the stolen money being removed. The best he could do is give his very rough description, his way of making the federal agents disappear. Federal agents hanging out in front of a Cayman Island financial institution was never good for business. So he threw the agents a bone, and gave them all he ever intended to release to them.

His description of the woman who came into to acquire the funds was that she was blonde. The exact report read, "Thin, attractive, and blonde." He'd said she had a dark tan with light long blonde hair that made the teller at the desk take notice. The manager refused to sit with an artist to do a rendering, and refused to ever identify the woman if ever apprehended. In any case though, it was now very clear, Tom had help. Her suspicion confirmed.

The fact that it was a woman bothered her, more than she wanted to admit. It made sense though; who else would Tom trust to take that much money other than someone he loved.

Just the thought of it made the taste of bile rise up in her mouth. She felt foolish now, she was being silly. He was a suspect, not a prospective suitor. She knew she needed to pull herself together because this wasn't helpful.

She sighed loudly and looked over her shoulder and out into room. She wasn't alone, there were two techs sitting on the other side talking with an FBI agent. They were leisurely sitting as if they didn't have anything better to do with their lives. "The other guy still at Williams' house?"

The FBI guy looked up and over at her nodding, "Yeah, seems to be sitting there watching TV, shows no sign of leaving . . . at last check in anyway."

"How long was last check in?"

"Twenty minutes."

Dawn pushed away from her seat, getting up and heading for the door, "I'll be here at least a couple more hours, I'm gonna grab a cup of coffee." She left the room without asking if they wanted anything.

She slowly drifted down the hall trying to fit all the pieces into place; this was all supposed to be so easy and now it was all so confused. The interview with Laura Netzly seemed to be messing with her thoughts. The more she put things together, the more she understood why Tom was looking to get even. She was almost to the point where she agreed with him; the downside to it all was that even if he was morally justified in taking his revenge, he chose the wrong way to do it. He broke the law. He got the NCUA and the FBI involved, and that meant he would go to jail. She just had to find the right way to get his sorry little ass on the hook.

Whether she wanted to do it or not was immaterial, it was her job, and it would get done.

She walked down the hall and curved into the break room and looked over at the very empty coffeepot. It took a few minutes to navigate the room, to find out where the coffee and filters were kept and get a new pot percolating. As she was doing it she looked out of the thick, glass panel window and saw the stars. Faint against the light radiating out from the heavily industrial area she was currently situated in, but there none the less. She stepped over to the glass, placing her palm up against it and stared up. She couldn't remember the last time she stopped to look up at them. In the background she could hear the pot starting to brew the tasteless office coffee that seemed to find its way into every corporation across America.

Back when she'd been a child starring up at the stars was her escape. What she did to help clear her head and think straight before going back into the house to face her parents and whatever medicine might be coming her way. It was as she got older it was taken away from her; Jerry never liked sitting still that long outdoors. He didn't see the beauty in the stars she did. When they'd lived together her chances to look at the stars dwindled, if she just sat outside quietly, he would go out and disturb her, take away the magic of the moment. After awhile she just stopped looking. She found that running was an activity that Jerry didn't much care for either, but one he at least understood. She shifted the focus for her thoughts for a five to six mile daily run. Looking out of the window, she couldn't remember why she forgot to stare upward after she and Jerry ended.

Suddenly her eyes flushed as a wave of memories swept over her, a thin smile creased her lips as she remembered back. She was hardly aware when the overhead lights went off and left her in the dark. She felt the other presence in the room, but didn't want to be disturbed just yet, so she just kept starring forward, into the night. Slowly the fake music HIL Fed funneled into their building was being turned up to the point where it lightly filtered through the room and she heard the sound of footsteps behind her. The footsteps weren't coming directly up to her though; they crossed over to where the coffeepot sat on the counter. She changed her focus in the mirror, the best she could to make out the man's shape.

"They're easier to see in the dark." It was a soft spoken statement, not a question, and not an invitation to speak further. The voice told her what she needed to know, the man behind her wasn't one of the NCUA techs, it was Tom Williams.

"Yeah," she said quietly, "they're beautiful." She wanted to scream at him; wanted to be mad. She understood why he stole the money, but the woman bothered her. She wanted to ask him who she was, but she knew he wouldn't answer. All she'd hear was another denial, and she just didn't have the strength or fortitude at the moment to go through another round with him on such a pointless subject. She also knew she shouldn't reveal she knew about the woman, it would only hurt her case, as it would give him the chance to create another future alibi.

"You should see them out on the water, at night when you're far enough away from the city . . . far enough that the lights don't dull the starlight, it's . . . It's amazing. It's like looking straight into the eye of infinity."

She kept her eyes focused on his dark reflection, her smile faded as she began to think about him all over again. She didn't want to; she wanted to stay mad about the woman. Something in the way his voice sounded stopped her though. She liked talking with him; he seemed different than anyone she'd ever met before. She was on the fringe of wondering what if? "You sail at night a lot?"

"When I can."

He was doing something at the counter, but she couldn't quite tell what and she didn't want to turn and face him at the moment. She heard a cup move against the counter and assumed he was making himself a cup. "Isn't it dangerous at night?"

"Sure, but if you know what you're doing, it's not too bad. Cream or sugar?"

He was getting ready to make her coffee; she'd assumed he'd only get his own cup. Once again Tom was proving himself different than most men she knew. She reminded herself about the blonde and all the other secrets he was keeping. She could keep her secrets also. She thought about the coffee and said, "This late? Both, please, healthy quantities too. Last time I drank it black this late I was up half the night."

She heard him rattling around, stirring sugar and powdered creamer into an empty Hil Fed mug, and then through both his reflection and the sound of his footfalls she could tell he was approaching. Slowly, with a gentle hand he reached the mug around her body to where she could easily take it from him. "You're working late tonight?"

She smiled at the gesture, as well as the comment. "And I will Tom, until the case is done," she said taking the mug. She noticed he stayed behind her about three steps. Even though he moved his arm back he wasn't trying to crowd her, their dark reflections merged against the dark of the room.

"Does that mean you're the one following me home tonight?"

"I've already paid my time doing recon, Tom, now other people get stuck with it. I run a desk anymore, not much else." It was a lie, and she felt guilty saying it, at least until she thought of the blond.

"You see a lot of stars from that desk?"

"Not especially, no."

"Hmmmmm, now that's a shame."

She wanted to joke with him, ask him questions about star watching from the water, but it wasn't prudent and she refused to start letting herself act like some foolish little schoolgirl with a crush. The silence however was killing her. A tactic she'd used so many times throughout her career was now like a huge weight around her neck, she needed to hear words, anything to fill the vacuum of darkness and piped music. "What are you doing here so late," she asked taking her first sip from the cup? The coffee was well blended and the cream and sugar didn't overpower the naturally bland taste of the coffee.

"Maybe I'm looking for you."

"Looking to confess are you?"

"Not to what you'd like to me to, no."

"Then why are you still here, your schedule says you got off a couple of hours ago?"

"Word's out that you went to see Laura today."

"Afraid I dug up some of your dirty little secrets from her?"

"Curious if I'm going to be arrested tonight."

"Does she know something incriminating about you?"

"No, she doesn't, but she can be very convincing when she needs to be."

"You under estimate my judgment of character, Tom, I'm not so easily swayed."

"So, no arrest tonight then?"

"Not that I know of, not yet."

"Not yet," he said questioningly, "does that mean you still think I did this?"

"We keep crossing over the same old topics Tom, I know you did it, I just have to prove it."

"Then can I make my last request, before everything starts to get ugly?"

"Ugly? You mean your arrest?"

"I can make a request then?"

She sighed; she didn't want to play this game, especially not today. Visions of blonds were dancing through her head, and in every image it was Tom dancing with them. What they danced on was a bed of money. "I make no promises, but you can ask."

"What's the song playing right now, over the speakers?"

Dawn stopped and listened, the music slightly off from its original version, but a sweet, simple song from the days of her youth. "haven't heard that in ages?" More old memories surfaced in her mind, memories of being with people she cared about at times in her life when she was still allowed to have fun.

"Wanna dance?"

"Tom . . ."

"Didn't ask if you would," he said as he took a step closer to her. Close enough that she felt his presence directly behind her. His voice softened to a whisper. "I asked if you would like to?"

"I love this song," she said surprising herself at the honesty, not wanting to go down this route with him, but at the moment not knowing how to stop herself. She was feeling him without actually touching him, listening to the music and sensing the darkness. "Yes." She stepped back again, against his body, rolling her head back on his chest, feeling as his hands reached up to her arms, taking her into him as he lifted the cup from her hand.

Tom took another step in and moved his hands into position, after he sat the coffee cup down on the edge of the windowsill. Suddenly she was dancing with him, alone in a dark room in the center of the very problem that lay between them.

They moved as one and she easily fell to the sway of the music. "It will you know," he said softly.

"What?"

"Get ugly."

"What makes you say that Tom?"

She felt him nestle in a bit closer as she found herself wrapping her arms around his neck, making sure to keep her face tucked down on his chest, not wanting to give him any kind of sign that he should try anything more than dance. She liked him, and the more she learned about him the more she found herself caring. She didn't really want to see Tom Williams spend the rest of his life in jail for getting even with the people who wronged him, but it wasn't her call to make. She certainly wasn't going to have his conviction over turned because of anything that might happen between them. In fact she knew she needed to break away from his arms and stop this foolishness she was indulging, but she couldn't quite bring herself to do it. Instead she just pressed her head in tighter against his chest and found her hands slowly moving up and down his back. The blond in the Cayman's didn't matter at the moment; the part of her mind that usually remained silent was starting to speak. It was telling her there was more to all of this then met the eye, that she was still missing something crucial to understand everything. Tom's secrets ran deep, but she would get to the bottom of them. It just wasn't going to happen tonight.

"It just will," he said, no longer caring about anything else other than the moment. Tomorrow everything between them would change; tomorrow it would all go downhill. He'd already made sure of it. He just prayed she wasn't a part of it.

* * *

THE BREAK

The Break 9.0

March 18, 2000

"Give us your position," Halstead said into the small hand held microphone as he sat in the camper the FBI was using as their portable command center, not far from the suspect's condo. Behind him, in the midst of the five other FBI agents who were gathered, Neal Johnson stood impatiently, thinking about Dawn and how upset she'd seemed all day, especially when he and Fred Halstead disappeared without telling why. She could tell they were up to something, and didn't like being kept out of the loop. Better she was left out of this, he thought.

"I'm within fifteen yards of target, sir," the radio hissed. Halstead lifted his gaze above the radio to look out over the canyon that sat between his makeshift command center and the condominium complex where Tom Williams lived. The decision was made as soon as Neal got back from the airport that they would make a soft entry, a private matter between Neal and Halstead, deciding that no one else needed to know. They'd send an agent up to the rear patio of Williams' condo and let him judge whether or not he could make a fast entry without being detected. They knew it would have to be at night, but ever since they'd started to watch him he'd been staying home most evenings. They assumed their best bet would be to try and get into his home in the small window of darkness between Tom leaving the office and his arriving home. They'd even imagined creating some kind of diversion for him to help give their agent more time. That's when they heard Tom Williams use his phone earlier in the day saying he'd be meeting his friend Bob for dinner that evening. He called ahead of time to ask what kind of wine he should bring, and whether or not he should bring any DVDs along to watch. With Williams' Saturday night plans made, the FBI made theirs as well while listening to his recordings.

Just after dark they watched from afar as Tom's Corvette pulled out from his garage and drove off. They followed him at a discrete distance, as Fred Halstead and Neal Johnson remained in the small command center. They waited for their tail to check in, saying that Tom was well on his way to Rancho Bernardo, an upscale community a good drive up the 15 freeway, and they listened to the small gush of rain that fell from the sky. They knew their opportunity was now.

The man on point was named Andy Crestin, and this wasn't the first time he'd entered a private residence quickly. He moved through the brush filled canyon between the command camper and the suspended back porch of Tom Williams' patio. Andy was dressed all in black and moved carefully, the closer he got to the large condominium complex the more cautious he became. It was only 7:00 p.m. and that meant everyone at the unit would still be up, so the possibility that someone might look out and see the man moving through the canyon existed. Andy wasn't terribly worried about this though because he knew the men back in the camper were scanning the police band, listening for any calls of a suspicious man in their general area. If the call came through, he was to turn tail and run, getting back to the Command Center as quickly as possible.

For Andy, it seemed like a fairly easy assignment. Similar to a dozen other jobs over the past few years, quietly in, quietly out. He'd get through the canyon, lift up onto the suspect's patio, pop the seal on the rear glass door, move quickly through the house to the room containing the computer and log onto the Internet using the suspects own password. There he would tap immediately in to a predetermined Web site where the government would effectively take over the computer and do a complete down load and copy every file contained within. The process was estimated to take about twenty to thirty minutes, and he would have that long to do a quick search of the residence, looking for anything else that might prove useful. It was a simple job; nothing would be taken, just noted. The one person who could catch him was on his way up north and being closely watched. Andy couldn't understand while Halstead was so tense; to his way of thinking this was a cakewalk.

Halstead peered out from the open door of the trailer, looking out with magnified night vision glasses, keeping a constant vigil on Crestin's position. Behind him he could hear Neal tapping nervously with his fingers against a card table they'd been set up inside. He wanted this part to be over with.

* * *

The Break 9.1

March 18, 2000

Andy's fingers gripped onto the rail of Williams' patio and he quickly flipped himself over, moving his tight, hard body in a controlled way over the edge as not to make a loud impacting sound when he landed. It burned a little as he did the maneuver, but it was a hard position to contort into when wearing a field pack and side arm

Lying still on the floor of the patio he waited for the go ahead. This was the part where everything could be lost. A strange man moving around a dark canyon was one thing, but it's a whole other matter when he starts to move into someone's home. It was a possibility that someone spotted him in the canyon and instead of calling it in right away would wait, watching him to see what his intent was. Andy knew that if anyone was going to make the call, it would be now. So he stayed still, not wanting to make any kind of additional noise, keeping himself alert and ready, just in case he needed to leap down and get back to the camper.

In a high exposure position minutes feel like hours, and to keep himself clam he began to silently mouth old nursery rhymes. After an eternity of time that actually only lasted five minutes he heard Halstead's voice in his ear, "do it."

With that Andy stood quietly and went to the door and pulled out a small muted motor to work at the back door screws where it sat near the frame. To do this quietly required skill and a proper placement of weight against the heavy door. The last thing he wanted was the mammoth piece of glass to come crashing down on him once he'd freed it. On his wrist he could see a dim red digital display telling him how long he'd been on the patio. It read ten minutes, twenty-seven seconds. Once inside he'd give himself sixty seconds to locate the computer, two to boot it, and thirty seconds to get online and to the Web site. After that he'd have thirty minutes to investigate and repair the back patio door, and then maybe another ten to completely erase his presence from ever being felt. Making his maximum total exposure time a little less than an hour. He knew that was a long time, and at any point the call could come saying Williams' was in route, and knowing this he worked harder at the door. He wanted out in less than fifty minutes, less than forty-five if possible.

The moment he felt the door pop he called it in, a dark heavy whisper as he disappeared into the condo. In his ear he heard Halstead say, 'good job,' but now wasn't the time to respond. He moved into the living room and huddled up just long enough in the small alcove between the couch and the now open glass door to put on his night vision glasses. Suddenly the darkness of the room came alive, shapes were everywhere. Andy took a quick, deep breath and let his sense adjust to the new settings they were experiencing, and then slowly started moving forward.

Moving through the room he stayed close to the ground, a force of habit from having entered way too many dangerous places in his career. He'd been shown a blue print layout of the condo and from using heat sensors in previous nights they knew exactly which room the suspect's computer was in. He twisted the corner to enter into what Halstead referred to as Williams' home office and saw the computer on a large component desk. To Andy's way of thinking, everything was moving along just fine.

It was then the lights came on without warning and he went momentarily blind, the sudden light burning his eyes with a searing pain.

His hands instinctively pulled up to cover his eyes, knocking the night vision glasses off his head and sending them falling to the floor with what seemed, to him, like an earth shattering thunk, a low hiss escaping his lips from the pain. Halstead's voice was stern now over the earpiece, wanting to know what the hell he was thinking turning on the lights, but before Andy could answer to declare his innocence he felt something hit him hard in the back, taking the wind out of him and sending him face first to the floor.

Andy's face went down flat onto the thin, neatly woven carpet and he felt himself coughing wildly as he tried to gasp, getting air back to his lungs. His body was trying to catch up to what was happening, but his mind was as sharp as ever, and he knew he was in trouble. Things had gone terribly wrong, and now all he could do was damage control. In this case that meant getting out of the area by any means necessary, and to his thinking that meant the side arm, holstered to his right side. It would be tricky, his eyes still couldn't see a thing other than bright circles of light, but he'd have to play it off. As he started moving his hand to this side he heard the hammer pull back on a heavy revolver. He knew it was revolver because they had a sound all their own when the hammer went back. A sound he'd learned years before at range training. It was, to his ear, a sobering sound. He froze his hand where it was, and he listened closely to the voice that followed.

"Don't even think it," the voice said, "move your hands out and as far away from your body as you know how. The Jig, as they say, is up."

Andy did as he was told and heard the voice add, "you lose."

* * *

The Break 9.2

March 18, 2000

"Oh shit," Neal said as he bolted up from his chair, "was that Williams!?!"

Halstead was running into the camper and killed the private communication pod that was supplying sound to Crestin, he looked fit to be tied and he was already starting to yell out orders with a sense of urgency, feeling already what was coming next. "You, dial Williams' phone now! NOW!"

Neal jumped into Halstead's face. "What the hell just happened!?!"

"Get on the line to the tail; have that damn corvette pulled over for something, anything! I want to know who's in it . . . because it's sure as hell is not Tom Williams!"

"Why did you cut the com line?"

"Why do you think, Neal? We don't right to be in there, we're fucked and this is damage control!"

"Shit," Neal looked at his hands and saw they were shaking, almost violently. "what do we do!?!"

"Do?" Halstead looked back out the open door to the trailer, staring briefly at the five FBI men who were suddenly frozen in place looking at him, trying to decide if any of them would still have a career with the bureau tomorrow. "Send the closest unit we have to his front door, now, we're making an arrest!"

Neal was screaming loudly, his hands flapping dangerously in the air as his skin turned deathly pale, "we have nothing to charge him with!"

"That doesn't really matter much anymore!"

One of the agent's chimed in at that point, "Suspects line is busy, Sir."

"What the hell does that mean?"

"Oh," Halstead said with a deep, regretful sigh, "that would just be our man calling the police, unless I miss my guess."

* * *

The Break 9.3

March 18, 2000

The First car the San Diego Police Department sent wasn't fast enough to beat the San Diego Union-Tribune reporter that arrived on the scene, nor the photographer who showed up just moments after the reporter. They did however beat the television news by about three and a half seconds.

By the time the first FBI car arrived it was pretty much a full three-ring circus.

Halstead, Neal and the other FBI agents sat listening to the police scanner in a hushed awe. Somehow Williams knew what they were planning, and out flanked them. The taps on Tom's phone would reveal the first call was made right after Tom gave his warning to Andy Crestin. That call however was not to the police. The first call out went to the cell phone of the reporter who was the first to show up on the scene. A contact Tom made years ago while working community relations at Hil Fed. The first call was twelve seconds long and consisted of a single word, Tom saying, "now!" A clear sign that the reporter's presence was prearranged and his close proximity to Tom's Condo, in Halstead's eyes, just confirmed it. The second call took place a heart beat after the first one ended and was directed to Tom's neighbor, three doors down, who happened to be a Santee Sheriff. He responded to Tom's call by running over in a pair of shorts, a tank top, flashing a badge and wearing an officer's belt. The neighbor came charging in, cuffing and disarming Andy Cretsin allowing Tom to make his third call to a local television station, telling them he just caught the FBI breaking an entering to his home. Only then did Tom stop to call the police and lodge an official complaint, promising to follow up with the State's Attorney Monday morning.

The police moved in and Tom's neighbor officially turned the intruder over to the San Diego Police Department, all under a fury of flashing lights of a camera crew that was rushing to take in as much of the scene as they could. Not to mention Tom taking a Polaroid of the man himself. All of his neighbors stepped out from their homes to watch the flurry of activity happening in their own quiet cul-de-sac. Tom just smiled as he stepped in front of the camera and began to give a statement.

While a large part of his statement was hearsay, the news media happily filmed it all, and as the police were dragging away Crestin, Tom produced a glass in a plastic bag, telling the news people he'd pulled the glove off the man he'd found breaking into his home to get a set of the man's prints, on his own, to ensure justice was really done.

By eleven o'clock, Halstead's cell phone was ringing like mad. Neal had already shut his off and simply sat and watched as Fred Halstead began to explain what happened again and again, and again. Neal listened to the scanner, hearing someone say Williams' lawyer arrived on the scene.

The agents Halstead sent to arrest Tom were called off, and the corvette was never actually pulled over. Neal assumed it was in fear over what his lawyer might do, considering the way the night had already gone.

Tom's face was the lead story on every local channel that night and Neal watched solemnly, feeling his gut twist as he heard Tom's words over and over in his head as he talked loudly about being wrongly accused of stealing 320 million dollars from the Hillsborough Industrial League Federal Credit Union.

The theft was no longer a secret; the suspect and crime were now public, and tomorrow, he knew, it was only going to get worse.

* * *

Saving the Case

Saving the Case 10.0

March 20, 2000

"My name is Marshal Elliott, and as of this morning the Federal Bureau of Investigation has officially taken over the case of the 320 million dollars stolen from the Hillsborough Industrial League Federal Credit Union at the early part of this month. Up until now, the case was being handled by the NCUA with only minimal assistance from our agency..."

The swirl of flashes didn't seem to faze the silver-haired man wearing the dark, pin-striped suit who stood before the podium set up on the steps of the Justice Department. It was just a whisper after 9:00 a.m. Monday morning, and right on his cue Marshal Elliott stepped out from the closed doors and addressed the media that were hungering for an official statement since late Saturday evening. Since the FBI got caught breaking the law. The man before the media was a highly decorated agent with over thirty years of experience with the FBI, a man who seemed to show no fear at the pack of camera-happy dogs that stood before him.

Questions were fired out and he answered them all with a charm and grace no one expected, but in the end very few questions were really answered. Ellictt having learned a long time ago how to speak and give appeasing answers while really saying nothing at all.

After thirty minutes, he turned on a stiff heal and walked away from the media spotlight and retreated to a meeting room within the building. Inside, he found Neal Johnson and Dawn McCafferty waiting. Each had cups of coffee in front of them that weren't being touched, and any fool could see that they weren't talking to each other; in a very noticeable way.

Stepping into the room, he shut the door and walked over, taking a seat as he unbuttoned his suit coat. "I suppose it's not too surprising for either of you to hear that the NCUA will no longer be point on this." He watched them silently for a moment, gauging their reactions. Neal closed his eyes in shame while Dawn just shook her head in reserved anger. "No," he said, "I suppose it isn't."

He leaned back into the stiff chair and pulled out a small notebook from his inside pocket, and then fished a pen out from the other side. "Mr. Johnson," he spoke with a reserved, fatherly tone, "at this point we will not be placing you under arrest, though I would advise you to get on a flight home tonight and stay put in your residence awaiting whatever disciplinary action the NCUA decides fit for you. I might also add that if you are not already a religious man, you might want to take up some immediate prayers, because if we cannot prove your Mr. Thomas Williams guilty of this crime, charges might indeed be filed at a future date against you. Do you understand this, sir?"

He could tell by looking at Neal that he was fighting back tears. "Yes," came a weak voice. A deep breath came next, and then Neal looked up through pooling eyes, "what about Fred?" Elliott thought a bit more of Neal here, wanting to believe his concern was genuine, but somehow suspected that Neal's real thought was whatever fate Fred Halstead faced wouldn't be too different from his own.

"Mr. Halstead has been arrested, because it was he who gave the order and made the official decision to knowingly break the law, at your suggestion certainly, but the order came from him. Worse still, he ordered another agent under his command to break the law in the name of the Bureau. That won't be tolerated I'm afraid."

"What happens to him?"

"Mr. Halstead's career with the bureau is over. His new concerns will be staying out of jail. You might also wish to consult an attorney. Mr. Johnson, undoubtedly your name will come up at his trial."

Elliott watched as Neal's head fell into his hands, no longer able to hold back the tears flooding down from his eyes. He watched the broken man cry for a moment before finally saying, "You are excused now, Sir."

Neal got up silently and stumbled out of the room, knowing his life was suddenly in ruins. His career was over, and any hope of finding another in a similar profession would be laughable. Not having a clue how to start over at his age, he left Dawn alone with Elliott, too lost in his own destruction to worry about what would befall her. "Ms. McCafferty."

"Mr. Elliott."

"So far this morning, you've been extremely quiet. I would think a woman in your position would want to be proclaiming her innocence in this affair rather loudly."

"I didn't think it would matter. Up until Saturday, I was under the impression this was my investigation. Therefore, I have to take responsibility on everything that happens on it."

"Both men, in their statements, indicated you had nothing to do with the decision, and in fact knew nothing about the illegal entry. Tell me, Ms. McCafferty, why do you think they didn't tell you about it?"

"Because they knew I never would have allowed it."

"Mr. Johnson was your superior. How exactly could you have stopped him?"

"Simple, Mr. Elliott, I would have turned him in myself.'

He smiled despite himself; he couldn't help it. The woman in front of him had fire; he could see how she'd earned her reputation with the bureau. She matched his stare perfectly, and finally said, "So, should I be seeing my attorney as well?"

"Only if you want to. I've asked the NCUA to leave you on . . . as an advisor only. The only upside we've had is the fact their error took place on a Saturday evening. That gave us all day Sunday to try and come up with a battle plan."

"And keeping me here was a part of it?"

"So far, you've been the only one to make any real contact with the suspect, and from what I understand he seems rather taken by you. I wish to use that against him, Ms. McCafferty. Besides, it's too late to bring in someone new. I feel this is exactly what Mr. Williams has been waiting for."

He watched as Dawn perked up here, "What do you mean?"

"If you are right, Ms. McCafferty, and Thomas Williams is our thief, why hasn't he fled the country yet?"

"That's what I've been trying to figure out."

"What if this is what he wanted? Your evaluation indicates this entire affair could be revenge-driven. If that is indeed the case, why would he want to leave before the credit union was humiliated before the eyes of the world? Thanks to his statement Saturday evening and the many statements made by his attorney all day Sunday, all the right questions are now being asked, publicly, and rather loudly. The credit union is humiliated. The damage, as they say, is done." Sliding the coffee away from her, he could see her starting to lean closer into the table, considering his words, starting to work through it on her own.

"Today, I gave a statement confirming the amount stolen. In about ten more minutes, the NCUA will be putting a man of their own in front of cameras somewhere and undoubtedly by the end of the day, so will the credit union. All of us are trying to put our own particular spin on things. Not that I believe it will matter, because we all know what the people listening will hear. Money is missing, a lot of it. The Credit Union's reputation is ruined, utterly and completely. I suspect, even from what little I know about the banking world, they will be out of business in no time, unless something drastic is done. The NCUA will be putting some form of moratorium on withdrawals today to limit the amount of runoff membership they fear will take place at the credit union. I imagine that will only generate even more media attention and fear, but my counsel on that particular subject was not requested. But let me ask, do you think that would please our suspect, Ms. McCafferty, do you?"

"Yes," she said softly, "I think that might please him greatly."

"So then, you see, right now we need to watch him very closely, and to be quite frank, we need to use every means at our disposal. Right now, that includes you."

"All these years and suddenly I'm just a skirt, huh?"

"I've read your file extensively. You are a more-than-capable investigator, but if you wish I'll happily provide you with my own resume, and you'll see that I am myself rather good at this. But a flash of my smile at the tender age of fifty-seven won't weaken the suspect's resolve. I believe yours might. As I stated, I think if Mr. Williams is going to run, he'll be doing it very, very soon."

"So then, what is it exactly you need from me?"

"I need you to start at the beginning, and I need you to tell me everything you think, know, or suspect about Mr. Williams. Take your time Ms. McCafferty, we have all day."

* * *

Saving the Case 10.1

March 20, 2000

It was nine o'clock that morning before Tom's Corvette managed to find a parking spot anywhere close to the Hil Fed building. It was literally surrounded with camera crews, and it was clear the story was no longer just of local interest. Over the course of Sunday the national media picked up on it; untold millions being stolen and the botched investigation, highlighted by the FBI's illegal break-in. By six o'clock last night Tom unplugged his phone because it wouldn't stop ringing and his answering machine tape was already full. He'd called Megan at about nine o'clock from his recently purchased cell phone to hear that her office was being inundated with calls as well; it seemed everybody wanted an interview with the accused. He'd just laughed, finding it all terribly amusing.

"No interviews Tom," Megan said rather sternly, "do you understand me?"

After about an hour he finally agreed. He was starting to see what Megan was telling him the other day about the way he lived his life. Pulling into the parking spot he realized he'd never really seen himself as a thrill junkie before, but all of this exposure he'd just thrust on himself, maybe he was. He liked it.

The approach of his car sent the camera buzzing and the hot lights were suddenly blazing right on him, a hundred questions all at once were being shouted, making it impossible for him to understand any of them, much less answer one. The closer Tom got to the building he realized that a private security team was present, brought in to guard the exterior of the credit union. Tom recognized the uniforms as a company they'd used before several times to provide security for public events. Usually they brought in a single guard, maybe two or three depending on the event. Today there must have been two dozen trying to hold the media at bay. As he got closer he saw two police cars with four uniformed officers standing nearby trying to help keep the peace.

Against the fury of lights and questions Tom lowered his head and pushed his way toward the door, the nearer he got the more cameras flashed and the more things grew into pandemonium. He kept his face tight, and tried to do exactly what Megan instructed him to, "never let them know what you're thinking or feeling Tom," she'd told him, "like a good stage actor, always leave them guessing." When the private security realized it was him approaching they fanned out and helped him through the sea of bodies that seemed camped out around every entrance. He thanked the guards and took the stairs to the Collections Department.

Inside he found his coworkers all waiting for him, staring at him with gray, solemn looks. Guilty of talking about him behind his back, asking each other questions about his character. He knew them well enough to know that's what they were doing in his absence, but liked them all enough not to call them on it. He just smiled, not a happy smile, but one that he hoped conveyed that he was going to be OK. Because they looked at him like he was man about to die.

Samantha was the first to say something as he moved deeper into the room, "You looked pretty good on TV, a little fat, but the camera does tend to add a few pounds."

"Yeah, but the half dozen donuts I had earlier that day didn't help much." They both smiled, not because either thought it was funny, but because they all needed the reassurance.

"Tom," Judy said with worried gaze, "I've been told to send you to Human Resources the moment you came in."

"Well," he said casually, "you always told me you'd nail my ass if I kept coming in late, guess I should have listened, huh? Though today, I have one hell of an excuse, if you want to hear it?"

"Tom . . ."

It felt strange to him, placing a hand on her shoulder, it seemed she was taking it much harder than he was. "Don't worry about it, J," he said looking her right in the eye, "it had to happen sooner or later." Looking around at everyone else he just shook his head, "though I have no idea who's going to do all your filing now."

"You know, Tom," Samantha said as she came up from behind him to give him a hug, "you keeping giving us those crappy ass jokes of yours and we're gonna be glad you're gone."

"Well, hell, Sam, if I'd known it was gonna be my last day at work; I'd have come up with some better material."

"What are you going to do, Tom?"

"Well, Judy, as per your instruction, I'm going to go to HR."

* * *

Saving the Case 10.2

March 20, 2000

Mark Dryerson sat at his desk dreading every second until Tom walked through the door; he could hear the clock ticking. He was given point on this matter after it was decided that it wouldn't be in the best interest of the credit union to make a huge production of what was coming. Being the senior vice president of Human Resources left this job to him.

They'd all been sitting together in the living room at Randy's house as the news aired and Tom Williams live statement came out Saturday night. They'd all been stunned.

The senior management team set aside all of their individual goals that they'd all boasted so proudly about at their annual company business meeting. Suddenly their new lot in life was trying to save their own asses instead of planning for the future. Randy, Megan, Roland, Doug, Craig, Robert, and him. All of them, the people who ran the credit union, utterly powerless because of the actions of one man.

"Hell, Roland," Randy bellowed at the top of his lungs as soon as Tom's interview ran, "why is it he's the only one talking, where's our statement!?!"

"We were waiting on the FBI, Randy, you know that . . . the fact they fucked up it hardly my fault."

"No," Megan Hertigin said shaking her head, "but I bet they'll make it look that way."

"This is a nightmare."

Randy looked at Robert Fetzer and nodded his head, "I agree, completely, Bobby. Your Mr. Williams . . ."

"He sure as hell isn't my Mr. Williams."

Doug Law was quick to snap up, "he works under your department, Bob, for all intensive purposes, he's yours."

"Kiss my ass, Computer boy, at least it wasn't my division that didn't notice a goddamn super-virus being uploaded into the mainframe!"

"No, just your boy who did it!"

"Well, I guess I must hire smarter people than you!"

"Enough!" Roland yelled out, trying to waive the tensions down in the room without spilling a drop of the scotch that was poured high in his glass.

"Listen people," Randy said sucking in a deep breath, "I think we've finally smacked this bitch open, and we need to talk openly here. If tonight's proven anything, it's the FBI ain't got a damn clue as to what they're doing. NCUA's obviously grasping wildly, they all know who did it. We know who did it. The thing of it is they can't prove it. Neither can we, but coming Monday we're gonna have a lot of very worried and pissed off members looking for answers. So I hope nobody was planning on taking tomorrow off."

A light chuckle swept through the room, something his southern drawl was often known to cause when he got a little whiskey bent. "Roland, you get on over to that phone over there and call up Laura, tell her, and her whole damn department they ain't going to work tomorrow onsite. They're coming here. We've got to have a battle plan for Monday. Full press kit and all. Got me?"

"Yes, Sir," Roland was saying as he turned to leave the room, headed toward the hall phone.

"And Mark," Randy said with a grim face, "the hell of it all falls to you. I'd do it myself, but after trying to take a pop at him the other day it'd probably be best if I wasn't directly involved."

"What?" He'd been honestly confused looking at Randy.

"Mark," he said stepping closer, "you're the goddamn head of Human Resources and the time has come to get the bastard out of the office. I want him fired, immediately!"

"We can't do that Randy."

"And just why the hell not!?!" Randy's eyes were about ready to pop as Mark told him what needed to be said, but the sound of someone entering into the Human Resources suite pulled him back to reality. Looking up he saw Tom walk through the outer office door, a gentle swagger about him. He'd called all his employees on Sunday and told them that they could all have the day off with pay. He wanted to be alone with Tom Williams, didn't want to help spread the gossip that would obviously come from what was about to happen.

He stepped through the office slowly, patiently even. Mark watched as he seemed to chuckle a little as he stepped up to the office door. The thing that caught Mark's eye the most though was the fact that his smile completely faded to a deadpan stare by the time he said his first words. "You wanted to see me, Mark?"

"Come on in, Tom, have a seat."

"Thanks," Tom said, "I'd rather stand."

Mark stared up at Tom, for a moment wanting to ask if he really did it, but instead he just nodded. He smiled uncomfortably at his visitor, knowing all along that it appeared fake, not that it mattered anymore. "That was quite a performance you made on the television Saturday."

"Sammie already told me I looked fat, not much to recover from there, eh?"

"I'm not joking here, son."

Tom just shook his head, and the edges of his mouth began to sag, "number one, you're not my father, I'd remember that if I were you. Number two, if you've called me here to lecture me, I'm not interested. Anything I say in my personal life is my own business, not yours, not this company's. If you don't like it, call my lawyer, I'm sure you remember her number."

"You're being suspended, Tom," he surprised himself with how easy it slid off his tongue, the fact that Tom was bugging him helped greatly, but the ease surprised him still. It would have been nice if he'd seen Tom react though, something he most certainly did not do. Tom just continued to stare.

"Obvious question," Tom said evenly, "with or without pay?"

"For now, pending the results of the FBI investigation that's currently going on, you will continue to receive your regular paycheck, in the event that the FBI decides to prosecute and that you are found guilty . . ."

"I owe you all the money back, right?"

"That's correct, Tom."

"Well, I'll be sure to put it with the other 320 million. That way you guys can come by and pick it up all at once. I'll keep it small, unmarked bills for you."

"I don't find that amusing, Tom."

"Well," he said, "that's because you don't have a sense of humor, Mark."

"I'm also going to have to ask that you don't return to your office, please just leave."

"My, so formal . . . not going to have one of your security guards escort me out?"

"Will that be necessary?"

"You know something, Mark?"

"What's that?"

"Do you have any clue how much people around here hate you?"

"Security is just a single phone call away . . ."

"Just wondering, Mark, that's all."

Tom turned heel and began to head for the door as Mark sat there watching. "No one goes into Human Resources to be liked, Tom." It was as the outer door closed he heard Tom say, "Congratulations then, you succeeded."

* * *

Saving the Case 10.3

March 20, 2000

Randy Carlson stood at the front walk of the credit union, beginning their own press conference; the media gathered about the small platform he stood on, aimed their cameras at the podium he seemed to be embracing with both hands and watched as the senior vice president and vice president of marketing stood at his either side. For the gathered collection of media personalities had already heard the story, and most strongly suspected what they would hear this morning from the credit union, but it was news, and when it all came down to the bottom line what the media cared about was ratings. 320 million dollars missing insured good ratings for the remainder of the week, and the fact that nothing new would be said at the credit union steps meant nothing to them. It was all about finding the one perfect sound bite that would be broadcast around the world within the hour.

No one could have expected the way it would all go down.

"Ladies and gentlemen of the press, my name is Randall Carlson." He started off with an even tone, hardly revealing at all how nervous and nauseous he felt inside, "I'm a simple man and I'm gonna do my best not to bore y'all too terribly much. That said, let's all come clean here, we're missing a whole truckload o' money. Now, I also know by now you've heard what the FBI has to say, as well as the NCUA. So, unless y'all have a specific question to ask, I'm gonna just go and gloss over all those parts you've already been listening to all morning long and just get down to the brass tax." It always made him nervous, standing in front of large groups of people. Even back in school when it came time to speak in front of his class, he'd go deathly pale and try to get out of it. In the boardroom, he was a giant. In a small group of people, he could bully his way through, but before a large congregation of people, he felt like throwing up after every other word. With hot lights the news cameras used blaring on him, he felt his stomach tying itself into a knot, and was suddenly wishing he'd taken Laura up on her offer to spearhead this statement. He did the only thing he could in times such as these—he let his accent come out thick and rich, hoping people would get lost in the rhythm of his voice.

"We're down 320 million dollars. Now before any of our members go out and start fretting too much, it's all insured. That's why the NCUA has been so actively involved in this investigation here. There is no chance of any member losing money. So no business or individual who does business with this credit union is going to be out one dime, nor will the handling of their accounts be effected. Everybody's gonna be just fine. All you gotta do is stick with us, 'cause we're gonna stick by you. We have our disaster plan approved by the NCUA and the transfer of funds from the government to our institution is set for early June pending the FBI's investigation of the matter. In the meantime, the credit union's reserves will be used to keep the business going, even if that means we have to temporarily liquidate some of our investment assets.

"Our credit union remains fully staffed and there will be no cutbacks or layoffs, while the investigation takes place. Our top concern remains the same, and that is the protection and service of and for our members. The same faces will be in our branches, the same voices you've always spoken with will be answering our phones. Right now, our top priority is showing people that despite this terrible incident, we are still a full service financial institution, with the goal of being actively involved with our community. Just like we always have been."

"Now, I'm gonna go ahead and open this up, so we can take a few of your questions. I know a number of you have been practically wetting yourselves to talk to one of us, but keep in mind we have a business to run and we just can't get to y'all." He knew Roland was squirming now, he'd sufficiently deviated from the script he'd been given to read, but with his stomach feeling like it did he knew he didn't have a hope of keeping to the script, so he'd gone to his heart to find his words.

Looking around him, he saw a sea of hands reaching to the sky; a flurry of voices calling out his name. He randomly pointed out to the crowd and said, "You, go ahead."

"What about the claims that one of your own employees took the money? Can you confirm?"

Randy was told to expect that one, and Roland and Laura both told him it was bound to be the first question thrown at him. They'd also told him exactly how he should answer it; say it was the FBI's show now, and that all information regarding suspects and accusations would have to come from them. They'd both been very specific with Randy all morning, saying again and again that he should refuse to answer any question pertaining directly to Thomas Williams, whether his name was mentioned or not. Randy was ready or at least thought he was, right up until the moment he saw Tom Williams step out from the credit union's automatic front doors. His tie was loosened and he walked with a casual swagger and an arrogance that seemed to reach out and slap Randy right in the face. Just his mere presence at their press conference caused Randy's blood to boil, and it was all he could do not to jump down and finish the job he started on Williams the other day. With the reporter's question still ringing in his ears, he watched Williams press his way right to the side of the makeshift stage, looking up at Randy as if he were hanging on his every word. "Well," Randy said coughing, trying to clear his throat and temper his rage, "I believe that's for the FBI to talk about, not me."

And as if he were on cue, Randy watched as Tom turned his face to the crowd of reporters and cameramen, causing an immediate buzz and ripple to pulsate through the crowd. Tom didn't smile as he turned; he kept his face passive, giving them what he thought would be the perfect media shot. Megan told him not to talk to the press, but as he recalled, she hadn't said a thing about posing for them.

Laura reached out to tug gently at Randy's cuff, seeing the building rage and knowing that nothing good would come from it. She saw that he was watching Tom's every move.

Roland, on the other hand, wasn't paying any attention to Randy. Instead, he watched Tom, as he turned slowly around, giving every camera he could a shot at his face before he finally turned back to look eye-to-eye with Randy. It was only then he thought Randy might actually leap off the podium at him.

"Come on, Randy, why don't you tell them what you did today? I mean, it was your handy work, wasn't it?"

Laura rushed forward, taking the microphone and speaking loudly into it. "This really isn't the time or place for this conversation, Mr. Williams. Why don't you just go home?"

"It's no problem, Laura," Tom said calmly, "I've suddenly found out I have all the time in the world."

The reporters buzzed in on this; the question in a hundred variations was being tossed out, all wanting to know what the accused meant by his statement. It was clear to everyone, though, that Tom wasn't going to answer. He, like all the rest, stared up to the three people at center stage, who were forced to look out at the crowd. Roland wanted to reach out for the microphone, call the conference there and then, just end it, and cut their loss where they could. But he would need to get through both Randy and Laura to do so, and judging by the tight grip she had on the microphone, she had no intention of giving it up easily.

"What Mr. Williams means is that he was placed on an administrative leave as of today, nothing more."

"Seems like a whole lot more from where I'm standing, especially since it wasn't phrased to me as an administrative leave. When Mark told me about it, he gleefully used the word *suspension*."

Roland just lowered his head when he saw Randy snatching the microphone from Laura's shaken hand, "Listen here, you just get the hell out of here!"

"Why? Afraid the truth might actually be heard? That you've suspended me without any proof of wrongdoing!?!" The fury of the press was growing suddenly. What most thought would be another dull press conference, where nothing of any real value would be said was rapidly turning into a shouting match between the two main principals. Live feeds were suddenly being turned on, and reporters were cupping their microphones and ears as they started saying they were sorry but breaking news was causing the interruption of their favorite morning programs.

"We have all the proof we need, you son of a bitch," Randy screamed down, not even vaguely aware that he was the center of the morning news, "you stole from us once, and now you just went and upped the ante, and I'll be goddamned before you get a chance at anything else here!"

And suddenly, the crowd was deathly silent; everyone was either looking to the podium or at Tom. Everyone wanted an explanation as to what Randy meant. Then the questions began to fly, and Randy realized he'd just opened Pandora's Box. Turning away from Tom and up to the crowd, he tried to compose himself as he said, "I can't get into the details, but Tom Williams was once almost fired over another theft he did, and based on the current FBI investigation surrounding him, we felt the need to remove him from all duties." Looking back down, he already saw Tom starting to push his way back through the crowd, but this time he swore he saw a smile on the man's face.

The next thing Randy Carlson knew was that Roland was indeed pushing past him to grab the microphone and end the press conference. Not that it mattered much. The damage was already done; Roland was wondering how long it would take before they were publicly chastised by both the NCUA and the FBI for once again interfering in their investigation.

* * *

Saving the Case 10.4

March 20, 2000

London was cold this time of the year, and he hated the cold. He longed to be back in the Cayman's, but it had been well over a week since he came to this place. He didn't understand the attraction to it, as he couldn't see what other people saw. History? He could care less. What he cared about were beautiful women in string bikinis bouncing around for his amusement. His place in Greece was already reserved for the summer, and after that he assumed the rest of his life would be spent foolishly chasing the sun somewhere.

Looking out at the heavy rain falling over London, he swore he'd never live in weather like this again.

The tabloid journalism of the city was so far the only thing he'd found any real enjoyment in. The food here was dull and tasteless, and the TV just plain boring. The tabloids made for an off-the-wall experience, though. The first thing he'd noticed was the page three girls who bared their breasts every day in a publication that could be sold to minors. To an American such as himself, it was all a great shock. But the real joy was their large coverage of an American Credit Union losing 320 million dollars, and the prime suspect Tom Williams. The British seemed quite intrigued at such a crime taking place by such an unlikely chap, and already British credit unions were saying that this could never happen to them.

He laughed and for a few moments thought about breaking into one of their computer networks just to prove them wrong.

The other thing he noticed was the tabloid's attraction to the woman being dubbed as the lead investigator, a striking beauty named Dawn McCafferty. He wondered if she was getting this much coverage back in America? Considering the way she looked, he suspected yes.

Looking over at his laptop, he saw the program running. Seeing the digital readouts, he was very happy at what displayed. He knew that with this much coverage his time was running out, and soon it would be time to disappear. The number at the bottom screen was growing though, and he gave a silent prayer to the memory of his wife, praying that this would last another two weeks to hit the target number.

Though thinking of another two weeks of the bland English diet was almost enough to make him change his mind; what he really wanted was a Pina Colada.

* * *

Saving the Case 10.5

March 20, 2000

"And now what do you think?"

Dawn watched Elliott's demeanor change throughout the day; he'd initially come on as a hard ass, but she'd quickly figured out he was the bureau's cleanup man. The one they sent in when lesser agents made dramatic errors in public sight. In all honesty, she'd found him so far to not be that bad a guy. She was a little uneasy about his plan to use Tom's attraction of her against him, but she knew all things being equal, it was the best plan anyone had at the moment. "The credit union certainly looks bad right now . . . I'd say that much."

"Hmmmm," he said musing, "would you like to take odds on how many depositors they lose on the morrow?"

"You know something, Elliott, not many people use the word 'morrow' anymore."

"Well, I benefited from a Harvard Education. However, I notice you are changing the subject. My question was as to what you thought of my assessment of Mr. Williams?"

"I knew what you were asking, but the thing is Tom defies reason."

"Really?"

"He doesn't need the money, so what he must be after is revenge. He's well educated enough though, that he realizes he can't honestly get away with a crime like this . . . so he must have a plan."

"And what would that plan be?"

Dawn nodded at him as she stood and began to pace, feeling sluggish just sitting there. Pacing wasn't as good as a healthy run, but seeing the way the day was going she figured pacing would be all she'd have time for. "Who would you trust with that much money?"

"What do you mean? His accomplice?"

"Yeah, as far as we can tell he hasn't maintained a serious relationship in quite some time, certainly not since he's been in the collections department. Who would he give that much money to?"

"I don't know... you know him better than anyone on the investigation team, who do you think he'd trust?"

"Honestly," she said with a thin, plaintiff smile, "right now, I'd say, Me."

"Then I'll have you arrested at once."

"I'm serious; I think he might honestly tell me ... if he just for a moment thought it wouldn't get him arrested."

"You don't have to tell me what a man will do to charm a pretty woman, you should have seen what I went through to marry my Emily... oh... it's a wonder she ever spoke to me in the first place, thinking back on all the foolish things I did."

She smiled brighter at seeing his human side coming out more and more, as the door to their meeting room suddenly burst open. Both of them turned to see Marc coming in, he was holding a stack of papers that he threw down on the table. "I think I've got something!"

The two of them moved closer to where Marc was quickly sorting out the pages. "You found the code," she asked as she started to look over his shoulder.

"No ... something odd though."

"What is it young man?" At that she took her cue to introduce Marc to the new lead investigator, but Marc gave the elder man little more than a head nod.

"Here, here ... look at this!"

"Marc, what is it?"

"This message board he's constantly posting on, the comic creator thing."

"Yes?"

"The problem was we were just reading his posts, no one else's."

"You'll forgive me," Elliott said as he began to stiffen his back, ready to dismiss anything further Marc said, "but I don't see the relevance of what you're trying to inform us of."

"We were just reading what he said, not the posts he was responding to."

"So?"

"So, in his answers, he responds to everything the original poster asks, but he also gives additional information. I never would have noticed but someone online today asked what the hell he'd been talking about. One of these smarmy posters who seem to feel the need to post about every goddamn topic brought up, even if every point he has to add has already been covered. He called Tom out, wanted to know what the hell he was talking about!"

"What was he saying ... the off topic part."

"He starts this post here, by talking about how much he enjoyed *Andrew Dabb's 'Happydale,'* going on and on over the points of what he thought made it such a great series, and then right here in the third paragraph he says, 'they tried to come in without knocking last night, look for the show.' Then he went back to talking about *Dabb's 'Happydale'.*"

"Get into that web server and find out who goes to it!"

"We already did that," Dawn offered, "the log in doesn't require any real information beyond an e-mail address. The site in question gets thousands of hits a day; it's in fact the largest comic book forum in the world. It's impossible to trace."

"Clever of him."

"No" she said turning away from them, "it's much worse than that. It's obvious he's speaking directly to his accomplice, but undoubtedly, he won't directly respond to this accomplice. They're leaving messages for each other, and since Tom seems to sit every night and read every subject header, and all of the messages within them, it's clear he's looking for someone's post.'

"Well, the good news," Marc said, "is we know how he's communicating with them, maybe we should just shut the board down."

"What do you think, Agent McCafferty?" he asked stepping up after her, now totally ignoring Marc.

"We might have to, but I have a sinking feeling, we may have found this out too damn late to be of use."

"So you agree then, he might be getting ready to run now that the credit union's been damaged?"

"Yes," she said, but in her heart, she didn't really believe it. Not yet.

* * *

Morning Rise

Morning Rise 11.0

March 25, 2000

Six Days Later

It was starting to get warm again, the light rain from last week confused her, but this morning it was clear she was staying in Southern California. It wasn't even 8:00 a.m. yet, but the cool night air already faded and the day's heat was starting to build. Even with her hair tied back into a ponytail she could feel the edges getting slick with sweat. She was pushing herself harder than usual, forcing herself to sweat before she stopped. This is what Dawn liked the best about coast cities, the way it felt like summer all year long.

The run was becoming very easy for her, a lot like running back home, she knew it instinctively. She'd been in town long enough and run the same course for far too long, so she was looking to vary it where she could. The only real change she made to her morning jog was the inclusion of a radio headset that kept her up to date on all of the happenings concerning Tom Williams. At first she wanted to use the time she had alone to keep her thoughts to herself, or channel her energies in constructive ways toward the case, now with Elliott having taken over she wanted something different. Suddenly she didn't have the illusion of being in charge; suddenly she was just another spoke in the wheel that was running the investigation. It wasn't that she didn't like Special Agent Marshal Elliott, she did. In fact she thought of him as a good man, and a rather stand up fellow. He believed in the law and was more than willing to talk things out and willing to listen to her ideas and theories. The problem was, she wasn't in charge anymore, she'd been pushed back on her own case and down deep inside, in a place she'd never admit to, it pissed her off. She'd earned the position she'd received, and she deserved the glory when Williams was brought down, now thanks to Neal she wasn't going to get it. Elliott would.

She felt her legs moving faster, pushing harder, the faintest edge of the early burn starting to rise up in her muscles.

This was where the real doubt crept in; she wondered if she'd ever really been in charge. Sure, Neal was the one to officially answer for things back at the office, with the higher ups, but he knew to leave her to the actual investigative work. Worse though was the thought that the real person in charge of all of this was Tom Williams, and that all along he was really just playing with them. Was he smart enough, she wondered silently as she ran at a full stride down the street? The part that really bugged her was he might be.

They'd all spent the better part of the week going over the Comic creator's forum, reading every message posted over the past three months. The total was over a hundred thousand messages, and they still didn't have a clue as to whom Tom might be writing to. The theory popped up that whoever his accomplice might be, was just reading for what Tom said, not writing back, but that didn't feel right to Dawn. Something deep inside told her that Tom would need updates from her. He would also need to know he wasn't being dumped for the money. He wouldn't be as confident otherwise.

In reading over Tom's posts again and again they started finding more and more odd references within them, but they weren't clear messages, not like the original one that Marc discovered on Monday, it was as if he were speaking in code. Dawn knew they didn't have time to crack a code.

Elliott was convinced that Tom was guilty and the only reason he hadn't run in the first place was he wanted to embarrass the credit union, to basically ruin them. Now that he'd essentially done it, he was just waiting for his chance to run. That was another reason she kept the ear piece with her at all times, Elliott placed Tom under full watch. There was nowhere he could go where he wouldn't be followed, and that meant there was always new updates being broadcast. Instead of four agents on him at all times there were now over a dozen. She listened to everything, and as she listened she tried again and again to figure out what the missing piece was.

She agreed Tom wanted revenge, to a certain extent she understood it. The people he trusted betrayed him, abandoned him, and he wanted to get even. She knew it. What she didn't know was what he planned to do with the money. It was the main flaw in all of her theories. The only thing she could come up with was he planned on giving it to his accomplice, maybe seeing some of the revenue somewhere down the line when he felt the heat was off him, she wondered why he didn't see that with this much money the government would never stop watching him. A crime of this magnitude needed a conviction, needed someone to parade in front of the public.

For her, the week was extremely tough, her face was suddenly everywhere. She could be seen on the evening news, whether local or national. She was on the front page of the newspapers, and someone from the FBI had already leaked to the press that she'd gone on a date with the suspect. One of the late night talk show hosts even made a joke about her, how government agents were so underpaid they were dating suspects for their money. The NCUA and FBI were both officially denying that the evening spent was a date, saying instead that she'd taken a full evening to interview Tom Williams, and they'd never been left alone. It was all true, but also a lie. It was a date, whether she wanted to admit it or not. They'd been on a date, and now she found herself wanting to go on another, wishing she'd let Tom kiss her on the elevator, even when she knew that it was something that she could never allow to take place. Wishing she was still dancing with him in the break room while looking at the stars.

"Garage opening." The voice said in her ear and snapped her back to attention. Their investigation showed him to be a nighttime kind of guy, not mornings. Being suspended from work, she figured today would be like every other this week where Tom stayed asleep until approximately ten or eleven. She looked down at her watch and saw the time was 7:58 a.m., and she wondered what Tom was doing up so early.

The credit union had a vigil of news teams set up to monitor everything that happened, and all week long was reporting the heavy loss of membership they were suffering in light of the announced loss. Tom's condo complex was the same; the press was everywhere through Monday and Tuesday, until the HOA board complained and got the police involved. The media screamed about their first amendment rights, but the privacy and domestic bliss of the neighborhood won out and they were pushed back far enough that few news crews even bothered to cover the general area of Tom's condo. The FBI didn't move and inch though, in fact under Elliott's control their positioning got better.

And the voice said, "what's he doing, Jack, can you see?"

There was confusion in the agent's voice which stopped Dawn in her tracks, it was only then she heard the heavy sound of her own breathing, how hard she'd been pushing herself. Standing there at the side of the street, half bent over from a sudden wave of exhaustion, she knew she'd never be able to run back to her hotel room.

"It looks like he's placing a large black duffle bag into the back of his vette."

"How large?" Dawn pressed her finger to the earpiece as she heard Elliott's voice pierce the morning.

"Four by Three by Three, sir, I think."

"No, bigger."

"I don't know, big though, damn big."

"Track him, anybody looses them better not plan on coming back in."

"Shit," Dawn whispered between breaths, "they think Tom's running."

* * *

Morning Rise 11.1

March 25, 2000

Agent Cole and Blackdale were following at a discrete distance as they cruised down the 8 freeway going west. They'd been warned that Tom previous broke his tail several times in the past couple of weeks by doing half crazed stunts, and using the power of his corvette to back him up, so they both remained alert. To Cole's eyes he just saw a standard owner of a corvette, who liked to dart in and out of traffic, going a little faster than he really should. In his experience that happened a lot when people bought a corvette. He'd owned his share of sports cars himself over the years, though he'd always preferred the Camero or the Mustang. To him the Corvette was an old man's car. An old man trying live through their second childhood at any rate.

Eventually the 8 West gave way to the 5 freeway headed south, and Blackdale who was in passenger seat called in their position heading, when they hit downtown San Diego they followed Tom right off the freeway.

* * *

Morning Rise 11.2

March 25, 2000

Dawn was going as fast as she could, she hadn't brought her cell phone so she didn't have a way of putting in her own opinion on what was happening, and they needed to hear it. The NCUA was no longer calling the shots, so carrying the cell phone seemed, to her, unnecessary. Having broken her rhythm in the midst of the run, she was suddenly having trouble trying to keep a good pace. Her breathing was heavy and labored, and the fact that she was now trying to rush back home to her hotel/apartment, or whatever she should call it, wasn't helping any. She just kept thinking about a large bag being stuffed into the back of Tom's corvette, what the hell was going on?

The next call that came over was Blackdale's voice, saying they appeared to be heading down to Sea Port Village, and Dawn suddenly realized exactly where Tom was headed, and she had a pretty good idea what was about to happen.

She tried to run again, but the pain in her side got to be too much and finally stopped, she was still a good mile away from her makeshift home, completely unable to stop what she saw coming.

* * *

Morning Rise 11.3

March 25, 2000

Marshall Elliott sat down his coffee cup and headed to the door. He was working downtown at the government offices, not wishing to add to the pandemonium of the Hill Fed main office. As far as he was concerned it was a lousy place to set up shot? He liked the surroundings of a bureau office, over having to watch what he said inside the boardroom of the place he was investigating.

He was only a few minutes' drive from Sea Port Village, and his gut feeling told him Tom Williams was finally ready to make his move. No wonder, he thought, Williams was lying in wait at his condo the other night, the money was right there inside.

He jumped on his cell phone and called a full alert, told the men in the Hill Fed building to locate McCafferty and send her down this way, he had a feeling this would all be over soon. Then he made a second call to a ready team and told them to head down to the water.

They all knew Tom kept his boat at the docks near Sea Port Village, and today was the day he was going to sail right out of town. Elliott admitted that as far as plans went, it wasn't bad. He could sail in a boat of that size for quite some time without having to hit a major port, and when he finally did land, the money could certainly set him up someplace.

It was all about the boat, he thought. He made a third call to the coast guard to put them on alert as well. He laughed as he got to his private car, thinking what a big surprise Williams would soon be in for.

* * *

Morning Rise 11.4

March 25, 2000

"He just pulled into the parking lot; we'll wait until he parks before we go in after him." The radio call was followed with Elliott's voice saying he'd be there in a second and how he wanted everybody on standby, awaiting his order. A chorus of voices began to check in acknowledging his order, there seemed to be a dozen men ready to arrest Tom Williams.

Dawn shook her head furiously, wishing like hell that the pain in her side would go away, before another drastic mistake was made. They didn't know Tom, but she did, and after everything he'd already orchestrated, she could see exactly what this was.

* * *

Morning Rise 11.5

March 25, 2000

Ron Tam stepped out of his four-door chevy and started walking the edge of the parking lot at Sea Port Village. He was dressed like any of a dozen people there, shorts and a loose fitting t-shirt, but he kept a rolled newspaper in his hand, and as discretely as he could he'd speak into it from time to time, or more appropriately would speak into the small microphone pinned to the top edge of the paper. Coming around the far edge of the lot he maintained a visual on Tom Williams, who was stepping out of the driver's side seat and stretching a little. "Looks like he's limbering up," he said to the newspaper.

He watched as Tom casually stepped to the backend of the car and popped the trunk with a button on his key chain. Ron lifted the paper to his mouth again and whispered, "Suspect has opened trunk."

Cautiously he began to move closer, watching as Williams began to lug out a large black duffel bag, lifting the newspaper to his mouth once more he said, "Christ. Whatever it he's got, it's large as hell. That duffel's almost as large as his upper body, and it's packed full . . . Looks heavy too."

"Stay on him," Elliott said over the air, wanting to make sure no one was slacking as he approached by car. All the agents could tell from the sound of his voice that Elliott wanted to be there when the collar was made.

Ron was now close enough that he needed to make a decision, one to turn around and act like he'd forgotten something in his car, or continue to move forward and pass Williams. He'd read the reports saying how smart Williams was, and felt it would be better to continue toward the suspect without directly watching him, then fall back as Williams moved out. His earpiece already telling him that agents Cole and Blackdale found a spot to park and were moving into positions. So he dropped the newspaper so it would hang loosely at his side and planned to casually pass the suspect.

He was about ten to fifteen feet away from the corvette when a hard gust of wind kicked up across the harbor and blew through the parking lot. The birds scattered in a flurry of movement as the wind shot through the, and in doing so rushed by Ron as well. The wind blew up his loose fitting shirt and a sudden chill ran down his spine as it happened. Not because the wind was unbearable, in fact on a warm morning the cool breeze was a nice respite from the pounding heat of the sun. The chill Ron felt on his spine was the fact that the moment his shirt went up the gun tucked in his waistband was in full and clear view of the suspect. Immediately he did two things as a reaction, the first was break from his plan; he looked directly at the suspect as he moved up the newspaper to block the view of his firearm.

The moment he looked up he realized he'd made eye contact with Williams, and then Williams eyes shot down to his waist. Ron knew at that instant he was made.

What happened next was a blur; Tom jerked the duffel bag over his shoulder, slammed his trunk and began to run for the more populated section of Sea Port Village. It was a frighteningly swift motion leaving Ron with nothing but a shot of Tom's back, as he carried the awkwardly heavy duffle bag as fast as he could, using his back to support the weight. Ron swore as loud as he could as he snatched the newspaper to his mouth. "He's running!"

* * *

Morning Rise 11.6

March 25, 2000

Dawn was almost to the parking lot of the executive resort hotel, she walked as quickly as she could with one hand clutched tightly at her side, the only thought going through her mind was how everything could have gone wrong so quickly.

"He's running.'

The call came with a fierce sound of frustration, and all she could do was say, "Shit."

"Take him down, *now!*"

The second call was from Elliott's, and she closed her eyes angrily, knowing she was too late.

As she opened her eyes again she could see two agents running toward her fast, waving their arms so she'd see them coming. She knew they'd have radios she could speak on, but she also knew it would already be too late, the call was out, and nothing she said could reverse it. She suspected by the time she could explain, it would all be over and done.

* * *

Morning Rise 11.7

March 25, 2000

Tom Williams was in fairly good physical shape as far as Cole could tell, but whatever was in the duffel bag was slowing him down fiercely. With Blackdale to his side they ran into the small upscale seaside shopping mall as they pulled out their badges and guns. In both their ears they heard Elliott's arrest order, and neither of the two men intended to let anyone else take the glory for the morning's arrest.

Cole leapt over two small children where Blackdale chose to go around them, which allowed Cole to get a good solid lead, as well as get into position to cut Williams off. He brought up his sidearm and aimed it directly at Williams' chest yelling, "Freeze!"

Tom stopped dead in his tracks and with a total look of shock raised both his arms upward, in doing so he was almost toppled over by the weight of the duffel bag which now tugged at his arm and threatened to take him down.

Blackdale ran up from the side his, gun aimed at Williams as well, Blackdale lowered his mouth to his collar, the spot for his remote microphone and said clearly, "we have suspect detained, orders sir?"

Cole heard it as clearly as Blackdale did, Elliott's voice coming over the radio proud and commanding, "Read him his rights."

"And the duffle bag sir, should we open it?"

"No, not there," Elliott said over the air, "best not to contaminate it until we have it under total control, understood?"

"Yes sir," Blackdale said as he came up to Williams side and tugged at the weight of the duffel. He then holstered his weapon and lifted it off Williams' arm while Cole kept the suspect covered. As the bag was lowered to the ground Ron Tam came running up to them, huffing and puffing from his own run.

Tom looked directly at Cole, who's eye never left the spot on Tom's chest where he was aiming and said almost gingerly, "be careful, Officer, that man over there has a gun, I saw it myself."

Cole didn't understand what Williams meant, and kept his aim solid until his partner backed up and pulled a set of handcuffs from the clip of his belt. Then Cole lifted his gaze right to Tom Williams' eyes and said, "Sir, you have the right to remain silent . . ."

* * *

Morning Rise 11.8
March 25, 2000

"Agent McCafferty, we've been looking for you everywhere . . . something's come up."

"I know," she said bluntly as she staggered past the first of the two men, "I'm wearing my earpiece."

"Elliott wants you downtown, right away."

"Sure," she said as she passed the second man, both of them confused by her demeanor.

"Ma'am, perhaps you aren't aware, they've arrested the suspect."

"I'm very aware, gentlemen, do either of you have a radio I can use to speak to Special Agent Elliott?"

One of the two men handed over their radio and Dawn immediately spoke into it between juts of breath, "Elliott, its Dawn."

"Dawn, about time you turned up, I need you down at the administrative building at once, we're about to have a 320 million dollar party, guess who's the guest of honor?"

"That's what I want to talk about."

"Talk . . . why?"

"What's in this duffel he had with him?"

"We haven't opened it yet, didn't want to open it at Sea Port Village in front of all the lookie-locs, and felt it would be better to do it at the office."

"Then can I ask you a question?"

"Of course, Dawn, go right ahead."

"If we don't yet know for sure what's in that bag, why have we arrested him?"

"He ran from an officer, he was made and he tried to flee."

"Uniformed or undercover?"

"What difference does that make?"

"Something tells me a lot, Elliott, listen, I'm on my way right now. McCafferty out." She shut off the microphone and tossed the handset back to the agent who gave it to her. "This is shaping up to be a hellava day, huh?"

"There's one more thing, ma'am."

"Yes," she said looking back.

"We've had someone calling for you every ten minutes for the last forty."

"Please tell me it's not my father."

"No, ma'am," the agent said smiling, happy he wasn't going to be giving her news she was going to dread, "This is from a Jerry Grayson, he sounds pretty eager to talk to you."

"Great," she half closed her eyes and the pain in her side fell from her thoughts, all she could think about was Jerry now, what he might want. How he'd found her wasn't a surprise, every television newscast in the world was reporting her name. Jerry, the ex-boyfriend who would never really go away loved to watch TV. She sighed deeply and looked up at the two men, "if he calls again, tell him I'm not taking any calls for the foreseeable future that don't have anything to do with the case, understand?"

"Yes, ma'am."

"Good," she turned and walked directly over to her rented car, she felt her hands shaking, but she wasn't sure if it was from shock that Jerry called, or her anger at it.

* * *

Morning Rise 11.9

March 25, 2000

She looked out of place at the Government building in her jogging shorts and tank top, but with everything moving so fast, she thought it was a smarter move to get downtown quickly, which meant there wasn't time for a shower and a change of clothes. She'd also brought a small running pack, instead of a purse. Just something to hold her identification in so she wouldn't be stopped while coming in. Finding a parking spot for her rented car was a nightmare on a Friday downtown, so she grabbed a parking spot for $10 two blocks away and hiked the rest of the way herself. Walking in she looked for Elliott, not finding him she went up to one of his assistants. "Where's Elliott?"

"What, the NCUA doesn't have a dress code?"

"Hey, fuck face," she said matter of fact, "I asked where your boss was, not for your take on the latest trends from Vogue magazine?"

"He just walked in to talk to Williams; you can look in through Observation Room One though," and pointed her in the right direction.

"Thanks," and with that she was off down the hall attracting strange looks from everyone she passed. Tank tops and shorts weren't a common an outfit in the justice building unless you happened to also be wearing handcuffs. She went around the corner and up a flight of stairs to a room where a sloppily dressed FBI agent stood outside. She flipped her ID and he motioned her into the observation room. Stepping in she saw only one other agent who raised an eyebrow at her appearance but said nothing, he went back to looking through the two-way glass. The room was dank and dark and overly chilled. She wrapped her hands around her arms to keep as warm as she could and stared through the glass. What she saw on the other side was much as she suspected; Tom sat behind one of the two tables; he was leaning back and seemed rather amused at his confinement. On the other table was the large black duffel bag she'd heard so much about. One of the arresting officers sat staring directly at Tom. Standing dead center in the room was Marshall Elliott in all his official glory. He was just getting finished reading Tom his rights, for what must have been the second or third time since his arrest, she assumed because it appeared as if Tom was mouthing the words to the Miranda warning as Elliott spoke them.

She stepped a little closer so she could hear their voices through the speaker, not wanting to disturb the man seated in front of her anymore than she had to. She knew how outlandish she was dressed to be in this room, and she didn't really want to have to explain why.

"So," Tom said casually, "has my lawyer been contacted yet?"

"Does that mean you would like your lawyer present then, Mr. Williams?"

"Boy," he said chuckling, "you're really quick on the uptake, aren't you?"

"This isn't the time for sarcasm, Mr. Williams; we just want to make sure you are receiving all the rights you are legally entitled to."

"We? You got a mouse in your pocket?"

"Again, Mr. Williams, I would like to take the opportunity to remind you this session is being recorded, and that this is not the time for sarcasm."

"Well, gee, I sure hope you let me know when it is time for sarcasm, I'd hate to miss my opportunity."

"Agent Cole, why don't you go and have someone contact Mr. Williams' attorney for him, will you?"

"Of course, sir." Cole stood up and quickly walked out of the room, leaving Tom and Marshal Elliott alone.

"So, you're the new guy they brought in to bust my balls, saw your face on the news. Marshall something or other, right?"

"Special Agent Marshal Elliott and I am in charge of the current FBI investigation of the funds missing from Hillsborough Industrial League Federal Credit Union, yes."

"So then, before your little friend gets back or my lawyer gets here, I was wondering, Marshy, can I ask you a question?"

"That's Special Agent Elliott?"

"Why exactly have I been arrested today, I mean, I've been fingerprinted and strip searched, it's been a big Friday for me, and I still haven't been told why I'm here as your guest."

"Well, tell me Mr. Williams, why do you think you're here this morning?"

"FBI ineptitude?"

"Mr. Williams," Elliott said with his voice severely tightening, "why did you run from our officer this morning?"

"I didn't run from your officer, Marshy, he held out his gun, told me to stop, and I did. Then his partner came up and took my duffel bag and together they joined hands in arresting me in public. Is this retaliation for calling the cops on your agent last Saturday? If so, it's a pretty cheap shot, he was the one breaking the law, not me."

From the other side of the glass Dawn started to shake her head, she didn't need to stay in the room to know what Tom was going to say next, from what she'd heard over her earpiece, she knew exactly where this conversation was going. She slid out a chair and sat next to the other man in the room, noticing as she did, that he seemed concerned. Dawn bit her tongue to stop herself from smiling.

"Mr. Williams, my name is Special Agent Elliott; please refer to me as such."

"Or?"

"I'm sorry?"

"Or what? If I don't stop calling you 'Marshy,' which by the way is short for Marshal, what are you going to do? Stop talking to me?"

Dawn's face was tight, fighting back the smile, she couldn't believe how Tom was acting, not that she was surprised, she knew as well as he did he was safe, but to actually have the balls to do it was surprising. The man next to her muttered something about Tom having balls the size of cantaloupes, but she just kept looking forward.

"Your disrespect will be noted for the record, Mr. Williams."

"Gee, let's see, here I am being accused of stealing several million dollars, that's nothing in comparison to having a bad attitude for being arrested by Laurel and Hardy at a place I go to all the damn time, whatever must I be thinking?" Tom raised an eyebrow to Elliott as he said it, as if letting the elder man know that he wasn't afraid of him.

"Our reports show that you ran from an officer."

"Then your reports are mistaken."

"Really," Elliott said in a condescending manner, "then you didn't run into Sea Port Village this morning with this duffel here slung over your shoulder?"

"Yes, I did run into Sea Port Village this morning, I don't recall saying I didn't."

"Well then, Mr. Williams, why were you running, or would you prefer to wait until your attorney arrives to answer that?"

"Not at all, Marshy, I'd be happy to answer that, while I was unloading my bag from the back of my car, a man with a gun started to walk up to me, I thought I was about to get mugged, so I wanted to get myself out of the parking lot and over where other people might be able to help me if I was followed."

Watching from behind the glass Dawn saw Elliott's feet almost give out on him, watched as he took a quick step back to regain his composure, she felt bad for him, because he never saw it coming. The man next to her was paying very close attention and Dawn found herself saying, "Agent Tam never identified himself, never showed his badge, Tom's got plausible deniability."

The man next to her turned to face her, his eyes wide and she realized this was a Federal Prosecutor who was watching any hope of a conviction go right up in smoke. "Son of a bitch," he said looking at her, "you've got to be kidding me?"

"Worse," she said softly, "any lawyer worth their salt will make the bag he's carrying inadmissible because of how he was arrested, so even if that bag is loaded with 320 million in large, traceable bills, you wouldn't be able to tell the jury a damn thing about it. Course, I'm not a lawyer or anything."

She watched as the Federal Prosecutor shook his head in despair and turned his attention back to the room on the other side of the glass. "You were running from a man with a gun. That's your story?"

"No, that's not my story, Marshy. That's what happened. It was an Asian man, about 5'10", 5'11", short-cut black hair, clean-shaven. Wearing shorts and a large baggy button down shirt, a Hawaiian print. He had an automatic pistol tucked into his waistband. I saw it when the wind cut through the parking lot, lifted his shirt up. The guy was headed right toward me, looked right at me when the wind kicked in, right at me. I was scared to death. He tried to hide the gun behind a rolled up newspaper, but by then I knew he was going to mug me, so I grabbed my bag, slammed my trunk and ran like hell. It seemed the most prudent thing to do. I figured you FBI guys were still following me, so all I had to do was get to a populated area and undoubtedly one of your agents would arrest the man, but the thing of it was, I was the one who got arrested, even when I identified the man to the arresting officer."

He could hear the shock in his own voice as he asked, "you pointed this man out to Agent Cole?"

"You bet, I told both he and his partner that the man had a gun, they ignored me though and proceeded with my arrest, and by the way, you still haven't answered why I was arrested, can we get back to that?"

"What's in the bag here, Mr. Williams?"

"None of your business."

"Well, that's where we differ then, I happen to believe it is very much my business."

Tom just smiled, "why was I arrested, Marshy?"

Inside the observation room the Federal Prosecutor was shaking his head back and forth, "don't open it you stupid son of a bitch, don't open it!" But he watched in horror as Elliott stepped right over to the duffel bag and began to unzip it. He then placed his head into his hands while Dawn kept her eyes wide open watching as the smile grew on Tom's face.

Elliott looked confused as the bag opened, and then he reached both his hands inside and pulled out what looked like a heavy white tarp, "what the hell is this?" His hands padded down the bag almost violently, searching for some trace of what the tarp must certainly be hiding, but found all he had was the tarp.

"It's called a sail, Special Agent Marshal Elliott, I guess you don't see a lot of those out at Quantico, eh?"

"What the hell were you doing transporting a sail?"

"It's my old sail, for my boat, you were aware I own one, right? Anyway, it's been sitting around, taking up space in my condo for over a year, I finally got sick of it, so I decided I'd just keep it in the master bedroom of the boat. After all, I rarely sleep in the boat, so I might as well make use of the extra space. Not that it's really any of your business, like I said."

Inside the small observation room the Federal Prosecutor stood up, "well, I think I've heard enough."

"You gonna release him?"

"I didn't arrest him, so it's not my call, but I sure as hell wouldn't prosecute, which means keeping him locked up would be career suicide. Not my career though. My guess, after everything that's happened, all the screw up's. The only way you get him, you gotta catch him red-handed, I mean this, last week, you practically handed him a get out of jail free card." He took another look at her, "you're that investigator for the NCUA, right?"

"Uh-huh."

"You think this guy really did it?"

"Uh-huh."

"Do me a favor then."

"Yeah?"

"Before you call me down here again, make sure it's something I can use to convict."

"Not the one who called you down in the first place. Now am I?"

"You're the smart one, aren't you?" With that he turned and left the room. Dawn looked back to the interrogation room to see how it would end. Elliott was standing perfectly still; while Tom was starting to make himself look very comfortable on the hard wood chair he'd been provided. His smile was now stretching from ear to ear. She saw that Tom wasn't saying a thing, instead he wanted to enjoy the moment, watching the FBI start their cold sweats, realizing they'd blown it again. She knew in her heart Tom set them up, he wanted this to happen, and he liked to embarrass the people who wronged him; she just wondered how long he had before it all caught up with him. Back at HIL Fed, their team was going line by line through all of the code from the last year, knowing that somewhere they'd find an execute line. Then trace it back to who placed it there. Sooner or later, they'd have a connection to Tom; she couldn't help but wonder why he wasn't running yet.

A knock at the interrogation room door snapped Elliott's head up and he watched as the Federal Prosecutor leaned in and motioned for Elliott to step out. He hissed out a warning for Tom to stay put and left the room; Tom just nodded at the elder FBI agent and then as the door shut, turned his attention to the mirror he was facing. He studied it, craning his neck to stare directly at it and finally he lifted his hand and waved "Hi."

On the other side of the glass, she said *hi* back, knowing he wouldn't be able to hear her. Then she watched as Elliott stepped back into the room alone, snarling out, "you're free to go, Mr. Williams, with our deepest apologies, of course." He then turned and left the room slamming the door.

Tom just sat for a moment before finally getting up and moving to collect his sail.

* * *

Morning Rise 11.10

March 25, 2000

Elliott stood in the main hallway, the one that led to the main exit, arguing with the federal prosecutor. Elliott was a smart man, and knew the only reason he was really protesting was to save face in the midst of an arrest gone horribly wrong. The federal prosecutor knew it, so he wasn't angry at being delayed further, after enough years in either profession you learn that's the way the game is played. It was clear Elliott was mad though, and he knew the FBI would come off again looking like idiots, that would make it twice in a week's time, and only help to muddle the eventual trial. At this point, Elliott realized all they were doing was helping his attorney establish reasonable doubt; she'd hammer the FBI's tactics, making it look as if they were slowly manufacturing a case against Williams even when they knew he was innocent. It was frustrating, but today they were left with no choice but to let him go free.

As soon as he was back in his office, he resolved to allocate more men to help the NCUA team going over the computer data. In his mind that was rapidly becoming the only way they were going to get him. Being old school, that upset Elliott, he liked the old ways, tracking the criminals down through hardcore investigative tactics, not waiting for a computer to tell them who to arrest.

"Hey, Marshy!"

Marshal turned to look at Tom Williams walking down the hall, his duffel slung over one shoulder, and mostly leaning into the weight of the bag. He still had a cocky edge to him, still wanting to rub it in that the FBI blew it, that he'd managed to beat them again. "I already told you, Mr. Williams, you're free to go."

"Well, that's all well and good, but you'll notice I'm a long way from my car or boat. Which one of your boys will be driving me back to Sea Port Village?"

It was a direct challenge of authority. Most of the time Elliott would turn his head and tell whoever asked such a question to call a friend, but here he knew he was playing with a live wire, and he was faced with an arrest he couldn't justify and didn't need to complicate the issue further. It was certainly in his best interests to have one of his agents drive Williams back to the car, but the problem was Elliott really didn't want to do it. His face showed it and that just made Tom happier. It was clear that Tom had no intention of backing down either; he was going to keep pressing, knowing that at least for the moment he had the upper hand. Elliott was sucking in a deep gust of air, when the voice called out from behind Williams, "It's OK, Tom, I'll drive you."

Tom didn't need to turn around to recognize that the voice belonged to Dawn, so instead he looked into Elliott's eyes, and eventually, after what appeared like an eternity to the aged FBI agent, Tom winked. Elliott stared back stone faced, wanting to do little more than lock Williams up for the evening in a cell. *Let him deal with the inmate population*, Elliott thought, *see how well the white-collar worker fared in general population*. He remained silent though, as Dawn stepped up next to Tom.

"Heavy load, Tom, wash day?"

"Yeah," he said turning his head to look at her, "you'd be surprised how many clothes you go through when you're not at work, but then again I can see by your outfit you could do with some laundry yourself. Wanna share a washer?"

"Nah," she said cocking her head, indicating he should follow her, "I can tell by the weight of that that it wouldn't fare well with my delicates. You ready?"

"Like you wouldn't believe." Tom started to follow her out but turned to look Elliott in the eyes once more as he passed by. "I'll see you later, won't I, Marshy?"

Elliott didn't answer; instead he just watched them walk out of the door in a grim silence. The federal prosecutor chuckled as they left, saying he couldn't believe Williams, asking if it was wise to let Dawn be alone with him.

"Right now, I'd say she's our best shot."

* * *

Morning Rise 11.11

March 25, 2000

"Quite the show you put on today." She pulled her car into the spot right next to his corvette, but left the engine running, having driven in utter silence the entire way over to the parking lot.

"Hey, I was just an actor in this particular drama. It was your guys that put on the show."

"You knew perfectly well what you were doing today."

"You think so, huh? Then tell me, why didn't you stop them?"

She was shaking her head, a light smile fading in and out of her facial expressions. "You overestimate my power over this investigation, especially after what happened Saturday evening."

"Yeah, I read in the paper that the NCUA was taking a big hit for that. What's his name? Johnson?"

"He's resigning on Monday from what I hear."

"Let me guess," Tom said, "he cut a deal to save his ass, so all he loses is his career, and he won't do a day of jail time?"

"I'm not privy to the details."

"But you're smart enough to make a reasonable guess, I'd wager."

"I'd be surprised if he wound up with anything more than probation."

"Just doesn't seem fair," he said as he hunkered down a bit. "If I broke into somebody's house, I'd be doing serious time, he orders my house hit. And he walks with a slap on the wrist."

"He's lost his career. He'll never be able to get a job in this field again."

"What about me, Dawn, how many banks or credit unions do you think would hire me now? He'll probably wind up going into private security, a consultant, or something. He'll still be able to find a decent-paying job. What happens to me?"

"So you want revenge, Tom, is that it? Against Neal?"

"I want what's right."

"In this world," she said, "it doesn't often work that way."

"Then let me ask you this. If 'it doesn't work that way,' why are you asking me about what happened today?"

She smiled and gently nodded her head. "How old is that sail?"

"It was the second one I ever had on her."

"Her?"

"Boats are referred to as she or her. It's tradition."

"Time honored by many feminists, I'm sure."

"Well, I'm gonna be honest with you, Dawn. I'm not really up-to-date on all my feminist reading."

"Such is your loss, Tom."

"It's getting easier for you, isn't it?"

"What?"

"Calling me, Tom."

"You just never give up, do you?"

"Do you?"

"No," she said softly, "I guess not."

"You ready?"

"To go?"

"No," he said with sudden burst of enthusiasm, "for your first time on a sailing boat?"

"What?"

"You said you'd never been sailing before. Well, today's your lucky day."

"Tom, I'm not going sailing with you."

"Look," he said leaning his head a little with a look that reminded her of a sad little puppy, "I really need to take the boat out. With everything that's been going on, I haven't had much time for it lately. That's not good for her, and I have the feeling, if I head out to sea by myself, I'll just have a huge hassle with the coast guard. That I don't need. If you're on the boat though, well, I figure the coast guard will watch, but they won't interrupt my day."

"So you just want me along for your convenience?"

"No, that's just the reason I'm using . . . it just happens to be true."

She started to laugh, not big, but a small, silent laugh that forced her to lay her head against the steering wheel, and then she reached up and turned the key, shutting the engine down. "OK, but I refuse to help you put the sail on."

He assured her this was just an extra, something he wanted to store on the boat. They laughed and joked, as they walked down to his boat and dropped the duffle bag off. She couldn't help but laugh and smile as they spoke. There was something about him. Even under as much pressure as he must feel, he seemed to be entirely at ease. He was also fun to talk with. He didn't make assumptions about his own intelligence. In fact, he was quite frank about the idea he wasn't very smart at all, just well read, which often gave him the illusion of being educated. They left the boat to stop off at the downtown Ralphs Grocery Store, a full-service megastore, where he picked up a few items he said he needed. He even bought her some candy to snack on as they walked back to the boat. As she looked around, she counted a half dozen agents placed strategically along their route, all watching them as they strolled back to the private dock. Once back on the boat, Tom disappeared below, unpacking the groceries to the cupboard, calling up to her, asking if she was on duty.

"I'm always on duty."

"Does that mean you don't want a drink?"

"I thought you weren't allowed to sail drunk."

"You planning to do the sailing today?" he called out from below deck.

"Tom, it's two in the afternoon."

"So that means beer or wine instead of a mixed drink?"

"Water, just water."

When he eventually appeared back up on deck to untie the boat, he tossed her a bottle of water and pushed off, carefully maneuvering out of his slip and then the stalls that surrounded them to get out of the harbor. Once he was out a good ways, he killed the engine and hoisted sail and headed deeper out into the blue. The wind sliced around them, and they picked up a decent speed as Tom settled in behind the controls. He yelled over to her, "So what do you think?"

"Yeah," she said smiling, "you're right. It is a fun. Beautiful even."

* * *

Morning Rise 11.12

March 25, 2000

She could tell they were out pretty far, but Tom was being careful not to let the city of San Diego fall from their view. Looking back at the city though, she began to see why Tom liked sailing so much. Staring out at the gray city, the contrast of the deep blue water all around her and the way the day's last bit of sunlight reflected off the water, it really was like being in paradise. Tom set the controls and lowered the sail. They were adrift on the waves, but they really didn't seem to be going anywhere. The sound of the waves lapping against the boat was soothing to her, like music she'd never heard but suddenly fallen in love with. Even as the night was starting to fall, it was still warm out on the water, even with the wind. She'd been very glad throughout the day that she hadn't changed into something more professional for her trip downtown. She did feel a bit exposed, wearing only the shorts and tank top, but while she did catch Tom looking at her a few times, he'd never been openly leering.

She watched as he came up again from below the deck, this time carrying a small hibachi grill and setting it up on deck. "Isn't it dangerous to cook up here on deck?"

"Talking like that, it makes me think you've already tasted my cooking."

"I'm serious."

"You're always serious, and no, it's not dangerous as long as you don't set the boat on fire."

"That's reassuring. Plus, it's starting to get dark, and I know it isn't safe to sail at night, is it?"

"You know, it's hard for me to believe you know that it's dangerous to sail at night when you end your 'statement of fact' with a question."

"You're going to make me work for this, aren't you, Tom?"

"It's not the safest thing in the world, no, but haven't you ever done anything a little dangerous?"

"I'm here now, aren't I?"

"Gee, am I dangerous?"

"Potentially, sure."

"Well, I promise you then, I won't set the boat on fire, OK?"

She just laughed. "What's on the menu for this evening?"

"Shark steaks," he said, "little rice, and some green salad, the best prepackaged bag they had in the store, I assure you."

"I can't believe I'm out here with you."

"To be honest, I can't either," he was setting up the hibachi and lighting the coals from a safe distance. He seemed to know exactly what he was doing. "I keep waiting to wake up and find that this entire day was some bizarre dream. Know what I mean?"

"Uh-huh."

"Can I ask you a question?" He watched as she nodded. "Can we at least have a real drink with dinner?"

She laughed wildly and told him sure, and then, "I thought you were going to ask me something serious. The look on your face, it seemed pretty intense."

"I was . . . I chickened out at the last minute."

"Go on, Tom, you have me out here on the water, and I think, from what I'm wearing, you can clearly tell I'm not wearing a wire this time."

"Why'd you come?"

She looked away from him, out to the water, then up at the city in the distance. "I don't know."

"Beer or wine?"

"Uh . . . what kind of wine?"

"Been a while since I last stocked up. All I have left is a couple bottles of blush, I think; I'm not much of a wine guy to be honest. But I usually have a couple bottles of something laying around for those who like it."

"That's fine, I'm not that picky."

"You OK?" he asked as he came up behind her.

"Why do you ask?"

"Don't know exactly. All of a sudden, you're not laughing anymore. You seem sorta lost . . . I was just wondering. You don't have to tell me."

"Nothing really," she said looking out at the water. "My ex called for me this morning, left a bunch of messages with the FBI guys back at my hotel, resort, whatever you want to call it."

"You talk to him?"

"No."

"Do you want to?"

"Not particularly."

"But thanks to all the press attention, he knew exactly where to find you."

"Pretty much." She could feel her head nodding, but it was as if her conscious focus was drifting further and further out into the lapping waves that glided gently past the boat.

"And him calling, it's brought up a lot of old memories . . . maybe you're even starting to feel a little of the guilt from the way you treated him while you were building up the emotional strength to leave. It's left you a little unsettled, and after this much time, you don't really want to talk to him, because you feel like you should confess what really happened, but in doing so you'd probably just hurt him more."

"Christ," she said turning to look at him, his face gentle and kind, his eyes deeply concerned for her well being, "I thought I was the one with a psychology degree."

"I took a lot of classes in school. Every guy knows if you want to meet the really hot chicks, you take psychology and drama."

Suddenly she was laughing again; he knew how to break through her defenses, slipping under her radar. She was confused over so many things. At the moment, she was having trouble keeping any of what she was juggling in the air. She didn't need Jerry back in her life, not now, especially not when she was playing such a dangerous game with Tom. "So," she asked, "should I talk to him next time he calls?"

"Can't answer that, only you can, Dawn, and it's not an easy question, not by any means." He stepped down below the deck long enough to pull up two good-sized shark steaks on a plastic plate and a bottle of wine in his free hand. He dropped the wine gently onto a cushioned seat and placed the steaks onto the grill. Once again he went below the deck to get an opener and two wine glasses. He sat the glasses down and used the opener on the wine. She stared out at the ocean, feeling the gentle rocking of the boat.

They ate their meal and drank their wine, and he pointed out to her how very beautiful the stars were which enthralled her completely all night long. She couldn't recall ever seeing the stars quite as clear as they were now, clearer here than at any point when she'd looked up at them as a child. When the chill of the night got to be too much, he brought up a sweatshirt and a blanket for her to wrap herself in. Looking at the clock she saw it was after 9:00 p.m. "When do we head back, Captain?"

"Whenever you like." He was resting at the far end of the boat, away from the controls and stretched out on the cushioned seats. She stood there staring at him, wearing his old sweatshirt that smelled like the fresh sea air, huddled into his blanket. Maybe it was the wine, or maybe the simple beauty of the moment, but everything just felt right. Looking at him, she suddenly realized she was attracted to him. She hadn't been at first. Not really. It was as she'd told Neal originally, he wasn't unattractive. He just wasn't the type of man she'd usually go for. Something had slowly changed: Maybe Tom was right, that she was just a drama junkie, and he supplied that level of needed drama in her life, or maybe he was just as messed up in the head as she was, and somehow in a world this crazy they'd managed to find one another. Even if it was in the worst set of circumstances possible. "If I told you to take me home right now?" She asked.

"I'll kick up the motor at your command."

She stepped forward, telling herself with every footfall she shouldn't and sat down right next to him. Suddenly she was resting her body against his, and then her head was on his shoulder, as she stared up into the night. His arm slowly came up around her, holding the blanket against her. *Nothing was really happening*, she told herself. His hands weren't anywhere they shouldn't be. She was positioned in a way that it would be impossible for him to try to kiss her. At the same time though, to her, it felt very sexual, and very, very comfortable.

They sat in a hushed silence for longer than they should, the awkward pause where all the words run out, but no one was willing to make that bold first move to take things to a new level. Eventually, he lifted his hand from her shoulder and began to lightly play with her hair. In her mind, the rational side of her knew she should make him stop, but she couldn't remember the last time anyone touched her in this way. Thinking back, she couldn't remember the last time she'd felt this comfortable with a man. She was sure it must have been with Jerry, but after this much time and distance, she couldn't recall. "This isn't going to happen, Tom."

"I know," he said, in a light whisper against the wind.

"Then why bother?"

"I'd like to be flip here, just tell you that nothing really matters anymore, Dawn. But the thing is it does and even though I know better, even though I know nothing can happen between us, I can't bring myself to give up the idea of it. I like you." He paused for a moment and then added, "And I honestly wish we'd met under different circumstances."

"Me too."

His fingers lightly ran themselves along her forehead, back into her hairline, combing through her hair. His touch sent a shiver down her spine, and suddenly she desperately needed to kiss him. To hold him like he was holding her, but she didn't move, she didn't say a word; she just stared up at the stars. *He was going to jail soon*, she reminded herself, *that or he'd be on the run forever*. Either way, there was no future with him. "I think, we better go back."

"OK" was all he said as he got up and headed for the controls.

* * *

Morning Rise 11.13

March 25, 2000

She didn't turn on her cell phone as she got back to her car. She was sure she'd find several messages from Elliott, wanting to know what the hell she thought she was doing. She'd love to tell him, but the truth of it was, she didn't really know.

They'd walked back to her car, his arm still around her. She was sure she was being photographed with him, but she just didn't care anymore. She wanted to feel his warmth touching her. She knew that when Elliott heard about it, he'd have a fit. The best she could think to do was say she was defusing the situation his bad arrest created. It was a half-assed excuse. They'd both know it when she used it, but all things considered, she was fairly sure he wouldn't call her on it. How could he?

He'd played by the rules when he walked her up to her car. He didn't even try to hug her good-bye, much less kiss her. It was honestly strange for her to walk away from him without any physical contact. She hadn't felt this connected to someone in years. To her, it felt like they were almost in a sexual relationship. It was an odd feeling to be this connected to someone, to be that close to someone from just words and thoughts. They'd talked about so many things, things she really shouldn't have said at all. While on the boat she'd started to think about her own future. This case was terrible, and even though Neal and Fred Halstead would be the scapegoats, her name was going to be drug through the mud as well. She'd been originally named as lead investigator. Her career was very much in jeopardy. There was a good chance the NCUA would let her go as soon as this case was over. Being seen with the lead suspect like this would only hurt her. Anymore though, the thrill was leaving her. She was tired of chasing people, tired of being the one to figure out all the little games. Even if the NCUA let her keep her job, she was sure it wouldn't be the same one they'd originally hired her for. She'd be put to the back end of cases, profiling and such. Something she'd hate, which left her with the choice of putting up with it or quitting. What would she do if she quit though? Become a psychologist? The mere thought almost bored her to tears. She'd told him she felt like she was rapidly running out of options; that her much-envied life was quickly starting to feel like prison. He'd held her even tighter at that point and whispered he knew exactly what she meant. For the past few years, that was all his life had been.

"Tell me the truth, Tom, you and Laura Netzly. You had an affair?"

Staring up at the stars, with his fingers playing through her long, beautiful hair, he simply said, "Yes."

"She slept her way to the top, while she was sleeping with you. She was also sleeping with Randy Carlson?" Again, he'd simply said, "Yes." "Why'd she back down, Tom? Sounds to me as if she had both barrels stacked against you eighteen months ago. Why didn't they just fire you? I need to know." Her head by this point had been deeply buried into his neck, and she could tell from the sound of her own voice she wasn't asking the question as an investigator, she was asking it for herself.

"Laura and I were an unofficial item for a while, a long while. One of those dirty little office secrets that lie hidden in the hallways of just about any company of our size. We'd managed to keep it quiet though, a few suspected, but no one really knew. She wound up getting pregnant."

"Was it yours?"

"According to her, no. But then, she wasn't about to admit to that. As far as she was concerned, it was her husband's baby . . ."

"But?" She asked reaching up a hand to hold onto him, wanting to let him know without saying it she was listening in support of him.

"But her husband, a carrot top, bright red hair, and she, a full blonde, natural. Their daughter, just go look at the pictures on her desk, Dawn. Her daughter, Karen. She's three and a half now. She's got dark brown hair, and in some pictures I swear she has my eyes."

"I'm sorry, Tom."

"It's weird having a child, even just thinking you might. It changes your perspective, and I guess I started fawning over her more than I should have. She used it against me, wedged me out of her life, and suddenly she and Randy were doing everything together, and the job I should have had went to her. I was pissed, and I'm not that good at concealing it. So she took a strike at me, tried to frame me. Probably would have worked too, but she wasn't ready to give up her secrets."

"What do you mean?"

"I had Megan, my lawyer, call her directly one day. Told her I was going to file a civil motion claiming I was Karen's father. I was ready to go down for blood tests or even DNA, and we'd use subpoenas to do it if necessary. She wasn't ready for her husband to find out about her little secret, meanwhile Megan, during one of her conversation with the credit union's lawyer, implied, just implied, off the record mind you, that I might have some evidence of her and Randy together, in a rather compromising situation. Randy was scared what his wife would do, how much she'd take him for, much less the hideous scandal it would cause in our tight little credit union community, and "boom!" Just like that all the supposed evidence about me stealing wasn't there anymore. Suddenly the credit union was ready to make a deal. I took it, for the exact reason I told you before, put in two to three good years, defeating their claim I'd done anything wrong, then leave to restart my life somewhere else. Then all this money turned up missing, and I'm back in the hot seat again."

"Do you really think her child is yours?"

"Yes," he said softly. "I do."

"How do you get yourself into so much trouble, Tom?"

"It's like I told you on the night we first met, I make bad choices. But I got to tell you, Dawn, I think I'm getting better."

His words clung to her, even now, as she drove back up the 5 Freeway, going north. There'd been a deep truth to his voice, and she knew that no matter what, she'd never tell anyone about what he'd said about Laura Netzly. Instead she drifted back again to the dock, right after they'd tied back in. It was as they got off his boat, he asked, "Hypothetical?" He wasn't smiling this time; in fact, to her, he seemed almost withdrawn and injured. "Another time, another place, I'm found innocent. I know you don't believe that's possible, but what if . . . my name's cleared . . . what if?"

"What if," she'd said softly to him, "nothing, Tom? Because there'd still be the blonde down in the Cayman's, and that's a helluva an issue of trust to block out of someone's head." She'd seen the startled look on his face as she said it. His eyes widened. The look of hurt he wore grew larger. She regretted instantly telling him she knew about her. It was a foolish thing to do, and took away from any future interrogation she would find herself in with him. It sprang from a childish place inside of her.

"And if I told you, you didn't know what you were talking about?"

"I'd tell you not to lie to me."

"I'm not lying when I say this, Dawn. The only blonde in my life right now that isn't a ghost is you, and right now, I tell ya, if the only way to convince you of that is to go to jail. I might just be willing."

"Don't say that, Tom. You don't have that much time."

"Time?"

"It's all just a matter of time, Tom. We just have to find the right line of code and trace it back, everything's recorded in the Logiterm system, everything. We also know about the message board. We just need to break the code you're using to contact her, piece it all together. You're down to days, Tom, at the most, and you're being watched tightly. If today showed you nothing else, you've got no way out, nowhere to run. All you have is moments." She'd said too much and she knew it. But even now, the look on his face, it was like he still didn't get it.

"If those moments are with you, Dawn, I'll take them all, every last one I can get, because I tell you, I'm not running. I'm too damn old, too damn tired, and I'm too damn scared you wouldn't follow."

"I already told you, I wouldn't be allowed to follow. Even if you did somehow manage to perform the minor miracle of escaping, with this much money on the line, they'd hunt you down like a dog. You can't really hide with that much money, and I'd be trapped back in Sacramento living a very ordinary life or a very frustrating one as I try, at the age of thirty, to learn a new career and build a new life."

"So then," he said softly to her, "no what-ifs?"

"Nope, no what-ifs. This is just what we have."

She felt ridiculous as she drove. She was actually crying. She didn't know what was happening anymore. She needed time to think things through; she needed to regain her perspective. Whether her corporate masters liked it or not, she was going to take tomorrow off. She needed to sit down and reevaluate her life, decide what direction she was going in, and what she was really going to do about the present. She was off her mark lately, and that made her a bad investigator, and she remembered a time in her life when she would have cared, something she knew at the moment, she didn't.

She pulled off the freeway and navigated back to her makeshift home, pulled into the reserved spot, and did her best to compose herself as she stepped out, just in case any of the agents was still floating around. As she got out of the car, an FBI agent stepped out from the shadows and walked up to her, he made sure to step out in the light as not to startle her. The agent wore a forced and concerned smile as he stepped up. Not having worn any makeup today, and being in this semidarkness she was sure he wouldn't be able to tell that she'd been crying, but she kept her head down anyway. As he got closer, she held out a hand. "I know, I know, Elliott's looking for me. Tell him, I'm having a bad day from playing cleanup. Tell him, I'm taking the next twenty-four hours off, and we'll talk Sunday, got it?"

"Yes, ma'am," he said. But he didn't leave, instead he looked like he was about to enter into an awkward situation, "You're right, Elliott does want to speak with you at once. But I'll tell him what you said. There's something else though."

With a deep sigh, she nodded her head. "What?"

"Someone's here for you, he showed up earlier in the day. We made him wait, but . . . well, he had your file password. So we assumed it was OK . . . We let him into your room so he could at least sit down. We reported it, of course, and sent up an e-mail to your Sacramento office. Like I said he had your password, so we figured it was OK."

"Sure," she said as she closed her eyes, a deep wave of regret coming over her. "Thanks for the warning."

"Yes, ma'am."

She walked away from him, thinking back to her first week on the job with the NCUA, when they'd asked her for a password for messages and visitors while she was on assignment. She'd just given them the same one she'd used back when she'd been with the FBI. It seemed logical. It was something she didn't have to worry about forgetting, and this way, she wouldn't have to tell her family anything new. She'd never really expected this to happen though.

She stepped up to the door on room number 8 and hovered outside of it for a moment, her eyes tightly closed, knowing that this late at night, and after the emotionally draining day she'd just had, she didn't want to deal with what was waiting for her on the other side of this door. She thought about turning and driving away, going to a motel, getting a good night of rest before dealing with it, but she knew this was too long in coming, and that it was better to finally get it over with, once and for all. With a nervous, twitchy hand, she reached up and turned the door handle, opened it, and stepped in, while she opened her eyes. The TV was on to some old '80s sitcom, but she wasn't quite sure which one, and without looking at him, she said in the most even tone she'd ever used, "Hello, Jerry, it's been quite a while, hasn't it?"

* * *

Moments

Moments 12.0

March 25, 2000

"I've been worried about you."

She couldn't believe he was here, much less that he was saying he was worried. The same thought kept running through Dawn's mind, "he shouldn't be here." He was though, the man she'd left behind, a piece of her past she'd much rather leave forgotten. No, she stopped herself, that wasn't entirely true; she had countless memories of him that were wonderful, times when he was her everything. She was angry that he was here, especially now. She'd long been dreading the next time they met, the things they'd say, the way she'd feel, but here and now when she was so confused over the investigation, Tom, and his blonde down in the Cayman's, she just didn't think she could handle Jerry too.

"You shouldn't be," it didn't even sound like her, she thought, listening to the sound of her own voice. It was huskier than normal, maybe from exhaustion or perhaps fatigue, but it wasn't her usual voice. What she heard was the sound her grandmother made in the years just before she passed—a dry, throaty voice that seemed to border on cracking. All around her the world seemed to be going in slow motion, everything was just a little off, distorted. In a very real way, she felt like she'd just been sucker punched, and again the question went through her head, "Why was he here? Why now?"

He was dressed in shorts and a T-shirt, his sandals kicked off carelessly to the corner. He'd been sitting on the edge of the couch watching TV, waiting for her to arrive. He seemed very pale to her, as if he wasn't getting anywhere near enough sun lately. Suddenly she was twenty-one again, coming home late after her night class, a little later than usual because a few of her classmates talked her into going out for a drink to wind down. He'd be back at their apartment waiting for her, sitting on the edge of their futon watching reruns on TV, worried about her. In her head it was like a repeating pattern, one she thought herself free of. Yet here they were. Shaking her head free of the white noise that blared in her ears, the confusion of her own jumbled thoughts; she stepped into the room and let the door fall shut. She flipped down the small running pack she'd brought with her this morning on a chair near the door. He stood and started moving toward her. Looking for a long, passionate embrace, she wondered? She turned her back to him as she moved through the room, picking up some loose papers lying about, trying to defuse the moment without hurting his feelings.

"I . . . uh . . . always worry about you, Dawn."

"I know, Jerry, but you shouldn't." She suddenly felt very exposed, realizing again how little she was actually wearing. With Tom, it wasn't an issue, be it because of trust or attraction, but suddenly with Jerry, it was. She could tell he was looking at her, in a way that made her slightly uncomfortable. He was remembering back, she could tell. If the last couple of e-mails she'd read from him were any indication, he was still far from over her being dressed as she was, wasn't going to help. "I . . . need to change," she said, but it came out awkwardly. To her ear, it sounded almost accusatory.

"How come?"

"I've been wearing the same thing since seven this morning, I need a change."

"OK." He was standing still, faced in her direction.

"I'll be right back."

"I . . . I thought you'd want to talk. It's been a long time."

"We will . . . I just need to change first, OK?"

"What's the big deal, Dawn? I've seen you naked before. We can talk while you change."

She just stared for a moment, her eyes wide, her mind racing, trying to find the right thing to say. Eventually, she settled for what she considered to be the nicest version of the truth, "I don't think I'd be comfortable with that."

"What are you talking about? It's just me."

"I know, Jerry, but I don't think I'd be comfortable, OK?" She sensed something different from him, a flash of anger in his eyes, at a level he'd never reached in the past. It didn't scare her, but it did surprise her. She watched, as he seemed to take deep, heavy breaths to regulate his temper and then in a very tight, controlled way, he nodded his head. "Sure," he said, "I understand."

But she knew he didn't. She stepped back into the bedroom and closed the door, lifting up the lid on her suitcase to try and find the most concealing outfit she'd brought. That's when she saw his suitcase. It was still closed, but it set off to the side of the dresser she'd never bothered to use. "What are you doing here?" she whispered looking down at the suitcase, finding herself angry all over again.

When she stepped back out of the bedroom, she was wearing jeans and a large pullover sweater. The TV was off, and Jerry sat on the edge of the couch, looking up as she entered. She looked at him for a second and then walked over to the kitchenette and took out a coffee filter to make a cup of instant coffee. She didn't particularly care for the taste of instant coffee, but she suddenly thought this would be a very long evening. Once the pot started brewing, she turned to face him. "You caught me a little off guard, Jerry. What are you doing here?"

"I came to be with you."

"What?"

"You've been all over the news all week, and I know how you hate attention, being at the center of it an' all. I figured you could use someone to talk with."

"I wish you'd called first . . ."

"I tried, but they said you weren't taking calls. Figured that meant you were upset, thought I better get right out here."

Her hand was up to her face, rubbing fiercely at her eyes, a low, dull throbbing was beginning just behind them. She was angry, she was confused, she didn't want to be doing this. "Jerry, I want you to know something," her words were tense, but she tried to keep them flowing at a smooth, easy pace. "I appreciate the fact you flew out here, I appreciate the fact you were concerned about me, but the thing of it is, I'm OK."

"Come on, Dawn, I've seen the news. It looks like this case is all messed up, and this guy you're after, Williams, he seems to be running around doin' all the talking."

"That's because we can't talk, Jerry. If we say something we can't prove, we'd be liable for it. So we stay quiet while we investigate, until we make an arrest. That's how it works."

"Is that why you were gone all day, because you made the arrest?"

"An arrest was made," she said coolly, "but it wasn't any good."

"I kept telling the agents to call you, to let you know I was here. They said your phone was off."

"Yeah," she said, "I think I would have been out of range most of the day anyway."

"Why, where were you?"

"Out on the water. I went sailing."

"I thought you were working?"

"I was." She could tell he didn't understand, and she really didn't feel like explaining it, unsure if she even could. She turned back to see that the pot of coffee was now full. She grabbed one of the ceramic mugs that were hooked above the sink. "Coffee?"

"Nah, I don't drink it, remember?"

"Yeah, that's right." She'd totally forgotten. Had so much of their little idiosyncrasies slipped from her mind? Something as small as him not drinking coffee was forgotten so quickly? How many times had she yelled at him when he'd gone to the store and forgotten to buy it for her? She began to wonder who the man was sitting in the other room. She filled the cup and took a drink; the taste was a bit sour, not like the coffee she'd make back at her apartment in Sacramento. "So where are you staying?"

She turned in enough time to see him shrug. She knew what it meant, the reason his suitcase was in her bedroom. He assumed he was staying with her. "I dunno, I really didn't have time to look today. I came straight here."

"Well, why don't you grab the phone book? We'll find something close to here, something economical."

"Why can't I just stay here?"

"Jerry . . ."

"I'm serious, Dawn, I'll sleep on the couch . . ." To her, it sounded like he was making a concession, like he'd always expected to sleep in her bed. Suddenly in her head she remembered looking up at the stars, watching them dance through the night, as they gently glided on the waves. She and Tom, arm in arm, lying closely to one another. She looked up and realized that Jerry was still talking; she didn't have a clue as to what he'd said.

"We need to talk, Jerry." She'd interrupted whatever he'd said. But she knew what was coming, knew what needed to happen, for both their sakes.

"That's why I'm here. It's OK. You can totally unload on me. I've been paying a lot of attention in therapy. I think I can help you."

She walked into the living room area and sat in the hard, curved back chair, facing him. She brought up her deepest and most sincere look. "You shouldn't have come, Jerry, really."

"Christ, Dawn, I came for you!"

Another flare of anger. She was impressed. For so long he'd been so passive it was an amazing sight to see him announcing his feelings. It seemed the past year in therapy helped him. He was starting to project all that he was storing up inside. Two years ago it would have thrilled her to see him like this, now it just reminded her of how sad and empty their relationship became. It also showed her how much anger he held inside toward her. She didn't blame him. If he'd played her over the years, the way she'd played him, she'd be angry to. The anger, she suspected, was mostly from the breakup and the subsequent breakdown. She would be the easiest scapegoat to use to help him start rebuilding; blame her before he realized he needed to blame himself. Therapy was odd that way; games were used as constructs to help people reestablish identity before they found truth on many occasions. Looking at him, watching the way he reacted to her, she could tell what his therapist was putting him through, which direction she was steering him. She was certain his mother was helping too; she'd always hated Dawn and she was certain his mother was cursing her name after every other breath. Poor Jerry would be caught in the midst of it all. He still loved her, still hoped they'd be together forever. His feelings would be the retaining wall against the hurtful words of his mother and the blame the therapist was assigning. It was all helping him release his anger, it was all helping him grow, but he still wasn't ready to face her yet. He still had a very long way to go.

"I know you did, Jerry, I know," her voice stayed calm, slipping delicately into her own therapeutic voice, trying to talk him through what he was feeling, trying to keep herself stable while she was at it. Saying his name with every sentence she uttered seemed important, her voice saying his name seemed to keep him calm. "But we're not together anymore."

"I know that," he said loudly as he lifted himself up from the edge of the couch. "I remember that night, my job wasn't good enough and you needed more."

She was impressed by the bitterness she heard. "That's an oversimplification."

"I had some bad months there, I know. But I have a regular job now, nine to five. I took a vacation day to fly down here. I've got health benefits and a 401(k) plan now. We can have kids now. I did what you said, I quit goofing off. I'm not the same guy anymore. I'm being responsible."

He was right; she knew he wasn't the same man anymore. He was worse in some areas and much better in others, but he still wasn't the man she wanted. He didn't want to wait for completion before implementing a new lifestyle. She shut her eyes and sat the coffee down on the small table to her left; she didn't know what to say. It was all too much; her emotions couldn't handle this roller-coaster much longer, not without something breaking. Suddenly she wished she hadn't given up her therapy when she moved to Sacramento. Right now she could use the advice. "Jerry, when we broke up, it was hard for me too. But I've started living a different life now, so have you . . ."

"I know what you're going to say, Hon. But answer me this, huh? Have you had sex with anyone since we broke up? Have you?"

"That's none of your business, Jerry, not anymore." It was getting close, she knew. They were a whisper away from getting into the subject she'd kept from him for what seemed like her entire life.

"You haven't, I know you. We were together forever, Hon, us, you and me. We've never been with anybody else. You can't just start up with somebody new."

And there she was, in the place she'd been dreading for so terribly long. Her anger at being thrust here made the moment a bit more bearable, but not perfect. "No, I haven't been with anyone since we broke up." That's when it occurred to her, she hadn't, and maybe a piece of what he was saying was correct. Added to what Tom said to her the other day, about needing a strong sense of drama in her life, perhaps it all fit together. When Jerry was no longer what she either wanted or needed, she began to look elsewhere, but never left the safety of their dysfunctional relationship. But since leaving it, she no longer felt safe in going off with someone new. She'd met many men in the past year in her new city. Plenty of coworkers offered to set her up, but she'd always steered away from it. She didn't want to be with just anybody. She'd told herself it was because she was waiting for the right man, but maybe there was something to what these two men who seemed to be at polar opposites of her life said. She'd never really let go of Jerry, because she needed the safety net of their relationship. Instead of actually having him in her life for the past year, she'd been using the drama of her guilt to keep herself pushed back, punishing herself for the way she'd treated him. It was amazing what guilt could do to someone. She'd seen it work in a million different ways over her life, but as her old professor said, "Once it strikes within your own life, you'll never be able to see it." Guilt was a part of it though, sitting across from him she could feel it welling up inside. She was still a prisoner of their relationship, the memory of it, and she knew there would only be one way to set them both free.

"You see, Dawn, what do you think that means? I'll tell ya . . . that means you still love me."

"Jerry," she asked hesitantly, "how many women have you slept with in your life?"

"You already know that, you. Just you! Always you. Only you."

They were staring at each other, and Dawn could see the confusion running over his face. In her own eyes, she could feel the first swell of tears. "Aren't you going to ask me?"

"I already know the answer. We were virgins when we first did it. You and me, baby, you and me."

"Six," her voice stayed soft, and the first teardrop fell from her eye and she looked up at him, trying very hard to contain the emotions that were starting to run high.

"What?"

"Six," she repeated. "You were the first, but there were five after you."

"You just said you hadn't fucked anybody since we broke up!"

"I know," she was nodding her head as more tears slowly rolled down her cheeks, "and I meant it." She watched him as his whole body seemed to fall back against the wall behind him, realization was settling in, and it was something he hadn't wanted to hear. Something he'd never even considered.

"You mean you . . ."

"Cheated. Yes. I cheated on you, Jerry."

"Five times?" The way he said it, she could tell he couldn't conceive of it, even as he repeated the number. It seemed too high, the whole idea too ludicrous.

"That was one of the many reasons I needed to leave you last year, Jerry. I couldn't keep cheating on you. I needed to break the cycle that our relationship had fallen to."

"You—you cheated on me?"

Looking over at him she could see the tears coming from his eyes now. She felt terrible, but he needed to know. She believed that otherwise he'd still think of her as that perfect woman, and there would be no way he could ever move on when he was anchored down by her memory. She could see that, and she wanted to set him free, even if that meant he'd spend the rest of his life hating her. "Yes." Mostly it was for her own sake though, for in saying it out loud she could feel a tight grip releasing from her heart, a grip she'd felt locked on it for several years.

"Why?"

"I've been asking myself that same question for years, Jerry, and to be honest, I don't know. At first I told myself it was because I wanted to have some experience that I didn't want to make a lifelong commitment to you without knowing what else might be out there. It was a good line, one I almost even believed. But once you cheat that first time, it gets easier to do it the next. The hardest part is over, the initial part of actually being willing to cheat. Why though, well, part of it was, I wanted more, and don't mean sexually. You were a good lover, but I needed more from our relationship than sex. I needed a man who would take care of me, and even very early on in our lives I could tell that if we were going to stay together I was going to have to be the dominant force in our relationship. With these other men, they took care of me. Some taught me things, some just talked to me in ways we didn't—each one of them offered me something that I wasn't getting from you. I probably should have left you back when I was nineteen, maybe twenty, but I loved you, and in a very real way I still do. I couldn't leave the man I loved. Maybe it was just the little girl in me not wanting to grow up and face the world alone, but I did love you, desperately. But as much as I loved you, Jerry, I never loved you the way you loved me. It was never a total, all consuming love. I'm not even sure if I even know how to love that way in the first place. I loved you out of the fantasy of being loved, out of the fantasy of loving somebody, and building a life. I loved you as a friend, and I loved you as a lover. Mostly I loved you because of the anchoring effect you had over me, and that was never fair to you. I should have set you free of the train wreck of my emotions a long time ago. I'd just never been brave enough to do it before last year."

She looked up at him; his eyes were like two running faucets, his face a mask of despair and heartache. She wondered how far back she'd just set his therapy; just to ease her own troubled emotions, just to free herself of the past. "And as for my celibacy over the last year, well, a lot of that has been about you I think, but not in the way you believe. It's been about me coming to terms with my past, about deciding what I really wanted out of a man. I was also bound by the guilt I felt over the way I'd treated you. But as much as I love you, Jerry, it's not about me coming back to you. You will always be a cherished memory of my past, but my past is what you will be a part of. I'm looking to the future now. And there's no place for us *together* in it. Do you understand, Jerry?"

"H—how can you say this to me?"

"Because I have to, because you need to hear it."

He brought both his hands to his face, using the heels of his palms to rub furiously against the flowing tears from his eyes. He was enraged and hurt, and she could tell he was bordering on having another breakdown, the kind of which she would not be capable of helping him through. He looked back at her, his eyes pleading more than his words and he cleared his throat to say, "It's OK, you know what, I forgive you."

She'd never seen it coming, the rage he'd shown earlier in the evening, the amount of therapy he'd already received. She'd never imagined he'd be able to forgive her, and this told her exactly how deeply in love with her he still was. He was ready to crawl back down into the same emotional hole he'd slipped into last year, to bury his head down in the sand, just to continue being with her. His desperation was exactly how unhappy he was without her. It also showed her just how happy she'd become. "Thank you," she said, feeling the first real sensation of exhaustion.

"We can still be together. We just won't, you know, tell anybody about it."

And looking at him she knew he meant it. He'd be more than happy to suppress this memory and never think or mention it again. All this time, he'd been using her as his anchor; he was working through the therapy to get back together with her. She'd become his goal, what he was striving to reach for, and here she was taking it away, pulling the carpet out from under him. "Jerry," she said as evenly as she could sustain, "I don't want to be with you anymore."

"What," he paused, an honest confusion engulfing him? "Is there somebody else?"

She froze as she looked at him; she was asking herself internally, *"Was there?"* Tom was so much in her thoughts lately that she wasn't entirely sure where thinking about the case ended, and where thoughts of them began. Jerry asking made her really consider it, and she was certain the question was clear in her eyes.

"What's his name?"

Tears still streaked down from his eyes, even as he asked it. His voice was that of her old friend's right now, and she found herself wanting to talk to someone about it, somebody who actually knew her. "It doesn't matter," she said shaking her head.

"Why?"

"Because I can't be with him."

"You could be with anybody you wanted," he said, choking a little on his own words.

"Not with a suspect."

"Suspect?" Jerry just shook his head, thinking about everything, working hard to stop the tears from coming. "Who were the others?"

"Does it really matter?"

"Yeah . . ."

"No one you knew. Maybe a couple of people you met once or twice through functions, back when I was still with the bureau. Other agents, a couple of guys back in college. No one important."

"Important enough for you to cheat," he said.

"Trust me, Jerry, they were never important . . . they were just there."

"Wasn't I?"

"Weren't you what?" He was once again bordering on hysterics, trembling before her, shaking his head almost violently. He was dealing with a lot, and she just didn't have the strength or the resolve to take him into her arms. She knew he really needed to be held right now, but she knew if she did it, it would only restart the process of him needing her. Something she was determined to break tonight.

"Important?"

"You were always important, Jerry. I just wasn't responsible enough to do the right thing, back when I should have, that's all."

"You were always the responsible one, everyone said so, and you said so. I was the lazy ass. You were the one who got shit done."

"I just wasn't as responsible as we both would have liked."

"I love you," he said desperately, and his look came just short of scaring her.

"I know," she said looking at him, watching a shift taking place, seeing something in him she wasn't really sure of.

"Say it."

"Say what, Jerry?'

"That you love me too."

"I'll always love you, Jerry, always."

"Say it."

He needed to hear it and she knew it; she also knew that he couldn't. She'd be lying to him, and a lie at this stage of his development would be impacting and lasting, and she believed cause more damage than good. "I can't, Jerry, I'm sorry."

"You mean you won't!?!" And he changed right before her eyes. Gone was the gentle childlike man she'd loved through her youth. Suddenly he was enraged, he was charging up at her, his eyes filled with madness. She couldn't believe what she was seeing; she couldn't believe what he was saying. His voice was screaming, telling her she was a "fucking bitch," and suddenly her training kicked in. The world which was moving in something like slow motion, ever since she'd come home, suddenly revved up to full speed. He was coming at her, a general madness of despair in his eyes, his hand was up and it honestly looked like he planned to hit her. In an instant she realized his rage was released, and in a way she never would have suspected possible. He wasn't thinking right now. He was just giving into his emotions; it was just that no one suspected his emotions would tell him to lash out physically, violently. Of course, being told their relationship was filled with lies, at a point where he still believed she was his saving grace, would certainly be enough to cause a traumatic trigger effect. She just never thought him capable of actually hitting her.

She bounced up from her chair as he came rushing toward her, moving with a dancer's grace, even as the panic of the moment filled her facial features. She didn't want to hurt him, but at the same time she wasn't going to let him hit her. In moving, she easily avoided his swing, an untrained, unskilled attack that was poorly timed. She then did a quick palm strike to his throat that caused him to start hacking and wheezing. She bounced around him and cut her foot into the back of his knee while twisting away from him. This sent Jerry falling down to the floor. He was completely under her power, and as soon as he was flat on the floor, she kicked down on his solar plexus. The attack was over less than thirty seconds from when it began, and she looked down at his helpless frame, feeling the burning of tears in her own eyes. *This is what love was to her*, she thought—*pain and suffering*. He loved her, and she drove him to this just to be free of him. Tears streaked from his eyes as he continued to hack and wheeze on her floor, and eventually, she began to sob.

She remembered the night she left him, just over a year ago. She'd manipulated him that night, and she couldn't help but feel that she'd done the same tonight. Her initial anger was at him as much as it was at herself. Tom was affecting her in a number of ways, and he was distracting her from what she was doing. She didn't want to admit it, but seeing Jerry's fallen body on the floor, she knew it was true. *His game was working*, she thought. It was the only thing that explained what she was feeling. She'd always seen herself as a master manipulator, but in this game Tom was playing her. He'd somehow wormed his way into her head. She'd spent the past few weeks chasing after him instead of the case. She needed to escape what was happening to her, and looking down at Jerry, she knew she no longer loved him. Not as anything other than a memory. It took this, to finally let him go.

She'd held onto an ideal of who he was for too long. The man she remembered would never have attacked her, not even knowing what she did. This wasn't her childhood sweetheart anymore, and she was no longer the little girl swept up in him. "Go ahead and stay the night, Jerry, but be out of here by morning."

She turned from him and walked to the chair where she'd dropped off her running pack earlier, picking it up, and moving toward the door. In her mind, a million thoughts suddenly surged forward. She couldn't help but ask herself how'd she let her life get so horribly out of control. Reason didn't seem to matter anymore, and the line between right and wrong was blurring. Seeing Jerry like this seemed wrong to her, totally alien. This wasn't who he was, back when they were together. *Or maybe*, she thought, *he was*. But she'd maintained so much control over him that his true nature was never allowed free. Throughout the last few years, she'd believed staying with Jerry as long as she did was for his benefit, that he'd been happier and healthier because of it. Now she found herself questioning that. Had her lack of interest and cheating done this much psychological damage to him? Had staying with him ruined him for anyone else? Was that the mark her wake left in his life? The idea didn't sit well with her, and she knew she needed to get out of this place, away from him, away from everything she was thinking. She needed to lose herself for a few hours, escape this life she found herself in, this roller-coaster ride she could no longer keep up with. She didn't know how much of this was really her fault, but she knew if it was broken down to percentages, she'd be the higher number. She'd never been honest with him, and now he was so much less to her she couldn't even conceive it. It was all too much to process. She needed an escape, and she needed it now. Opening the door she felt the cool night air sweeping around her, and she looked back at the sad little man on the floor, "And before you ever attack someone like that again, Jerry, get back into therapy, or you'll be lost forever in your own pathetic rage, and I'd like to believe you were better than that."

With that, she left.

* * *

Moments 12.1

March 25, 2000

He lay still on the floor for almost an hour, before he finally got back to his feet. All he could think about was the number five. Five times he'd been played a fool. He couldn't believe how much he hated her right now, how she'd treated him.

No wonder she'd left him, Jerry thought, *he couldn't even tell what she was doing, what she was feeling.* He felt like the loser she must have always thought him to be. *Why'd she even bother to keep me around,* he wondered? *To laugh at, make fun of?* The thoughts pulsed through his head, blurring his vision.

He grunted as he moved. His throat was sore and his back ached. The worst part was, he knew she'd been gentle on him. She could have hurt him much worse. Suddenly the room seemed very large, and he felt very small within it. He was still crying, for so long now that the tears actually hurt. He was lost, and he didn't know what to do. Sitting on the dresser in her room, he'd seen a portable radio, an FBI issue, something that would allow Dawn to keep up on the case. He knew she still did it; instead of listening to the radio or a CD, she'd tune the radio in and listen to the ongoing watch on a suspect. She'd always done it, even back when they were together. He stepped in her room and turned it on, listening for any sign that she'd gone back on duty, or would call in and say where she was going. He needed to talk to her.

The pain was still there, and he felt like he wanted to throw up. His throat was raw and sore. He checked the bathroom to see if she had any painkillers, but found both her medicine cabinet and bath bag had nothing but aspirin. He knew he needed more than that. He stepped back out in the main room. The sound of an agent named Lindy called out; saying she just spotted Dawn come over the air, asking of anyone was expecting her. He smiled at the fact that he'd soon know where she was. Looking around the room he saw her purse and stepped over to it, wondering if there was anything in it, a painkiller or two, she'd never miss them. He flipped open the cover flap and saw it at once. A new shiver went through him as he looked down into her bag and saw it. No painkillers, well, not really. He pushed the thought out of his head, and tried to focus away from the pain, listening to the radio, which suddenly seemed frantic with activity. It was after he'd been listening for awhile that he heard something that dropped him to his knees, something he never wanted to hear at all. Suddenly everything Dawn just confessed to him became clear and he stared blankly at the radio in disbelief, and he felt the rage building up inside him once more.

His tears, he knew, were all cried out, and he once again opened the flap to her purse and stared down at it, and with a quivering hand grabbed it.

"I'll show you," he said in an unsteady, trembling voice. "I'll make you love me again."

* * *

Senses of Night

Senses of Night 13.0

March 25, 2000

"Command Unit One, this is Lindy. Is anybody expecting McCafferty tonight?"

"Lindy, this is command. No, from what the agents at her boarding said, she was deactivating herself until Sunday. Why?"

"Because her rent-a-car just pulled around the corner."

Agent Roberts stiffened up in his seat from their mobile command trailer they positioned to spy on Tom Williams' condo, "Come again?"

"I said her car just went around marker #1."

He shrugged it off. "Probably needs some hard data for one of the NCUA reports. Thanks for the head's up though." He looked around the trailer where he and Agent Camden sat. It was clean enough, and they didn't have anything in here they weren't supposed to, so he didn't really care if they had a visitor tonight. He stretched a little in his seat, longing for the day he'd be off nightshift, could get back to sleeping with his wife, instead of rotating shifts for sleeping. Looking over at Camden made him gaze down at his watch. On nights like these, when they wasn't any supervisors with them, they traded off taking naps. They each got an hour at a time; Camden had fifteen more minutes to his, then it was his turn. He turned to look back at Williams' house, the drapes were drawn as they always were, but his light was clearly on inside.

"Command Unit One, this is Lindy again . . ."

"Go ahead, Lindy. It's just you and me online tonight, no need to be so formal."

"McCafferty just passed marker 2."

"Say again?"

"You heard me."

"Thanks." He clicked off and walked over to the door of the trailer, opening it and looking out at the long stretch of road that led to where the condo units began. He saw a car moving up toward the entrance. He walked back in and flicked Camden's ear to wake him.

"What the—"

"Relax," he said, "just me."

"What the hell are you doing? I've still got time before it's your turn, don't I?"

"McCafferty's on her way up."

"So, she's ex-FBI, she can't touch us."

"She just passed marker 2." It seemed odd to Roberts because marker 2 was the point where you needed to turn to get to their command unit. In passing it, she was now heading directly toward the condo units themselves.

"She's probably doing her own surveillance run. Now, seriously man, let me sleep."

Something still seemed odd to Roberts, but he hunkered back in his seat waiting. Lindy's next call said McCafferty's taillights disappeared around the bend; she was now out of sight. Roberts sat uneasily, listening as Baker radioed in that he saw McCafferty's car approaching. Baker was positioned just inside the condo lot in the van, the FBI having paid one of the homeowners a little extra to use their parking spot. "She's turning in."

"What?" Roberts couldn't believe what he was hearing. "Are you sure?"

"I see the two headlights coming right at me."

"Then please tell me she's coming to talk to you."

"I wish."

Robert's fingers began to thump down on the tabletop, as he considered what he should do. He was trying to guess what she might be doing. Was she running the grounds looking to see if they'd missed some kind of alternate escape route? Why the hell wasn't she calling in? Sure, she wasn't FBI, but she used to be, she knew the protocol. She could at least do them the courtesy of acknowledging them. He picked up the phone and dialed her cell. A prerecorded message told him her phone wasn't responding at the moment. He then tried to raise her on the open channel they'd been using. "Agent McCafferty?" But all he heard was the silent hiss of dead air. "Baker, what's happening?"

"She's pulling into his extra parking space."

"Aw, Christ," he again held the microphone to his mouth, "Agent McCafferty, this is Charlie Roberts of the FBI. Please respond."

Baker's voice again filled the air instead of hers, "She's getting out of the car."

"Why?"

"Listen, man, I'm a field operative, not a psychologist. How would I know?"

"Well, what's she doing?"

"Hard to tell because of the other cars, but it looks like she's locking her car."

"McCafferty," he said sternly into the radio once more, "I insist you respond and state your intent!"

"That's probably not going to work, Charlie."

"Really," he found himself snapping at Baker, "Why's that?"

"She doesn't seem to have her radio with her."

"Of course not."

"Should I intercept?"

"Shit," he said into the mouthpiece of the radio transmitter, "how would I know?"

"She's headed to his unit, Charlie. If I don't go now, I'll never be able to stop her."

They'd all been briefed directly by Elliott, and he'd told them all he planned to use McCafferty's relationship with the suspect against him. "Negative, Baker. Let her go."

"Christ, Charlie, are you sure?"

"No, not sure at all, but I really don't see how we can stop here either. She's NCUA, not FBI. Know what I mean? Just do me a favor. Take a lot of pictures. I want it documented."

"Gotcha."

He reached over and dialed the phone again, as he kicked Camden in the leg; he snapped to attention, looking very angry with his partner. Camden was about to start yelling, when he heard what Roberts was actually saying. "Yes, sir, Mr. Elliott, I'm aware of what time it is. However, I thought you should know Agent McCafferty has pulled into the suspect's parking spot." Camden suddenly realized things had taken a weird turn since he last dozed off. "No, sir," he said, "she has not called or radioed in with her intent . . . Yes, sir, I did try to raise her by both cell and radio. Her cell is off, and she is not responding. Agent Baker says she is not carrying her radio. I thought you should be informed."

Baker's voice again filled the command center, "She's going up the stairs, right to his door."

"Yes, sir." Baker continued, "That's correct, she's approaching his front door."

"She just rang the bell."

"Sir, it appears as if she's initiating contact with the suspect. What are my orders?"

* * *

Senses of Night 13.1

March 25, 2000

Tom looked through the peephole, as he flipped on the porch light. He couldn't believe it was her. He undid the deadbolt and chain lock and opened it to face her. She stood a few steps back looking at him, her face seemed thinner than earlier, and he could tell she'd been crying. She seemed, for no apparent reason, more delicate to him than before, and he wanted to wrap his arms around her, but knew he couldn't. He stood in a startled silence, before finally managing to utter out, "Hi."

"Hi," she said back sheepishly.

"You're about the last person I expected to turn up on my door tonight." Then a thought hit him, "Are you here to arrest me already?"

She released a small laugh, more of a chuckle, as she gently shook her head and said, "No." She looked up at him, and he could tell she was trying to figure something out, but for the life of him he didn't know what, so he said, "you changed clothes."

"It was cold."

"Damn weather," and he saw her smile gently at his joke, but she still seemed sheepish and undecided. "This outfit looks pretty good too. If you don't mind me saying."

She looked behind her for a moment, thinking of where she knew the agents to be placed, wondering how many pictures they'd already taken of her as she walked to his door, and then she thought about the fallen body of her former lover, lying on her living room floor, crying lonely tears for a love that no longer existed. She felt very alone right now, empty. She didn't like the way she felt, and somehow, coming here seemed like the answer. "Did I wake you?" she asked.

"No," he was shaking his head, "I was actually just getting ready to go to bed."

"Yeah," she said softly, "me too."

Something in the way she said it told him everything he needed to know. He wanted to say something, but no words came. All he could do was look at her, his mouth dropping in amazement. She smiled at his reaction; in fact she confessed to herself it was the best she'd ever seen him look. Since they first met, he'd always come across so confidant, the man with a plan. She'd never once worried him with what she was doing, until this moment. She took great pleasure in that, especially when she saw the edges of his cheeks starting to color. It was the first time she'd ever put him on the ropes, and she knew he'd never make the first move. Not even here on his own home turf. Without saying another word she stepped forward, keeping her eyes locked into his, thankful that he didn't back away as she moved in. Suddenly they were a whisper apart, suddenly everything was changing. Though it only lasted a moment, it was a moment that seemed to last forever, each hovering on the edge of a dream. They both kept their eyes open, as she pressed her lips to his.

The kissing began slowly, at first just their lips, hints of more as they each slowly opened wider as the moisture between them grew. He was never one to kiss fast. He enjoyed it and wanted to savor each kiss that came his way, bringing himself back to a time in his youth when kissing was everything. He'd been with women over the years that seemed to slide their tongue into his mouth as they first started leaning into one another. Dawn wasn't like that; when she kissed, it was to state intent, and tonight, that was exactly what she was doing. Her first kiss was soft, delicate, tasting like a cool rain. At first, it almost took his breath away, but then he lifted his hand to her neck and looked into her eyes, and he saw what she wasn't saying. She was past the point of caring about right or wrong, and she needed to be with someone, someone she felt close to, someone that might even understand her, if only just a little. He'd wanted to be with her from the moment he first saw her for the most obvious of reasons, but since then he'd been watching her in an entirely different way. He'd been studying her, and the more he saw of her, the more he liked her. Remembering back to his own childhood when his elders would ask him what he was looking for in a woman, he'd told them he wanted her to be beautiful, smart, funny, and have something inside her that would make him never want to let go. Looking at her now, it was like he was reading off a checklist.

He also knew as he gently glided his fingers around to the back of her neck, slowly bringing her forward again for their lips to meet; the kiss lasted for minutes as they just stayed under the dim light of his porch, both knowing that others were watching, and neither wanting to do anything to stop this sleek, elegant moment from unfolding. He knew this was about her, not him, not the case or what he might be accused of. This was about something she needed, even if only for this one moment, and as her tongue did finally part his lips. He knew he didn't care how long this magic would last; he was committed to this to the very end. Being accused of any crime was more than worth it, he thought, if meeting her was the reward.

They were close now, close enough that their hands and arms began to wrap around each other, until finally where two people stood, only one really remained. Their eyes closed as their kisses lingered, and the weight of the moment struck them. They pulled their faces apart for only a minute, and without a word both knew what would happen next. Slowly he pulled her inside, her body practically knocking him over as she wrapped her arms hungrily around his neck and seemed for a second to swing on him lifting her feet completely off the ground. It was gleeful and childlike, and completely unlike anything she'd done in years, but with him it felt right. The door closed with a loud, rambunctious bang.

* * *

Senses of Night 13.2

March 25, 2000

"Son of a bitch!" Baker screamed into the airwaves.

"What is it?" Roberts was screaming back as he instinctively reached for his sidearm, thinking immediately of the worst possible scenario. "Hang on a moment, sir," as he did his best to keep the phone Special Agent Elliott was on fitted between his chin and shoulder, looking around at the radio speaker as if that might help Baker know he was looking for clarification. "Baker, what is it? Is McCafferty OK?"

"You're not gonna believe it, Charlie . . ."

"*What?!?!?*"

"She kissed him."

"What?" Suddenly the inside of his stomach was doing a free-floating somersault, because if he heard Baker correctly that would mean he would need to be the one to relay this sudden development to Elliott, something he definitely didn't want to do. "Say again, Baker, say again?"

"She kissed him, he pulled her inside, and they shut the door. Before that though, they were goddamn making out right on his front stoop. What the hell happened out on that damn boat today?"

"Christ Almighty," Roberts said, as he relayed the message to Marshal Elliott, who waited angrily on the line for an update. When Roberts finally hung up, he looked back at his partner and spoke into the radio, "Everyone, hold your positions and be advised. Special Agent Elliott is on his way down. Right now."

* * *

Senses of Night 13.3

March 25, 2000

They fell back against the wall facing the door; he couldn't believe it was really happening. But it was, his hands were finally touching her, caressing her skin, and suddenly the rules she'd been so concerned about didn't seem to matter. He didn't understand what happened, what changed, but at the moment, he didn't really care. The look in her eyes said three things: One, she didn't want to be alone, and the second was, she didn't want to talk about the reason why. The third thing he could tell was the happiest for him though, it said she wanted him, just as much as he wanted her. He wanted to keep the moment alive, keep it going before her more rational side took over her senses. He feared, at that moment, he was just a temporary fix to whatever ailed her. The thought saddened him, but the feel of her body allowed him to push it aside. There would be time for sorrow of what might have been later.

All he wanted right now was her, and he got the intense feeling she felt the exact same way.

Nothing else mattered; the pain from falling back into the wall at full force didn't faze him. His feet were still sliding, and he didn't seem to be able to get his footing as she pressed herself tightly against him, kissing him madly. It was a moment out of some teenage movie, two kids experimenting with sex, starting with the passion of the kiss. He shrugged off the blow to the wall as if it were nothing, keeping his mouth pressed to hers. Feeling the moist smoothness of her tongue as it rolled in his mouth, teasing and exciting him with every twitch. It was eighteen months since he'd been this close to anyone and a lifetime since it seemed to mean so much.

She was digging one hand into his hair, tightly combing through the strands while scratching down his head, her other hand was pressing tightly against his ribs, squeezing sensually. Her flat palm cascading down his side and then rubbing smoothly back upward, sending sensations throughout his body. His own hands circled around her, pulling her in. For Tom, it was like waking up for the first time in years. It was moments like this, he mused, that inspired poets to write love sonnets, a moment like this that kept people up to all hours trolling singles' bars. Each of them looking for that one hit of ecstasy that could only really ever come from the fulfillment of desire. Honest desire, true and real.

He couldn't remember the last time he'd felt like this.

The sweatshirt she wore wasn't terribly thick, and he could feel her firm, tight body beneath it. The outline of her spine as it rose softly up. His fingers pressed in rhythmic pulses up and down, and her body contorted, pushing her deeper into him.

He'd been getting ready for bed, when the doorbell rang; he wore nothing but an old pair of sweat pants and a credit union T-shirt he'd gotten years ago. With her pressed so tightly against him, there was no way of concealing his excitement. She didn't seem to mind though, as she just kept leaning into him.

Slowly they slid against his weight to the hard, cold tile floor, and rolled their way to the carpet of the living room.

* * *

Senses of Night 13.4

March 26, 2000

"There are still a few things I don't understand."
"Like what?"
"You and Netzy. When did it end?"

"End? You mean us sleeping together?"

"Yes."

"About four months before she was promoted. She stayed late, told me she didn't think it was right. Said she loved her husband. She wanted to work on it at home, fix things, she said. I mentioned Karen again, always a sore subject between the two of us, and she told me to go to hell. It was as she was leaving that night, storming out, more to the point. She told me she intended to apply for the VP job too. I thought, you know, well, hell, maybe you don't. I thought she was just upset about something, me, maybe. Blowing off steam, I guess, is what I really thought. I never dreamed she'd do what she did."

"So you're saying she used you right up to the point where you could no longer benefit her career?"

"I'd say that was fairly accurate, yes. Is that what was bothering you?"

"No. That I was just curious about."

"What's bothering you then?"

"Why do you think I'm bothered? Maybe I'm always like this afterward?"

"Nah, it's your eyes, they give you away. You're bothered."

"If you think Karen is really your child, Tom, why didn't you file the paperwork, take a stance? It sounds to me like you could have, and should have, long before you were accused of embezzlement."

"That's not an easy answer, Dawn . . . mostly because it makes me look bad . . ."

"That mean you're not going to answer?"

"No, I'll answer . . . I just don't think you'll like it much. I was scared. Scared that Karen was my daughter, scared she wasn't. Scared about what that would mean to my life, my reputation, even to a certain extent my career and the way I lived my life. Her husband for instance, he's a good man, someone I actually like. Back when she first got hired, I even went out with him for beers on several occasions. I like the guy . . . and the idea she might cheat on him . . . it'd ruin him. Completely . . . that Karen might not be his . . . But hell . . . When it all comes out, I guess I didn't want to admit she could be mine . . . I didn't want to be a father . . . especially not with her . . . and being quiet was just an easier way of dealing with it."

"Funny, I think that's the most honest you've ever been with me."

"No, it's not. I've told you a lot of true things."

"But never something you didn't want to tell me."

"True . . . So how about you? You gonna tell me why you came here? Why you really came here, because I saw the look in your eyes . . . and there was a reason, and as much as I'd like it to be me, I know that's not the case. So tell me, Dawn, tell me why are you here?"

* * *

Senses of Night 13.5
March 25, 2000

She couldn't believe what she was doing. In her mind, she knew this meant she was essentially throwing her career with the NCUA down the drain. But with the fresh thought of Jerry lying on the floor of her rented room, she just didn't care. She needed to feel a man's touch; it had been far too long, and tonight more than ever she needed that sensation. More importantly though, it needed to be the right man touching her, and to her, that meant Tom.

She didn't know how long she'd really been thinking of what his touch would feel like against her skin, but the thought was there nonetheless, haunting the edges of her investigation, and clouding her judgment whenever he'd been around. Jerry was the catalyst, his rage, his maddening attack, she needed to be free of the past, and that meant leaping toward the future. That meant taking a chance.

Tom was being gentle, she could tell, she wasn't. For her it had been over a year since the last time she'd been with a man, Jerry, a few days before their breakup back in Washington DC. Tom was nothing like Jerry; so far their entire approach was different. Tom was working hard at being a gentleman, despite the fact she'd lunged into him at the end of a Friday night just before he'd headed off to sleep; he wasn't presuming anything. He was braced for the idea she might stop, get up, and walk out on what she'd started. She knew he wanted her, in the exact way she was currently offering herself, but he refused to play the role of the cad. She knew in her head and heart that if she said stop, even now as they rolled from the tile onto the carpet, he wouldn't argue.

Before, back when she'd been with Jerry, if something was started, it had to be finished, no matter what. Back then, she understood it, accepted it even. Tom was older though, he understood that not everything worked out the way you assumed it would.

It was all crazy, she knew it. This was insane, and wrong, and the worst possible choice she could make; she knew it all, but couldn't stop herself. Even as the thoughts surfaced for her to stop and run away, she felt Tom take her finger into his own mouth. She couldn't recall how many times she'd taken a man's finger into her own mouth, to stimulate nerves and senses leading up to a larger picture for later that evening, but never before had a man been willing to do it for her. *A small thing*, she thought, but something that stood out to her. The power of his mouth on her skin was revealing and sedating. Once again, she didn't care about the NCUA or the wrath that would most certainly be coming from Special Agent Marshal Elliott. All she knew was that she wanted Tom Williams, in exactly the way she was now experiencing him.

She'd been with a total of six men prior to this evening, in the entire course of her life; she'd known friends who were with that many through high school. This wasn't her life; she wasn't the kind of woman to run from one man to another, especially not a man in trouble with the law. At the same time, she realized she was the one who drove a reckless amount of miles to get here, coming with one intent on her mind. She wanted to know how Tom Williams tasted when he kissed, and she'd been very pleased with the results. He was a gentleman, the kind her mother always referred to as a real man. The kind that cared about the person they were with. Most men, she'd always told Dawn, cared only about their own temporary satisfaction; it was a rare gem that cared about pleasing their partner first. The key, her mother said, was in the kiss. A man who kissed selfishly, like they only wished to get it over with, was not worth her time, but the man who lingered or better yet enjoyed the subtle passion even in the quickest of pecks could bring, that would be a man she should take notice of. With only a few, real minutes of being able to judge, Dawn realized that so far, Tom was exactly that kind of man.

She'd surprised him; she knew that. But what lay beneath his sweats gave way to the fact he was not displeased with her surprise visit. As far as she could feel, he was very pleased indeed. But unlike most of the men she'd been with, the fact he had an erection wasn't the only thing he fixated on. Most men would have been forcing her hand down to grab it, something that lacked any element of subtlety in her opinion. All women knew the reaction such activity would have on a man, they'd known since their teen years in most cases. Still, most men felt the need to present the issue as if no woman had ever given a man a hard-on before. To Tom's credit, she thought, he didn't conceal it, but he didn't draw any unwarranted attention to it either. His hands remained on her, lightly touching, caressing, and at times even massaging. Never forcing her, he let her decide where her hands would go, how she would rub his body. He seemed to concern himself with her and how he moved his wandering hands.

And she liked how he moved his hands.

Again, she found him very unassuming. His main focus was her, dancing his fingers in pulses of pressure and tickling up her back, over her ribs and caressing in and over her spine. Occasionally his hands would drift lower, cascading over her rear, something she could tell by his touch he wanted to grab tightly, but it was a rare indulgence. To encourage him, she began to give out small, subtle moans of pleasure whenever his hands dropped below the small of her back. Not enough so that he would completely forgo what he was already doing, but enough that he realized he shouldn't be ignoring her ass either.

And that was the way she thought of it at the moment, not her rear end, for at least the moment, and probably the rest of the night, it was her ass. And she wanted to feel his hungering advances, his guttural grabs, and his rustic reaching. For at least one night she didn't want romance, she wanted sex.

She could tell he wasn't the kind of man to go for that, especially when things had already run so deep between them, but she could also figure out his tells, the way he moved, the way he touched. He was looking to judge her responses to what he was already doing, ready to make any necessary changes to his technique or form. He was there for her.

And that made her want to be there for him.

Slowly, making sure to make a spectacle of it, she began to slide both her hands down beneath his waistline. Already he was making this a very special night for her, and as long as he continued on at this rate, she'd do the same for him.

* * *

Senses of Night 13.6

March 26, 2000

"Jerry's in town."

"When?"

"Sometime yesterday . . . I didn't know until I got home. He was there waiting for me."

"Did you talk?"

"Yes."

"I meant . . . I meant, about the past?"

"Uh-huh, yeah . . . I knew what you meant, and yeah, we did."

"How'd he take it?"

"I could lie and say well."

"That bad, huh?"

"Worse."

"Anything I can do?"

"I think you've already done quite a bit for one evening."

"Yeah, well . . . look at the clock, Dawn, it's not evening anymore. It's morning. Whole new set of rules apply."

"It's amazing how the night seems to hide all our fears and doubts, isn't it? How it lets the true nature of a person free."

"I suppose, though, I tell you, Dawn, I've done some wild, crazy shit come the dark of night."

"Haven't we all?"

"Well, if we're judging by last night . . ."

"Come on, Tom, look at me, look at us. Walking up to your door last night, I might as well have put in my two weeks' notice. It would have been cleaner and had far less ramifications."

"They're going to fire you for coming here?"

"Directly, no. They'll find another way I'm sure. Maybe hook me onto the same sinking ship as Neal, or, who knows, maybe they will fire me for consorting with you. But in any case, it's all but official. My career with the NCUA is over, probably as of Monday morning."

"Then why'd you do it?"

"I needed you out of my head. You were taking up too much space. I needed some room to think."

"Did you get it?"

"**Beg your pardon?**"

"You have a nice smile, very teasing . . . when you want it to be."

"**Thank you, Mr. Williams. I'll take that as a compliment.**"

"Seriously though, am I out of your head now?"

"**Partially, part of the block anyway. The frustration I was feeling at not being able to act on my impulse, it's out of the way. Now I'll start to think a little clearer in regard to you and this case.**"

"So you still think I'm guilty, even after all this time."

"**Tom, let's not do this, OK? I know what you have to say, I do, but . . . I don't like it when you lie to me. I know you're guilty, you know you're guilty, everybody knows you're guilty, but here I am anyway . . . What does that tell you?**"

"That you probably shouldn't have stopped seeing that therapist."

* * *

Senses of Night 13.7

March 25, 2000

Her laughter filled the room, and it was more intoxicating than any wine he'd ever tasted. He remembered for a brief moment a woman he'd been with many years before, a struggling actress from the small theater circle San Diego offered to locals. She'd told Tom that sex was never like it was in the movies, and he knew she was right.

In the movies everything was perfect, right down to the lighting. In real life, people got rug burns as they moved a bit too quickly across the floor. They broke out into spontaneous laughter while looking at their partners' faces, reacting at the things they were doing or having done to them. There were screams, moans, and even the occasional whistle. Heads got bumped, and lovers fell off beds. Awkward positions were fixed and each started to sweat as the heat of what they did consumed them. Mostly though, the difference was laughter, people in the movies never seemed to stop and talk, tell a joke, make a funny face. In real life these things happened, especially with Tom. He looked at the act of making love as an enjoyment, and in his opinion anything enjoyable needed to be fun. That meant laughter was a must. He'd been with more than a few women over the years that were temporarily put off by his less than serious or intense approach. He always liked to show them he was as intense in the moment as they were, he just chose a less serious way to do it. In the end, they'd always seemed to enjoy themselves, and seeing how a good portion of the women he'd been with over the years were still friends, still people he could talk with, he was fairly sure none were too traumatized by his quest for laughter. Looking at Dawn's face he wasn't worried about her. He could tell that tonight she needed to laugh, that tonight she needed many things. But her life was very serious, and she needed a break from it.

Tonight was one of those nights. The clothes were already starting to be pulled wildly from their bodies as they rolled onto the living room carpet, and both were sure they'd each wind up with a few interesting bumps, bruises, and perhaps even a burn. Neither stopped to reposition themselves though, both kept the moment going. They'd said what they needed to say on the boat earlier, and both felt the time for talking was done. Anything else that still needed to be hashed out would need to wait for the sun; right now it was time for the night to reign. And tonight was not for talking.

Beneath her sweatshirt, Tom found she was only wearing a thin T-shirt, telling Tom that whenever she'd changed out of what she'd been wearing at the boat, she hadn't planned on leaving the house again. She'd been planning to settle down for the night. He pulled his mouth away just long enough to pull her shirt upward, making it disappear from her body. He then pulled her mouth back to his.

She seemed incredibly warm as she pressed her naked body to his, warmer than any other woman he'd ever encountered. Her body was lean and tight, well cut from many years of physical training and exercise. Dawn knew how to take care of herself; she also knew how to take care of him. He wasn't pressing too much, but he was reacting to every move she made. He seemed to be everywhere, as the heat continued to build between them. Rising up to the point where she could hardly think straight, rolling around half naked on the carpet, she lost track of time. Had she been in his house an hour? Or was it three?

She was still dressed from the waist down, while he was now completely exposed. This was the first time in her life that she remembered not being naked first. It seemed the men she'd been with were always so desperate to have her; they didn't consider what she wanted. Maybe they'd just been self-conscious about their own appearance, none of them having been in the same kind of shape she kept herself in. None of them realizing that she slept with the men she did for one reason only, because she'd wanted to. There was always something that attracted her to one partner or another, some level of physical attraction, but most often the attraction began with their mind, with the person they were. Not an image they tried to carry. She'd never set out looking for some bronzed, chiseled man. Most of those who she'd encountered in her life offered her little she actually cared about. What she'd always really wanted was a man, someone who knew what it meant to be a man. Not the image of one.

His tongue slid from her mouth, down to her neck, where he loosely suckled at her skin for a moment, before rising up to the delicate feel of her earlobe. Her nails dug sharply into his back as he embraced her tightly. Tightly against her he could feel her every breath she took and react to her every need.

This was the time for the foreplay, and neither of them felt the need to hurry.

This was a job that could easily take all night to complete.

* * *

Senses of Night 13.8

March 26, 2000

"So if you really think your career is over . . . what's next?"

"Next?"

"Yeah, you know, what do you plan to do when you grow up?"

"You know something, Tom? I haven't got a clue."

"Essentially then, you coming here tonight was about the worst thing in the world you could do. It's going to send gigantic ripples through the threads of your whole existence for many years to come."

"My, my . . . aren't we the melodramatic one?"

"Am I?"

"A little . . ."

"But I'm right. I'm concerned."

"About me?"

"You're the one here, aren't you?"

"I'll be OK."

"How?"

"I'm not destitute. I may not have the kind of cash you do, stashed away in the bank, but I do have a halfway decent nest egg. I can survive until I find a new job. I'll be OK, honest."

"Is there . . . I don't know . . . hell . . . anything I can do?"
"Sure . . ."
"What?"
"A full written confession . . . that would help a lot."
"Would that need to be double spaced?"
"It's not going to end well, Tom . . . It's not."
"I know, but I don't think it'll end the way you think it will."
"It's very rare I'm wrong."
"So let me ask you this, OK?"
"Sure, go ahead . . . ask away."
"What if you're wrong about me?"

* * *

Senses of Night 13.9

March 26, 2000

"What the hell is she doing in there?" Roberts asked, standing a step behind Marshal Elliott. Elliott just continued to stand, staring forward. He held a lit cigarette that he hadn't actually placed in his mouth since igniting it.

He wore loose-fitting khakis and a short-sleeved button-down that was straight out of the 1950s. The other agents nearby assumed this is what Elliott thought of as casual wear. He wore dress shoes and his socks were black. He'd done little more than grunt words since arriving. He was angry and seemed more than just a little disturbed, standing there outside the trailer, looking across the field toward the back of Williams' condo.

They all watched in silence as the lights went out in Williams' unit.

Elliott turned and looked down at the radio speaker, no word from Baker saying she was leaving the residence. He tossed his cigarette to the ground and stamped it out in a lingering way. His face grew tight and pained as he looked up at Roberts. He was clearly annoyed, "Son, if you can't figure out what the hell she's doing in there, turn your badge and gun in at the end of your shift, because frankly, you have no future with the bureau."

He walked up to the trailer, looking to the other assembled agents. "Find somebody up in Sacramento," he shouted. "Get me whoever McCafferty answers to, now that the other one's quit. We need a new field representative immediately."

"You're going to fire her?"

"She's not employed by me. I wouldn't have that authorization."

"Arrest her then?"

Elliott looked at the agent, keeping himself calm and rational as he shook his head. "Sex isn't against the law."

"But the investigation?"

"We'll see about that tomorrow, but for right now, get me her boss. I don't care how many people you need to wake up, understand?"

* * *

Senses of Night 13.10
March 26, 2000

The journey back to the bedroom took at least an hour, but as with life, quite often the thrill is with the journey, not the destination. Neither rushed, both knew what was happening and where they were going. Both knew this was something different.

They didn't leave the floor until they made it to his unmade, crumpled bed. Even then they didn't stand. Instead they pulled themselves up to it, both naked now, their bodies completely wrapped into one another. On the bed, they laughed and giggled at how slick their bodies had become, sweat built up, even when rolling on the floor. Pressing themselves together they could actually feel each other's heartbeats. Both pressed forward.

They both needed this moment, this freedom, this release from the lives they'd been living. This was their escape, no matter what terrible things it would later bring. With slow, easy moves, he entered her, and with a dark longing, she pulled him deeper. Her nails clawed at his back, in heated pulses, as he moved in and out, teasing her in the only way he could.

They never once stopped kissing throughout it all. Never once stopped holding on as if everything in the world depended on what they were doing. It was dancing in the dark of night, a naked symphony of energy and passion. Each of them drowning their fears and troubles that plagued them in their lives, here in the sweet, quiet darkness that surrounded them. They had no other responsibility than to each other. The weight of the world lifted from both their shoulders as they gave in to the delights the other's body offered, as they allowed themselves the indulgence of giving themselves completely to the other. Here where every movement they made was a fantasy, a secret delight of forbidden romance. Neither imagined themselves to be Romeo or

Juliet, but at the same time, the forces that surrounded their lives would take issue. Her employers, the FBI, for him his friends and his lawyer would be having conniptions if they knew. That made the thrill behind what they were doing even sweeter. For each, it was like being a teenager again, having sex in someplace dark and hoping no one would find out. Some things people don't outgrow, and the initial rush sex brings is something all people crave, that pure unadulterated wave of hunger that consumes someone when they are finally receiving the person they desire. The heat only smolders more when the friction between the two lovers burns not only from passion, but from rebellion of the soul as well.

When they were finally through, they knew it was just for the moment, their sweating bodies clinging tightly, each breathing in the others' breath because their mouths stayed so closely together. This was a reprieve, a chance to rest before the next round began. This was a game that wouldn't end until the night was long behind them.

* * *

Senses of Night 13.11

March 26, 2000

"What are you going to tell them?"
"**About last night?**"
"Yes."
"**I haven't a clue.**"
"I could say I called you."
"**Your phone's tapped, you know that. They could trace mine easy enough as well. Besides, they would have seen us kissing on your stoop.**"
"We could say you suffered a seizure. That I was just trying to give you mouth-to-mouth."
"**They aren't as stupid as you tend to believe they are, Tom.**"
"I think I might dispute that. Besides with all the errors that have already been made in this case, we might just get reasonable doubt."
"**Is that what you're going for, with all of this? Reasonable doubt?**"
"I'm just trying to live my life. It's everyone else that keeps messing with me. First the NCUA, then the FBI, and now I'm on home restriction, thanks to the credit union."

"Once it went public, Tom, what else could they do? They had to suspend you."

"I suppose."

"And you, I saw the tape on TV, you and Randy going at it. You pimped him into blowing up that day. Why?"

"I . . . I . . . Hell, I was pissed, I was just told to leave the building, to not even bother returning to my own office, saying good-bye to the people I care about. Just leave . . . how would you have felt?"

"I just walked out that day. I didn't go back to my desk. I didn't say good-bye to anyone. I just left."

"What?"

"At the FBI, I was once placed on an administrative leave pending an investigation of actions on a field case. I wasn't angry. In fact I really wanted to leave the office, wanted to go back home and curl up into my bed. I didn't go pimp my section head into a cheap fight."

"You were suspended? For what?"

"I shot someone."

"You kill them?"

"Yes."

"Wow."

"Two squeezes of my trigger, and suddenly someone, who was alive and breathing, wasn't anymore. Another two shots out of the barrel and you couldn't even tell he had a chest anymore. It all happened so goddamn fast, it's hard to keep track of it all, even in your own head. You just know that other people will die if you don't pull your trigger, if you don't take the bad guy down, so you squeeze and hope your nerves don't make you miss."

"Is that why you went to therapy?"

"Yes."

"Did it help?"

"I think so, it made me see what I was doing wrong and the changes I needed to make."

"That's why you left the FBI."

"You ever fired a gun?"

"Sure. A few years ago. A friend of mine's a sheriff, you know, my neighbor, he took me to their firing range. We spent a couple of hours unloading a few clips at pieces of paper with man-shaped objects on them."

"Did you enjoy it?"

"Not really, no."

"How come?"

"I guess I don't much like guns."

"Even though you own one, even though you were able to jam it into an FBI agent's face?"

"Gun's have their use. They're a shorthand answer to temporary power. If I hadn't had that gun, your agent would have probably kicked the shit out of me and run off. He'd have effectively gotten away with breaking the law."

"Have you ever killed somebody?"

"No, no, I haven't."

"Trust me then, Tom, you'd really hate guns if you had, and you'd probably never want to pull one on anyone again."

"You carry a gun though."

"I do a lot of things I don't want to do in life, but you're right about the temporary power a gun provides . . . that's why I carry it. Protection."

"I noticed you weren't wearing it last night."

"Does that disappoint you, that I didn't consider you a threat?"

"No, that actually makes me happy."

"If it makes you think I'm not still going to bust you, you're wrong."

"I thought you said you'd be off the case."

"I will be. But to get a new agent to replace me on a case of this size and scope, it'll take a few days to move a replacement in, and they'll probably need me to remain at least long enough to bring the new investigator up to speed. More than enough time I expect."

"Will you leave then?"

"I don't think I'll have much choice in the matter."

"I'd prefer it if you stayed."

"You'll be leaving soon. Federal penitentiaries don't exactly allow coed cells?"

"Stay until I'm arrested then."

"You mean here?"

"Sure."

"You just don't get it, Tom. You're going to jail. Soon."

"Hopefully not dressed like this. It would give the boys in the cellblock the totally wrong impression."

"I'm being serious."

"Yet you still came last night, you're still here now. Am I wrong, Dawn? Tell me if I am, really. But I think there's something between us, and I don't just mean the sex. I'm talking about something else."

"Tom . . ."

"I'm serious. Maybe it won't amount to a thing. Maybe it'll all collapse in our faces. But shouldn't we at least try? See where it all leads?"

"I already know, Tom. I know exactly where it leads—you in jail and me sitting at home alone, crying empty, lonely tears."

* * *

Senses of Night 13.12

March 26, 2000

She awoke to the sound of the shower going; she was still tired and couldn't imagine how Tom could be anything less. The drapes were still pulled shut giving the room a very dark tint. Despite the fact the clock told her it was already twelve twenty in the afternoon. She was relaxed though, despite a few sore spots on her body. She couldn't remember the last time she'd felt this relaxed. She pushed her head deep into his pillow, trying to force the girlish smile off her face. He'd been everything she'd needed him to be, and despite how good it all felt, that wasn't necessarily a good thing. The pulled drapes weren't for her to be shielded from the sun; she knew it was to keep the prying eyes of the FBI out of his life. To shut out the people she would very quickly have to answer to.

She got up and stretched, listening to the running water coming from the bathroom. For a moment she thought about going in and surprising him, but decided against it and walked down the long hallway toward his main room, the place where all her clothes were loosely scattered. Entering the living room she could smell coffee brewing in the kitchen. She stepped in and saw two mugs set up and a large pot of coffee finishing its brew cycle. She reached out and filled one of the mugs, blew at the rim to cool it, and took a drink. It was a dark, expensive blend, maybe even something tropical. Once again his accomplice came to mind, and she felt foolish standing naked in his kitchen holding a cup of coffee that was most likely purchased by the woman he planned on spending the rest of his life with.

Using a mirror in the entryway, she twisted her body to see a large rug burn that began toward the top of her thigh and stretched up to her rear end. She wanted to laugh; the entire night was an adventure ranging from the absurdly comical to the height of erotic sensation. Taking another drink from her coffee, she realized that she very badly wanted to walk into that shower, let the hot water pour down over her and start the process all over again, spend another few hours wrapped tightly in his arms, and wake up once more as the sun was starting to fall from the sky. Instead she sat the cup down and started to pick up her clothes and get dressed.

Her hair was a mess, and she knew there was very little she was going to be able to do about that until she got home, a home she prayed would be empty. She knew she wouldn't be able to stand seeing Jerry this morning. She wouldn't be able to face him after everything that happened. She didn't really blame him for attacking. She wished he hadn't, but still, hadn't she deserved his rage after her confession of sins against the very fabric of their relationship? She'd been hard on him as well, she could have stopped him a lot easier than she chose to; he'd never be a match for her, not with her training. For that matter neither would

Tom, but somehow she couldn't see him attacking someone physically, unless all other choices were gone. Tom was a subtle form of smart; he was a watcher, and he seemed to know how to pull people's strings. That was what he had done so far throughout the investigation. Being arrested yesterday hadn't affected him in the slightest. He'd known he wasn't doing anything wrong, but why would he have carried his old sail back to the boat at that moment, and in that way? He'd been pimping the FBI, just the way he'd pimped Randy Carlson in front of the credit union on Monday. It was like Tom was playing a very elaborate game, and he didn't care if he got caught.

That's when it hit her; what Tom was really doing? Why wouldn't he care if he got caught? Two obvious reasons: The first, he was innocent, but the problem there was, Tom Williams didn't act like an innocent man. Innocent people accused of crimes were scared, frantic even. These people usually proved their innocence by showing how comically inept they were. Tom wasn't inept, and he'd never been scared through any part of the investigation, that left only one other option. The second reason, he didn't care if he was caught. He had a plan. A plan he thought was foolproof. Reasonable doubt came to her mind once more, hadn't they given him that with the break in and the false arrest? It seemed to be his best bet, but even that didn't seem like the game Tom was playing. Not to her it didn't.

She knew his plan wasn't about running though, that's where she and Elliott disagreed. She knew if he was going to run, he would have done so by now. His plan was certainly to get even with the credit union. But how did he hope to get away with it, or had he simply fallen so far in his own life that he didn't care about going to prison? She'd met people like that before, those who no longer cared for their own safety or welfare. They cared about getting even, and as long as they took their enemies down with them, they didn't care what the price for their victory was. She wondered if that was what Tom was doing. They'd been monitoring his accounts from the beginning, looking to see if anything over the past few years had changed, if he was shifting his money. But everything was consistent. She took another drink from her cup as she heard the water shut off in the bathroom. She stayed her ground, drinking the coffee as he stepped in wearing only a towel. "I see you found the coffee. Hope you like it."

"It's good," she said struggling to remain casual.

"Hope I didn't wake you?"

"No, just woke up. I always thought you were someone who liked to sleep in. I was surprised to see you were already up."

"I guess I was a little wired from last night. I know I should be utterly exhausted, but somehow . . . it was like waking up for the first time in years."

"It'll probably be better for both of us if you didn't talk like that."

"Yeah . . ." He started to walk toward her, and she instinctively found herself moving away. Picking up on her uneasiness, he moved into the kitchen and made himself a cup of coffee. Unlike her, he added a lot of cream and sugar. Something she only drank with coffee very late at night, in the morning she needed it black and hot. "You're mad?"

"No."

"You want to talk about it?"

"No."

He nodded, but he also knew there was a lot she wanted to discuss, things she wanted to ask, things he knew she wouldn't. Things he knew he'd never tell. He walked to the living room and lowered himself down the doorjamb that led to his home office, the spot where a week ago he'd placed a gun to the back of a man's head and opened the investigation to the public. He didn't want to be comfortable, not really. He knew that, right now, any sense of comfort coming from him would make her want to leave, so he put himself somewhere cold and sterile. Below him the entryway tile led into the office carpeting. His towel slid a little and exposed his legs, and he drank his coffee looking up at her.

She looked back and forth, not wanting to look at him, but needing to. Fighting herself from asking the questions, she eventually stepped into the kitchen to refill her cup. He remained silent the entire time, drinking his coffee, trying to give her the space she obviously needed. After taking another drink, she stepped over to the door and lowered herself down to the floor and rested her back against him, placing her head gently on his chest. His hand came up and began to play with her hair just slightly.

She tilted her head back a little further and asked, "There are still a few things I don't understand."

"Like what?"

"You," she said softly, "and Netzly, when did it end?"

And for a while they talked. She enjoyed the comfort of lying against him, though she was sure fixed into the doorjamb as he was, he couldn't be comfortable. It began by talking about the investigation and his connection to Laura Netzly and ended with her talking about the lonely tears, she expected to cry very soon.

She sat her cup down on the tile floor and stood, "I need to go."

"For what it's worth, Dawn, I'm sorry."

"About what?"

"Pretty much everything. Both what's come and what will."

From the way he said it she couldn't tell if he meant her pending dismissal or something else. She smiled and started to move toward the door. "Can I ask you one more thing?" And she stopped and turned to face him, wondering what question he could still have left to ask.

"What?"

"Another place, another time?"

"Another place and time, Tom, and we would have never met. This is all we have."

"Was it worth it?"

Looking up at his door, she realized that neither of them locked it last night. They'd been totally vulnerable to anyone who might have turned the handle. She thought back over everything that happened, both last night and the last few years, the whole set of choices she'd made to lead herself to this place, and she smiled. "In my opinion? Yes. I'm free now, of a lot of things, some of that I even owe to you. I carry no regrets about last night. And if it does make you feel any better, if things were different and by some small chance we would have met otherwise, maybe something could have happened over the long term. I don't know, but I think I would have tried."

And having said her piece, she turned and walked out, letting the door fall shut behind her. He sat drinking his coffee for a moment, watching the door carefully, hoping she'd come running back in, and eventually, stood to go lock it. He turned and walked to his office and booted up the computer. *She was right*, he thought, *they were almost out of time.*

* * *

AFTER

After 14.0
March 27, 2000

Paul Westin scanned the pages slowly, reading line by line on the ream of paper in front of him, looking for any line of code that might indicate something was placed on the system. He'd worked for the NCUA only a few months, and suddenly he was doing a job that wasn't in his employment description.

He was a gifted computer tech, he could write seamless code, but didn't really enjoy it much. He preferred maintaining systems and going over other people's work. He'd oftentimes referred to himself as a computer editor. He'd never imagined himself being involved in a high-level FBI investigation, yet here he was hundreds of miles away from home, sitting behind a computer desk looking for something to help the investigators catch a criminal.

He and a team of men, mostly FBI men who resented being stuck in such a tedious part of a very large case, sat in the computer conference room at the bottom floor of the Hil Fed building going over the code sheets that were produced over the year 1999. They'd all picked different starting points and pulled code printouts from random days. They had no way of knowing how long ago the virus was inserted in the system. Most guessed that it would have been inserted during the latter half of 1999 when so many other code patches and fully automated programs were being installed, but there was no guarantee. A plan executed this seamlessly on a computer could have been uploaded years ago if the person had the proper computer skills.

He'd been in San Diego since March 12, and had seen almost none of the city. Just the short stretch of road between his rented living space and the Hil Fed main office. All he could think about was getting back to Sacramento, getting back to Alison. Her e-mails were starting to take on a nervous edge; she was actually worried that he might be cheating on her. All she knew of San Diego was what she'd seen on the live TV shows that promote it as a beach paradise, filled with nothing but bikini-clad girls prancing wildly about and getting drunk. He could now speak from experience when he said San Diego was no such thing. It was city pretty much like any other that happened to have a beach nearby.

Every line of code was starting to look the same to him. All he could really think about was Alison, and because of that he almost missed the one most important line in the sheet he held. The ream of paper was file stamped as being run from the tapes of Wednesday, September 15, 1999.

The entry in question was time stamped at 9:15 p.m., entered from terminal number 118, and the user number was 241.

He stopped and read the line carefully, seeing nothing around it that made any sense. He then rolled his chair over to the live system and began to physically trace the record. After all, he didn't want to alert anyone before he knew for sure, but something in his gut told him, he'd just found what everyone was looking for.

* * *

After 14.1

March 27, 2000

"So Friday I'm off then?"

Marshal Elliott just nodded his head as she spoke. He didn't understand her at all, much less how she could be so nonchalant about it. To listen to her speak, it was so incredibly matter-of-fact, and yet all he could see was that she was callously throwing away her career. He wanted to ask what she was thinking, but he strongly suspected she wouldn't tell him. That or she'd give him an answer he wouldn't want to hear. So he sat sternly looking at her, behind the rickety table setup at the command trailer looking up at Tom Williams' condo. He'd sent the other agents outside so he could talk to her privately, though gauging her reaction it wouldn't have mattered if he'd let them all stay to watch.

She was dressed in jeans, a dark-colored T-shirt with a blazer cutting over it. She didn't seem at all worried about looking professional. This told Elliott she knew she was on her way out and didn't want to play any games in the time remaining. He also noticed something else about her; she seemed different, more relaxed. He couldn't help but wonder why she was calming down. He'd seen more than his fair share of agents "lose it" under high-stress cases. Having read her file though, he'd expected better of her. Every profile she'd been given, while working for the FBI, placed her at a top ranking, even after she shot a man to save the lives of two fellow agents.

"Yes," he said stiffly. "With your new supervisor yet to be announced, it would seem the investigative office is in the midst of change, and getting someone reassigned down here will take a few days. To be quite honest, they can't even guarantee Friday, though I was insistent."

"You despise my being here so much?"

"No, Ms. McCafferty. But I do have an investigation to run, and the moment that your interests ran contrary to mine, you needed to be removed."

"And you believe I no longer wish to see Tom Williams go to jail."

"No, Ms. McCafferty. I do not believe you wish him to go to jail. I think you would still arrest him, but I no longer feel your heart would be in it."

She nodded at his words and then looked him directly in the eye. "I may be relieved from my duty when the new agent arrives, but mostly likely they'll need me to stay on a few days to bring them up to speed on the NCUA side of things. You're aware of that, yes?"

"I assumed as much, but that part doesn't concern me. What does concern me is the next five days."

"Meaning?"

"Meaning," he said, "you are not to go within a hundred yards of Mr. Williams unless accompanied by a federal agent who has my expressed authorization. You are not to contact Mr. Williams, not even to say good-bye."

"And if I do call him to say good-bye once I am no longer the assigned agent?"

"I can't do much about that, now can I? I can warn you though. If you do anything further to endanger my investigation, I will do what everyone of my junior agents wanted on Saturday morning, I will have you arrested for interference. Are we clear?"

"Yes," she said quietly.

The radio squawked on. An agent's voice came over the airway telling anyone on channel that Tom Williams stepped out of his front door. Dawn chose not to react.

* * *

After 14.2

March 27, 2000

Tom's neighbor was a seventeen-year-old boy named Alex, who sat on the front steps in front of Tom's house bouncing a basketball on the ground. He looked up at Tom as he stepped out on his front stoop and said, "'bout time."

"Sorry," Tom answered, "I'm not as young as I used to be."

"Sure, sure," Alex said grinning as he stood. "Always an excuse for why I'm about to kick your ass."

"We'll just see about that, kid."

"You're darn right we will." And with that the two walked to the basketball court the condo complex provided its residents.

The hot, noon sunshine beat down. Most of the residents were at work or school. Tom didn't ask why Alex wasn't at high school, mostly because he could tell it was a subject he didn't want to talk about. He'd heard his father mention something the other night about a fight on school grounds, but Tom believed in letting people keep their secrets. He certainly had enough of his own, so he casually walked over to the court, talking about a TV show he knew they both watched.

They started off easy, Alex the entire time joking about the poor shape of the near-forty-year-old man who ran around the court, even though it was clear that despite his age, he wasn't in that bad of shape. He'd always told Alex that sailing was a great way to stay fit, especially when you most often chose to sail by yourself. In the case of basketball though, Tom knew he didn't really have a chance at beating his young neighbor, who seemed to have an unlimited source of energy to keep him going. Long after, Tom started to sweat. Alex looked up at him with a keen, hungry eye that said he was ready to run the full court as many times as it took to show the old man up.

After twenty minutes of constant movement, Tom could already feel the first burning sensations in his chest. He was pushing himself hard, almost like he needed to prove something. He was also losing badly. How much of that had to do with him being overmatched, instead of just being confused about Dawn, he couldn't quite tell.

He'd called her Saturday evening and left a message on her recorder, so far she hadn't responded. He knew he didn't really have the right, but he was concerned about her nonetheless. He wanted to know if she was OK. Though one part of him, deep down inside, just really wanted to hear her voice again. It was less than two days, and he missed her. For him that was something rare, almost unheard of.

It was only as Alex began to go soft on him that he started to make points in the third go-around of twenty-one.

The game continued on though. Every time Tom would start to get ahead, Alex would push himself back up to full speed and begin to run rings around him. From time to time, the other community residents, who didn't work, would stop and watch the two men dribble the ball back and forth, shooting hoops and running themselves ragged under the hot sun, but none stayed very long. Tom knew what they really wanted. His picture was in all the papers. He was featured nightly on just about every news channel. They all wanted a glimpse of their crooked, thieving neighbor. He just intently focused on the game and utterly ignored them. After all, he knew Alex didn't care about what the neighbors thought. *One of the joys,* Tom thought, *about being seventeen.*

As the game went on, neither of them bothered to look up at the pale stranger, who seemed to almost stumble as he came upon them. He held a brown paper bag, clutched tightly in his hand and appeared nervous and scared. *Another looky-loo,* Tom thought and worked twice as hard to ignore him. It was really only by chance that Tom looked up when he did. What he saw froze him place, the stranger pulling a gun from the paper sack.

The ball whizzed right past him, and Alex started to say something, complaining that Tom wasn't paying attention that time. Tom's eyes were transfixed on the gunman, who was aiming directly at Tom. He could only think to do two things: The first, perhaps the only noble thing he'd done in years, and the second, incredibly self serving. He yelled for Alex to get off the court, praying that the gunman planned to kill only Tom and not the kid, who still had a real chance at a future, and then at the top of his lungs, Tom yelled out, "*Gun,*" praying the FBI would hear.

* * *

After 14.3

March 27, 2000

"Son of a bitch." Agent Cole screamed into the radio. "Someone just pulled a gun on Williams!"

And as if someone just screamed out her name, Dawn was up from her chair, ignoring Elliott's protestations and grabbing up one of the many pairs of binoculars lying about, running out of the trailer. The agents assembled outside, waiting to get back in. All had strange, paranoid looks on their faces as she came charging out with such intensity. They were all wearing earpieces and heard Cole's message. Dawn brought the binoculars up and tried to look past the edges of the building to where she knew the basketball court was located, but found no acceptable angle. She was suddenly frantic, her hands trembling in fear.

Elliott's voice came from behind her, snatching the binoculars out of her hand. "Just get back in the trailer," he said and began to turn away.

"What's the gunman's description!?!"

"None of your business, Ms. McCafferty!"

"Tall, lanky, pale, holding a 9 millimeter?"

Elliott stopped and turned back to face Dawn. He saw an honest panic in her eye, but it was more than just concern. He saw guilt. "And how would you know that?"

"I think he might be my ex-boyfriend."

The rage he was struggling to contain was obvious, but she knew better than to back down from it, even now. "How," he screamed, "or more importantly, why would your ex-boyfriend be here holding a gun on our chief suspect!?!"

"He's my ex, and he's recovering from a mental breakdown that he suffered after I terminated our relationship approximately one year ago. He arrived in town sometime Friday after seeing me repeatedly on the news. He wanted to get back together. I told him, 'no.' I told him that we were through."

"I still do not see how that brings him here?"

"He didn't take the news that I didn't want to get back together with him well, OK?"

"Meaning?"

"He attacked me. I think his therapist was teaching him to express his rage, but probably didn't know how volatile he would become when confronted with a serious, emotional defeat."

"Why didn't you report this attack on your person?"

She shook her head. "I didn't want to see him arrested, and I was never in any real danger. I took him down and left him in my residence Friday evening to sleep it off. He was gone when I went back home Saturday afternoon."

"Why is it, Ms. McCafferty, I still feel there is something in this story you are leaving out?"

"I haven't been able to locate my sidearm since."

"That's your gun?"

"Technically, it's the FBI's gun. It's on loan to me. But to answer your question, I believe it is, yes."

"And the reason you didn't report a stolen weapon was?"

"I thought he was going to kill himself, or, more to the point, threaten it. I notified his mother Saturday evening, and she contacted his therapist. We were hopeful he would try to contact one of us, as we all knew Jerry really doesn't want to hurt himself."

"And he's here looking for you then?"

"No," she said as it all came together, as she filled in all the blanks in her head, "I don't believe that's the case. I have a radio in my residence, tuned to receive all of the reports on this particular investigation. I imagine it's possible he awoke and turned it on, and he listened to whatever reports were being made Friday evening over the open channel as I entered Tom's condo."

"If your ex kills our suspect, McCafferty, you can count on your career being over," Elliott's voice was direct. Dawn nodded and turned to look at the road leading up to the condo community. "Where do you think you're going?"

"He'll listen to me. I can stop this."

"You are not to go anywhere near them. You're likely to make this situation even more volatile!"

"Then you better order your men to shoot me. Because listen up, Elliott, there's no way in hell you're stopping me any other way!"

And with that, she took off running up toward the condos.

* * *

After 14.4

March 27, 2000

Paul Westin triple checked his reports, and what he was looking at didn't have any foundation for being there. One odd line of code led to a second line that seemed to have been loaded in month's before, telling the Logiterm system to load a file stored to quadrant 76970. The problem unfolded slowly from there. There was nothing located in quadrant 76970. In fact, when he'd originally gone looking to see what was lurking in that quadrant, the system didn't want to even acknowledge that that quadrant existed. As if the Logiterm system was turning a blind eye to that whole file allocation. Paul suspected that even a full-scale, shutdown and scan of the network hard drive and database would reveal nothing there.

When he finally cracked his way into the area, it was completely empty. No program lurking to run. The trick of it was that the line of computer code. It told Logiterm on the night of September 15, 1999, to run a program. If the program hadn't been there, an error message would have been issued to whoever the standby man was during the nightly processing. An error in the internal operating system of Logiterm would have effectively shut down the system, but the elegance was it went to a code line that didn't exist either. That meant to Paul that there was indeed a program run that night. Undoubtedly, the last line in the program's command code would have been to erase itself from the system, effectively erasing any trace the virus existed, even from the reports that were stacked up all around him. He just stared at the readout in front of him, smiling. He knew it. Could feel it down deep inside. This was where it began.

"What is it, Paul?"

Paul turned his head to see Marc standing behind him. He looked annoyed and was trying to do his best to convince people that he was now the senior ranking officer on call from the NCUA. Everyone there knew Marc was one step up in rank from the parking lot speed bump and tended to treat him as such. This led to a lot of run-ins between Marc and the techs, and Paul knew that at least for today, he needed to avoid the conflict. He'd resolved to just spoon feed Marc if that's what it took.

"I think I found it."

"Found what?" Marc's voice was obviously annoyed, and his eyes rolled while speaking.

"Gee," Paul said quickly, trying to contain himself, "where the code started, and who did it."

Marc froze and looked at Paul with what were rapidly becoming hungry eyes. Paul just smiled. "I've already sent a few notes back up to Sacramento and copied the FBI field team down here, but I think I found the execute line."

"And . . ."

"And," Paul smiled, "it belonged to an entry placed by user number 241, namely Thomas Williams."

"Are you sure it's the correct code?"

"Of course not. I have a line of code that leads to an empty quadrant. But if a program hadn't been there, the system would have stopped in the midst of its nightly processing. Which means the code line perfectly executed, run, and then deleted a fully functional program, seamlessly integrating it into the Logiterm system before that nightly processing completed. We're talking a processing time of less than fifteen minutes, which would have to reconfigure several lines of code throughout the core system. I'm talking about a drastic alteration, if it was done like I think it was."

"And for those of us who were criminal justice majors instead of computer science graduates, what are you saying?"

"A system the size of Logiterm especially for a version as large as this credit union is running, has several safeguards in it to prevent a virus being inserted. Technically speaking, it just shouldn't be able to happen. You'd have to be one helluva programmer to pull it off, and that would be with a huge program and a lot of time when you weren't being watched. This program, like I said, wouldn't have been executed from the way this code line reads until nightly processing of the Logiterm system."

"So?" Marc said, while starting to sit down next to Paul.

"So the line's deep enough in the code that it would run pretty deep into the processing, and the Logiterm system is advanced enough that no programs can run independently on top of it of the nightly processing. So this line of code executed a program that could reconfigure their entire on—and off-line systems in less than eleven minutes' time. There's only one way I can conceive of that it went completely undetected."

"And that would be?"

"Since from what I've been led to believe, none of the money or system ghost numbers occurred until the beginning of this month. To wait that long without anyone in the Information Services Department noticing code changes or rerouting of files and lines would mean that the code that executed on September 15 literally disassembled the virus code, scattering it throughout the system. Then on February 29, an execute line must have been placed to come up only on that date of the year, which sent the whole viral code running. Which is pretty clever since February 29 only comes up once every four years? We're talking about a very sophisticated virus program, Marc, and that's important to mention."

"Why?"

"Because a system that sophisticated, we'll probably never be able to prove it even existed. Because the erasing happened in each case, I would assume, while the nightly processing was being run, which means there will be no trace of it. In fact, the best we can probably ever hope to find of this virus is this execution code line right here."

"Son of a bitch . . . ," Marc said shaking his head. "But was it Williams who placed this line of code?"

"Yes."

"And I take it you've already checked to see that Mr. Williams had no authorization to place this line of code."

"That's correct."

"So what you're telling me then is this is the best evidence we will likely ever find against Mr. Williams?"

"Yep, and that's what should concern you."

"Don't worry, Paul. It does."

"Not for the right reason."

Marc looked at Paul coolly. "What's the right reason?"

"From everything the FBI guys have told me about this Williams guy, I mean, come on, he's a marketing geek who wound up in collections. I've seen the code he punched in for this lame-ass collection package they spent most of 1999 putting together, and if it wasn't for the info systems guys down here, it would have been unworkable. Knowing how to use a computer well and being able to program are two radically different things."

"That's why you're a computer tech, Paul, and not an investigator!" Marc stood and reached for the phone, dialing the command trailer with the information he now possessed. He was shocked at the number of times the line rang, before someone finally picked up.

* * *

After 14.5

March 27, 2000

"Who the fuck is that!!!!?" Alex wasn't thinking straight and was yelling loudly at the sight of the man with the gun. Tom was thinking clearly though and seeing that the pale stranger was fixated on him, he was trying to slowly inch his way in an opposite path from where Alex stood frozen in fear.

The pale man didn't appear too upset at the sound of Alex's voice; his eyes seemed fixated completely on Tom. Tom felt the twinge inside and knew immediately it was fear. He couldn't believe this was how he was going to die. He could only assume the man in front of him was some angry investor at Hil Fed who hadn't bothered to read all of his funds were secured by the NCUA. To Tom, it seemed like a stupid way to die. The only thought pounding through his head was *where the hell the FBI was when he needed them,* but then it occurred to him, after the embarrassment he'd caused them over the past week, perhaps they didn't care if someone shot him. It was only then it hit him, the true desperation of what was happening. He could already feel off kilter, that he wasn't perceiving things properly. Everything around him seemed to be moving at a million miles an hour, his heart beating faster and faster. Everything was speeding up all around him except for himself and the two people closest to him, Alex, and the gunman.

"If I die," Tom said softly, "I want it to be with a clear conscious, OK? Why don't you let the kid go, OK?"

"You did it!" The gunman said and did his best to steady his aim dead center on Tom's chest. His finger was tense on the trigger but not yet firing, as if he wanted to make him suffer first.

"Fine," Tom said as he inched forward a single step, "if that's what you need to hear, OK . . . I did it. Now come on, can we just let the kid walk?"

"*Fuck you!!!!*"

"We can talk about this, can't we?" Tom said nodding his head, as he chose to inch a step further away from Alex, trying to separate them as much as possible. "No one cares if I die, really. Hell, you'd probably please at least a half dozen people to no end, but the kid still has a future. He can't hurt you, so let him go. Then you take care of me. How's that? He doesn't need to see this, huh?"

"I love her goddamnit!!!"

"What?"

"You took her away. She loved me! *Me!*"

"I'm sorry," Tom said baffled, "I, uh, I don't understand."

Jerry was already angry, hearing what Tom said didn't help. In his head, he perceived Tom as being purposely dense and fired a single shot into the ground just to the left of Tom's foot. As the bullet embedded itself into the grass at the edge of the basketball court, they both heard Alex drop screaming to the ground, for the first time realizing he was in trouble. Face to the ground, Alex crawled wildly to the small picnic table off to the other side of the court and went under it, a makeshift form of cover. Tom jumped at the sound of the gunfire; the wave of panic and fear he'd been trying to suppress bolted him back three feet in the matter of a second.

"Fuck you, you don't understand," Jerry screamed at the top of his lungs. "Fuck you!"

All Tom could feel was a wave of sweat coming over him; how much was from the basketball game, how much from adrenaline and fear, he couldn't tell. He could see the look in the man's eyes; he was enraged, and it scared Tom deeply. "OK," Tom said nervously, trying to maintain his composure, when all he really wanted to do was run. "Let's just talk about this. What do you say?"

"I say you took her from me!"

"Her?" That was when it hit him, when it all became clear. "Her . . . you mean, Dawn? Dawn?"

"Fuck, Dawn, fuck Don't say her fucking name. You don't have the right, fuck!'

"You're right," he said as softly as he could, wondering how far a man would have to fall to become as fragile as this. He wondered for a moment if he could ever fall that far, but decided there was only so far to drop before hitting bottom, and where ever his bottom was it would never be like this.

"Don't fuck with me!"

"I'm not, really. Jerry, right? Your name is Jerry?"

"Fuck, she told you about me?!"

"Sure," Tom said dryly, "not a lot, but some. You're big in her life. How could she not tell me about you?" Looking at Jerry, he realized the poor guy was monumentally confused, and Tom had no idea if what he was saying was helping or hurting, but it seemed to be making him think, and to Tom, him thinking seemed to be stopping him from shooting. "You've got to think, Jerry, about where you're at. The FBI, they're watching me, man. Do you understand? We're under surveillance. You need to get out of here."

"N-n-not," he stuttered out, "until I kill you!"

"OK, less than comforting, Jerry, but let me ask you this . . ."

"Freeze, sir, drop your weapon!"

Tom looked over to see Agent Cole running up to the scene, his gun held confidently and aimed directly at Jerry. His voice calm and solid, "I repeat, sir, drop your weapon. I am a federal officer!"

"Why couldn't I have just stayed at work?"

* * *

After 14.6

March 27, 2000

"This is Marshal Elliott," he spoke, but there was an urgency to his voice. A distraction. It was clear he didn't want to be on the telephone right now.

"Sir, this is Marc, with the NCUA."

"That's very nice, son. Now if you'll excuse me, I'm a bit busy right now. I'll return your call in a half hour or so."

"No," Marc screamed, "you don't understand, please . . . listen."

And Marshal Elliott did, as a smile slowly started to creep its way across his face, and he grabbed up the handset and coded in the personal code for Agent Cole's earpiece.

* * *

After 14.7

March 27, 2000

Jerry didn't move his gun nor change his aim. He seemed to have his sights set for Tom. Tom stood before him with his hands outstretched wide, as if trying for some form of surrender or communication with him. Cole was down on one knee, a ready-to-fire position, his own sight line aimed directly at Jerry's chest.

"Hi, Agent Cole," Tom said in a rather light voice, desperately trying to conceal his panic, "nice of you to join us. How you doing today?"

"This might not be the best time for levity, Mr. Williams."

"Really," he said, while keeping his eyes directly on the end of Jerry's gun, "'cause I gotta tell you, I could really use a good joke right now."

"This guy, a friend of yours, Mr. Williams?"

"Fuck," Jerry screamed again. "He fucked her. He took her from me."

"Friend of Dawn's actually."

"*Fuck you. I told you not to say her name!!!*"

"Yeah," Tom whispered, tensing his whole body. "Sorry, Jerry. Won't happen again. My mistake, really, sorry."

"You've got to be kidding me," Cole said as he looked over at Tom.

"What can I tell you, Cole? It's a crazy ol' world we live in. First you arrest me for stealing 320 million dollars, thinking I'm driving it around in my 'vette, and now he's come to kill me."

"He's not going to kill you, sir."

"The fuck I'm not!"

"Yeah, Cole. I gotta tell you, it's nice to hear, but that gun he's holding, it's loaded. He's already fired it once."

"I heard the shot, Mr. Williams, I think everyone did. It has a distinct sound."

"Fucking shut up! Both of you!"

"Jerry," a familiar voice called out, a little winded but unmistakable. Tom didn't bother to look back, as she came running up from somewhere behind him. What scared Tom was what Jerry's reaction would be seeing Dawn.

She ran up at full speed, stopping just shy of the basketball court, looking on with amazed eyes and a weary stance. She'd sprinted the entire way. Seeing her, Jerry held steady aim at Tom, but his eyes were completely on her.

"Dawn . . . baby?"

"Jerry, what the hell are you doing?"

"Getting you back."

"How?" she cried. "By killing someone I care about!?"

"You fucking care about him?" he said thrusting the gun in Tom's direction.

"Dawn, not that I didn't want to hear that, but could you maybe lay off that kind of talk while he's pointing that at me!?"

"Sorry."

"You know, you could have just called me back," Tom said whimsically. "I didn't expect you to call in the old boyfriend card. If you didn't want to see me again, all you had to do was say so."

"Is there anything you take seriously, Tom?"

"Sure, I just can't seem to remember what it is right now what with the gun aimed at me an' all."

"*Stop talking to her!!!*" he screamed loudly. Jerry was growing more and more agitated and confused. He was blinking every other second. He was coming unwound.

Dawn stepped forward. She was five paces to Tom's left, standing on the grass. Her hands were empty and held clearly in sight. Her eyes were sad though. "I'm being fired, Jerry, not officially, but they plan to give me the worst cases until I quit. We can go back home together, OK?"

"Dawn!" Tom found himself yelling.

"Don't you fucking say her name!"

She took another step forward, trying to keep Jerry's eyes focused on her. She'd seen the look on Tom's face though. He looked deeply concerned and no longer just about his own life. "We'll talk to your doctor together. How's that?"

"*I want him dead!*"

"You're not a killer, Jerry. Come on, baby, you know that."

"*He touched you!!*"

"Jerry, you're not a killer."

"*I hate him!!!*"

"Jerry," she said calmly, "I went to him."

She watched as he began to cry, tears streaming down his face without control. All around him he saw other FBI agents starting to run up. She was suddenly very worried. After what happened when Jerry got upset on Friday evening, she wasn't sure how he would handle the stress of being boxed in. Feeling trapped wouldn't help the situation. She wanted to give the order to back off, but she was no longer in charge, and she knew they wouldn't listen to her anymore. She also feared desperately for Jerry if this wasn't stopped at once. While none of the agents present had any love for Tom Williams, he was still the man they were assigned to watch, and any agent on duty would take serious issue to having their principle shot while under direct observation. That meant the one in the most danger, at least to her way of thinking, was Jerry, and she also knew the only reason Jerry was here was because of her. She could see the growing look of confusion on Jerry's face; she was scared to death that someone might die. Someone she cared about.

"*Die!*"

"Whoa!" Tom said instinctively at the gun that was once again being thrust in his direction, taking a step back, and as he stepped back, he saw Dawn taking a step forward.

"Jerry," she said behind pleading eyes, "please don't do this . . . this isn't you, isn't who you want to be. I know you better than this. You don't want to hurt anybody. You just want to feel less bad inside, and, honey, we can talk about this. OK?"

"*I loved you!!!*"

"And I loved you."

"*No,*" he screamed, "*you cheated!*"

"So," Tom whispered, "I guess you told him."

"Yeah," she answered, whispering, "I think I may have mistimed my confession a little. Sorry you got thrown into it."

"What? And miss all this fun?"

"You know," she whispered a little louder, "for a guy with a gun aimed at him, you're fairly calm."

"You'd be amazed, Dawn, at what freedom death might be right now."

"I wanted to call you back."

"But," Tom said as he continued to hold his hands up at shoulder level, palms facing flat out toward the gun that still hung on his every move, as if his bare palm might be able to shield him from the destructive force the weapon would unleash. "You were in too much hot water for having spent the night."

"Something like that, yeah."

"*Stop fucking talking to him!!!*"

"OK, Jerry," she said as she took yet another step closer to him.

"Dawn," Tom whispered, praying she would hear him, "I'm sorry for everything that's led us here. I never once imagined I'd ever meet someone like you, not after the life I've lived and the things I've done. If I'd known, I'd have just quit Hil Fed and moved on."

If Dawn heard him, she gave no indication. She just continued to stare forward at her former lover, large eyes looking for any sense of hope she might be able to expand on. "Jerry, you need to give me my gun back."

"Holy fuck," Agent Cole blurted hearing the gun belonged to McCafferty, as he centered in on what he thought was his best shot, slowly lifting back the hammer on his weapon, ready to end a life, just to save a guilty man. His earpiece came to life, and the sound of Marshal Elliott came directly to him through an undercurrent of static. He listened intently to what his supervisor said, and it was the only time after taking his direct aim he looked away from the target, for just a moment to look at Tom Williams.

"*I loved you, Dawn!*"

"I know, Jerry. Now please, honey, the gun."

And suddenly the gun was no longer aimed at Tom Williams; he shifted his aim to point directly at Dawn McCafferty. She didn't flinch for even a moment. She just took another step toward Jerry. It took Tom a second to figure out what happened; he was no longer under fire, it was Dawn now. Good sense told him to run for cover. Out of the corner of his eye, he saw an agent motioning for him to move. He knew it was the right thing to do. Instead he took a bold step forward and screamed as loud as he could, "Hey, fuckhead, you take the gun off me again and I'm gonna shove it up your ass!"

"Tom, *no!*" Dawn prayed he'd run but knew better. She knew Tom wasn't the kind to run; he was the man who was just standing next to her cracking jokes while his life was threatened. She also knew that Tom's outburst was meant to save her; he didn't realize that in Jerry's fragile state, it would only cause him to become increasingly unstable. She watched as Jerry swung the gun back around to point at Tom. Knowing she needed to do something quick, she screamed out Jerry's name again looking at him as he cried, as he constantly blinked, as if trying to clear the fog that had overtaken his mind.

Jerry was falling apart, piece by piece, and she could see it. She was literally watching it happen, but with the gun in his hand, he was a danger to everyone, and every one of the approaching FBI agents knew it. Against Tom's life, Jerry meant very little to anyone but her. "Please Jerry, we're running out of time. I need you to give me that gun before someone else does something that none of us will be able to live with. You haven't hurt anybody, Jerry. This can all still go away, but the longer you draw this out, the more serious it becomes, the more dangerous. Do you understand what I'm telling you?"

"*You lied to me, Dawn!!!*"

"Dawn," Tom's voice cried out from behind her, "get out of here. Just let the guy shoot me and end this. I don't want you hurt!"

"Not gonna happen, Tom, no way!" And that's when she finally saw Cole's position, the ready-fire stance and the look of remorse already on his face. She could tell he was waiting on the perfect moment to fire, the order to kill already given. Suddenly she was Jerry's only hope.

"Please, Jerry," she said as the first wave of tears hit her own eyes, as the desperation of the moment encircled her, "please, let me walk you out of here. Right now. Just you and me. We'll leave today. You and me."

"*You're fucking lying!*"

"No, I'm not, Jerry. I'm trying to save your life though, please!"

"*Save my life! Christ, Dawn, that's what you always tell me, but you always lied, fucking lied!*"

"I'm not lying now."

Tom saw the look change in Jerry's eyes. The loss and the anger switched. He saw the man before him transform. The gun was still aimed at him, but his eyes were totally and completely focused on Dawn. Suddenly all sense of fear for his own life left him, because he didn't feel he was in danger; the anger was all being directed toward her. He knew when the gun fired, it was going to be at her, and he was also sure that every FBI agent was either watching the scene as a whole was keeping their eyes on him. No one was going to be worried about saving Dawn McCafferty, just him. He felt his body start to tense and his front foot lead forward as if ready to launch off on it. Slowly, he began to move forward, very slowly as not to attract the gunman's attention.

"*You fucked him!!!*"

"Yes, Jerry, I did. No secrets, not anymore. I'm all lied out." She was moving forward as she continued to keep his eye contact on her. She was praying that as long as she kept him focused Cole wouldn't shoot, and neither would any of the other approaching agents, because she was sure before this was through, several open shots would present themselves. "You know everything now. I cheated on you, I kept things from you, and I outgrew you. I confess it all. Both in private, and now, here in public. You were the good guy in our relationship, and I was the bad guy. You were right, and I was wrong. But what you're doing now, it's going to change all that. But there's still time. Now give the gun."

"*Fucking bitch, don't play your fucking-head games on me!*"

"I won't . . ."

"*Don't get any closer!*"

"Jerry!"

"*Fuck!*"

"Jerry, please . . . talk to me . . ."

But the time for talk was over. Jerry was too far-gone. He swung his aim off the spot, where he believed Tom Williams to be and took a quick shot at Dawn, an unmistakable rage in his eyes. "*I fucking loved you, you bitch!*"

And half a second later, the second and third shots rang out, and everyone nearby began to close in.

* * *

After 14.8
March 27, 2000

Agent Cole's finger was tight and ready on the trigger; a part of him still couldn't believe this was going down. He was looking at a mad man, a man obsessed with a beautiful woman, a man who was obviously wronged if what he was saying was true. Cole could feel a certain degree of sympathy for the man. His own ex-wife cheated on him. He'd come home early from a field assignment to find the neighborhood letch in bed with her in the midst of the act itself. It had been all he could do not to pull his service revolver and blow them both away, but he hadn't. That was what separated him from being an animal. He'd always told himself, he had the chance and the ability to think about his actions before taking them. He didn't just act on rage, or any other primitive emotion lurking inside. He called an attorney from the hall phone and arranged for the divorce papers to be filed the next day.

A part of him still loved his ex-wife, but he knew he'd never trust her again. So any hope of a future between them was gone. But even if he could imagine a future with her, he knew he'd never pull his gun on some guy that was seeing her, and he'd certainly never pull a gun on her.

He didn't want to kill that man in front of him. But on the first clear shot where neither Williams or McCafferty were in jeopardy, he would take the kill shot to end this, just as he was trained to do. Dead center to the chest, an almost impossible target to miss at the range he was at. So he stood, watching, as the man became more and more agitated, more and more erratic. It was eerie to watch a man crumble so completely, and he wondered for a moment what kind of woman Dawn McCafferty was to consume a man so completely.

Then it all happened.

Jerry swung his gun off Williams and took a shot at Dawn. Suddenly the world was in slow motion, and nothing made sense. Agent Cole realized that he'd been paying so much attention to the shooter that he hadn't been paying enough attention to Tom Williams. While Jerry was so focused on his conversation with Dawn, none of them saw Tom inching his way forward, getting himself closer to Dawn while staying out of Jerry's direct line of sight. Tom hadn't been in danger of being shot for several seconds, and in that time, he hadn't bothered to get himself to safety; instead he'd gotten himself closer to everything that was happening. When Jerry moved the gun to fire, Tom charged forward plowing his shoulder squarely into Dawn's and knocking her off her feet and into the damp grass she's been standing on, knocking her out of the way.

The shot rang out in a deafening blast, and Cole saw Tom take the shot meant to go directly through Dawn's chest.

Cole didn't focus on that though. He knew one thing instinctively beyond all else. Now was the time to shoot. Jerry was far too confused to make another sudden shot. He would need a second to concentrate and aim, redirect himself down to the ground where both of the people he'd been aiming at were. Cole squeezed the trigger twice, and he watched cool and detached as Jerry's chest exploded in a wash of blood.

* * *

After 14.9

March 27, 2000

It all happened so fast she didn't have time to react. Jerry lost it, and as she started to stumble backward. She realized that she'd be too late to do anything to protect herself. Jerry was firing the gun, and he was aiming at her.

There was a blow she only partially felt, as her body lifted off the ground, something slamming into her from the side. She didn't understand. It didn't seem to feel the way a bullet would feel. But having never been shot, she couldn't say for sure, only that nothing made sense.

She was off her feet and falling. She knew that much. A deafening sound was ringing through her ears, and she felt a distinct sense of panic come over her.

Wet, sticky grass, from the morning dew, was everywhere, and she felt the wind knocked out of her as she hit the ground. She did her best to stay alert. She knew everything still hinged on her. Looking up she saw it was too late. Jerry's chest erupted in blood and gunfire, and she saw his legs collapse backward as he wore a mask of devastation and pain where his lovely, sweet face had once been. She tried to scream in protest, but it was all over too quickly, and she could only feel the tears running down her cheeks.

She dropped her head to the ground, into the grass as the tears continued to burn their way from her eyes. She was near hysterics. She knew Jerry was only there because of her, and what she'd done to him all those years, she would blame herself for the rest of her life that he was dead.

It was only then she thought of Tom and realized it was Tom who saved her. Otherwise she would have beat Jerry to the grave by a full second.

* * *

After 14.10

March 27, 2000

He knew he wouldn't have much time. So the moment he saw Jerry's rage building out of control, he gave up trying to move subtly and started a maddening charge, rushing forward like he was planning to charge through a herd of linebackers. His shoulder was out and aimed directly at Dawn's.

She was in far better shape, he knew that. He watched her while she was on the boat; she never lost her footing and remained stable. Most people who stepped on a boat for the first time took a while to adjust to the motion of the sea. He knew that she wouldn't just crumble down if he were to lightly bump her; he knew he needed to slam into her. So that was what he intended to do.

As his shoulder connected to hers, he immediately felt her being thrown back. She wasn't braced or ready for him, so he was afraid he'd hit her too hard, too fast. But he saw her falling out of the way as he heard the shot ring.

For Tom, it was the last thing he heard clearly. There was an impact against Dawn as the shot cracked out. The ringing in his ears overpowered him, and suddenly there was a burning in his arm, and he felt himself falling backward. He wanted to stabilize himself but he couldn't remember how. It was like his body was no longer listening to what his brain wanted. All around him the world blurred and got out of focus, and he could feel himself screaming, even if he couldn't hear himself doing it.

He felt himself falling back to the wet grass, and then everything continued to go dim and dark. A wave of nausea came over him, but nothing came up. The burning continued in his arm, and he couldn't bring up his head to look.

He was in pain, but he didn't know why. He wanted to scream, but couldn't remember how to speak.

Everything was out of focus. He could see images circling him and felt the presence of many hands touching him, but he couldn't tell who.

He wanted to ask for help, but found he wasn't able.

* * *

After 14.11

March 27, 2000

An FBI agent was helping Dawn to her feet as she looked over at Agent Cole who was rushing in. He didn't come toward her, his weapon already re-holstered. He carried a pair of handcuffs, as he stepped over Tom Williams and grabbed his good arm.

"What are you doing?" she screamed, but Cole just turned briefly and told the agent who was helping Dawn up to move her back to a clear area.

She wanted to be with Tom, to see how he was. All she could see was a stream of blood that stretched out far behind him in the grass and a growing pool of blood forming under him. She wanted to know if he was OK, but she also wanted to know what was going on.

As the agent pulled her back, she saw that Tom was still conscious, but clearly disorientated. That's when she realized Cole was reading Tom Williams his rights, placing Tom under arrest. She tried to break away and move forward. But at the first sign of her struggle, another agent came up, and with one agent on each of her arms, she was quickly escorted away, and she knew the only way to stop them would be a fight. Knowing that nothing good would come from that, she reluctantly walked away from the scene.

* * *

After 14.12

March 27, 2000

"Don't know if you can hear me or not," Cole said as he stared directly into Tom's blurry eyes, "but what you did just now, whether you're guilty or not, it took some serious stones, man, and no matter what the outcome, you'll always have my respect for that." He could see that Tom Williams was someplace else, as his body and mind found a way to deal with the wave of pain coursing through him.

Cole looked back at the other approaching agents and said they'd probably have to do this again at the hospital. But for now, he wanted to make it official. He turned back to look at Williams and in a very clear voice, said, "Mr. Williams, you are under arrest for the theft of 320 million dollars from the Hillsborough Industrial League Federal Credit Union . . ."

In the back, he heard McCafferty starting to make a commotion and told them to get her out of here and then turned back and finished reading Tom his rights.

But in the face of getting shot, the man he was arresting placed his own life on the line and saved someone else selflessly, and for a guilty man it just didn't make any sense. As always, Cole did his job, but for the first time in a very long time, he felt a bit of doubt.

In his ear, he heard Marshal Elliott shouting orders and arranging for emergency vehicles to be coordinated in. He wanted Williams taken to the nearest hospital immediately. He wanted a twenty-four hour guard placed on him, and he wanted Dawn brought directly back to the trailer. He was screaming about warrants and court orders that would be needed at once. And it sounded to Cole like Elliott was having the time of his life.

Looking down at Tom Williams, he just saw a man in pain, a man, who'd never been shot, stuck in a pool of his own blood that seemed completely and utterly alone.

The frequency was abuzz with chatter, everybody talking about the found code line that would incriminate Williams. How it was his user number in the system, and they finally had the necessary proof to get their arrest. Despite it all, Cole felt sorry for the guy, and couldn't help but wonder what must be going through the poor man's head.

* * *

After 14.13

March 27, 2000

It was all almost like it was happening to someone else, as Tom couldn't really perceive it. Even as his vision cleared and the pain in his upper arm became more predominant, it was a lot to take in. He was being lifted off the ground in a stretcher by an ambulance crew, and men with guns were surrounding him. His left hand was handcuffed to the bar of the stretcher.

The man who'd arrested him seemed sad and kept moving his lips, but all Tom could hear was a small buzzing, the sound the TV makes when you've left on and it wakes you in the middle of the night. Everyone seemed concerned about him, but suddenly he was very calm. The ambulance people injected him with something and he wondered if that was why.

He felt the tips of his fingers on his right hand shaking violently. There was also an odd tingling sensation; something told him this was bad, but he couldn't find it within him to panic. He was just really tired and wanted to take a nap.

It was only then Dawn crawled into his head. He remembered trying to knock her out of the way of a bullet, and it was then the panic started. Had he done it? Was she all right?

He knew it would be impossible to outrun a bullet, even with the head start he'd created. All he could think about now was Dawn, and he felt his heart begin to pound wildly. The crew of the ambulance was suddenly swarming around him; they were saying things to him, but he didn't understand. He was trying to yell Dawn's name, but he couldn't hear himself. So he just started screaming louder and yet still, he only heard the buzzing.

He was trying to move, but was restrained, and the world around him kept getting darker at the edges.

And then suddenly everything was dark and black and quiet, and he couldn't stay awake any longer.

* * *

SUSPICION OF GUILT

Suspicion of Guilt 15.0

March 29, 2000

Monday

She came through the door just past noon on Monday. He was watching the TV news from the set mounted to the wall where he saw Marshal Elliott holding an official press conference, *claiming victory*, Tom thought, though his words were chosen carefully. All the main channels in San Diego preempted regular programming to carry the conference. Tom couldn't believe how famous he suddenly was. In the back of his head, he could hear his mother telling him to mind himself, lest his vanity run amok. His left wrist was still handcuffed, this time to the bedrail. He was twelve stories high at Mercy Hospital, and the open window gave him a breathtaking view of the San Diego skyline and just a bit further out the Pacific Ocean. Two uniformed policemen stayed watch outside his door, and every time Tom needed to go to the bathroom, he was forced to call one of them in to uncuff him and escort him. He appreciated the fact that they at least turned their back as he went about his business. All in all, it was a pretty miserable place to be. His right arm was constantly throbbing, and the painkillers did little more than ease the pain.

The doctors told him that he'd been incredibly lucky, which to him seemed a rather odd statement, as he would have much preferred not to have been shot at all. They told him the bullet went through fairly clean, and the worst part of the damage was where it flaked some bone. He'd be sore; they told him, for quite a few weeks but would recover just fine and have full use of his arm. With that said, he'd made a few good-natured prison jokes that made the doctor laugh and the nurse blush.

The rest of the time spent in the hospital over the past two and a half days was almost comical. Tons of people wanted to see him, and in his head, he imagined a waiting line for him down in the main lobby. He figured the hospital must be making a killing off the price of parking alone. When he was first brought in, he'd been drugged out of his mind and was told all he'd said throughout the entire process of getting him through surgery and up to his room was Dawn's name in a hysterical, panicked way. That evening, his doctor refused to let anyone in to see him, telling the FBI and everyone else that he needed rest. Very late that evening, they let Megan in who was very intense in her tone about how Tom was not to talk to anyone about anything that didn't concern his health unless she was present, and even then she wanted to be involved. She was very specific to ignore the press, no matter what, poking him in the chest with her finger to make her point. Tom, through a drug-induced haze, agreed. When Marshal Elliott appeared in his room Sunday morning, Tom told him to leave unless Megan was present. He lingered just long enough for Tom to ask him if the FBI intended to ignore privilege also. He left quickly after that, muttering something under his breath.

He watched TV and was constantly amazed how often he saw his face on the screen or heard mention of his name. He'd laughed hysterically when he was informed that at the time of the shooting he was still covered under the Hil Fed health plan, suspension or not, so inadvertently the credit union that now hated him was stuck paying for all of the very large medical bills he was racking up. Not that money was his largest concern at the moment, but to his mind, he thought it fitting.

On Sunday afternoon, Megan came by again with a full briefcase, a portable radio, and a sour disposition. The portable radio played loud enough so that no one out in the hall would be able to overhear anything said inside the private room Tom occupied. It was then Megan let Tom know what was going on, about the line of code they'd found, and she grilled him hard on what it meant. Tom did what he could to answer her questions, though neither were entirely happy with his answers. Despite her reluctance at talking about it, she finally gave in and answered the one question no one else would provide; she told him Dawn McCafferty was fine, and Tom was being credited with saving her life. It seemed though that Dawn was being kept under wraps and no official statements were being made. She'd even heard a rumor that Dawn left town on Saturday evening, not long after the shooting occurred. She also informed Tom that his shooter was killed as well, two shots to the chest.

"Is she OK?"

"I just told you. She's fine. You saved her."

"No, about Jerry. Him dying. Is she OK?"

It annoyed Megan how much Tom wanted to talk about Dawn, and often through their conversation, she was forced to steer Tom back to the matter of his defense. It also annoyed her to no end how nonchalant he regarded the whole matter, as if the idea of going to jail for the rest of his life didn't matter. They spoke for several hours, and the only interruption Megan allowed was when the doctors came by. Anytime Elliott or any other official came by, she stated only that every answer Tom would give would be silence. Every time this approach was taken, the official in question got angry and stated quite loudly that the moment Tom was discharged from the hospital, he would be brought before a judge immediately. Megan would only smile and say, "Fifth amendment," while suggesting they go look it up.

She and Tom spoke throughout the entire day Sunday, talking about many things, and it was only when it got late, Tom took over the conversation and brought up a whole different side of the case which startled her. It made perfect sense to her, and she felt a little foolish that she hadn't thought of it. It was something she hadn't expected to hear from Tom, but in listening to him she knew exactly what she would need to do, and she couldn't help but be amazed at how much thought Tom put into it.

But now it was Monday, and Dawn McCafferty stepped into his private room. She was dressed in much the way she was when they'd first met. A short businesses skirt and a stylish blazer/blouse combination, her hair tied back gracefully. She wore hose with delicate heels, a clear sign that she was there on business. He didn't care though. Seeing her became the brightest spot of his day. Just hearing she was alive and well hadn't really been enough; he wanted to see her.

He felt embarrassed to be seen like this; he was sure he looked terrible. The doctors gave him several blood transfusions for the blood he'd lost in the shooting, so he was sure he was still deathly pale. His hair was undoubtedly a mess, and he couldn't even recall the last time he'd shaved. His left wrist was shackled to the bed. He was wearing only a thin hospital gown and a small cover sheet. She looked radiant.

"Am I disturbing you?" she asked quietly as she came in. He noticed she held what appeared to be a greeting card, sealed in a colored envelope.

"Nah, can't really sleep anyway. I usually sleep on my side. Hard to do with this on."

"Sorry."

"Why, you didn't put it on me."

"No, Tom," she said with a deep look of sadness and regret, "you did." She stepped forward and handed the card over, setting it down on the small tray that held a cup of water with a straw on it.

"A get-well card?"

"Yeah, I thought it was appropriate."

"Depends, is there a file hidden in it?"

She smiled and watched as he shifted uncomfortably in the bed, pushing himself to sit up a bit more. "I . . ." she started, and then settled on, "Thank you."

"Shhh," he said quietly, "you don't owe me any thanks."

"You saved my life. The other agents said that your arm took the hit exactly where my heart would have been a second or two earlier."

"You don't owe me any thanks." He repeated, his eyes were deep and clear. He meant each and every word.

"I'm also sorry, it came down to this."

"You warned me it would."

"Yeah," she said nodding slowly. "Can I ask you a question, Tom?"

"Probably not," he said chuckling a little. "Megan was very direct in her instructions to speak to no one unless she was around."

"Not about the case, not about the arrest. About this whole comic book thing of yours. They got the warrant to search your residence by the end of the day on Saturday."

"Yeah, Megan told me."

"How many boxes of those comics do you have?"

"Just under a hundred. I once dreamed of opening my own comic book store."

"How many books does that translate into?"

"To be honest, I wouldn't even want to guess."

"OK," she said, "why at almost forty years old does a reasonably intelligent man still read comic books?"

"That's an easy question. When I was growing up, comic books taught me how to read. They taught me right from wrong. Each individual issue was like its own little morality play. It taught me what heroes really were, not people in tights, but the people who went above and beyond to do the right thing, even in the face of adversity."

"Like throwing yourself in front of a bullet?"

"I'm no hero, Dawn. Just look at me, not too many heroes wear handcuffs to bed."

"Another thing we found interesting?" she phrased it as a question, but she saw Tom only stared at her blankly. "We took apart your computer. The drives inside had all been recently replaced. Both of them, brand new, less than a week old the techs tell me. No trace of your older drives." She waited for a moment for him to answer but saw he wasn't going to. Instead he just smiled.

"There was this one issue of the "Amazing Spider-Man," written by a guy named *Roger Stern*. It almost made me cry. It was a deep story about Spider-Man explaining why he did what he did, explaining it to a kid who was dying—a kid who worshiped Spider-Man. Peter Parker even reveals who he was to the kid. He didn't know how to deal with the fact that the kid was going to die. It was incredibly well written. It was a short backup story in **"Amazing Spider-Man" issue #248**. It really shows what can be done with the genre. I hear people all the time talk about how comic books are just for children, that if you mix story with art you don't get anything worthwhile. They're all small-minded fools though, because it doesn't matter how you present a story. It's still a story. Comic books are just a form of entertainment that requires a little bit of intelligence and imagination. I've always loved comics, always wished that one day I'd be able to contribute something to them, but I guess I just wasn't cut out for it. Tried to write a couple of stories for them once. All I ever got was rejection letters."

"So you gave up trying?"

"I started to build a career for myself, build a life. I still got to be creative, working in marketing. I wrote a lot more than anyone would ever think. You just don't get to put a byline on the vast majority of what you produce, and it all winds up getting credited to a whole department instead of a single person."

"And then Hil Fed took it all away from you?" He just nodded and stayed silent. Finally she reached out and touched his hand. "It was a good plan, Tom," she said as a wave of concern overtook her face. "It just didn't stand a chance of succeeding. You did hurt them though. My sources tell me that Hil Fed has lost about half of their worth in the past two weeks. The blow you gave them, they may never really recover from it. They'll try, sure, but no one at the NCUA thinks that they'll be able to succeed, if that's any consolation to you."

"Can I ask you a question, Dawn?"

"Sure."

"Do you consider me a stupid?"

She smiled, as she moved her fingers gently along Tom's hand. "I think you were angry, and you probably weren't thinking all that clearly."

"Dawn, please, answer the question. Do you think I am a stupid man?"

Looking deeply into his eyes, she was surprised at how clear and levelheaded he appeared. "No, Tom, I don't think you're stupid."

"OK," he said nodding. "Can I ask you another question then?"

"Sure, go right ahead."

"Megan was telling me what you guys are saying, about how this was a massively complex program, a masterwork of industrial espionage. You really think I spent however many years a program like this would take to design, just to upload it under my own teller number? That I just sat at my desk one day in the middle of my office with all of my coworkers around me and uploaded a program without anyone asking what I was doing. And then when it all finally goes down, I just sit around waiting to get caught. If what you guys are saying is true, Dawn, I designed a brilliant program virus that went totally undetected for months in a high security system, but didn't realize that I could be tied to the upload of it."

"Sounds to me like you're already building your defense, and you probably shouldn't share it with me."

"Yeah," he said, "I guess we are. But what I want to know is this. Do you think I'm that stupid?"

She sat looking at him, slowly rubbing the tips of her fingers on his hand. "It doesn't make much sense, I'll say that."

"But you still think I did it?"

"Yes."

Tom leaned his head further back into the pillow and for a moment stared up at the ceiling. He looked hurt. "How are you?" he said softly.

"Me? I'm holding on."

"I heard rumor you left town the other night. I suspected you went back to tell Jerry's mother about the shooting yourself."

"Yeah," she said nodding her head, "I thought I owed her that much. All things being equal."

"How'd she take it?"

"Not well."

"Blames you?"

She realized she was still nodding her head and forced herself to stop as she spoke, "Yes."

"Do you?"

"What?"

"Do you blame yourself too?"

She didn't want to answer, but she knew she would. Something about him always made her answer the questions he asked, whether she wanted to or not. "Yes, partially."

"You shouldn't, Dawn," he said as he stared directly into her eyes. "You can't control what other people do in life. You can only ever take responsibility for what you yourself do. This I have learned the hard way."

"I'll try to keep that in mind, but right now I should go. I'm not really supposed to be here in the first place. Elliott would have a conniption if he knew."

"Are you holding up?"

"I don't think I want to talk about this."

"Even if you desperately need to?"

She was shaking her head softly. "I thought I was supposed to be the shrink in this relationship."

"You loved him once, Dawn. Hell, I bet on some level you still do. Two days ago you watched him die. How can something like that not affect a person? Not affect you?"

"You seem, OK. You don't even seem angry."

"I understand."

"What do you mean?" she said as she used the tops of her fingernails to slowly trace his hand up to his wrist just under where the handcuff began.

"How can I be angry at a man who's already faced his judgment, a man who obviously wasn't in his right mind any longer, a man who couldn't bring himself to let go of you?"

"He shot you, Tom."

"And the doctors say I'll be fine. What about you, Dawn, are you going to heal as well?"

"I'll do," she said quickly, "what I need to do."

"Nightmares?"

"A few, yes."

"You gonna see your therapist again?"

"I think, yeah, I am."

"He did it to himself, Dawn, not the other way around."

"That doesn't change the way I feel, Tom, the way I remember things, or what I put him through."

"Never will either," he said looking back at her softly, "but you will work past this. You just need to focus on something else in the short term."

"Yeah," she said. "Maybe. But there I'm fresh out of luck. The case I'm on has been solved. I'm just sticking around for administrative purposes. I'd really like to completely throw myself into an investigation of some sort right now."

"You told Jerry the other day you were being fired, is that true?"

"You're caught, Tom. Why are you so worried about me?"

"Just am."

"When you get convicted, a lot of heat will be off me. It looks like I'll be able to keep my job, but I won't get the same kind of cases. I suspect I'll mostly be stuck doing heavy office work, pushing the paper around into different piles."

"Sounds like something you'd hate."

"It won't be the kind of job I'll keep very long."

"Let me guess," he said as he felt her hand lift from his, as she stared to move away. "You'll stay in the job just long enough to erase any allegation that could be held against you. Then you'll find something else."

She smiled as she moved closer to the door. He knew the story well; it had been the same plan he'd intended after what happened to him originally at the credit union. "I probably won't be able to come back to see you again, Tom. I really am sorry you know, that things weren't different."

Her hand was reaching for the door, when he spoke again, "One last thing, Dawn."

"Yes?"

"I've had the same two passwords for Logiterm since the day they installed it. I go back and forth from one to the other since the system makes you change it once every thirty days."

She stopped and took her hand away from the door, turning to look back at him and his sudden intense stare. "Why tell me?"

"You're not supposed to let anyone at the company know what your password is, but I've got to tell you, Dawn, my password is one of the worst kept secrets out there. With as many years as I've worked there, a couple dozen people know it as well as I do, especially the people I was closest to. Everything on the Logiterm system is designed to work off seniority. I can do a lot of things on the systems others couldn't, because I was technically trusted, supposedly I knew what I was doing. Things change, what can I say, huh?" Seeing she wasn't responding to his joke, he said, "Seriously, do you have any idea what a pain in the ass it is to get up every time someone needs an override?"

"So you just told people what your password was, and because they knew, they effectively had all of the privileges you did?"

"Uh-Huh."

"You're saying you were framed?"

"I'm saying I don't have the money, and I never have."

"You should tell all of that to your lawyer, Tom, not me." She stopped for a second and then quietly added, "There's been enough errors made in this investigation. Who knows, that might just meet the reasonable doubt you were looking for." She turned and again reached for the door.

"I heard I made the front page of the *Union-Tribune*. Tell me something, did I make *USA Today* as well?"

"Why would you care about that?"

"Vanity."

"Tom!"

"I want to know if I'm internationally thought of as a thief, as well as nationally."

"Tom, you stole 320 million dollars. It's a pretty safe bet you're on the cover of every newspaper in the world today. And if not today, at least by tomorrow. I'd be willing to bet you'll make the cover of both *Time* and *Newsweek* soon."

She looked back at him, not understanding why he cared about the fame, smiled and then walked out.

"Good-bye, Dawn," he said to the empty room, as he closed his eyes and pushed his head as far back into the pillow as he could. Suddenly very afraid, he'd never see her again.

* * *

Suspicion of Guilt 15.1

March 29, 2000

He was in Victoria Station when he bought his copy of *USA Today*; the face of Thomas Williams was in full glossy color. The copy read it was a promotional picture donated by Hil Fed Credit Union, taken back when he'd been active in their marketing department. Waiting in the long line at the bookstore to purchase the paper, he read the article from start to finish. It consisted of reporting an arrest was made in the largest credit union heist in American history. Tom Williams was the only suspect throughout the entire investigation, and evidence recently discovered showed he uploaded a massive virus onto the Logiterm system.

He couldn't help but laugh.

He paid for the newspaper and gingerly walked away, a spring to his step as he walked down to the underground station and took the first tube back to his hotel, and once back inside, he booted up his laptop computer.

He went immediately to the program he'd designed and keyed in the password to remove the useless gibberish from the screen and reveal the actual information he needed. The whole program, he had to admit, was a masterwork of genius. He scrolled down to the current total and laughed out loud all over again.

He then called up the command system and began to make the necessary adjustments for the final stage the program was designed for.

Across eight different screens that he could access with a simple roll of the mouse, he looked at the total lines that added up to 355 million dollars. This next part would be heartbreaking, he knew, but it still needed to be done.

He hit the sequence code to start compiling the funds digitally into two separate accounts he'd set up in Hong Kong. It was going to take a while, and there would undoubtedly be a few losses along the way, but even if by some small chance the FBI was watching all accounts in Hong Kong, by the time they could be alerted, he'd already have the money gone. "Who'd ever think I'd give up 320 million dollars?" he said laughing as he pushed the enter button, setting everything into motion.

* * *

Suspicion of Guilt 15.2

March 29, 2000

When Dawn walked into the small conference room in the Information Services Division at Hil Fed, she saw Marc at once. She walked directly up to him, grabbed him by his shirt collar and dragged him to the corner without a word. At first, he protested loudly, but his reaction only started the people around him laughing at how he was being bullied by a woman. He knew they wouldn't understand Dawn McCafferty could probably kick the stuffing out of most of them, especially when she was angry, and Marc worked with Dawn enough times to know that the first spark of anger was clear in her eyes. So he let her pull him over to the far side of the room where they could speak privately. "Jesus, Dawn, what is this?"

"The code line you found, tell me about it."

"Why should I? In case you haven't heard, you're officially off this case. They're only keeping you around now because replacing you after the arrest might look bad when it goes to trial."

"Listen to me very carefully, Marc. You're a little worm of a human being, and the only reason you've come as far as you have was because Neal liked the way you kissed his ass incessantly. Me, I'm already on the outs with the NCUA. We both know it. So if I take a moment to beat your silly little ass around the street once we're both away from any witness, we both know you won't have the balls to press charges, and even if you were to report me, all you'd do is become a laughing stalk. So I want you to start talking right now, or start looking over your shoulder later. Your call, hot shot."

He looked around him, making sure that no one else could hear what she was saying. He knew Dawn well enough to know she didn't make idle threats. He'd also constantly heard of her fierce temper and that she'd once shot a man while working for the FBI, though he was still unclear on why she shot and killed someone. It was one of the many subjects he'd been too afraid to ask her about.

"What do you want to know?"

"I read in the report that it was uploaded in September at night. 9:00 p.m.?"

"Uh-huh," he said looking around nervously. "It all happened during one of the board meetings that they were having, right under their nose."

"He stayed to work late that night?"

"I suppose."

"Did you check his time card?"

"Of course, we did, and of course, it wasn't listed. It showed him as leaving three hours earlier that day. Our guess is he left and then waited until everyone left and snuck back in."

"Surveillance tapes?"

"They erased them after three months, Dawn. Standard procedure."

"No video evidence then?"

"Dawn, it's a password-coded system. It was his user number."

"It was done at a collection computer terminal?"

"No."

"What?" she said with far more force than she meant to.

He backed up a step, unsure of what she might do. "I said, no. It wasn't done at a registered computer in the collections department."

"Well, where was the computer located?"

"The marketing department, OK?"

"All the terminals here are independently registered, right?"

"Yes . . ."

"Whose computer uploaded the virus?"

"We're not supposed to get into that."

"Well, I'm already in it, Marc, so go ahead and tell me. It'll certainly be brought up at trial anyway. So why not just tell me now and save me the trouble of reading the transcripts?"

"The vice president's terminal, OK?"

"The virus was uploaded at Laura Netzly's terminal?"

"Yes. Now are we through?"

"Yes," she said quickly, as she turned quickly on her heel and hurried upstairs.

* * *

Suspicion of Guilt 15.3

March 29, 2000

"Marshal Elliott speaking."

His phone voice showed the perfect tone, polite but steady. "Hi, Marshal," she said boldly.

"Hello, Ms. McCafferty. What is it I can do for you?"

"The upload was done at Laura Netzly's terminal back on September 15, last year."

"I'm aware of that, but thank you."

"Are you also aware that Tom Williams is shown on his time card as leaving from work early that day?"

"Ms. McCafferty," he said with a gentile ease, "while I appreciate the thoroughness of your investigative instinct, I think, I must, at this point remind you that you are no longer an active investigator for this case. Your position now is simply to represent the NCUA in an administrative capacity."

"And I appreciate you're reminding me, Marshal, but I wasn't sure if you were aware Ms. Netzly knew Tom Williams's password for the Logiterm system. Or no one shared with you that she had also carried on a sexual affair with Mr. Williams for several months prior to her being named as the VP of Marketing and I would suppose you were also unaware that she just happened to have been on a Caribbean cruise during the early part of this month, at the same time the funds were being transferred from the credit union down to the Cayman Islands."

"Wait, what was that?"

"I did a little checking over the past few hours. It turns out while looking through Ms. Netzly's employee file that she majored in marketing back in college. Want to guess what her minor was?"

"Offhand, I cannot say I am aware of Ms. Netzly's school history, mostly because I don't believe it to be relevant."

"Computer Science," Dawn said in a cool, detached voice, "Programming to be exact. It seems she originally wanted to write computer software for marketing purposes. Guess where she interned one summer while in college? It was one of her selling points when she was getting hired here at Hil Fed." She could hear a shift in his voice; he was growing uncertain. She was sure he was standing in the exact same spot he stood when he first picked up his cell phone.

"Where?"

"Logiterm Systems. The Programming Department."

"Ms. McCafferty, is there some reason you didn't bring this up earlier in your investigation, back when you still had authority?"

"I only recently found out that Tom, ah, I mean, Mr. Williams only used two different passwords since the advent of the Logiterm system, and he went back and forth between the two. Also it was only after his arrest that he stated he told people he believed he trusted what those passwords were."

"And I suppose, Ms. McCafferty, you have a very good reason why you were talking to my suspect after I gave you your specific orders not to."

"He saved my life. I went to thank him, nothing else."

"And yet," he said with a slight edge of anger, "he wound up discussing his situation with you."

"Only briefly, and he wouldn't elaborate. It seems his attorney told him not to trust anyone. But I suppose you were right all along, Marshal. He does trust me, even if it is only the sexual tension that makes him do so."

She was in the Hil Fed boardroom, surrounded by stacks of employee files that the FBI kept locked up. She'd gone through them wildly looking for Netzly's file, going over every word of it.

"So," Elliott said quietly, "Mr. Williams claims to have freely given his password to the people at the credit union whom he trusted?"

"That's correct."

"And you now believe that Ms. Netzly is the guilty party?"

"I didn't say that."

"Well, then Ms. McCafferty, perhaps you should be more specific, because to my tired old ears that sounds exactly like what you are indicating with this telephone conversation."

"I'm saying, sir, perhaps we should take a close look at Ms. Netzly. From what my techs have said in their report, it wouldn't seem that Mr. Williams wouldn't have the technical know-how to create a virus such as the one they believe was inserted into the Logiterm system. Ms. Netzly has extensive programming background, and she's worked directly on the raw Logiterm system, and the program upload was initiated from her terminal on a night she would have been in the building."

"Now wait just a moment, Ms. McCafferty, how do you know that Ms. Netzly was in the building that night?"

"I read the board minutes for that night. The credit union keeps them on file here in the boardroom where we've been stationed for the past few weeks. I looked them up. She was present that evening. Also I did one other thing."

"And that would be?"

"I called in a favor to an old friend at the FBI, and no, before you ask, I won't tell you who. He tracked down Ms. Netzly's itinerary for her recent Caribbean cruise."

"Why am I extremely positive that I will not like what you are about to tell me?"

"The cruise took wrapped around to the Cayman Islands. She would have been docked there for a stopover . . ." and before she could finish her sentence, he did it for her.

"On the day a thin, attractive blonde went into several banks down there and transferred the 320 million dollars out to the four winds."

"The very same day, yes."

"Tell me something, Agent McCafferty?"

"I'm back to being Agent McCafferty, am I? You stopped calling me that after the night I slept with the suspect."

"Well, perhaps that is because this is the first time you've acted like an investigator since prior to that evening."

She couldn't help but smile at his words; he was right. "What's your question, Marshal?"

"Do you still believe that Mr. Williams is guilty of this crime?"

"My opinion?"

"Yes, McCafferty, your opinion."

She stared forward, looking all around the boardroom that was stacked high with files and reports, "Yes, I do."

"Then why are you calling me with this?"

"Because," she said not believing the words that came from her mouth, "what if I'm wrong?"

"All right, Dawn," he said as he softened his voice, "what do you want to do? Call her in, talk to her?"

"No," she said closing Laura Netzly's file, "I want to work up a profile of her and see if we turn up anything else we should know, and for the sake of her privacy, I want it done quietly. The only way I can go any further on this would be with your authorization."

He was silent on the phone for a full thirty seconds, before he finally spoke, "Do it. Let me know what you find."

* * *

Suspicion of Guilt 15.4

March 30, 2000

Tuesday in London

It was all done, and the early morning hours surrounded him.

He checked out of his hotel earlier that evening, and went to a new hotel. *An unnecessary precaution,* he was sure, *but why tempt fate? It was all over now.* All he had to do was wait for morning to go collect what was his.

It was still miserably cold in London, especially down by the Thames; he huddled deeply into his jacket, a jacket ill equipped for this kind of weather. Under one arm he carried his prized laptop, his beautiful program already thoroughly erased, all trace of it gone. The only part where any of the code remained was in his head.

He'd even formatted the drive, completely cleared out everything twice. The laptop he carried was utterly useless until a new operating system was loaded onto it. With the time he'd spent sterilizing the computer, he was sure no one would ever be able to retrieve anything that was once been on it. But again, he wasn't the kind of man to take chances against the unknown. *Who knew what the technology of the future would bring?* He'd spent twenty minutes bringing down the hard wooden chair inside his hotel room on the keyboard, smashing it down deep into the guts of the computer, shattering the processing unit, hard drive, and assorted card hookups.

His precious laptop was no more than junk, and when he hit a deserted stretch of walkway, isolated from the nearby street, he hurled the remains as far out into the deep, murky water of the Thames as he could.

He smiled a dark, almost sinister smile and then let it fade from his face, as he thought about his wife. *This never would have happened,* he thought, *if she hadn't been taken from him.* Not a day went by that he didn't think about her, and he knew he would never stop loving her.

He could have been a good man, he thought, *but instead this was what he'd become.* The only upside was, he was incredibly good at being bad.

He turned to head back to his new hotel, ecstatic that he wouldn't have to stay in the city much longer. He knew that somewhere in this world there was a warm, sunny beach calling his name, and he was determined to get there as soon as he could.

* * *

Said and Done

Said and Done 16.0

March 30, 2000

At three o'clock Tuesday afternoon, the FBI, accompanied by a small group of San Diego police officers, as well as NCUA Agent Dawn McCafferty, marched into the marketing department of the Hil Fed building holding an arrest warrant. Marshal Elliott looked regal in a charcoal gray suit that was perfectly cut to his anatomy. It was easy to tell that he thrived for moments like these. Bursting into the room, they startled the receptionist, Corina, so badly that she spilled her half-full cup of coffee across her desk. Elliott, followed by two bureau agents, moved right past her, despite Corina trying to stop them.

"Ms. Netzly?" Elliott called out, and she met them halfway down the hallway to her office, looking very confused as to why they were there.

"Can I help you with something?"

"Yes," Elliott said with a very casual demeanor. "As a matter of fact, you can."

Dawn stayed in the back of the party, as two FBI agents read Laura Netzly her rights. She was indignant and loud as her rights were recited to her and was swearing she'd have someone's ass for this miscarriage of justice. Elliott remained polite and even courteous through the entire reading, until he finally insisted that she acknowledge that she understood the rights as they were read to her.

"Fine, fine," she screamed, "I understand them. Now will you please tell me what's going on here?"

That was when Elliott stepped up close to her and asked, "Tell me, Ms. Netzly, how do you account for the Cayman Islands' account in your name with just under 320 million dollars in it that we located this morning?"

"What the hell are you talking about?" she snapped angrily.

"Would you also care to explain how you paid off your home this morning? Both your first and second mortgage? Not to mention both your family cars?"

"I did no such thing!"

"We also," Dawn said, as she gracefully stepped forward, "have an e-mail trace to a hotmail account that sent the instructions to the Cayman Islands Bank to pay off your home and cars, as well as the homes and cars of all your family members." Dawn smiled as Netzly glared at her.

"Or, Ms. Netzly," Elliott said smoothly as the two worked together in an attempt to rattle her a bit, "why your computer terminal this morning was logged onto the hotmail server for several minutes?"

"That's a lie. I haven't been on the Internet today, much less go to a hotmail account, which I do not have. What are you people doing? Is this a game you're trying to play, an early April fool's joke of some kind?"

"No joke, Ms. Netzly. That's why these agents just read you your rights."

"This is insane!" she screamed at what seemed like the top of her lungs, causing Dawn to step back a bit wanting to put some distance between herself and a woman, who was obviously bordering on hysteria.

"I take it then you don't wish to comment on our inquiries at this time, Ms. Netzly?"

"You can take it however you like, because you haven't got a clue as to what you're doing! Tom Williams is the thief, not me!"

"Or so," Dawn said in her most coy voice, "we were led to believe."

"This is your doing, isn't it, you bitch? Everyone around here knows you slept with Tom. Did he sway you over to his dark little fantasy world?!"

Dawn just smiled. "Sleeping with Mr. Williams would hardly be an exclusive club, now would it?" And with that, Dawn turned to walk away. She heard Laura Netzly screaming her head off as she was handcuffed and marched out of the building. It seemed altogether too amusing, and Dawn knew she wouldn't help the situation by being present.

Yesterday she put together a profile of Laura Netzly's life, running what information they had on her. In fact, she stayed up very late going over what she could discover from the credit union files. It was when going through computer logs that she found that the Information Services Division could monitor Internet use; she'd discovered that periodically Netzly used her work terminal to check a hotmail account.

She'd also pulled a credit report to find out where she owed money. She'd assigned out the report to an FBI agent to verify all balances and history, and he'd called her this morning to say that she no longer owed any money, anywhere, to anyone. She'd received several wire transfers from a Cayman Islands Bank to all of her creditors paying her accounts off in full. The wires were traced back to an account under Netzly's name, a bank that was less than a block from the bank the 320 million dollars was originally deposited to at the early part of the month down in the Cayman's. This new account under her own name was opened over the Internet, using the hotmail account.

In the first part of the morning, a large wire was transferred in from a bank in Hong Kong to the bank down in the Cayman Islands. Not long after that, an e-mail arrived, digitally signed by Laura Netzly, from the same hotmail account authorizing them to release funds to her creditors. The Internet bank account was controlled by an authorization code, an authorization code which was included in the hotmail e-mail.

The FBI immediately issued out warrants so that they could verify the information they'd received and ran a check on the electronic computer signature that all computers inside the Hil Federal credit union are assigned. An IP address which can determine any computer and track it if necessary.

Dawn sat in the main lobby and watched as they brought Laura Netzly through, leading her to the black sedan parked illegally in front of the building. After a moment, she saw Marshal Elliott stroll through the lobby smiling. He stepped up to her, and she smiled back at him. "I guess we were both wrong about your Mr. Williams."

"I suppose."

"Now, now, Dawn. There's no need to take it so hard," he said as he sat down next to her on the posh bench. "We all make a mistake while analyzing crime evidence, sooner or later, at any rate. This just happened to be your turn. Not to mention you are the one who caught the real criminal, red-handed as a matter of fact. That will be placed in the report I'll be writing, a copy of which will be sent to the NCUA director."

"And you think they might not go so hard on me then, right?"

"Well, now, Dawn, you just saved them having to pay out 320 million dollars to reimburse the fine folks here at the Hillsborough Industrial League Federal Credit Union. I suspect they will view you as something of a savior. After all, I don't think many government agencies account for an expected loss of that size when compiling their annual budgets, do you? Insurance funds or not."

"I'm rather sure they don't," she said letting her smile grow just a tad brighter. "What else did she say? I heard her caterwauling up a storm?"

"This vacation of hers, the one that took her down to the Cayman Islands, she says she won it, by placing her business card in one of those fishbowls that they have at restaurants. She couldn't remember which restaurant though."

"Let me guess," Dawn said trying to hold back a small burst of laughter. "She's the type who drops her card in every one of those fishbowl contests she sees?"

"That is what she was trying to lead us to believe."

"But how could she know that I'd already had a copy of her travel plans and spoke to her booking agent to find out that she had arranged for the entire vacation via her hotmail account where we have a record of her IP address here being online at all of the times those e-mails were sent? Or, that when we contacted the travel agent, located in Iowa, who said he received a Federal Express package with a return address for the Hil Fed credit union on it that contained the cash for her vacation tickets?"

Elliott leaned back a little, letting his back lightly touch the back wall of the lobby. "Very clever of her. Sending cash wouldn't leave a credit-card trace to prove that she paid for it. Since she's an American online customer, at home, there's no way to track her IP number, because they randomly assign it each time a user signs onto their network. She obviously didn't know that each of the credit union computers was assigned a direct one."

"Obviously."

He was looking directly forward, across the lobby toward the elevator, when he finally asked her, "You're not going to ask?"

"About what?"

"Him."

"What's to ask?"

"Whether or not we have released him yet?"

"I already know the answer to that."

"Do you?"

"There's no way you would have released Tom Williams from custody until this arrest was complete. You wouldn't have wanted to alert the press, or Netzly. I imagine, on your way downstairs, you phoned someone to have him released, someone to contact his attorney and then step into his hospital room and eat a little crow against Tom's righteous rage at being falsely accused yet again. How am I doing?"

"Remarkably well, Agent McCafferty. Perhaps you should come back to the bureau?"

"No, thanks."

"Do you think you will continue to find happiness with the NCUA?"

"No," she said as she stood up. "But I think, I'm tired of carrying my gun."

"Hard to escape in your kind of work."

She just nodded, suddenly feeling very uncertain about her future.

"Agent McCafferty," he said with a stiff smile, drawing back her attention, before softening. "Have you thought about him? About his intentions through all of this?"

"You're starting to sound like my father now."

"Perhaps a father is what you need right now."

"I think," she said, "I have a fairly good idea of his intentions throughout this investigation."

"Here's a question then. Why did he save you? Why take the bullet? If he was guilty, I'd think it would have certainly been easier for you to fall out of the investigation, at least for him."

She stood slowly. "It probably would have, but Tom Williams isn't exactly what I would call a conventional man."

"No, I suppose he isn't, is he?"

"I better go pack my stuff."

"Yes, and I had better get started on all of the many reports that I need to complete by the end of the day. Though I hope you will find, Dawn, that the world isn't always this confusing, and that perhaps, somewhere out there is a job for someone like you will enjoy that doesn't require a gun."

She started walking across the lobby, headed back toward the elevator. "Yeah," she said nodding her head, "everybody needs a dream. Good-bye, Marshal. It was nice meeting you."

"You as well, Agent McCafferty, you as well."

She didn't look back at him as he got on the elevator. Something was nagging at the back of her skull, something that was bothering her for a while, but now she was starting to see it all very clearly. She needed to talk to a couple of people in the building first though, before she could be sure of what she suspected. There was no need to tell Elliott, that die was already cast, that game already played.

* * *

Said and Done 16.1

March 30, 2000

Megan walked into Tom's room a little after 1:30 p.m., a bright, sunshiny smile on her face. "How you feeling, sailor?" He was still shackled to the bedrail and looked up from his book with weary eyes and matted, unkempt hair. Back when they dated, all those years back, she'd seen Tom look what she thought to be his worst on many occasions; something about the image she walked into today put all other memories to shame. She could tell by a single look that he didn't want to talk about the case, his arrest, or any other future dealings; he was lost and alone, chained to a hospital bed, and she was sure he'd much rather be on the water. Something she'd told him rather bluntly the other day he might never be able to do again.

"Better. I'm on less painkillers. Why are you so cheery?"

She strolled over to his bed, her smile growing with each step. "I got a call from the FBI, Tom. I've been told to walk you out of here as soon as the doctor discharges you. You're obviously not doing anything here but taking up space."

"What?"

"It turns out they found the money, and it wasn't in your possession." She slapped his cuffed hand in a playful, flirty way.

"So I'm free?"

"Yup," she said, "lock, stock, and barrel."

Tom just smiled, as Megan sat down beside him on the edge of the bed. "Thanks for representing me again, Meg. I guess I really owe you this time."

"I hate it when you call me, Meg. You know that, right?"

"Uh-huh," he said smiling, "I know. It's one of the benefits of being free."

She started laughing with him, a contagious bit of energy. She'd been more worried than she cared to admit. Even with all the flaws the FBI and NCUA made, the line of code with Tom's name on it was going to be damning in a court of law, especially since they wouldn't be able to prove what was supposed to have been loaded. There was a huge hole in Tom's defense, and she hadn't really known how they were going to get past it. Tom insisted he was being framed, but she knew it would be a hard battle to get reasonable doubt on that. After a few minutes, the laughter died down, and she looked at him sweetly, "OK, kiddo, next pressing question, your plan for how we were going to pay for the very expensive trial we were anticipating. What do you want me to do on that front?"

"I want you to press forward," he said moving his eyebrows up and down like he was acting out some cheap vaudeville act. "Now that the name of the game isn't finding a way to pay, it's called recompensation. I'm still in the same boat, yeah?"

"Oh yeah," she said making the same foolish eyebrow motions.

"How soon can you have the paperwork prepared?"

"Hey, what do you think, you hired some amateur attorney to represent you? I was worried about how you were going to pay for this trial. I started to work on the pleadings Sunday evening. My staff and I finished them yesterday. I just wanted to double check with you before we filed anything."

"When do they get filed, served?"

"Let's get you out of here first. I don't want any complications with that, and then we march forward with payback. What do you say?"

"What do I say? I say hand me my pants and get that goddamn guard in here to take this cuff off."

"You sure you're ready for discharge?"

"If I have to sign out against medical wishes, I am out of here, now. I want to go home, Meg! Home, home, on the range! Give me some damn deer and antelope to play with!"

"You know," she said looking at him, "this plan of yours is probably going to affect your friend too?"

"She didn't do anything wrong. It was her boss."

"You know as well as I do, Tom, maybe better, shit has a way of rolling down hill." She got up from the bed, moved the wrinkles out of her skirt by pressing hard on them with her palms and smoothing them out. "I wanted to make sure you were aware of that possibility before I did anything. But I tell you, if we don't go after them all, we can't go after just one."

"Do it, Megan. You have my OK. Nail their asses to the wall."

* * *

Said and Done 16.2

March 30, 2000

Dawn stepped briefly into the office of the senior vice president of finance. Craig Peterson was on the phone, and his tie was completely off, discarded to the mess of papers that seemed to line his desk from one corner to the next. Looking up he saw her and motioned her in. He was busy and really didn't have time to talk to anyone that wasn't on his meeting schedule, but she moved into his office, closed the door and sat down.

Listening to his call she heard him speaking to someone important at another banking institution, she suspected it was one of the banks that received a pay off wire from Netzly's Cayman bank this morning. Dawn sat quietly and waited for Craig to get off the line. In all, it took about twenty minutes, even as he mentioned three times to whomever he was speaking with that he had an NCUA representative sitting in his office.

When he finally sat the phone back in its cradle, he looked a good five years older than when she last saw him and she watched as he slumped back in his chair apologizing to her for making her wait. "It's OK," she said. "I imagine it's a pretty hectic day."

"Yeah, you guys are being great and so's the FBI. We should have all the money back in a week or so. But I've got a lot of angry banking people, who aren't happy with being involved in this. Something tells me that we'll be putting out fires for a long time to come." He clapped his hands together, as if trying to start a new thought. "What can I do for you though?"

"I need to ask a stupid question."

"Sure, go ahead. I'm a master at those. I work in finance."

"If you were given 320 million dollars, Craig, how much interest do you think you could make on that in an approximately a month's time?"

"What? I mean, that's really variable, market conditions and such."

"Is it possible you wouldn't make any interest on it?"

He was shrugging his shoulders a little. "Possible? Sure, likely, no."

"So theoretically, how much interest could you make on 320 million dollars in a month's time?"

"The market's been strong so far this year. A lot of booms in the dot-com industries . . ."

"No," she said, "imagine the foreign market, where the FBI wouldn't be able to trace you as easy."

"Are we assuming the person knows what they're doing?"

"For the moment, let's assume yes."

"OK," he said as he leaned his head back trying to consider far too many variables. "It's really a lot like throwing a dart at a board, Dawn. No set answer, but I would assume if you had that kind of money to back you up, well, you could actually help create rushes and falls. Undoubtedly the person wouldn't use all the money in any one stock, and if I'm reading you right, you wouldn't want to be transferring around 320 million dollars if people are looking for it. You'd have it broken up into a lot of little, more untraceable pieces. If you used those pieces effectively, you could steer a market in small ways with that kind of money."

"So bottom line?"

"Bottom line, who knows? But I'd like to think I could probably create a false impression of a boom, and probably in a month's time net somewhere around thirty to forty million dollars. Of course, you'd need a lot of people to manage that much money, especially if you were trying to stay under someone's radar."

"Thanks, Craig," she said softly. "You've been a big help."

As she stood, he asked, "Do you think Laura stashed a bunch of money somewhere?" As she opened the door to his office to walk out, she just turned to look at him and with a casual glance, said, "No."

Dawn's next stop was back on the first floor, back to Jim Krieder's office. She hadn't spoken to him in almost two weeks. But as she stepped into his office, she saw his face light up and his hand come up to wave. "I wondered," he said gleefully, "if you were going to say good-bye?"

"Not gone yet, Jim."

"Something tells me that you will be soon enough." He motioned for her to take a seat.

"Can I ask you a question, off the record?"

"Sure, Dawn, shoot."

Inwardly, she cringed a little at the term "shoot," and suspected she would for quite some time. The thought of Jerry haunted her mind for a moment—the thin, fragile look he had right before he died. She closed her eyes and pushed it out of her head. Looking back up at Jim Krieder, she asked one simple question, "If you had the technical know-how, Jim, could you clone an IP address?"

* * *

Said and Done 16.3
April 4, 2000

Megan sat in front of the entire board of directors in the Hil Fed boardroom. Intermingled amongst them was the senior management team, as well as their corporate attorney. None of them looked happy. Megan looked very pleased to be there, alone, against them all.

For Megan, it was an extremely busy week. She'd filed two lawsuits against three defendants. The first filed against both the FBI and NCUA for illegally breaking into her client Tom Williams private residence without a warrant, a clear violation of his civil rights. Considering the FBI agent was caught red-handed and arrested by a local San Diego sheriff, it was fairly open and shut. But it still amazed her how quickly both defendants offered up settlements to have the matter dropped.

It was Tom's plan to sue all the people who appeared to have been set against him, use their own money to pay for his trial when the time came. With the violations that were perpetrated against Tom, it was a clear case of victory as far as she was concerned, and all the FBI and NCUA really wanted in the settlement was a hold harmless against all aspects of the investigation from this point forward. They knew they both feared a wrongful arrest case, even though they would have certainly won. It would be embarrassing and costly. Better to settle out on what they did do wrong and get everybody to agree that the entire matter was completely and forever dropped. Each agency combined forces and negotiated her down to a sixteen-million-dollar settlement, eight million dollars to be paid from each. Certified checks from each agency would arrive tomorrow.

Still, she knew they weren't the people Tom really wanted to hurt; he wanted the credit union, and that was why she sat before them now. Today was their turn.

"We had nothing to do," Randy Carlson said loudly, "with the NCUA breaking into Tom's house, they did that on their own." The credit union's lawyer did what he could to hold Randy back, but Randy just kept ranting on.

"Mr. Carlson," Megan said gracefully, "I think you may have misunderstood what my filing against Hillsborough Industrial League Federal Credit Union was about. We have never asserted that the credit union had anything to do with the illegal break-in to my client's home. That's not what our case against you is about."

"Then what in the good Christ are we doing here?"

"Well, Mr. Carlson," she said, as she pulled a tape recorder out of her briefcase, "it has to do with a confidentiality agreement you and the Hillsborough Industrial League Federal Credit union entered into with my client Thomas Williams, a contract that the credit union broke."

"What the hell are you talking about?"

She simply pressed the play button and leaned back into the plush leather chair she sat in. Randy Carlson's voice was distinctive, even on a poor-quality recording made from a television news reporting, "We have all the proof we need, you son of bitch. You stole from us once, and now you just went and upped the ante, and I'll be goddamned before you get a chance at anything else here!" Other voices popped into the recording, people asking questions fast and furious, and then Randy's voice returned clear as a bell, "I can't get into the details, but Tom Williams was once almost fired over another theft he did, and based on the current FBI investigation surrounding him, we felt the need to remove him from all duties." Megan hit the stop button and looked back up at the assemblage of people.

"This recording," she said, "was taken from an official Hil Fed press conference you held outside your own front doors. The voice belongs to Randy Carlson, speaking as the head of Hil Fed credit union, and the words he chose to use that day violated the agreement we made, an agreement we have in writing. My case against you has to do with that violation, and my client is prepared to go all the way with this case. After all, what's a little bit more embarrassment for your credit union here in what you're undoubtedly looking at as the rebuilding stage? A public lawsuit from Mr. Williams should catch a lot of press attention, especially when it's revealed that Hil Fed was not only unable to keep depositors' monies safe, but cannot honor their agreements either."

Everyone was silent; everyone knew what she was saying. This case was largely about revenge and would come at a time they were fighting to hold onto the membership they had left. They were already in a public relations nightmare, and to have this added would make their recovery process impossible.

Their attorney cleared his throat and looked across the table at her. "Megan, we're not recording here, and we all know what you're saying. Tom just received two large settlements from the FBI and the NCUA. He doesn't need to work anymore and would certainly donate whatever funds it took to hurt this organization. We understand, so let's cut to the chase," he said. "What do you want?"

"Well," she said holding back her laughter, giving the line exactly like she'd been rehearsing all morning, "my client would be willing to entertain the thought of a settlement, but we think we have a very good chance of winning this case. We have audio, video, and plenty of witnesses that can be subpoenaed. So if you're going to settle, think big." She looked around the room at all the tight, angry faces, and suddenly wished she'd brought Tom along; he really would have enjoyed it.

* * *

Saying Good-Bye 17.0
April 7, 2000

Tom was packing things from his desk into boxes, while Samantha sat at hers trying to finish up a week's worth of work on a late Friday afternoon, just past regular business hours, they were the only ones left in the department. He wore jeans, a button-down shirt, and a nice sport coat that seemed to work well with the blue-jean image he was going for. *A casual style of retired excellence,* he'd thought. Officially, this was Tom's last day at the credit union. He'd been quiet when he walked in with a set of boxes to pack up the knickknacks that lined his cubicle. There was a genuine sense of sadness. Everyone hugged him, before they left saying their official good-byes, everyone but he and Sammie. They'd been good friends in a very unconventional way; she was one of the few employees around from almost the beginning, from when Hil Fed first opened their doors to serve the public. She'd started in the branches and found her way up to the administrative department and inevitably into collections. When Tom was still a fresh, new employee, he'd go out to the lunch tables around the back of the building, seeking out the companionship of other employees. Sam was always there chain-smoking away, a lively joke ready to be told at all times, and despite her hardened exterior, she was the most decent person he'd ever met.

Even after Tom stopped heading out to the lunch tables, when he was suddenly the king of the power lunch in his high-flying days in marketing, they always spoke. Even if it was just as they spotted one another in the hallways. Tom couldn't begin to picture what a different place this company would have been if not for Sam. He certainly knew collections would have been a far more miserable job without her wry sense of humor and sarcastic wit.

The day was an emotional one; Tom hadn't even arrived until well after one. He was no longer on any schedule, other than his own. That wasn't the reason he arrived late though. He wanted to avoid as many people as possible. It was a well known that a lot of the executives took off early to start their weekends, and with so much bad blood between him and the senior management team right now, he really didn't want to see any more of them than necessary. He'd cost them a tremendous amount of money this past week. Their insurance bonds would help pay the settlement, but Hil Fed was still a long way away from recovering from their recent state of bad press. The talk of a massive layoff was already starting to spread its way around the building. Tom heard from fairly reliable sources that offers for early retirements were being discretely made, and some suggested, the credit union would be forced into a merger by the NCUA to protect assets. Reading *Time* magazine on the back deck of his condo yesterday, he found an article saying that analysts were expecting that Hil Fed would never completely recover from this mar on their once-great record, which in his mind gave a lot of credence to the NCUA forced-merger rumor. It also shocked him to be reading about Hil Fed in Time magazine.

Even though he was being declared innocent and wrongly accused at every turn, there was anger in the eyes of the faces he saw. Whether misdirected or not, Tom felt he was better off avoiding as many people at the credit union as he could. Credit unions were like any business. They largely thrived on gossip, whether good or bad, and it was fairly common knowledge that Tom received a large settlement and would not be returning to work. With a circling rumor that a lot of people would soon be losing their job, his face would mostly likely not be a welcome sight. He felt bad for everyone who would be affected and decided not to rub his newfound financial freedom in anyone's face. He went late and planned to sneak in and out, as quickly as possible.

But the collection department was there, and they were waiting for him. They knew he'd be coming sooner or later, so they planned a small going-away party. Just the five of them, some punch, and a cheesecake they'd been saving in the fridge for whenever he showed up. The workday stopped in the collections department as soon as he walked through the door. A quiet, unsteady office changed into a pleasant atmosphere, and the coworkers spoke freely. They laughed and talked, and as each left, they hugged. It was their way of saying good-bye and wishing Tom the best. Tom could see it in each of their eyes. They weren't worried about losing their jobs; the delinquency for the credit union had been growing steadily since the announcement of the theft. It seemed a tremendous amount of people assumed that Hil Fed would go out of business and didn't think they would need to pay their debts. Not realizing whether the credit union survived or not, the debts would wind up being owed to someone. In collections, job security was always a joke, because they would always be people who didn't pay their bills. Good times or bad.

But now, several hours later, Tom didn't think about that aspect of the job, because it didn't matter anymore. He was here to go through the remains of his past, the possessions someone collects over many years service in one place. Looking at his desk he was amazed at how much junk he'd amassed. Knickknacks and whatnots; these were his keepsakes, small, little toys to pull him from his workday, if even for a moment. Reams of funny memos and e-mails collected over years of service. For a moment, it had seemed so important that he come back and collect his things. Now as he sat looking at them, they all seemed so worthless and foolish.

"Not much, is it?" Tom looked up to see Sam looking at him, a knowing smile on her face; she could tell exactly what he was thinking. He couldn't even fathom the life she'd lived. It was clearly the school of hard knocks, and somehow she'd managed to come out on top. She was one of the smartest, sweetest people he'd ever met. She'd been through hell and always came up smiling, always with a joke or a story to brighten the mood. She was one of the few people at Hil Fed that he honestly admired. No matter what kind of mood Tom was in, no matter how hard he might try to conceal it, she could always see right through him. He smiled back at her and shrugged a little. "No . . . not much at all."

"I don't ever plan to clean out my desk."

"Just leave it all for the next person to sort out."

"I suppose," she said, "but mainly it's because I plan to die right here at this desk, so it won't be an issue for me."

"That's rather gruesome."

"Anything of value?"

"Doesn't look like it," he said as he tossed another stack of papers into the trash. "'course most of the stuff that I really cared about found its way home after I left marketing." Once again, he looked around the desk, shaking his head at all of the meaningless things that for so long shaped his days, miles of paperwork that didn't really matter, and did nothing but create bullshit jobs for other people, things that really didn't matter. It broke his heart to see how his credit union fell over the years. Years ago, when he was first hired, his boss had given him a speech about what credit union's stood for, "People helping people." He'd been told, and that was what Tom always believed, because for years, that was the way Hil Fed acted; they treated their members with such love and tenderness that Tom was shocked that any financial institution could work so well with their members. But then, the management shift took place in the highest ranks, a replacement CEO, who started to bring in his own people for the senior management positions. That was when Hil Fed encountered the number crunchers, where everything went down to the bottom line. Suddenly, a not-for-profit credit union began to require bottom-line sales from all branch staff, even Tom, who'd remained unaffected by the sudden change, thought it was wrong. Suddenly, the people on the front lines were being marshaled into a sales force, and if they didn't meet their projected sales quotas, they wouldn't get their raises and might even lose their jobs. Tom pointed out, almost tirelessly, that as a not-for-profit organization, they shouldn't care about sales. He never received a proper answer. The idea of the credit union again being an extended family, not just a financial institution seemed lost. The moment the old guard left, risk-based principles began, and the people running it didn't care about the members, just the money. There were hundreds of little changes Tom saw with the coming of the new regime, too many to think about. He looked back up at Sam and said, "Why do you stay?"

"Where else would I go?"

"With your years of experience, Sam, you could go anywhere."

"Kid, take a look at me. I'm too old to be taken serious in a job interview, too damn close to retirement. Leaving here, I'd lose a ton of vacation, and it would screw up the 401(k) and retirement benefits I have going. It's safer to stay, just in case I don't die at the desk. I've made my bed, and I'll lie in wait for a few more years. It was you I was always worried about, Tommy."

"Me?"

"Yeah, I was scared to death that you'd wind up a collector for the rest of your life. Woulda broken my heart if that happened. You weren't meant for this kind of shit job."

"Really," he said feeling a slight coat of red coming to his cheeks, "what do you think I was made for?"

"Something creative, not this."

Tom stood at his desk looking over at her and then glanced over at the small table with the food. "You guys really shouldn't have gone to so much trouble."

"If we'd known for sure when you were coming, we'd have done a lot more."

"Gee," he said chuckling, "I'm not sure whether I should be disappointed or relieved."

"Probably relieved," she said, as her eyes grew very intense, "since I save all of the old company newsletters they wanted me to pull all the ones you were in and put it together like a little scrapbook for you."

He stiffened a little as he looked back at her. "Yeah," he said, "relieved is probably the word."

She looked about ready to say something, when the door to the suite opened, and Dawn McCafferty walked in. She was wearing the same dress suit that she'd been wearing on the day they went out to dinner; she looked just as radiant as she had that night. She didn't say a word as she entered, but suddenly all eyes were on her. She looked nervous and more than just a little confused, and as Sam looked back at Tom, she saw the exact same look on his face. Sam knew she'd suddenly become a third wheel and stood at her desk. "Well, I've got something I need to do over in Lending. Can I trust you two not to tear the place apart?" Without waiting for an answer, she moved to the door, passed Dawn with an approving smile. As she crossed right in front of her, blocking Dawn's view of Tom for just a moment, she whispered, "He's a good man," and left the room.

Alone they stared at each other without saying a word, until finally she opened her mouth, "I'm sorry I didn't return your call the other day."

"I figured you were probably busy," he stepped away from his desk, out to where nothing would block them.

"I have been," she said, "but that wasn't the reason I didn't call you back."

"Too weird?"

She wrapped her hands around her arms, cradling herself, as she entered into a conversation she'd obviously been dreading. "I needed you that night. Jerry was waiting for me when I got back, after you'd taken me sailing."

"You told me."

"He tried to attack me after I told him about the other men. I hurt him, both physically and emotionally, and then left him to be with you. I left my radio behind. I assume he heard the watch team talk about me going to your front door, undoubtedly heard the call go over when we started to kiss. I've since heard a recording. They weren't subtle. They broadcasted the kiss loudly, repeating it over and over. I think hearing that, especially after I'd just admitted cheating on him so many times, I think it tore apart whatever shred was left of his sanity."

"Dawn, we've already covered this ground," he was slowly stepping forward, realizing how very tense she seemed. "You don't owe me any explanations."

"He's dead because of me, because of the choices I made. You told me that you stopped dating because you finally realized the choices you were making were so horribly bad. I think I've come to the same place. I don't trust what I'm thinking anymore, not after everything that's happened."

"I understand. I mean, no, I don't, not really, but I do. I'll hopefully never know what it's like to see someone I love die like that. I don't have the same kind of baggage you do. I freely confess that, I do. But I know about having a fucked-up life. I know about being persecuted for no reason. I know what it's like to suddenly feel like an outsider in a group of people you always believed were your friends."

"I know, Tom, you've run your own gambit in life, and I respect that. I know how smart you are. I know what you've accomplished, even if I am the only one who knows."

"Dawn, what's the matter?" he was now right up next to her, and she was looking deeply into his eyes as she fought back tears. "Talk to me?"

"I'm going, back to Sacramento. I gave my testimony today under oath. I'll probably be called back for the trial, though I suppose there's an above-average chance that the trial won't be held here in San Diego. Who knows, maybe she'll take a plea. Anyway, this, this is good-bye, Tom."

"It doesn't have to be, Dawn. That's one of the things I wanted to talk to you about when I called."

"Yeah," she said slowly, "I think it does. I know too much about you."

"Or maybe you just think you do."

"No, look at me, Tom. I know."

He reached inside his coat pocket and pulled out a British Airways ticket envelope and placed it in her hand. "Take this," he said.

"Tom . . ."

"It's a round-trip first-class ticket on British Airways to London. I plan to spend the summer there. You said before you didn't want to stay with the NCUA. Fine, quit, come to London with me."

"Tom, that's not going to happen . . ."

"I've got a flat rented for the summer—two bedrooms, two baths, all the amenities you'd ever want. No expectations, Dawn I think we have something—a connection, a spark, you told me before you felt it too. We said before that if things were different, we might have a shot. Well, things are different now. I'm cleared of the charges you wanted to bring me in on. You've arrested someone else. I'm suddenly rich, madly rich, and with what I've set up with my accountant, I'll never have to work again in my life. Take the summer, take a leave of absence from work if you're not ready to quit, but come with me, and let's see what we have. The ticket is yours, no questions or expectations. If after three hours alone with me in London you decided you want to go back, you hop on the next plane, or maybe we'll fly back arm in arm in September. I can't predict what'll happen between us anymore than you can, but I'd like the opportunity to find out. This money I have can be the answer for both of us. Let's see if we're as good together without the drama as we are with it. Let's find out how bad our decisions really are, but let's do it together."

"I can see," she said quietly, "why you were so good in marketing, that was a very persuasive speech, it doesn't change my answer though."

"Why?"

"Because, Tom, I know the truth, even if I can't prove it."

"What are you talking about?"

"I know you did it. I know you're guilty, and that all of this. Everything that's happened was a setup to get back at all the people who wronged you, and worse, you used me and my position to do it."

"Dawn."

"I know, Tom. I've learned a lot about what an IP address is. If you were smart enough to create this super virus, you're certainly smart enough to copy an IP address, or clone it. From there you just use it on another user terminal. If you have a backdoor onto a system, you can even create an e-mail coming from someone who didn't send it. And in all the time the money was missing, it seems no interest was earned on it? How is that even possible, Tom, huh? Let me clue you in. It's not, no matter how small a monetary unit you broke it down into. You'd have earned at least some bit of interest on it, but in the case of this 320 million, there wasn't so much of a dime earned. So you sued the FBI, the NCUA for breaking into your home, and the credit union for violating their agreement, and you've become a rich man, plus somewhere in this world you have a bank account with the interest you earned on the 320 million. Sweet deal, especially since all of the people who ever wronged you are in ruins. Laura Netzly is going to jail, all because eighteen months ago she falsely accused you of embezzlement. Most of the senior management team is going to be replaced in the next several months. I can guarantee you that, Tom, I've heard that directly from the board members. Randy Carlson will be placing his resignation in on Monday, but his desk was cleared out this morning. You got everything you ever wanted and you walk away rich because of it. And because I followed the chain of evidence you laid out for me, I became a part of your crime, an accessory after the fact. I should file everything I said in a report, give it to both the NCUA and the FBI, maybe even pass a copy of it along to Netzly's attorney so she can try to use it to get an acquittal. But I won't, and you want to know why, Tom?"

His stare was blank. He didn't know what to say, and finally she just stared down to the ground. "I would really like to fly off with you to London. I'd like to find out what there was between us. But if I do that, I think I'd just be chasing after that same sense of drama the thrill of being with someone who actually got away with it. I can't bring myself to turn you in, Tom, because I believe you were wronged, and more to the point you set up things so well that I doubt we'd ever have enough evidence to convict. So Netzly does the time you should be doing."

"Dawn," he said in a very tired, weary voice, "just think this through for a minute."

"I've been thinking about nothing else since the minute we arrested Netzly. I saw it in her eyes, Tom. We have all the evidence we need against her and more. But her eyes said it all. She's innocent, and your eyes read guilty."

"Fine," he said, feeling himself losing hope at the one thing he really wanted. "Just keep thinking about it though, go over it again. Because, and I mean, this with all the respect in the world here. I don't think you're seeing the big picture. That ticket in your hand is completely exchangeable. You can use it anytime you want. There's a card, the address I'll be staying at, tucked in with the ticket, though you probably already know where is, since you were investigating my life. This is about freedom, and you have it. That ticket can be used any time, and you know where I'll be. All I'm asking is that you just think about it. That right now we can just start over in London, see where we would go, with or without the drama. This isn't about the money anymore, Dawn. That isn't over our heads. All that matters here is us and what we do about it. And for you, there's no risk. You can walk away anytime you want. We both know I can't stop you from doing what you want, and hopefully you know I'd never try. What I'm looking for is a chance. I'm not looking to just pick up where we left off from that night, that beautiful, wonderful night. What I'm looking for is to spend time with you. And right now, just for the record, I think you want to come with me, despite anything else going on in your head. But you don't think you should. I understand, hell, I even respect it. But think it over, because time has a way of changing things, making what would have been perfect a fractured memory of regret down the road. Maybe we're not perfect for each other, maybe we are. The only way we'll ever know for sure is if we take the chance, right now, away from the newspapers who still want to interview us and the trial that will be going on all summer long. I need to be away from it, and so do you. Here's our chance. Take it."

"I saw your car in the parking lot," she said. "I came up to say good-bye. I thought I owed you that much."

"Dawn . . ."

She turned away and moved toward the door and without saying another word left. He fell back against the wall and closed his eyes; he couldn't believe the wave of loss he felt. Then a new thought occurred to him, something he'd almost missed. When she left, she was still holding onto the ticket. He didn't know if it would be thrown away the moment she got back home or not, didn't know if she'd dare take the chance to use it. But she'd held onto it, and that at least gave him some inkling of hope.

He turned to his desk and realized he didn't care about a damn thing in it. Anything he might accidentally leave behind could easily be purchased again. The door opened behind him, and he turned frantically only to see Sam walking back in. She looked at him with a sweet smile and said, "How'd it go?"

"Ahhh, not too well actually, Sammy, but what did I expect, right?"

"Shame, you two looked cute together, and the tension between you two, wow!"

"Yeah well, I guess she's looking to release some of the tension in her life."

Sam walked back to her desk and sat down. "Never know, Tommy. She might just change her mind."

"One can hope," he said picking up the box he'd been filling and then suddenly setting it down on top of the trashcan beneath his desk.

"Decided it wasn't worth it?"

"Uh-huh," he said, "I can buy whatever else I want. Whoever takes my job can have all this stuff. Do with it as they please. I just don't give a shit anymore."

"You're a good man, Tom. I want you to know that I honestly believe that."

"Thanks, Sammy, I appreciate that."

"Were you scared?"

"You mean while I was being hunted by the FBI? Sure, a little."

"So," she said looking across at him, "I told you I started to dig through all of my old company newsletters I'd saved."

"Uh-huh," he said as he sat down on the edge of his desk looking at her.

"I found the newsletter announcing you'd been officially hired. You made the front page. You were hired in to handle a lot of the new accounts that marketing was picking up. It was a big coup for marketing at the time. The industrial league was growing steadily, and we were working hard to secure new business so the credit union could keep growing."

"I remember," he said smiling, looking at her curiously as he said, "the first day on the job I was told quite specifically that I was not to fuck up and cost the credit union business."

"Do you remember what else was on the cover of the newsletter you were ushered in with? What incredible mark the credit union reached? All the deals marketing helped us increase our asset size substantially. It was so long ago, and our assets had grown so much since then that I hadn't even realized, it took me back a little. You remember what the headline to that issue of the newsletter was?"

"Sure," Tom said as he smiled at her, slowly nodding his head. "It read, 'Marketing hires Thomas Williams to help manage our new record-breaking assets of 320 million dollars.' Something close to that, at any rate."

"No," Sam said looking back at him, "that what it said exactly. 320 million dollars in assets, and you were hired to help marketing, to manage the business they were bringing in."

There was a different flash of a smile from Sam. Tom saw it and smiled back, and he realized she knew. He got up and walked closer to the door with a look of a cat that just swallowed the canary and said in a voice just above a whisper, "The funny thing is I kept waiting for someone to find that newsletter. No one bothered to check back that far, match up my hire date with our asset size. I thought it was a great clue, that I was being so clever. It's what I counted on them tying me into the crime. I half thought I was going to have to mention something to someone just to get the ball rolling. I mean seriously, what's it take to get arrested in this day and age?"

"Because," Sam said, "you needed to be arrested. You needed to be publicly wronged so that you could sue everyone in the end."

"Uh-huh," he said with a childish grin. *He'd been so good*, he thought, *at not letting it show, but here was a friend who discovered it all on her own*, and the thing Tom hated most about this whole game was how no one would ever know how brilliant the plan was. It was hard to have a secret that good and not share it. "Without being arrested, the rest of the plan fell apart. I mean, it wouldn't have been a total loss. But it wouldn't have been anywhere near as sweet. The money would still be out there, and there would always be the risk that they'd finally trace it back to me. Then the FBI screwed up by breaking into my place. It was just dumb luck I found out about it first."

"And the Logiterm programming," she said, "as I recall, you were the one who brought Logiterm in back when we were first converting over from the older system. The credit union was out shopping for a new system, and you set us up with Logiterm because you had a friend who was a senior programmer over there. You said you could get us a deal. I remember hearing that."

"David Wing," Tom said looking directly at Sam. "He was one of the first generation of real computer hackers. He could do amazing stuff with computers. He always seemed to be a step ahead of anyone who was chasing him. Given a system like Logiterm, which he basically rebuilt from square one, after he turned legit that is, a guy like that, he just loaded the system with backdoors and entryways that you wouldn't believe. Every programmer does. It just seemed no one could ever find his."

"You told me right before you came to collections, out at the lunch table one day that his wife died. You were worried about him."

"Yeah," he said almost laughing. "David only ever stopped hacking for Donna. She didn't want to live a life of a criminal and made him promise he'd stop, go legit, and David, he loved her like you wouldn't believe. He gave up everything. Found a job at Logiterm and rose up the company ranks at a job he absolutely hated. Nine-to-five, boring code, annoying clients whose asses he needed to constantly kiss. He had the mind of a genius, a criminal one sure, but genius nonetheless.

But for her, he was willing to put up with it all, and I never heard him complain about it once. Then, out of nowhere, she passed away. It was like a bomb went off in his life after that. He didn't care about anything."

Tom shrugged his shoulders as he looked up to Sam's face. She stared back at him, a dark, approving smile on her face. "We were out for beer one night, about a month and a half after she died. He just stared up at me and said matter of fact that I might not want to be seen around him anymore. That I might be safer as a part of his past instead of his present. He didn't need to explain it to me," Tom said. "I knew exactly what he was talking about. Without Donna, he didn't see any reason to play by the rules anymore. I guess it all really started that night. We started to talk a lot about what he did over the years at Logiterm, specifically how it related to Hil Fed. I gotta tell ya, Sammy, you'd be amazed at how easy it all was. All these people think that they're so superior and secure, and they can't even see past the end of their own noses. They never saw it coming."

"Like I said, Tom." Sam looked up at him. "You're a good man."

"You can't ever tell anyone, Sam."

"Who would I tell?" she said smiling. "And what would I care? This place ain't done nothing but screw me since new management took over. As far as I'm concerned, they got what they deserved, and so did you."

She walked over and hugged him, kissing him gently on the cheek, and with a smile he left, leaving his cluttered desk behind. Walking out the door very differently than he imaged he would when he first joined the HIL Fed team.

She sat back down at her desk and laughed for a while and wondered, *if Tom Williams could fraud the company, couldn't she do it too?*

It was there and then that her own plan started. She didn't think that she'd ever be brave enough to use it, but it comforted her to know she had her own way of revenge.

* * *

Epilogue in London

Epilogue in London 1.0

April 17, 2000

He walked down the street toward Scala House, up from the Goodge Street station on London's west end. He carried his new laptop, slung over one shoulder in its protective case. He also had a large suitcase on rollers that trailed along behind him, bumping along the uneven sidewalk. In his hand, he carried a large manila envelope. He looked ready to leave the country. Very soon he'd be out of the dark gloominess of London and on his way to the warm beaches of Greece. David Wing couldn't wait.

He popped into Scala House and looked at the lovely lady behind the reception counter and asked, "Excuse me, but has Thomas Williams checked in yet?" He already knew the answer, but he didn't mind playing along with Tom's silly little plan for a little while longer. He owed his friend that much.

"No," she said pleasantly looking up at him, "he's not due for a few hours yet. I'm terribly sorry."

David knew Tom stayed here several times in the past, so it didn't come as a surprise that the people behind this family-run business would remember who Tom Williams was. He placed a look of disappointment on his face. "Darn," he said trying to make it sound real, "I was hoping to have a drink with him before I flew out. Tell me, is it OK if I leave something for him?"

"Of course, sir."

"Thanks," he said, as he handed over the manila envelope and watched as she marked it with a sticky note and slid it into a room slot.

"I'll make sure he gets this when he checks in."

"I appreciate it," he said, as he grabbed up his suitcase and started to get ready to roll it back out to the street. She interrupted him to ask if she should leave his name with the package.

"Just tell him, a friend stopped by. He'll know when he opens it."

With that, he was back on the move, a fugitive in a sense, even if no one else knew it. On Goodge Street, he hailed a taxi and instructed the driver to take him to Heathrow Airport.

Sitting in the back of the cab he could still remember how it all came together. Even he wasn't sure if it would all go off the way it was supposed to. The risk for Tom was huge. His was only marginal at best. He'd be out of the country for the most part, when it would all hit. Of course, he also knew that Tom didn't mind the risk if he could get even with everyone.

It all started back in July 1998; he couldn't remember the exact date anymore, not that it really mattered. He and Tom met up for their monthly brewery trip, after being best friends since they were thirteen years old. They made time to meet. Their schedules were twisted apart by the lives they were leading and it was hard to find the time for even once a month. But they always did. This trip to the brewery was different than others though. This time they were both on the down end of luck. It was that very trip where everything began.

His wife was dead for just over a month, and he was devastated. Tom was just accused by his new boss of embezzlement—a woman he confessed to having an affair with. Neither was very talkative at first. Both just wanted to support the other. But faced with their own personal tragedies, about all they could do was be there for the other. He remembered that Tom felt guilty, being so distracted by something as insignificant as work when he was still dealing with the death of his wife. David let him know he understood. Tom poured his heart and soul into the credit union for a number of years. He knew everything that was going on at Hil Fed as far as it concerned Tom. The job that was taken away from him, the lies, and now this, an ultimate betrayal of being accused of something he didn't do. He saw the look in Tom's eye that night, something he hadn't see since they were back in high school, pure rage. Tom wanted to strike out at them. He wanted to get even, and David wanted to help him.

Tom was an honest man by nature, so he couldn't just suggest something. Whatever the revenge would be would need to grow naturally. So he said the only thing he knew to, "You might not want to be seen hanging around me anymore, Tom. Not that I want to stop having our monthly beer, but things with me are gonna change now that Donna isn't around."

Tom knew what he meant, and nodded his head, took a slow sip of his beer and then asked a startling question, "You told me once that you filled the Logiterm system with a ton of backdoors. That true, or were you just bullshitting me?"

"Thought you didn't want to know about that sorta stuff."

"Tonight, tonight, I do."

"I loaded every program I've ever written with backdoors. No one will ever be able to stop me from communicating with the programs I created."

"Including the one at Hil Fed?"

"Yup. Just because you worked there, I didn't see any reason to change my standard operating procedure. Besides, I never really figured it would matter."

They both stared across the table and began to smile. They didn't have a plan yet, but they had an inkling. More importantly, David could see Tom was past the point of being concerned of ever breaking the law. He could see it clearly in his friend's eyes. He wanted revenge. Their monthly brewery trips became weekly, and sometimes, it seemed, nightly. Slowly the kinks started to get worked out. Plans were discussed and tossed out as the pros and cons of it were discussed. David kept himself on the clean side of the law, though he did place his resignation in with Logiterm, wanting to distance himself from what would happen. The fear of the Y2K crunch already flooding the market place, programmers of David's talents were in high demand. He traveled across the country as a consultant and building a huge supply of cash, and that's when Tom called him and told him that one of his new responsibilities in collections would be to help build and create an on-collections system in Logiterm. They both laughed hysterically, because despite the back doors, they would need to insert a trigger line to start the virus he would place in through the backdoor. It was the only way Tom's plan would work, being able to link the theft back to him, and then through evidence over to Netzly. In December 1998, they had a fully working plan. After all, why not feed into the fear already plaguing America about Y2K?

Tom knew the risks and demanded on taking them. He wanted Netzly to pay and the whole senior management team to be caught up in it.

"They'll wind up arresting you, Tom. You know that, right? If we do it like this, it'll be your ass on the cross, while I'm off someplace tropical having a piná colada in the sun."

"I'm not worried, David," he said as he finished up his glass of dark ale. "I'd have you watching my back, and we've known each other far too long, too well, for me to even begin to think you'd hang me out to dry. Besides," he said, "for this to work, I need to be arrested."

"I'd never let you down, buddy," David said toasting their plan and the revenge Tom would have. "I think I have a good trigger code too," he said boastfully.

"Yeah, what's that?

"We use a date to do it, I'm thinking February 29." They both laughed thinking about it. Knowing that all video surveillance in the credit union of him loading the virus in would already be destroyed in that amount of time, and the date itself would seem completely arbitrary.

A few months later, they sat at David's laptop in a rented hotel room about a mile and a half away from the Hil Fed main office and entered the active Logiterm system by remote modem access. The moment they logged on, it was through a backdoor in the system, not the standard prompt system that the other employees would use, so as not to create a record that anyone was there. From that point on, David began to work his magic, finding out Laura Netzly's IP address' and setting things up for Tom, making sure the bulk of the virus program would be loaded in very slowly in several different regions inside Logiterm. So when Tom had to physically enter the command codes in person from Netzly's keyboard, he wouldn't have to be there more than a few seconds. This would give any investigator working the case something to find, allowing the blame to fall on Tom while they set up Laura Netzly to take the fall.

David worried a lot about the amount. To him, 320 was too obvious a tip to Tom's past with the credit union, having been hired in on the day they hit that point in assets. But Tom shook his head. "It'll take them at least two weeks to make that connection #1," he said teasingly. "Laura will be out of the country, and it's her department that runs the archives for the old newsletters."

"What about the cops?"

"It won't be the cops who find it, trust me," Tom said in the background, as David continued to type fast-paced code directly into the live Logiterm system, using a backdoor-code-feed method he'd designed years before, back in his hacking days. "It'll be the NCUA at first. With this much money, I figure, the FBI will be involved too. But straight procedure states that it'll be the NCUA through the door first. They won't start going back through newsletters. They'll be too busy at first figuring out where the money went. I'd lay dollars to donuts, its Laura who finds the connection first, and I assure you, she'll take weeks to look backwards. History isn't her strong suit."

"Still seems like an unnecessary risk, Tom."

"You worry too much."

"It's not that," David said. "What I'm worried about is having to pull out too early and us not making any money on this deal. Interest isn't a guarantee. Making a profit isn't even a guarantee, buddy. Have you considered the possibility that the investments we make won't turn a profit? What happens then? What if I start to lose principle and can't bail out the full 320 million dollars when you do get locked up?"

"Again, you're worrying too much, Davey. Listen to me; you've watched me over the past couple of years. I've done OK on the stock market, eh?"

"Sure, but we won't be investing on the local market. We've already gone over how much safer it'll be going international."

"And let me ask you this, did you plan on investing the money in a bulk sum of 320 mil?"

"No," he said quickly, taking a moment to look up from his laptop, "I told you I'm in the process of designing a program so that I can break the money down into literally into groups of thousand dollar deposits, while still tracking the whole. Meanwhile, I'll be running the money through an equal amount of accounts. In fact, our biggest concern there will be transaction fees eating into the principle."

"Right," Tom said smiling brightly. "So once you have it broken down into thousands of controlled pieces, like the many heads of the hydra, I want you to invest it in the same things."

"What?" David said turning his full attention to Tom.

"What would happen to a stock, especially a small to midlevel stock if a sudden influx of 320 million dollars were funneled into it over the course of a day, or even hours from several different sources?"

David was nodding his head here. "The stock would automatically rise in value, easily. We'd create an artificial market. Legitimate investors would suddenly jump on board. The lines of our money versus anyone else's would be so incredibly blurred that no one would ever be able to trace it."

"Exactly," Tom said leaning back in his chair. "And then, even with the heavy transaction fees, we're guaranteed to make money on every investment. Yes?"

"Yeah," David said shaking his head at the simple brilliance.

"But it only works if your program is fully functional. The foreign markets are just as regulated as ours here at home. If anyone can trace large portions of the money to a single source, we're made."

"We won't be made," David said with an extreme confidence. "That I can guarantee. In the last few months, I've found out about literally thousands of banks and finance companies worldwide, and I currently have a good chunk of code working to regulate routing transit numbers to our use. They'll never see us coming. It's a shame though we can't keep the 320 million. That would be one hell of a nest egg to fall back on."

"That much money, Davey, they'd never rest until they found it, and without the money, even if we gift wrap Netzly for them, they won't stop looking. We'd never be able to spend it. We'd be the richest paupers in the world."

"Yeah," he said, as he turned to look back at the code he was now automatically entering into Logiterm and asked, "So how do you know for sure you can get Netzly out of the country at the right time?"

Tom laughed and said clearly that would be the easiest part of the entire plan. Having eaten out with Laura many times in the past, back when they were together, Tom knew Laura had a compulsive habit of placing her business card in every fishbowl setup in the restaurants around town, all offering some fabulous prize if her card was selected. Tom decided it was time she won. They set up a bogus Web site on a free server and sent her a congratulatory e-mail, saying she'd won a Caribbean cruise. Netzly was so excited at winning a real prize that she never bothered to ask which restaurant she'd won at. The restrictions for the trip were that she could only utilize her free week at certain times in the year. Tom selected all the times very carefully, all of them at busy moments in the marketing year—times when there would be no way she could leave the office, with the exception of the week of March 6 through eleventh. The trip was expensive, but Tom took the money out of his accounts slowly to pay for it, giving it to David, and he paid for it all with cash or money orders. They made sure that there was no direct connection between the purchasing of the vacation and their money. Complete and utter deniability. They made it all look as if Laura was the one setting the trip up, including taking down the Web site that they'd originally used to entice and convince her. David then hacked into the free server's site and deleted all record their fake site ever existed. David never met Laura Netzly, so he was the one who contacted her when she had questions about the free trip. She fell for it hook, line, and sinker.

The rest of the plan was simple; the virus did all the hard work. David finally packed up and moved to Florida in March 1999, and that was when he and Tom perfected their "code speak" over the Internet forum. That way, they would still be able to communicate with one another while the investigation was happening. They both agreed that when Tom's arrest hit the news, that was when the money would then be discovered in Netzly's accounts. After all, Tom didn't want to have to spend too much time in jail. Just long enough to make him look guilty. Just long enough to get the credit union's senior management team to bring up Tom's past, as publicly as possible. David hadn't thought they'd do it. To his way of thinking, it would be far too stupid for a credit union of their size and stature to make such a foolish financial error. But Tom was sure that he could goad the CEO into it; in fact, he'd said that he was positive.

The tricky part for David was to find a blonde to do the first transfers down in the Cayman's. To officially put the money into play, they needed to get it out of plain sight, start filtering it, and hiding it away from prying eyes. For Tom's revenge to happen, it needed to be done on the exact day that Netzly would be at the Cayman's. Finding the girl was easier than he thought, all the while making the girl think he was a drug dealer. She was the only weak link to their plan, an additional witness who wasn't in on the score and had no reason to stay quiet. David was fairly sure he'd played up the drug angle heavy enough that she'd never say a word. But he also suspected if she was just stupid enough to fall for him as a drug dealer she was stupid enough to hear all about the stolen 320 million and never connect the dots. Still, David made Tom promise to leave the country the moment he was free of custody, just in case. If the ditzy blonde down in Florida actually had an original thought and spoke up, Tom's life could get very complicated, very quickly. He'd have far more leverage outside the country than he ever would inside. With the money they'd always figured they'd make, he could easily slide off the face of the earth. It was one of the few concessions that Tom ever made to David through the course of the plan. But it forced David to set up shop in London, all because Tom loved it there.

Tom being seen with the investigator, that was something David hadn't expected, but then Tom always did like to play on the dangerous side of life. He'd told him once long ago about having too much drama in life. Tom laughed out loud at the expression, swore he'd use it ever after. It was classic Tom, he thought, playing everything close to the vest. It was a side of Tom he hadn't seen in years. It was nice to have his friend back, even if it was an incredibly stupid plan.

On the cab ride to the airport, he reached into his coat pocket and pulled out his new passport, his new identity. William Cascade, listed occupation stockbroker.

It was a good enough identity for now. If worse came to worse, he had three others he'd be able to fall back on.

Now though it was time for a vacation after almost two years of planning and worrying, the next year of his life was for him and him alone. After a year or so, after he soaked up enough sun, he'd contact Tom and see how he was holding up. He agreed with Tom it was best they went their separate ways for a while. They could always get a hold of each other through the message board if they needed to.

For now, he'd happily settle for the fact that they won. They beat the system and the FBI to boot. But mostly he was happy because they had enough money they'd never have to work again. The one big score all criminals talk about, the one they'll end their nefarious ways on, he'd done it, and it all went off without a hitch. He was out, he was free, and *damn it*, he thought, *he was rich*.

Tomorrow was wide open for him, and it was finally time to see if there was any living left to do.

* * *

Epilogue in London 1.1

April 17, 2000

"This is for you, Mr. Williams," the young lady behind the counter said, as she handed him the manila envelope. "A gentleman dropped it off for you earlier. He seemed rather disappointed you weren't yet in from Heathrow."

Tom was weary from his flight. Ten and a half hours on a plane, even in first class tended to tire him out. He thanked her and had one of the gentlemen behind the counter help him with his things upstairs. Usually, he'd just carry everything up himself. But he'd packed a lot heavier knowing he was going to be here for several months, plus his arm still bothered him, and carrying anything over ten pounds caused fatigue after awhile. The doctors told him to expect it and even arranged for a physician in London to make a regular series of appointments with him for his visit. Tom didn't concern himself with that, as he took the envelope with a smile and made his way upstairs. With the bags dropped off in his room upstairs, he tipped the man, locking the door securely behind him. He walked back to his bedroom and collapsed on the bed. The last thing he remembered seeing was the alarm clock next to him reading 6:36 p.m. *The envelope and the remainder of his lifelong vacation would be waiting for him in the morning*, he thought, *and he was just too damn tired to do anything about it now.*

* * *

Epilogue in London 1.2

April 17, 2000

The steward at the counter looked at her with a genuine concern as he asked, "May I help you?"

She sat with the ticket in her hand, tapping it at the edge of the counter, totally and completely unsure of what to do. In her other hand, she held a hundred-dollar bill.

Her long blonde hair was tied back in a ponytail and she wore jeans, a T-shirt, and a short pullover sweater. At her feet was a suitcase, not her usual travel case. This was larger, holding more clothes than she usually traveled with. It's what she used when she planned to stay on an extended visit.

She was nervous, even though she knew there was no reason for it. The things she was thinking were crazy, and she was fairly sure that no matter what she decided, it would turn out to be the wrong decision. The tapping at the counter with the ticket was nervousness. She knew it, but found herself unable to stop. She was making a spectacle of herself, but the real battle was going on inside her head. Her analytical mind weighing out all of the possibilities for the action she teetered on. To do what she was contemplating would throw away everything she always worked so long and hard for. In a sense, it would invalidate the adult entire life she'd built. It was foolish and stupid, and she knew she should stop at once. "Just turn around and go home," she told herself.

"Ma'am," the steward's gentle voice broke into her thoughts as a deeper trace of concern filled his voice, "are you alright?"

She looked at the man behind the counter of British Airways and said very passively, "I don't know."

* * *

Epilogue in London 1.3

April 18, 2000

Waking up in the morning, he felt like an old man, the jet lag still shuddering through him. Part of him imagined, this is how he would feel daily if he lived to be too old. Touching his arm for a moment, right at the impact point, he thought very seriously about how if the bullet was aimed just a little different, growing old wouldn't have been a problem. It was a thought that still made him shudder. Getting up from bed, he stretched a little, and in looking over again at the alarm clock by the bed, Tom realized it was only 5:23 a.m. The hot water in his unit wouldn't even turn on for another two hours. He continued to stretch trying to work out the knots that seemed to be everywhere on his anatomy.

Stepping out to the main room, he flipped on the TV to watch the morning news as he strolled into the kitchen. Watching the morning news had become a lot more important to him lately, a new habit. He'd heard a comedian once say that every morning he got up to check the obituaries, just to see if his name was listed. For Tom, watching the morning news was something very similar. He watched for a trace of his name, a whisper of his crime, and what the day ahead might hold for him. He'd e-mailed ahead and had provisions placed in his kitchen for him. That way, he could have his cup of morning coffee until he could find the closest Starbucks. With the TV playing in the background, he made his way to the kitchen and started grinding and brewing his way to his first cup of coffee.

With a fresh cup in hand, he sat in the living room watching the telly for a good half hour, through the local news and right into the international report. He was relieved when his name wasn't mentioned. There was brief mention of Laura Netzly and how her lawyers were challenging venue, and he smiled enjoying his coffee. The TV was different in England than it was in America. To Tom, it appeared they still had a sense of humor over here about life, and it reflected in their television programming. He loved England and was seriously considering moving. He no longer had any financial reason not to. In fact, there was only one thing about England that he didn't like, and that was their food. Bland and tasteless for the most part, as a culture the English seemed to have an aversion to spices. Not that it was much of a problem for Tom. He'd always loved to cook, and maybe living in a country like this would finally stop him from eating out so much.

After he felt a bit more alert and awake and well into his second cup, he walked back to the bedroom and picked up the manila envelope and ripped it open. Inside was exactly what he expected. A passport, driver's license, and even a few credit cards for a man named Craig Fiest, his new identity if he should ever need it. The picture on both the passport and the license was a quickie picture that David had taken of him right before he moved to Florida; he looked utterly terrible in it. He took these items and buried them in a hidden compartment in the inside of his suitcase. The next item out of the envelope was a key to a safety-deposit box taped to a note with directions to the proper bank. The last item inside was a handwritten note from David reading:

> *We did it, buddy, we really did it. Sorry to hear you got hurt, but hopefully what the key holds will ease the pain, if only just a little. I'm off to Greece. If you need me, contact me through the board, as I'm not entirely sure where I'll*

be staying, or even which name I'll be using. I'll be around though, and I'll always keep an eye on the boards in case of an emergency.

As far as the money goes, if I read the code right, you told me you got eight mil a piece from each of the folks you sued. Totally twenty-four mil. Meg would get a third, and taxes would rake you pretty good on what was left., But I figure, you still walked with eight to ten million in your pocket free and clear, but hell, let's round down for ease. So that eight million is what I'm placing into the total pot. If I'm wrong about that, again, send me a note, and I'll correct it next year when we hook up for our next drink. It has been far too long since we split a pitcher.

In the time I had the money, I did pretty good. We played the market hard from several different directions. The one downside is, I think, we may have inadvertently ruined a few foreign startup companies with our little games. What are you gonna do?

Anyway, I made a total of 33.6 million after all the costs. Combined with your eight, we have a new total of 41.6 million dollars. That's 20.8 apiece. Since you already have eight, if you follow the key, you'll find your kitty comes to 12.8.

If my math's at all funky, let me know. We'll work it out, bud, I figure neither of us can foolishly spend almost 13 million before next year. So, until we see each other again, stay cool, don't freak, and remember if you need it, you've got a totally new ID to fall back on. So be smart, destroy this note the moment you've read it, no evidence. We'll do drinks someplace warm in 2001.

Note: I said someplace warm, which means any of the piss-ant countries that you love so much are unacceptable, got it?

We did it . . . We really did it. Now go enjoy. You deserve it.

The note wasn't signed, but that didn't surprise Tom. He crumpled it and placed it deep inside the pants he'd been wearing when he left the flat. He unpacked his things and waited until the hot water clicked on to take a shower and got dressed. Before he left, he made sure that he had his identification for his alter identity instead of his normal passport. He didn't want to be caught by anyone carrying two different sets of ID. He grabbed the directions and key and headed out to the early morning streets of London.

In all the time this was going on, he'd never been nervous, not really. He knew that he always had an out. He knew that even if his game was called early, he'd planted more than enough evidence for Laura to take the fall, not him. But today, he was actually going to be in contact with the money. If he was still being followed, he'd be leading them right to it. Plus he'd be caught with a fake ID, a clear sign of guilt if there ever was one. With everything he'd done so far, this would be exposing himself to the most to risk. Even back on the night he'd entered into Laura Netzly's office to load up the key code that would run the virus, he hadn't been this nervous. That night he waited until the board of directors' meeting was taking place on the fourth floor took a planned break. He'd left early that day complaining of stomach flu, and when he returned to the building, he parked in a neighboring complex's parking lot and cut through the bushes to cross over to the Hil Fed building. Since the board meeting was taking place, all of the normally locked doors on the building weren't, so he strolled right in. He knew a route through the building where he would be filmed as little as possible on the security cameras, but there would be no way he could have entered without being filmed at all. That was a very minor concern for him though. What he worried about was someone actually seeing him. He knew the security tapes from the evening would be erased and reused long before so much as a dime was stolen from Hil Fed, so they would never be able to be used against him. If someone saw him though, everything would go to hell. While he could easily explain his presence in the building by simply going into collections and doing some coding work on the collection package, it would leave a traceable record of his presence that night. So he'd been careful. He waited in the stairwell, in a non-monitored section, just in case anyone happened to be looking at a security camera. They wouldn't see him just loitering about. He sat there for a good ten minutes while he waited for the regularly scheduled break in the upstairs meeting. Laura Netzly never left the boardroom during the board meetings, at least not to return to her office. Instead she would linger in the break room, walk around the executive suite, or occasionally go back to Randy Carlson's office, but she would always return to the marketing department to file a board report before going home, and that meant she always left the marketing department unlocked while the board meeting took place.

Tom walked boldly down the hallway from the stairwell and flipped the handle to the marketing department and went right in without a moment's hesitation. He'd gone through those doors a million times while working in the department; he didn't feel out of place doing it that night. The inside of the department was not monitored at all, so he cut right back to Netzly's office and found that her computer was even on. He entered the trigger code and hit enter.

He could see why David was so festive in the note; everything really did go off exactly as planned. He still remembered reading Laura's e-mail to the prize company as she arranged her Caribbean vacation. How he and David laughed themselves silly! The best part was how much time Laura seemed to spend online at home. One night, David did a test against Laura's home system while she'd been online, to see if she had any kind of security screen or firewall protecting her home system. Since she'd gone through extensive computer training in school, they'd both expected she would and while with enough time David was sure he'd be able to beat whatever system she had, they didn't want to risk alerting her to what was going on. One night, however, David gave it a try and discovered that she didn't have any kind of protection at all. So he planted a file one night into her C drive, right into the program files, and placed bits of the code, and then erased them. Knowing fully well that if the FBI ever did a throughout test on her system, they'd easily be able to find traces of the partial code that was used against Hil Fed. They hadn't read anything about that yet in the papers, but Tom was sure they would before her trial was over.

Leaving his rented flat he didn't go to the nearest station on Goodge Street, instead he walked the backstreets of London, to see if he could get an idea if he was being followed. In all the time the NCUA and the FBI were following him, he'd never really spotted anyone doing so, except for maybe once or twice, though even then, he wasn't sure. Without knowing who was following him, he'd taken up driving a bit more reckless, figuring they wouldn't give him a ticket and blow their cover. Here in London, he felt he'd have a better chance than back at home. He seemed to be more alert here, less relaxed. Back home, he was comfortable on all the streets. He knew his way around. Here everything was new and fresh, and since he was on foot, he'd be able to see anyone tracking him easier. At least he would until the crowds came out. It was still brisk and early and not many people were out. He walked the backstreets, where he could see everyone around him and took numerous twists and turns. He'd been to London enough times to know his way around, but he didn't have the comfort level he did in San Diego. He cut into an underground station and bought a pass to use their version of a subway. He traveled the city at random, going from one underground station to another, jumping out to the street level and walking vigorously for blocks to another underground station. If anyone was following him, he knew he was taking them on one hell of a crazy ride.

By eleven o'clock, he walked into Harrods and bought several large bath towels. The clerk behind the counter loaded them into two large green bags. He thanked her and left.

An hour later, during the busy noontime madness that covered London, he walked into the bank, where the safety-deposit box was held. He showed the bank manager the ID saying his name was Craig Fiest and was shown back to a private area, where he could casually go through the contents of his locked security box.

Opening the box, he found the money, 12.8 million dollars and he began to laugh hysterically.

Ten million was in American dollars, the rest was converted into English pounds. Looking over at the trashcan at his feet, his tossed several of the towels into it. He then loaded a good percentage of the English money into his bags to walk out of the bank with a set of towels on top of the money to conceal it.

He locked his safety-deposit box back up and had the security guard return it and then walked out and opened a real account with the bank for three hundred and fifty thousand pounds, an account the bank manager was more than happy to help him with personally. He then walked back out to the streets of London.

The city was busy, but the lunch rush was over, and the streets were starting to empty a bit. It was a surprisingly sunny, warm day out, and he stood very still in the sunlight waiting for someone to come and arrest him. When ten minutes went by and no one came by to take him in, he decided to return to the flat.

This time he went simply to the nearest tube station and took the most direct route back to Goodge Street. He sat with a smile from ear to ear on his face as he rode along in the car, surrounded by people on the underground who had no idea of the kind of money he concealed inside his Harrods bags. Anyone looking into his bags would simply see the towels.

Getting out at Goode Street, he took the elevator up and out to the street, wrapped around the corner past the outdoor fruit and vegetable stand with his head down. Chuckling lightly, he strolled casually up the street toward the flat. The only thought going through his head was *he'd really gotten away with it. He'd beaten everyone. He'd actually won.*

His only disappointment was he didn't want to be in London alone. It just didn't seem right without her. Because just anyone wouldn't do. He wanted Dawn.

If later asked, he would never be able to say what caused him to look up when he did, never be able to tell anyone why he decided to look down the street to the entryway of the building to his rented flat. He froze in his tracks the moment he did. Because the moment he looked up, he saw her.

She stood wearing wrinkled jeans, obviously from sitting for far too long on a commercial flight over the Atlantic. She had on a T-shirt and a short; pullover sweater, her hair tied back into a semi-ragged ponytail. She looked tired, weary, and more than just a little out of it. But to his eyes, she was still the most beautiful sight in the world.

She looked down the street at him, shrugging her shoulders, a playful gesture, and he noticed a large suitcase at her feet. They shared a smile from half a block away, a real smile, one that didn't have anything to do with the past left behind them.

Tom felt a surge of happiness wash over him. *He couldn't believe it. Dawn McCafferty was really there!*

* * *

Epilogue in London 1.4

April 18, 2000

The steward at the air counter for British Airways was almost at the point where he needed to call security before she'd made up her mind and made her request, asking to trade her ticket in for the next available flight from Sacramento to London. That was the first thought that flashed in front of her eyes, as she saw Tom Williams walk around the corner from the tube station. She was exhausted, the jet lag beating her down. She remembered in her younger days being able to fly without any repercussions. Those days were obviously behind her. She was in London now though, and she knew her life was going to change.

She was going against everything she knew to be true, fighting against her ever-rational side and living on an impulse. She was courting a thief, and the moment she saw him, she felt something inside her soften. He looked different than he did back in America. He seemed happier, freer, more of the man he spoke like, instead of the man he pretended to be. He'd beaten the system, she knew that, but he hadn't beaten her. She knew he was guilty, had even figured out the how and why. If she'd wanted to, she could have continued to press him, gone to the FBI with what she knew, and what she suspected. Even if they hadn't believed her, they would have had to follow up on it. Tom's entire life was in her hands, and he didn't have a clue.

She didn't want him in jail though. Her entire life, she fought the good fight, right versus wrong, good versus evil, and she'd always played the game correctly when it came to the law. Morally, the only questionable action was how she treated Jerry and the result of their tragic relationship. Now, faced with Tom, she knew she wasn't doing the right thing. She was letting him get away with the largest domestic theft a credit union ever faced, and she didn't feel the slightest bit bad about it. There was something about him or more importantly, how they fit together mentally and emotionally that was more important to her.

She watched as he suddenly looked up and saw her. He'd been smiling since the moment he turned the corner, toward the flat, but she watched the smile grow, and she felt her own starting to appear. The connection between them worked on many different levels, even at a distance. He stood there for a moment, just staring, and she knew why; he needed a moment to process it, to make sure he wasn't just imagining her. He needed to know she was real; he needed to make sure she was here for him, not to make an arrest. She shrugged her shoulders at him as she motioned to her large, cumbersome bag sitting at her feet, and she saw a wave of happiness wash over him.

He wanted her, she knew that, but not in the way Jerry had. It wasn't a need-based relationship. In fact, she admitted that he would be better off without her, since rationally speaking he would never really be able to trust her, not with where her loyalties might lie, not with what she knew. She could turn him anytime, if he even hinted that he really was responsible for the crime. She could always hold it over him. If whatever they had ended badly, she could see him arrested and prosecuted. For him, entering into any kind of a relationship with her was incredibly stupid, dangerous even. Yet he wanted to.

For her, entering into this relationship meant the end of her career. Rumors would always haunt her, and she knew no one would ever take her seriously again, even if she were to eventually bust him. She'd slept with a suspect, while under surveillance no less. She quit her job without a moment's notice and chased off around the world to be with him. No one would ever hire her now and certainly never again with the kind of respect she once held.

She didn't care.

This was the right thing for her to do. Seeing him look at her, she felt it, down deep, down where things really mattered.

It was crazy, but true.

After a few moments, he came walking up, and she noticed immediately the bags he held were weighted awkwardly, heavy, and carried low to the ground. *What would someone like Tom Williams need on his first full day in London from Harrods that would be that heavy?* The closer he got, she saw large bath towels at the top of his bag, and she knew immediately what lay beneath. She didn't need to look to know, it was money. She could feel it. Whoever his partner was made the drop-off, but probably not all of it. This was the money Tom expected to spend and start leaving legal traces off. This would be the money he would launder into the system, so he could spend without question. She looked away from the bags and decided to look simply at him, still feeling the girlish smile on her face.

"I wasn't sure," he said stepping up, "if you'd show."

"Sure you were," she said taking a step closer to him. "That's why you bought me the ticket."

"This is gonna sound stupid, but London just didn't feel right this trip, not without you here. Stupid, huh? I've never been here with you, never been anywhere with you, and the city suddenly isn't right unless you're here. What do you make of that?"

She smiled at him, and suddenly she didn't care about the money inside his bags, didn't care at all about the life she was leaving behind or the past they were escaping from.

"You're really here," he said in total disbelief.

"I wanted to see what might be, without all the drama. Isn't that what we talked about?"

"Suddenly, Dawn," he said shaking his head smiling wildly, "I can't remember a damn thing we ever said. I'm just glad you're here."

"Me too."

And the next thing either of them knew, his bags were on the ground and their arms were wrapped tightly around one another. Someone passing by would have thought that they hadn't seen each other in months from the way they held each other.

He was a thief, Dawn knew. She'd seen his game and watched it unfold, and now she was a part of it. Not just an accessory after the fact, but truly a part of the crime. Suddenly her drab little world was filled with hope and promise. She didn't know if she and Tom Williams would wind up together, but she knew she was at least willing to take the chance on that possibility. That unlike the change she'd made fourteen months ago with Jerry, she was changing her life to be with someone, not get away from them.

They were both entering into this relationship with a past, but this time the sky was the limit. Money wasn't an issue, and more importantly for the first time in as long as she could remember, she had thoughts about only one man, and suddenly she couldn't imagine being with anyone else. Suddenly all she wanted in the world was him as she felt his lips touch hers.

The kiss was warm and inviting and perhaps really did hold the promise of forever.

The End

Made in the USA
Lexington, KY
04 September 2012